Thoroughbreds
and
Trailer Trash

Bev Pettersen

Editors: Pat Thomas & Rhonda Helms
Cover design: Hot Damn Designs

DEDICATION

To Barb, Becky and John,
the best siblings in the world.
Love you!

Also available from
Bev Pettersen and Westerhall Books

Jockeys and Jewels

Color My Horse

Fillies and Females

Horses and Heroin (Fall, 2012)

ACKNOWLEDGEMENTS

To Brenna Pettersen who cheerfully and patiently answers every trumpet call, whether it's to brainstorm, proofread or travel to the track.

To Lauren Tutty and her dad, Briar, who found a stall for Penny and helped a horsecrazy kid's dreams come true.

To Jessica McLoughlin, equine massage therapist, who answered all my questions and took such good care of Nifty.

And a very special thanks to Sally Goswell, Bruce Jackson, Kathee Rengert and all the helpful folk at the Fair Hill Training Center, truly horse heaven!

Chapter One

It wasn't stealing. But Jenna peeked over her shoulder as she fingered a bag of horse vitamins, aware Wally didn't want anyone to see. She slipped the precious supplements into her backpack, along with a tube of dewormer. Her little pony needed all the help he could get.

Her phone buzzed, making her jump. She noted the Philadelphia number and eagerly flipped it open. "Hi, Em," she said. "How are classes?"

"Fine. Other than biology, the spring semester's a cinch. But I need more money. When are you getting paid?"

"Hopefully today. And I'll transfer it right away." Jenna rubbed her warm forehead and forced a smile, determined to match Em's carefree spirit.

"Thanks, sis," Em said. "You're the best. How's Peanut?"

"His hair is falling out but good vitamins help." Jenna dropped a guilty glance on the bulging backpack. "Today he even trotted a couple steps."

"Good to hear." Laughter bubbled in the background and Emily's voice drifted. "Look. I gotta go."

"Wait—" But a harsh beep replaced her voice. Jenna slowly pocketed the phone. She understood college courses were demanding, but it would be nice if Em would visit some weekend.

Wally Turner, manager of Three Brooks Equine Center, poked his balding head into the feed room. "There you are." His gaze drifted over her pack, and his voice lowered to a conspiratorial whisper. "Keep that bag shut. And if you drop by my office on the way out, I'll give you the rest of your overtime in cash."

"Great." She blew out her relief. "I'll be right along. I told Frances I'd sweep for her. This place needs a cleaning." She grabbed a broom, wishing their longtime receptionist did something more than crossword puzzles.

"No worries. It's another week before the new people arrive." But the lines around Wally's mouth deepened, and it was clear he was worried. Little wonder. The Center had just experienced a messy buyout, and the incoming owners had a history of ruthlessly culling management.

She swept every inch of the tiles, grimacing at the stubborn clumps of gum mingled with the spilled grain. Fortunately Wally planned a cleanup. However, she had bigger problems than a messy workplace. She dumped the waste into an overflowing garbage bin and detoured to pick up her pay.

The extra money was a blessing. Wally had definitely thrown a lifeline by offering cash for massaging additional horses. She didn't want to agonize about her sparse checking account, but Em's living expenses seemed to be skyrocketing.

Wally's door was shut when she arrived, his voice droning incomprehensibly through the office wall. His closed door always meant stay out, so she dropped her loaded pack on the floor and flexed her stiff shoulder.

Other than a hang-up about office privacy, Wally was usually lenient and it would be no problem to duck out early, send Em the money and still have time to massage Peanut. Of course, that was assuming her shoulder held up. Massage was physical work, doubly hard since she was trying to learn a more traditional technique. She'd found a new library book on equine therapy, but was stuck on page thirty-eight and so far hadn't learned much of value. Her mom had taught her more than anything she'd ever found in a book.

The door slammed at the far end of the aisle and a workman stalked in, dented hard hat clamped under his arm. The construction crew had been working nonstop, rushing to build a storage shed for the new owners. Occasionally they ducked into the air-conditioned Center to grab a drink from the pop machine. But this man didn't stop for a drink.

His stride was long and forceful. Metal-toed boots pounded the concrete then quieted on the rubber mats. Sweat-stained shirt, eyes as dark as his hair, and heading this way. She straightened, prepared to defend her spot in line.

"Wally Turner in there?" Impatience roughened his words and he barely looked at her. A bit of a surprise. Men were usually a sucker for long legs and blond hair, and often just a smile had been enough to extricate her from a tight spot. A smile wasn't going to work with this man though. Clearly he liked to bulldoze.

"Yes." She squared her shoulders. "But I'm also waiting—"

His scowl jerked from Wally's door to her face, cutting off her words with the force of his displeasure. The female exercise riders had been detouring past the construction site all week, smiling and flirting with the crew, but it was doubtful they'd sent many jokes this guy's way. There was something hard about him, the same ruthless element that had emanated from her father's cellmates.

He dismissed her as though inconsequential, the muscles in his arm bunching as he reached for the door. However, she was accustomed to fighting for every inch and had certainly faced much tougher men.

Lifting her chin, she squeezed between him and the door. "Sorry but you'll have to wait your turn."

The scowl deepened as he loomed above her. His annoyance mixed with the smell of freshly cut lumber, something piney that was actually quite pleasant. She was tall but he was taller, and for an instant her attention was riveted to his big workman's body. Damn, she hated when that happened. She quickly snapped her attention back to his face.

He frowned for a long moment then something lightened. His mouth twitched, a tiny movement, almost imperceptible, but enough to crack that ruthless expression. "Of course." He inclined his dark head and stepped back. "It wasn't my intention to butt in."

Sure it was. However, his smile definitely softened her. Wow. If he ever cut loose and actually grinned, he'd be devastatingly handsome. "I won't be too long," she said, rubbing her sore shoulder, trying not to stare at his lips.

"Did you hurt yourself at work?"

He hadn't appeared to look at her earlier and she blinked; no one had asked about her health since her mom had died. "I'm fine. Sort of a chronic thing." She dropped her hand, hiding the discomfort. "And I won't be long with Wally. Just need to pick something up before I go."

"Leaving early?" He checked his watch and his mouth flattened.

"Yes, but Wally doesn't mind."

"Nice of him."

His tone was definitely disapproving and she crossed her arms. "Not much sense hanging around if the work's done."

"If it's done." He glanced pointedly down the aisle at an abandoned wheelbarrow, still brimming with manure. A blue pitchfork leaned perilously against the wooden handles.

"That's not my job," she said, surprised at the defensiveness in her voice. "I'm the masseuse."

"A masseuse? Of course." His dark eyes flickered over her in a thoroughly masculine assessment, nothing lecherous, just simple approval that made her pulse kick. She swallowed and realized she'd been wrong. Very wrong. The gallop girls would definitely have noticed this guy.

"We're one of the best therapy centers in West Virginia with massage, hydrotherapy and oxygen chambers. For horses," she added, just in case he was a bit dense. The gorgeous ones usually were. "Are you with the construction crew?"

"No."

"Looking for a job then?" she asked. "Because Three Brooks is a great place to work." She didn't usually babble but his sparseness with words was rather unnerving. "Wally's nice, really easygoing."

"Obviously." His gaze flickered down the dirty aisle.

Resentment tightened her mouth. Wally wasn't the most organized manager, but he was a family friend and genuinely loved the horses. And while it was okay for her to criticize, it wasn't acceptable for outsiders. This man reeked of disapproval.

He seemed like a tight-ass and probably wouldn't be good with animals either. Compassion could usually be sensed, and there was nothing coming from him but autocratic authority. She hoped Wally didn't like him either—in fact, she might be able to help with that.

She unzipped her pack and groped for her keys, beaming her most magnanimous smile. "Since you're in such a hurry, you can see Wally first. I need to drop off my pack in the car anyway. But don't wait by the door. He prefers that visitors knock once, then walk right in."

"Really?" His eyebrow arched and his gaze bore into hers. Clearly he wasn't quite as gullible as she'd hoped, and the force of those laser eyes sent her into an unexpected fumble. Her hand jerked, knocking her pack sideways, scattering the secret supplements across the floor. Shit!

She rammed the plastic bags back into her pack, annoyed her hand trembled. At least no one was around, only this construction guy, and he wouldn't have a clue about horse wormers. She peeked up, her breath flattening at his odd stillness. It was clear he was quite capable of drawing his own conclusions.

"What's your name?" he asked, so quietly she wasn't sure she heard him correctly. Which was perfect as it was probably not a good idea to give her name.

"Could you help me with this please?" she asked, her mind scrambling. "These supplements are past the expiry date. We're clearing out the supply room. Getting ready for a big inventory... Never mind. I have them."

She jammed the last bag in her pack and hoisted it up, so desperate to escape she forgot about her sore shoulder and winced at the sharp pain. An arm flashed. The weight disappeared.

"You shouldn't be carrying around something that heavy." He tossed the backpack over his shoulder with careless ease.

"It's okay. I'm fine." She glanced longingly at the door. "Really."

"Show me your car."

His expression was unreadable. Maybe he *had* swallowed her story of expired supplements. Best to humor him. Let a man help a little and their protective instincts always kicked in. She'd pick up her money tomorrow. Em would have it by Friday. Not a big deal, just a slight change in plans.

"This is so nice of you." She rubbed her shoulder, pretending simple gratitude as she accompanied him down the aisle. "My shoulder is rather sore."

"Shouldn't fill your pack so full."

The feed room is usually locked, she thought, and Wally wanted her to take the supplements before the inventory. But she nodded as though he'd imparted valuable words of wisdom. "You're absolutely right." She beamed another grateful smile. "Lucky for me you came along."

He'd opened the door, pausing to let her pass, but the corner of his mouth twitched again so she quit talking and stepped outside. Despite his solemn expression, she'd almost swear he was laughing. Her father had taught her to read faces, taught her about all the little 'tells' in poker—a lip twitch was a dead giveaway.

"My car's over there." She gestured toward the green Neon, a mere twenty feet away. Normally the rust spots weren't so glaring, but today it was parked beside a sleek black Audi with the shiniest wheels she'd ever seen.

"That's the visitors' lot," he said. "Thought you worked here?"

"I do, but everyone parks where they want. No big deal." Although no one ever took her customary space, next to Wally's, the second closest slot to the door.

She glanced over her shoulder at the construction crew, anticipating their usual good-natured waves and catcalls. They were all oddly subdued so she inserted her key. The Neon's tiny trunk creaked open.

A bag of empty cans needed to be pushed aside, and it was a relief when he finally maneuvered the pack of supplements between the blue bag and her spare tire. Usually she was fairly cool with this type of thing, but today she felt jumpy. Hesitant even.

"So that's it? Nothing else to load up?" He paused, one big hand on the trunk, watching her with an odd expression.

"Yes, that's all. Thanks." He seemed to be lingering so she reached out and slammed the trunk, hit by a rush of regret. He was rather nice in an uptight way, even gallant enough to load her car. Yet she'd deliberately fed him misinformation. And he might need a job as much as she did.

"Actually Wally's been a little stressed lately." She retreated around the fender to the driver's side. "Maybe it *is* best to wait until his door opens. But he's planning a big inventory and cleanup so needs to hire some muscle. I really hope you get the job."

His eyes hooded as she slid behind the wheel. He didn't seem the indecisive type, but he definitely appeared to be thinking now.

"All right," he finally said, as though settling something with himself. "Anything else I should know?"

"No. That should do it. Although it does help if you like horses. And maybe smile a little more." She grinned, turned her key and the engine sputtered to life. "Better hurry before someone else gets in line. Maybe I'll see you tomorrow. And you can help me...load more things."

He smiled then, a real smile that made her hands squeeze the steering wheel, and part of her fervently hoped he would land that job.

"What's your name?" he asked.

"Jenna, Jenna Murphy."

"I'll see you tomorrow, Jenna."

The raw promise in his voice jolted her more than the Neon's aging clutch, and the little car bucked twice as it rolled from the parking lot. Definitely a cocky guy. But oh, so cool.

She was still smiling as she sped down the winding driveway, her heart thumping a tad faster than normal. Her gaze drifted to the rearview mirror and she blew out a sigh, inexplicably disappointed to see he'd already vanished.

CHAPTER TWO

"Vitamins, glucosamine, flax. Nothing but the best for you," Jenna said as she moved her hands over Peanut's hindquarters, concentrating on the large gluteal muscles at the top of his rump. The pony stretched his shaggy neck, as usual loving his massage.

A pity Thoroughbreds weren't as tiny as Peanut. It was easier to work on a pony, less than twenty minutes for the little guy, and his massage didn't leave her shoulder throbbing.

She gave Peanut an affectionate pat then led him across the driveway to graze. Technically the grass on the other side belonged to Three Brooks but it hadn't been harvested in years, and it saved on buying hay. In better times, her chief worry had been that Peanut might overeat, but now his teeth were worn and his tattered coat hung in chunks. The poor fellow used to be a good-looking pony.

She returned to her sun-dried yard, trying not to look at the ragged shingles hanging from the trailer's roof. Peanut was showing his age, so was her home. Last year Emily had helped her patch a portion of the roof. They should have fixed it all.

A diesel pickup rumbled over the hill. She shot an anxious look over her shoulder, relaxing as the big vehicle slowed fifty yards out. Wally. A couple of the maintenance men for the Three Brooks mansion drove too fast, but Wally knew to watch out for wandering ponies.

He lowered the window with a wry smile. The fading sun emphasized the deep lines bracketing his mouth. "I need a beer, Jenna."

It was getting late and her shoulder ached, but Wally looked even more drained. Besides, it probably wasn't beer he wanted but conversation. Sometimes she thought him lonelier than she was, if that were possible.

She nodded a welcome, slipped into the kitchen and grabbed a couple cold beers. By the time she stepped outside, Wally was stretched on the porch swing. Flies buzzed over the brook but thankfully stayed off the cooler porch. They didn't seem to bother Peanut who chewed contentedly, swishing his tail and looking like a pygmy in the tall grass.

"Talk to Emily lately?" Wally asked, his gaze fixed on Peanut.

"Today, just for a minute."

"She should get a part-time job. Her college support is wearing you down."

Jenna waited a beat, trying to control her annoyance. Wally was like an uncle, but he was always much too critical of Em.

"I don't want her worrying about money," Jenna finally said. "Not while she's studying. She's barely twenty."

"You're only six years older. Look at you."

Jenna leaned her head against the swing. *Yeah, look at me.* A crumbling trailer, an ancient pony and a sister who no longer needed her. She felt old, alone and rather scared. But at least one of the Murphy girls was going to college.

Wally tilted the bottle. *Glug, glug.* He swiped his mouth and glanced longingly over his shoulder. "Got another beer in there?"

So much for studying her massage book; Wally seemed really down. She rose, clicked open the screen door, grabbed another beer and filled a plate with spicy pepperoni. This was better anyway. Wally was always good company—as long as he didn't snipe at Emily.

"You're a sweetheart," Wally said, gratefully accepting the second beer along with the sliced meat. "There's something damn special about this front porch. Looking over the valley makes me feel like a king. Your dad sure set things up right."

"He was a lazy asshole who spent more time in jail than out, and made Mom miserable."

"Agreed, but he sure built a nice porch."

Jenna sighed, enjoying the smells, the reddening sunset and the nostalgic sound of peeper frogs and their promise of summer.

Wally was right. Her dad had done one good thing. He'd found the most beautiful spot in the entire county.

Wally's arm moved and a white envelope dropped on her lap. "Unfortunately things are going to change a bit," he said, his words muffled with pepperoni. "That's the last of those."

She opened the envelope and flipped through the bills. Two hundred and twenty dollars. Em would be thrilled. "What do you mean, the last?"

"The new owner is tough, a stickler for rules. And the sale went through much quicker than expected." Wally burped, and Jenna inched away from the overpowering smell of pepperoni and beer. "He's going to be a pain in the ass," Wally went on. "Even clamping down on the construction crew. Staff will have to walk the line."

She shoved the bills back in the envelope, quickly crunching numbers. After sending Em's money, there'd be sixty dollars to last until the end of the month. It'd be tight. "I always walk the line," she said, tucking the envelope into her back pocket.

Wally chuckled. "But sometimes it's the wrong side."

"Can't help it. Bad blood and all." She tried to speak lightly, didn't want to reveal how his words hurt, but the fact was undeniable. The Murphy family was trash.

"Jenna," Wally said quickly. "What I meant is we can no longer look after every sick animal that knocks on our door. These people want to see a profit." He took a thoughtful sip of beer. "Should be plenty of work though. The Burkes have a lot of contacts. They're in the process of negotiating contracts with major race stables so eventually we'll receive quality horses. Unfortunately Three Brooks will be closed to the public."

"What?" Jenna blinked in dismay. "What about the locals? If a horse is hurt, you mean we can't help?"

"Not anymore." Wally blew out a resigned sigh. "Derek wants to offer pricey rehab to an elite clientele, along with top staff and expanded facilities. He'll be explaining all this in a staff meeting tomorrow."

"Who's Derek?"

"Derek Burke, their cleanup guy. He's moving into the big house…taking over for a while."

Jenna stiffened, straining to see Wally's expression through the gloom. "The Three Brooks mansion? But you'll stay in the apartment at the Center? You're still the manager?"

"Far as I know." Wally ripped a slice of pepperoni into three ragged pieces, his voice gruff. "But frankly it would have been better if the Canadians hung on to ownership. They didn't come down much. Never interfered."

Jenna squeezed her hands, her heart aching for Wally. He loved the town, the people, the horses. To her knowledge, he'd never turned down a fundraiser or any sponsorship request. But paying clients were few, and business had slowed to a trickle. It was a miracle he hadn't laid anyone off. For his sake, she hoped the new boss would be easy to work with...and didn't know much about massage.

She swallowed and glanced over her shoulder, resolving to stay up late and study another chapter in the library book. All her knowledge had been learned from her mom or by experimentation, and her massage technique was rather unorthodox. Maybe the new guy wouldn't approve.

Maybe there'd even be a test. Her stomach churned at the thought. She always felt stupid when people talked about college and university and degrees. Street smart, book dumb, her father had always said, usually with an approving wink.

"Thanks for the heads-up," she murmured, scrambling to her feet and scooping the empty bottles off the table.

Wally rose with a rueful smile. "You know I'll always look after the Murphy family. Long as they let me."

She waited until the lights of his truck disappeared then crossed the road and whistled for Peanut. He ambled from the dark and poked his muzzle into her hand, whiskers tickling as he snuffled for the tiny piece of carrot.

"Time for bed, mister." She guided him by his forelock to the kennels. Luckily he was small. Years ago, they'd raised foxhounds and the old mesh kennel was perfect for a tiny pony.

Perfect for her father too. He'd been too lazy to build a shelter or paddock, or perhaps he'd been in jail at the time. Memories blurred. She did remember her mother selling eggs and puppies, desperately trying to raise money for her horse-crazy daughters. Now it seemed natural to keep Peanut in a dog kennel and compensate by giving him the run of Three Brooks' vast acreage.

"Sleep tight, little buddy," she whispered. He pressed his head against her stomach and blew out a long sigh, his version of a goodnight kiss. She latched the gate and trudged through the dark toward the illuminated porch.

Beer always made her drowsy and she settled at the kitchen table, yawning as she flipped open the thick book: *Massage and Chiropractic for Equines*. Everyone assumed she had a college diploma. Wally had desperately wanted an effective horse masseuse on staff so had quietly fudged her resume, and everyone had been happy.

Besides, she *did* help horses. Clients were always pleased when their animals walked away much improved. Peanut was a great testimonial, still very limber for a senior citizen. She'd been massaging him for years so she must be doing something right.

Still, it was best to be prepared.

She propped the heavy book on the table. Her sister was probably studying too, and the notion that they were doing the same thing was rather comforting. Hopefully, Em wasn't missing home too much and could concentrate on her courses, especially since her high school marks hadn't been great, and Jenna was no longer around to help.

Fluttering moths distracted her, bumping loudly against the porch light, and she forced her attention back to the page. So much of this massage stuff was common sense, so simplistic her mind wandered. She needed to fertilize the vegetable garden, check on a lame donkey and she'd intended to ask Wally if the scowling man with the hint of a smile had landed a job.

She yawned twice, closed the book in defeat and crawled into bed with an equine heat pack tucked against her shoulder.

The sound of a vehicle woke her sometime during the night, but she was too tired to check the clock. She fell back to sleep, vaguely curious as to why the maintenance people were working so late.

Chapter Three

Derek Burke strode into the meeting room and scanned the group of silent, anxious faces. He didn't have to check his notes—thirty-seven employees, including a manager, grooms, handlers, exercise riders, and technicians—plus one masseuse. It was the masseuse who intrigued him.

She'd been stealing and his first impulse had been to hand her a pink slip. Yet she'd bristled when he'd criticized the manager and he admired loyalty. It was going to be a tough transition and unwise to alienate employees at this early stage. Most of the staff lived in the district, an area plagued with high unemployment. Some unpopular policy changes had already been implemented and it seemed likely he'd have to replace the affable manager.

He glanced sideways at Wally Turner and his disdain churned. Staff might like Wally but the man didn't even have enough initiative to keep the aisles clean. The accountants had also reported disturbing discrepancies and Three Brooks, operating at thirty percent capacity, should have achieved a healthier cash flow. There definitely needed to be an accounting, and he was prepared to cut and slash.

But first, soothe the masses.

Wally introduced him to a cautious scattering of applause. He studied the faces, memorizing the truculent who might cause trouble, and outlined the new goals and policies of the Center. "There will be no immediate layoffs," he said. "In fact, all employee credentials will be reviewed and salaries adjusted to industry standards."

The Burke public relations people had advised that his expression was much too grim so he concluded his speech with a tight smile. A big-busted lady near the front returned an inviting smile but his scowl was quick and automatic, and she averted her head.

And then they were finished. More applause, louder this time and clearly spiked with relief. Plenty of time now to weed out the poor performers, the hapless, the liars.

He lifted a hand, raising his voice so as to be heard over the buzzing crowd. "One final item. I'd like Jenna Murphy to meet me in my office." He deliberately refrained from saying 'please.' He had nothing but scorn for the Canadians and the permissive corporate culture they'd fostered.

"What do you want with Jenna?" Wally asked, his voice taut with an emotion Derek couldn't define.

"Pardon?" He scowled to show his displeasure and Wally dipped his head, nervously shuffling papers. Lazy and a coward as well, Derek decided, notching another tick in Wally's debit column.

Employees stepped aside as he strode toward his new office but he didn't look sideways. He was rather impatient to interview Ms. Murphy and actually surprised he hadn't spotted her regal head in the crowd. Perhaps she was shorter than he'd initially thought.

He left the door open, gratified to see the office was much cleaner than yesterday. Wally had been slow to vacate despite the Burke directive he was coming, and obviously the man had hoped the sale would flounder.

He yanked open the filing cabinet and flipped through the employee files. Jenna Murphy. The file was thin. Not even a resume. A copy of an insurance application, barely legible: Jenna Lynn Murphy, twenty-six, local address, one sister, parents deceased, unremarkable health, five-foot-nine inches, one hundred and twenty-two pounds, blond hair, blue eyes. Single.

Ah, so she was single.

He pushed the drawer shut, glanced impatiently at his watch, then crossed the room and checked the aisle. That too was much cleaner than yesterday, with stable hands knocking down cobwebs and sweeping furiously.

The outer door slammed and Jenna sauntered in, walking with a graceful sway of her hips, the proud tilt of her head unmistakable.

She stopped to greet a groom pushing a wheelbarrow then continued down the aisle. Paused when she spotted him, and a delighted smile lit her face. God, it had been a long time since anyone smiled at him like that.

"Good morning," she called. "I'm glad you got the job!"

He scowled but she didn't stop smiling and actually seemed genuinely happy to see him. An unusual reaction and his impatience seeped away. "Are you always this late?" he asked mildly.

"Not always, but a lot. Depends on my massage schedule." She gave an unrepentant smile. Stuck her head past him and checked the office. When she saw it was empty, she immediately backed away. "Better get out of there," she said, tugging at his arm. "Wally doesn't like people in his office. It wouldn't be smart to piss him off, not on your first day."

"So," she added, once she'd herded him to the middle of the aisle, "will you be working with the inventory or the cleanup? I can give you a quick tour if you want. Introduce you to everyone."

He paused, not usually at a loss for words, but her openness was refreshing. As the heavy for the Burke operations, employees either feared or disliked him. Not a problem, just the way it was. Still, this couldn't go on.

"I had a tour last month, Jenna." He crossed his arms. "My name's Derek Burke."

A flash of dismay then her expression shuttered, and she stepped back. "A pity. I liked you better with the hard hat."

"Come in. Shut the door." He pivoted and walked back into his office.

She followed but neglected to close the door. "What have you done with Wally?" she asked.

"He's moved into the receiving office at the other end of the barn."

Her shoulders relaxed as though that was the extent of her worries, and he frowned at the door, irritated she hadn't followed his simple order. "Maybe you should be worrying about your own job," he added.

"Maybe, but not yet." She tilted her head, eyeing him with sharp intelligence. "If Wally's still here the rest of us are probably safe, at least for a while."

She was absolutely correct but in spite of his desire to keep staff intact, theft was cause for dismissal. He leaned back in his chair, studying her over steepled fingers, waiting for a fidget. It didn't take long, fifteen seconds.

She crossed the room and picked up one of his framed degrees. "Wow, you're a smart guy."

"Put that down."

"Why do you have it here then?" she asked.

"Certainly not for employees to handle." He tilted his head and waited, realizing she wasn't going to confess or beg. Obviously the job didn't matter. Rather a pity. She'd shown him a simple kindness yesterday, and he'd already decided to let her stay.

"I'm still an employee then?" She replaced the frame and swung around, her shoulders relaxing, and he realized then he'd made a mistake. The job mattered to her; it mattered very much.

Good. It was always easier to control staff if he understood their motivations. "Of course, you're still an employee," he said. "At this stage, you're my closest friend in Stillwater."

Her mouth curved with irrepressible humor. "Kind of like your number one employee?"

"Let's not push it," he said, trying not to smile back. "And I don't want to see you lugging any more company supplies to your car."

"Oh, you won't see that again, Burke. Promise."

She flashed him a jaunty wave. He stupidly waved back, and she was gone before he could tell her not to call him Burke.

The next ten interviews were tedious and much more routine, ranging from a stammering receptionist to a brown-nosing groom. Derek turned his chair, glancing out the window at the construction site, watching as wood was expertly planed. Yesterday they'd been resizing planks, and he itched to get his hands on a power saw.

"Three Brooks is very important to me, Mr. Burke. I'm hoping to make head groom in five years."

Derek nodded, adding another doodle on his yellow pad.

"I've been working here for three years and always intended to take courses on animal husbandry. There's a college close by—"

"Yes, yes. That's excellent." Derek waved a hand in dismissal. "Your salary will raise ten percent when you complete a diploma. That will be all."

The man—pointless to remember all their names—rose and rushed away with a bounce in his step. Derek stretched his legs and exhaled. Clearly high unemployment in the area would make changes palatable and also help keep the most qualified staff. Tiresome though. Everyone had been nodding and bending over backwards, telling him anything they thought he wanted to hear, everyone but Jenna.

He swiveled his chair toward the big window, checking the parking lot for her car. There it was, jammed right beside his Audi, along with Fords, Fiats and a couple other rust buckets. That motley mix was definitely not good for Three Brooks' image. If he were to establish this as an elite facility, it had to look the part. He scrawled a notation on his pad, then rose from his chair and stalked down the aisle. It was time to see his new staff in action.

The hyperbaric oxygen chamber, in his opinion the most valuable technology at Three Brooks, was his first stop.

When he walked into the room, the technician sitting by the blinking control panel slammed down her mug and jerked upright in the chair. "Good afternoon, Mr. Burke."

Behind her, a horse's flicking ears were visible through the porthole window of the oxygen chamber. "Good morning," he said. "How many minutes is your average session?"

"Sixty."

"And you never leave the controls? You're always watching the horse?"

"Absolutely." The technician's head bobbed. "This is a pressurized environment. Someone always has to watch the monitors."

His eyes narrowed on the steam rising from her mug. "You never leave? Not even to grab a coffee?"

Her gaze darted downward. She flushed but didn't speak.

"Well?" he asked.

She withered under his flat tone. "Maybe just to grab a coffee, but it's only for a second—"

"When a horse is in the chamber, you do not leave. Ever. This is a flammable environment. If you need a break, call on the phone for a technician to replace you. I assume we have other trained staff members?"

"Yes, sir."

He nodded in dismissal and pushed through the end door, watching as two handlers held a bay gelding on a treadmill. Water bubbled against the transparent sides, swirling around the horse's legs.

The digital display showed one minute remaining.

"How many times has this horse had hydrotherapy?" he asked.

"At least five times, sir," the shorter handler said, frantically scanning his chart. "It's noted here somewhere."

"So you would assume he'll be quiet and not scramble out, possibly injuring himself or his handlers?"

"Yes, I'd definitely assume that. But horses are always unpredictable, sir."

"Exactly. Which is why you should have a chain over his nose."

"Of course. We were just…hurrying. Sorry, sir."

Derek nodded and stepped back. The second man grabbed a chain and looped it over the gelding's nose. Clearly this animal wasn't going to cause any problems. However, the Center's future patients would be fresh off the track and powered up from racing. He'd wait a few weeks before treating any top class horses. Let the staff practice on cheaper, more expendable animals.

He pushed through the swinging door and into the solarium. A chestnut mare stood under the infrared lights, head lowered, hind leg tilted, clearly enjoying her light treatment.

A slim brunette nodded but didn't meet his gaze. "Good afternoon. I'm Anna," she mumbled.

"I'm Mr. Burke." He stepped closer. "If you have owners or trainers checking on their horse, what would you tell them about this treatment?"

"That infrared stimulates circulation and helps skin issues or dermatitis. That it promotes their general well-being."

She faltered and he nodded encouragingly.

"I might also say," she added, "that they sometimes fall asleep under the lights and that it's especially beneficial after a massage. And that they love it."

"Very good, Anna. Now jog my memory—where exactly is the massage room?"

"Down the hall, to the left. But Jenna wants people to knock before entering."

He strode down the hall and pushed the door open, deliberately not knocking. Jenna glanced up from a thick textbook, her eyes flashing with annoyance. "Hey, Burke. Next time knock. Don't scare my horse."

"There's no horse in here."

Her smile was slightly mischievous. "But you didn't know that. Have a seat."

He didn't like to be offered anything that was already his, but it had been a tiring day and she, at least, wasn't uptight. He stretched out his legs, folded his arms behind his head and watched her through narrowed lids. Rather odd to have a textbook beside her. None of the other technicians had books.

"Studying for something?" he asked.

Her hesitation was almost imperceptible but it was there. "I have my massage diploma but I'm finishing my...equine sports certificate."

"Burke policy is to increase salary with all post secondary education."

Interest flared in her blue eyes. "Yes, I heard. Actually, I'm pretty much finished. So that's a ten percent increase, right?"

"That's right. How many horses can you massage a day?"

"As many as you want." She laughed. "And it also depends on what's wrong with them and how quiet they are."

"I need an exact time for scheduling. Is there an appointment book somewhere?" Massage was probably the least important treatment offered with less tangible results. If the profit margin was negligible, he intended to drop the service. Not that he'd tell her, not yet. And for now, it would increase profits to squeeze in as many massages as possible.

"Of course, there's an appointment book. Wally keeps it up to date." She subtly shifted on the chair, but his senses were honed and he knew the signs of guilt. "Would you like to see the next patient?" She gestured at the end doors. "Molly will be arriving soon."

And indeed Molly did arrive. He'd never seen such an ugly mare, with cow hocks, a swayback and a dragging left hip. "Jesus, why don't we just shoot her," he said.

"Shush, Burke. You'll hurt her feelings."

The handler's eyes widened. Jenna really shouldn't be telling him to shush—and she definitely shouldn't be calling him Burke—but he was too stunned by the horse to bother with a reprimand. This unsightly animal couldn't possibly be a Thoroughbred.

Jenna dragged a blue plastic block behind the horse's hindquarters and stepped up. He hadn't seen many massages before, but the ones he'd viewed had always started at the front. Maybe she was doing a shorter version since the horse was evidently on its last legs.

Made perfect sense, he decided.

"Is this a ship-in?" He cautiously lifted the mare's front lip, surprised to see a tattoo. Old and faded, but clearly a tattoo. Definitely a Thoroughbred.

"Molly's more like a lead-in," Jenna said with a smile. "Now please stop talking. I need to concentrate on my patient."

Her face set in concentration as her hands moved slowly down the horse's rump. The mare's trusting eye followed as Jenna circled to her side—clearly the mare believed she was in competent hands. Always a good sign.

But he was puzzled by Jenna's technique. This was like no massage he'd ever seen. "What exactly are you doing over the sacrum?"

She shot him a warning frown. "Be quiet, Burke."

He tightened his mouth and scowled at the attendant who ducked his head and scraped the rubber matting with his boot. At least one of the people in this room was respectful.

"There," Jenna pronounced, stepping gracefully off the block. "She should move better now."

Derek snorted. If this were Wally's clientele, no wonder Three Brooks operated in the red. He doubted anything could improve this nag, and it wouldn't help the Center's image to have animals collapsing in the aisles.

Clip, clop. His eyes widened as the mare walked evenly from the room. Nothing could ever be done for her conformation but her hip no longer dragged, at least not at a walk.

Jenna was leaving, following the mare without so much as a word, and he stalked after her. "Tell me what you did."

"Of course," she said. "But first I have to talk to the owner."

Talk to the owner. Of course. That was good. Owners and trainers appreciated full reports, would pay a premium for the service, although it was preferable to present them in writing, complete with a glossy folder. More efficient, better publicity and with the right clientele, the Center could draw horses from all over the eastern States.

He joined the parade, following the handler, the mare and Jenna down the aisle and through the wide end doors. He didn't see a trailer; in fact the receiving lot was disturbingly empty, a fact he needed to remedy.

A freckle-faced boy popped up from the grass, sporting ripped jeans, a stained shirt and a gap-toothed smile. "Thanks, Jenna. She looks way better now." The kid reached over and plucked the rope from the attendant's hand.

"Not so fast, Charlie." Jenna stepped forward, hands on her hips. "Have you been racing Molly again?"

"No, ma'am."

"Don't lie to me, young man. I know you've been racing."

"Maybe just a few times." The kid's gaze darted to the ground and he twirled Molly's lead rope. "I didn't mean to hurt her," he added sheepishly, "but I have to practice for the big race."

Jenna's voice softened. "It's not the galloping. It's the hard start. If you want to race, ask your friends for a trot start. She'll hold up much better."

"Yeah?" The kid brightened and tugged on the rope. "Can I ride her home?"

"Walk her down the driveway and mount past the gate. But take it easy and stay on the soft shoulder. Molly's a nice horse. You need to take care of her."

Derek dragged a hand over his jaw. "Leave us," he snapped, jerking his head at the handler who quickly fled back into the building. Derek waited until Charlie was out of earshot. "What the hell was that?"

"Local boy with a horse." Jenna shrugged. "I made the mare feel better."

He stared down the circular drive, watching as the kid angled his horse to a rock, scrambled onto her bare back and trotted away. "We treat ride-ins?" His voice sounded strange and he had the absurd notion he might laugh.

"Sometimes. This place is never busy so of course we help the community." She squared her shoulders. "Wally said you wanted to stop that, but I really think you should reconsider."

"This is a profit center, Jenna, not a charity. Our plan calls for treating an elite animal with a high profit margin. You can't have nags like that stumbling up to the back door. It weakens our image. Besides, who knows what contagious diseases they might carry?"

He shook his head, still scowling. Wally must be an imbecile, probably charging half price to locals. He stiffened, his eyes narrowing. "What price do the locals get?"

She stuck her hands in her back pocket, shrugging, and he was momentarily distracted by the way her shirt tightened over her breasts. Momentarily.

His voice hardened. "How much did he pay, Jenna?"

Her gaze darted to a blue bag half full of cans and he couldn't help it. The corner of his mouth twitched.

She grinned then, flashing him a conspiratorial smile that would lighten any man's mood. "Maybe we should charge a full bag next time?"

"There can't be a next time." He forced a frown, purely out of habit, but it was obvious he didn't scare her. Christ, she must be used to some hard-assed men. "We don't have insurance for walk-ins," he added, still trying to figure out how to stop this practice without raising the town's ire.

"I never let the kids mount until they're off the grounds," she said, reaching for the bag of cans. "I'm not that stupid."

"You're not stupid at all. And where are you going with those cans?"

"Putting them in my trunk."

"Ah, ha. But that would be stealing, Jenna."

"I usually collect them for the school. But I'll leave them in your office if you want."

He blew out a long and resigned sigh. "Please. Put them in your trunk."

Chapter Four

Peanut's ears flicked toward the crest of the road and Jenna guessed a car was coming. Despite his age, the pony's hearing was excellent.

Seconds later, she heard the purr of a powerful engine, definitely not a diesel.

She considered whistling for Peanut but feared he'd be hit when crossing the road. Besides, most of the caretakers tending the Three Brooks' mansion knew enough to slow down. Probably safer to leave the pony where he was.

A black car streaked over the hill and Peanut, for some obscure pony reason, ambled to the middle of the road, tiny ears pricked in welcome. Rocks peppered the bottom of the speeding car as it skidded to a halt. The driver's door snapped open.

Jenna sauntered down the steps and across the yard, hiding her fear the only way she knew how.

"What the hell is that?" Burke asked, stepping out.

"That's my racehorse, Peanut. You'll have to drive a little slower on this section."

"I'm not talking about the pony." His eyes widened as he stared over her head at the crooked trailer. "Please tell me Three Brooks doesn't own that."

"Three Brooks doesn't own that."

"You live there?" His normal scowl darkened to amazement.

"Happily."

"Indoor plumbing?"

"Installed last week." She laughed then because despite his growly exterior, he really was quite a good sport, not even complaining about loose livestock nibbling away at his property.

"I guess my place is a little further down."

"Yeah, another half mile," she said. "Wally had some extra cleaners working around the clock."

His scowl darkened and she regretted mentioning Wally, but Burke was still scrutinizing her property with a mixture of disbelief and revulsion. "This place needs a bulldozer."

"Absolutely not. It's my home."

His eyes narrowed. "Doesn't Three Brooks own this land?"

"Not this strip."

"I'll have our lawyers find a loophole and make you an offer. What's cooking?" He sniffed the air. "Chicken?"

"It's not ready yet."

"I'm in no hurry. And I want you to look at some appointment books, if you don't mind."

They both knew it wasn't a request and she turned away, pretending to admire the red glow settling over the valley. "You're working late?" she asked.

"Checking out a few things." He reached through the open window, grabbed the green appointment book and Wally's private blue one. Pocketed his keys with a wry smile. "Think my hub caps are safe here?"

"Peanut's pretty honest."

"Good to know."

Her feet dragged as she walked toward the porch. He, on the other hand, glanced around, assessing everything with a clinical stare. "Kennels? No hounds?"

"No hounds, not anymore."

He nodded as though he understood, but she knew he couldn't and she tugged her pride tighter, trying not to see the property through his eyes—the rusty hubcaps nailed to the shed, the crooked porch, the forlorn kennels. Deserted by everyone but her.

"Have a seat outside." She jammed her hands in her pockets, pretending a nonchalance she didn't feel. "Tea, water or beer?"

"Beer, please."

He was polite for a hatchet man and she opened the screen door, hurried to the stove and flipped off the oven—dammed if she'd share her chicken—grabbed two beers and kicked the fridge door shut with her foot.

She passed him the bottle, challenging him to ask for a glass, but he didn't say a word. Just nodded his thanks and took a long drink. His strong throat rippled. She took a second to admire the sight, but pulled her gaze away before he noticed.

The appointment books lay between them and she glanced down once, then stared at the reddening skyline. He hadn't spoken, and she was determined not to make it easy.

"Nice view." He settled against the seat, looking much too comfortable. "That pony always loose like that?"

"Only for an hour in the morning, a couple hours in the evening."

"I'll watch out for him then."

"Appreciate it." Her grateful smile faded as he reached down and picked up the books.

"You in this with Wally?" His voice was curiously flat, as though discussing the weather and not their deceit. However, anger radiated from his big body.

He was too savvy to trick and she blew out a weary sigh. "Yes, it started with a couple sore horses, worried owners who couldn't afford the treatment. The Canadians didn't care but didn't want the auditors to discover we were giving away free services. They asked Wally to keep a separate log. We probably do ten a week now, at free or reduced cost."

"I understand that. You made it perfectly clear this afternoon. But what about the other horses?"

"That's it." She shook her head in confusion. "There are no other horses."

He pulled out a sheet, pinning his gaze on her face. "Last week you massaged thirty horses. Yet in the official books, it's reported as thirteen. And it's physically impossible for anyone to massage thirty horses a week."

"It's not impossible. You saw how fast results came today."

"Strange massage." He grunted. "Looked more like chiropractic. And where's the money for the rest of the sessions?"

"I was having trouble with some bills," her throat thickened, "and Wally offered to pay me cash."

"How much does he pay per horse?"

"Twenty dollars."

"I see." But Burke didn't sound appeased and, if anything, his voice roughened. "That volume of horses can't be good for your shoulder."

She swallowed, ripe with misery. She'd blown it. He was going to fire her and rightly so—Emily would have nothing. "I'm sorry," she said, her voice thick.

"From now on, it's five horses a day, max. Don't push yourself. And no more under the table stuff."

He continued his lecture in a solemn voice, but she couldn't concentrate after the 'from now on.' Seemed she wasn't going to be fired after all. Her bottom lip quivered with relief. And gratitude.

She wasn't exactly sure when he turned silent or when his enigmatic eyes settled on her mouth. But she sensed his sudden awareness, the thickening of his breathing, the subtle shifting of his body.

"Want another beer?" She scrambled from the swing, holding her bottle in front of her chest like a shield.

"No, I'm good." He rose gracefully for such a big man. "I better go." He strode to his car without a backward glance.

Well, that's a relief. For one crazy moment, she'd thought he might kiss her and that could have turned out to be extremely problematic. So it was a relief he'd chosen to leave, most definitely.

He paused by his car. "We'll have that chicken tomorrow," he called, before sliding behind the wheel and roaring away.

Chapter Five

"Trevor's dad is a doctor," Emily said. "I can't bring him home. It would be way too embarrassing."

Jenna's fingers tightened around the phone, and she kicked the trailer door shut with her foot. "I'd never want to embarrass you, Em."

"Then you understand why I can't visit this month. Maybe later, when Trevor likes me enough."

Enough to overlook her dubious background. Jenna flung her purse on the passenger seat and jerked into the car. "Of course," she said, but it was hard to keep her voice from cracking. "Come when you can. And good luck with the biology paper."

"Thanks for helping with the research. I'd still like a summary though. At least this semester, you can help while the material is so basic. You won't understand once it gets complicated."

Jenna jammed the phone against her shoulder, fighting her frustration. Emily was ashamed—ashamed of her family, their home and once she had a degree she'd probably be more embarrassed. "I really have to go to work."

"Why the rush?" Emily's carefree laugh filled the phone. "Just tell Wally you're helping me with a course. He never cares when staff are late, as long as they do their job."

"Wally's not in charge, not now anyway. Three Brooks was sold. There's a new guy here."

"I heard something about that. Is he cute?"

Jenna paused. She wouldn't call Burke cute. He was too dangerous, circling like a panther, looking for a weakness and poised to pounce. She checked her watch. Thirty minutes on the cell, bills to pay and now late for work. "I'll work on your paper tonight, Em. But just the research. You have to do the rest. And remember not to use your cell phone so much. Texting is free."

Emily gave a long-suffering sigh. "I wish we had more money. Trevor doesn't understand when I ask him to text. And it would be a big help if you could do the summary too. Everyone else can afford to buy their papers. Bye, bye."

Jenna closed the phone, rubbing her forehead as she bounced the little Neon over the dirt road. Maybe on the weekend she could massage some local animals and make a few extra bucks. Unfortunately her friends and neighbors expected her to work for free, or else for a token bag of recyclables. Most people in the area simply couldn't afford high-priced pet care. However, she simply couldn't ignore animals in pain, not if there was something she could do to help.

Possibly she could buy some chickens and sell eggs again, but that wouldn't cover Em's phone bill or even come close to paying for new shingles. She'd grown to rely on the extra cash Wally paid and despite the toll the additional work took on her shoulder, its loss left a gaping hole in her paycheck.

She zipped into the parking lot and rammed her car into its usual spot. Stared through the windshield in dismay. A bold white sign jutted two feet from her bumper. Visitors Only, it proclaimed. She glanced around but there wasn't another car in the upper lot. No surprise that everyone else had listened.

At least *his* car was parked in the lower staff lot too, beside Frances's blue hatchback and Wally's Chev truck. The visitor section, however, was empty—a ridiculous waste of prime parking. Grumbling, she rammed the Neon in reverse and backed up, past the row of cars and Burke's gleaming Audi, hunting for a vacant spot. Finally found a slot, but it took an extra three minutes to rush up the winding walkway.

The clock in the main aisle showed eight forty but her first horse wasn't booked until nine, so it shouldn't be a problem. A hard hand grabbed her forearm, tugging her into the alcove between a wheelbarrow and a stack of blue feed bins.

Wally's flushed face was only inches from her nose. "What did you tell him about the books?"

"Hey, Wally, back off."

"Sorry." He immediately released her arm, dragging his hand over the dots of sweat beading his forehead. "Derek told me he saw the books. I tried to call but your phone was busy. So? What did you tell him?"

"Everything's fine," she said. "But we can't do community horses anymore, at least not at the same rate." She tried to remember everything Burke had said, but the words blurred. All she could remember was the primal intensity of his eyes, his hard mouth, the way it twitched when he tried not to laugh.

"But what about the cash horses?" Wally's voice rose. "You didn't say anything about those, did you?"

"Well, yes, I did, but he already knew about them. He had both sets of books."

"Goddammit."

Jenna stiffened. Wally was usually easygoing. She'd never seen him so agitated and he definitely needed to back out of her space. She tilted her head. "What's going on? Have you been pocketing money?"

"A little, but we can cover it. All you have to do is say you were paid a hundred dollars per horse."

"But I already told him the truth. That you paid me twenty."

"Just say you forgot." His voice tightened with impatience. "Come on, don't look at me like that. I helped a few people out. The money's gone."

"But you took eighty dollars a horse?" She gulped. She'd been so happy to earn extra money, she hadn't questioned how much the cash horses were paying in total. No wonder Wally was considered a local Santa Claus. No wonder the Center struggled.

"Christ, Jenna, the Tuttys couldn't afford colic surgery. I had to raise the money somehow."

She crossed her arms, caught in a moral tug of war. "Did the Canadians know?"

"They didn't care." But he averted his gaze. "Come on. My job's on the line. It's just a little lie. Make sure you think about this."

She jerked away and rushed down the aisle, too stunned to look at him. She'd never guessed he was using the Center's money to cover outside vet bills, hadn't even thought about the reporting requirements. Probably why he was so paranoid about anyone going into his office. Maybe she should have questioned him…or maybe, deep down, she'd known.

She gave her head a shake, not liking that idea. Sure, sometimes she was a little creative but only if it didn't hurt anyone. Yet if Wally felt the need to cover up, this couldn't be good. Her breath escaped in a tormented sigh.

"Your nine o'clock was moved to eight-thirty," Frances, the receptionist called. "The horse is in there now. Better hurry."

Jenna grimaced, still thinking of Wally. "Guess the mare won't mind if I'm a little late, Frances."

"She won't mind at all because someone else is massaging her."

Jenna jerked to a stop, forgetting about Wally and his troublesome Robin Hood tendencies. "You're kidding. Who's doing the massage?"

"Kathryn Winfield. She's pimping for a job now that she finished that massage program in Kentucky." Frances shrugged, her shoulders returning to their perpetual hunch. "Mr. Burke said he'd watch her work on a horse. Glad it's not me. He's scary."

But Kathryn Winfield wouldn't be intimidated, Jenna knew. Kathryn was smart and was armed with a degree as well as a diploma from that new center in Kentucky. Her dad, Leo, was a town bigwig. Kathryn had never really liked animals though, and it was doubtful she'd be effective as a therapist. So if Burke wanted results and was astute enough to ignore the bullshit, Jenna's job wasn't really in jeopardy.

Oh, God, please. She prayed her job wasn't in jeopardy.

She detoured by the staff room—heck, she was already late—and made herself a fortifying cup of tea. On impulse, she poured a coffee for Burke. Kathryn would be busy with the horse and besides she was much too nasty to be served a cup.

Jenna knocked quietly—this mare was rather skittish and needed little excuse to jump—before pushing the door open. She spotted Burke, looking rather bored, his hip propped against the back wall as he watched Kathryn work on the mare's left shoulder.

"Good morning," Jenna said, passing the coffee to Burke. Everyone thought he never smiled but that lip twitch spoke volumes. Unfortunately, his lip wasn't twitching now.

"Oh, you're finally here, Jenna," Kathryn called, tacking a smile onto her snide greeting. "I was just telling Mr. Burke that this mare would benefit from some craniosacral therapy. I certainly hope you're doing that?"

"Of course." Jenna took a quick sip of tea. *What the hell was craniosacral therapy?* She did know the mare had a displaced sacrum, and she itched to make it right. She peeked at Burke over the top of her cup.

From the jaded look on his face, it was clear he'd rather join the construction crew outside than watch his technicians do boring things with their hands. Maybe he'd already been on the work site. A car had roared past her trailer early this morning but it had been deathly dark, and she'd merely dragged a pillow over her head. The smell of fresh pine clung to his clothes though—that appealing earthy smell—and the way his chiseled throat rippled when he drank was also pretty darn appealing.

He lowered his cup. "How did you know I like my coffee black?"

She jerked her wayward gaze back to his face. "Going with the odds." His type would consider it a weakness to add milk or sugar. "What exactly is happening here?" she added, trying to sneak a peek at Kathryn's resume, curious as to what fancy title they bestowed on the elite Kentucky grads.

He raised his arm, deftly blocking her view. "We need a massage therapist on the grounds from eight to four. I don't care *who* it is, as long as someone's here." The warning in his clipped voice was unmistakable, but on the bright side he seemed to be enjoying his coffee.

She'd been late and with a man like Burke, the best defense was to go on offense. She shook her head and moved one step closer. "Well, you should care who the therapist is. Did you notice how that mare walked?"

"Short in the right hind."

His quick analysis surprised her, but she nodded. "Exactly. So she needs manipulation over the sacrum."

"But that's chiropractic, not massage." His eyes narrowed. "Where exactly did you get your diploma?"

"A local college." She didn't want to meet his penetrating eyes so took a hasty gulp of tea. Almost burned her mouth. Luckily he seemed to have forgotten she'd wandered in late, but this college topic was also very sticky. Her workmates had been buzzing about possible raises but in her opinion, far too much credence was placed on formal education.

It was a pity simple, old-fashioned results didn't matter. She'd been helping animals since she was nine and truly loved her job. Heck, she could probably make up fancy college titles and no one would be the wiser.

She studied him over the cup, her mind churning. Wally had said Burke was an exceedingly busy man and wouldn't be staying in Stillwater long. Certainly not long enough to check diplomas.

She drew in a fortifying breath and lowered her cup. "I went to a local college and as we discussed yesterday, I just finished another update for my Equine Sports Massage Certificate. Does that qualify for a raise?"

"We need documentation, of course," he said, "but there's a pay bump on top of your upgrade. And you're presently underpaid for the diploma you have."

Jenna's eyes widened. "Underpaid? By how much?"

"Eight percent. Plus you'd get another ten percent for the completed certificate. Burke Industries encourages education. We stand behind our promise of having the most qualified employees in the business."

She shut out his rah-rah-Burke speech, too busy with calculations. Eighteen percent! Her last raise had been a two percent cost-of-living almost three years ago. She bounced on her toes, almost spilling her tea. This was awesome. Burke Industries was awesome. Her face split in a delighted grin. "You're awesome, Burke!"

The words leaked out with bubbling joy. She saw his blink of surprise, the lip twitch, then an actual smile. He had such a beautiful mouth. Not even the perpetually timid Frances could be scared of a man with that kind of mouth—tolerant, kind, amused.

She gave a guilty jerk as Kathryn's voice cut their connection.

"See what I mean, Mr. Burke?" Kathryn called. "This mare would definitely benefit from an intensive schedule of craniosacral therapy. They've pioneered that program in Kentucky and taught us how to perform at a deeper and more intuitive level. We can do so much more," she glanced pointedly at Jenna, "than the basic massage they teach locally."

"That's fine, Kathryn," Burke said, his voice clipped. "Thanks for stopping by. We'll certainly keep your resume on file."

He turned to Jenna, his dark eyes inscrutable. "Can you work your magic on that mare? I'll be back in an hour to check her walk. Then send her for thirty minutes of infrared. Thanks for the coffee."

Jenna watched in stunned appreciation as he strode from the room. Maybe he was results oriented. Wally was generous and wanted to help every horse and person he encountered, but his knowledge of lameness was rudimentary. The door snapped shut behind Burke's broad shoulders.

Kathryn scowled. "Dad said they were upgrading staff. Said the new people should appreciate a college grad. I don't understand. You just have a measly certificate, right?"

Not even. Jenna lobbed her empty cup into the metal garbage can and walked toward the mare. Even now the horse rested her right hind, tail and hip cocked at an odd angle. Poor girl. "I'll be sure to let you know when they're hiring, Kathryn," she said politely.

"No need. My dad's a member of the Hunt Club. He'll talk to Mr. Burke there. You know what the Club is like...oh, sorry." Kathryn gave a disdainful sniff. "Guess you don't."

Still a bitch, just like in high school, Jenna thought. She deliberately widened her smile. "Oh, but I've been there a few times. Colin took me on several occasions, remember... Oh, sorry, guess you don't."

Kathryn's lips narrowed to a malicious line. "Well, you won't get there again because I'm dating Colin now. And you and your tramp sister still live in that dog shack."

"My sister's not a tramp!" Jenna charged forward.

"Relax." Kathryn raised her palms, backing to the door. "A tramp is actually a step up for your family. And I will have this job." She gave her fingers a sarcastic flutter and sashayed from the room, her designer boots clicking on the concrete.

Jenna unclenched her fists and turned back to the horse. Nothing to worry about. The Center had always been safe from Leo's influence. Wally was a rock. But her breathing remained ragged, and the mare's soulful brown eyes seemed to reflect Jenna's growing concern.

The powerful saw roared in Derek's hands, slicing through the wood with an aggressive thrust. He flicked the switch and the air hushed. "A couple more like that," he said to the foreman. "I'll be back tomorrow morning."

The man nodded and if he was resentful of Derek's hands-on style, he hid it well. "Certainly, Mr. Burke. As you suggest, we'll start at six."

Derek nodded, wiped his forehead with his arm and headed back into the Center, grateful for the diversion. Construction work always provided an outlet. It was no coincidence he'd approved the building of a storage shed. Generally it was the only release he had. Employees steered clear of him, tiptoeing with wary eyes, as well they should.

He was the Machiavellian arm of the organization. But when he left, companies were leaner, more profitable, much improved.

Often he was in and out in a few weeks; at other jobs he remained much longer. Three Brooks needed some streamlining but it shouldn't be too long a stay. Add a much-needed facelift and good horses would be clamoring for appointments, engendering the fees every elite stable expected to pay.

Of course, Three Brooks also needed a new manager. Wally Turner was lazy, incompetent and dishonest. Termination wouldn't even require a payout if the theft could be proven. Jenna had already admitted she only received twenty dollars per horse. If that were confirmed in writing, they'd have Wally by the balls.

Shouldn't be too many issues with this assignment, other than the usual loneliness and boredom. His one meal at the Hunt Club had been spoiled by constant intrusions from social climbers, and their groveling aroused nothing but his annoyance. Typical. People in small communities generally were either hostile or fawning although Jenna was totally unapologetic about anything. He rather liked that.

Long hair and legs didn't hurt either, but it was her honesty he most enjoyed. That and the fact she'd stood up to him on his first day, yet had been inherently kind enough to offer advice on landing a grunt job. Amusing really.

But she was a thief.

He shoved aside that thought, annoyed by his ambivalence. Stealing supplies wasn't something he condoned, although technically it hadn't been on his watch. And at the last second, she'd warned him not to barge into Wally's office. That counted for something.

He strode into the building, scanning the reception area. Everything looked fine except the way the receptionist shrank whenever he looked at her. Jesus. People would think they beat horses here.

Unthinking, he wheeled and barged back into the massage room, scaring the jumpy mare. Jenna calmed the mare, returning to work on the horse's muscled rump. "How many times do I have to ask you to knock?" she asked.

"Apparently more than once," he said, "but I need your help. Please tell that woman out front to smile. We're supposed to be a happy, healing environment."

"Then maybe you could set a better example." Her voice was mild though, and it was clear she was focused on her job.

"Unlikely." He grabbed a chair and sat, tilting it against the wall. She leaned back into the mare, and the horse lowered her head seeming to enjoy Jenna's ministrations. And why not.

Jenna was a looker, and this was an excellent chance to admire. Her legs were almost as long as the mare's, shapely and elegant in those faded jeans. When she raised her toned arms, her shirt tightened, and if he looked hard enough he could almost imagine the outline of a nipple.

Damn, when had he slept with his last girlfriend? Must have been awhile. He'd taken Theresa to dinner that last week in New York but couldn't remember any of the details.

He dragged his head away, switching his attention to the mare. She stood evenly now and her hip no longer appeared broken. However, Jenna was holding her shoulder oddly high and didn't seem to be using her right hand with as much pressure.

"Your shoulder bothering you again?" he asked.

"It's fine," she said quickly. "I can do my job."

He rose, shaking off his impatience. "Obviously you can do your job. But we don't want any workplace injuries either. Are you finished? Let's see her walk."

"Sheesh, just give her a minute. She's all relaxed here."

"We have to keep a schedule. Have to be able to handle a lot more horses." He watched critically as Jenna led the mare along the rubber walkway. Stared in disbelief as the mare stepped out with a loose, swinging stride. Unbelievable. Just like the horse yesterday.

He shook his head. Obviously the massage end of the Center was in good hands. He'd match Jenna against anyone in North America. He still wasn't confident of the infrared benefits though. Some of the holistic elements here seemed a little left field, but if horse owners wanted it, Three Brooks needed to provide it.

At this point though, he was definitely satisfied with his masseuse. "Damn, Jenna, but you do good work."

She gave him that hundred watt smile, like a model on a runway, a model with a slightly sore shoulder.

"I want you to stand with that mare under the infrared light," he added, checking his watch, "and we're going to move your second appointment to this afternoon."

"But that means I only do three horses today." Her smile faded. "I can't buy groceries with that."

He scowled, unused to being questioned. "You're paid the same, no matter how many horses you rub. And you need to follow orders, without all this debate." But she was watching him with that hostile look and he much preferred her smile. "Besides," he softened his voice, "I really want to see if the infrared will help your shoulder."

"Oh, so you're using me as an experiment? That's neat. I've never been in the solarium before. It's fifty dollars a session."

He walked over and pried the mare's lead line from her hand. "And the price is going up. Now lift your arm and see if you can reach my shoulder."

She raised her right arm, face set in concentration. There was some sort of shiny stuff on her lips and her hair smelled like flowers. However, pain shadowed her face and he grabbed her wrist, sensing she wasn't the type to quit.

"Don't push it," he said quickly. "We'll try again after the infrared, okay?"

She nodded, staring with those vivid blue eyes. He realized he still held her wrist, could feel the pounding of her pulse and knew she wanted to get away. Not good. If he was going to nail Wally, he needed her loyalty. Needed her trust. "I can't have my top employee getting hurt," he said, forcing a smile.

She rolled her eyes. "Bet you say that to all your employees."

"Actually, no." He chuckled and this time his emotion wasn't at all forced. "Only the ones who make me dinner."

"Sorry. The chicken's gone—"

"I need you to sign some papers. And I'll bring the food."

She tilted her head as though pretending she had some say in the matter, then slowly nodded. "All right. See you around six." She plucked the lead line from his hand, patted the mare's neck and led the horse toward the exit.

"Make sure you stand under that infrared," he called. "And drop by my office afterwards so we can check your range of motion. I need to know if that thing works." He didn't want to admit he also appreciated her company, that she was the only person who didn't freeze in his presence.

Maybe he should call Theresa back and invite her down for the weekend. But then he'd have to entertain her all day. Nights were okay—he could do nights. But all day? He sighed, reluctant to admit that he preferred to pound nails.

Chapter Six

Jenna swore, almost hitting her finger with the rusty hammer. She gave the nail one last whack then stood back and admired her new certificate.

Two actually. She now had a Diploma in Equine Massage Therapy as well as a Certificate in Equine Sports Massage. All in one day—impressive. It probably hadn't been necessary to add 'Graduated With Distinction' but it seemed reasonable that, when forging, you should go whole hog. And maybe Burke and Company had another pay hike for exceptional marks. She had to admit the certificates looked wonderful on the wall.

At first she'd been scrambling for an excuse to avoid supper with Burke but this was perfect. She'd invite him into the kitchen where he could see her impressive qualifications, and maybe he'd overlook the fact that her employee file was empty.

She didn't want him to have a copy, too easy to check validity. However, Wally had said employers rarely checked resumes after a buyout. She tilted her head, debating. Maybe it would be prudent to offer help with file organization—yes, she definitely should do that.

Once Burke left, Wally would be back in control. So far, the main change was that employees had enjoyed a pay review. Certainly new ownership hadn't been the disaster Wally predicted. It sucked she couldn't treat local horses at the Center anymore, but she'd already promised to be on hand at the county fair and steeplechase. And she could still volunteer on weekends.

In contrast to Wally, Burke believed only expensive horses deserved treatment—a totally asinine concept. She'd continue to help needy animals. If owners couldn't afford it, no problem; she'd treat them outside the Center's hallowed halls.

Just like Peanut.

She grabbed the dewormer and hurried outside, ducking her head at the spattering rain, debating if she should put him in the kennel. The years had stiffened his joints, and little Peanut hadn't wintered well. It didn't seem to matter how much glucosamine or other fancy products Wally kicked her way. Peanut still creaked when he walked, and his once-shiny coat was dry and dull.

She shoved her fingers in her mouth and whistled, a sharp blaring noise that rang in her ears. Peanut trotted across the road, bright-eyed and eager for his daily treat.

"Hey, boy." She fed him a piece of cut carrot then carefully shot a fifth of the tube of dewormer into his mouth. Enough paste left for four more treatments. The dewormer might outlive Peanut, she thought with an ache.

It was a shame the infrared machine wouldn't fit in her backpack. No doubt it would help. The session today had proven its effectiveness, and she was grateful Burke had made her hold the mare under the lights. She rolled her right shoulder, amazed it was still loose and pain free.

This morning she couldn't lift her arm high enough to reach Burke's shoulder; yet when they'd repeated the experiment after the infrared, she'd been able to grip him with ease. Well, not quite with ease since her fingers certainly couldn't stretch over his brawny shoulder. No doubt about it, if Burke decided to boot employees, he'd have no problem single-handedly tossing them out the door.

Peanut gave her elbow an impatient nudge. She jerked her attention off men and muscles and back to her pony, wishing she'd led him down the path for some infrared sessions while Wally was still in charge.

She scratched his damp neck, saw his ears prick and a moment later heard the purr of an engine.

Aw, shit. Burke was early. And her shirt was too wet, too faded. She considered making a dash to change, but his car had already swooped over the ridge.

He opened the door and stepped out, giving Peanut a dismissive glance before reaching in and grabbing two big brown bags. Yummy odors wafted on the breeze and her mouth watered.

Garlic, onion, tomato, and suddenly it didn't matter so much that he was intruding.

"Italian, right?" she asked, pressing a hand over her stomach, hoping he hadn't heard its delighted rumble.

He nodded, his gaze drifting over her shirt. "Let's get inside. You're soaked."

She had a problem taking orders and didn't move. However, her cheeks flamed when she glanced down and saw how wet her shirt really was. "You're early," she muttered. However, his eyes narrowed on her chest with open appreciation so she crossed her arms and retreated toward the trailer.

"Hope you brought something to drink with that," she called over her shoulder, aware she sounded churlish but needing to have the last word. "I've got stuff to do too, so you can't stay long. And my company always sits on the porch."

"I have wine," he said. "Dessert too."

"That's the best kind of company. Guess you can come inside for a minute." She swung around in time to catch the twitch of his lip and couldn't help but smile back.

His gaze swung over the trailer's aluminum siding, its patchwork roof, and she braced for the inevitable flash of disdain. Even Wally was never quite able to hide his revulsion. Sure, he tried but no one could totally conceal it.

"Jenna, every time I drive by this place I want to order a backhoe."

He wasn't trying to hide anything and her discomfort fizzled, blowing out her mouth in a ragged laugh. She paused on the steps, no longer worried about her wet shirt or about how she didn't want him to see her cramped kitchen.

"It's pretty bad, isn't it." The admission left her strangely light. "My mom was born here. Her dad kept foxhounds for the local hunt. Peanut is older than me." She sighed. "It would hurt so much to leave."

"It's a beautiful location." His smile was quick and understanding. "And you're one up on me. My father had six houses and a horse farm, and I never cared for any of them."

"Well, I do care about this. So please don't call in your wrecking crew." She glanced at the bags in his arms and held open the door. She'd give him a minute to stand in the kitchen, see her fancy certificates and then they'd go back outside. The porch really was the nicest part of the trailer anyway. No one could possibly criticize the view.

"I'm going to change," she added. "There's a corkscrew in the left drawer."

When she returned five minutes later, he stood politely by the kitchen table. The wine bottle was open and cartons of food were spread on the table, but she had the feeling he'd absorbed every detail of the room—the crooked linoleum, the leaky tap, the water-stained ceiling.

"Is that a picture of your sister?" he asked.

"Yes. She's away at college." Jenna couldn't hide her ring of pride but deliberately let her gaze settle on the wall where her own certificates now hung. Unfortunately his attention remained on Jenna's face.

She brushed past him and reached for two plates, making sure her arm rubbed the wall close to the glistening new frames. He still didn't look.

"Is she coming back?" he asked.

"Em? Of course. She loves it here. Has lots of good memories of the place." Excellent memories. Emily didn't seem to remember the fights, the fists, the constant fear. Plates rattled as Jenna drew a ragged breath. "Let's eat on the porch."

He silently helped her carry everything out. Once settled, he passed the containers of pasta and salad, waiting as she scooped some fettuccine onto her plate.

"Is this from Claudio's?" she asked, taking an appreciative sniff. "They have the best food in town."

"That's what I heard but I hate eating alone." He expertly poured the wine. "So thank you for the company."

She rolled her eyes. "No need to pretend, Burke. We both know any number of women would be delighted to join you. But you need me to sign some papers, you probably want information on some unfortunate employees and Claudio's is a good exchange. I get it. But let's eat first."

He arched an amused eyebrow. "You're smart, Jenna. I like you."

Her heart gave a little kick but she plunked herself onto the swing. He wouldn't like her quite so much when she changed her statement about earning twenty dollars per horse. But if it saved Wally and he promised to keep better records, what could it hurt?

Besides, she wanted Wally to remain as manager, not be fired and have some new guy parachute in. The town needed Wally. Best to tell Burke after their meal though. No doubt, he'd be furious when she retracted last night's statement.

And that was truly unfortunate because he was easy company. He appeared relaxed on the wide swing, crammed next to a scarred wooden table. Drops rattled the roof and fresh rain thickened the air.

He nodded at Peanut, grazing placidly across the road. "Your little guy doesn't mind wet weather?"

Jenna swallowed another delicious bite of gnocchi and shook her head. She hadn't eaten at Claudio's since Colin had taken her. "Peanut doesn't even notice it. He loves that green grass over there—your side of the road is always fertilized—and I'm hoping the rain will help his coat." She sucked in a fortifying breath. "I was thinking a few sessions under the solar lights might help him too."

"Absolutely not." Burke's refusal was swift and dismissive. "That pony is not the clientele we're targeting. And who knows what kind of communicable diseases he has, something that could infect a million dollar racehorse."

"No worries. His lice are gone. I treated him yesterday." She peered sideways, searching for the flinch of disgust, but Burke only reached for the wine and topped up her glass.

"Have you always had such a chip on your shoulder?" he asked. "Drink a little more wine. Sweeten up."

He obviously wasn't going to give her pony any breaks, but it was hard to summon much annoyance when he spoke so reasonably. And he had brought some very good wine.

The containers were still half-full when she wiped her mouth with a napkin and reluctantly conceded she was stuffed. And Burke was looking way too relaxed, long legs stretched out, glass tucked in his large hand, like he wasn't going anywhere soon.

Almost like a date.

"So, what are these papers you want me to sign?" She deliberately clipped her voice, knowing she had to get things back on a business footing.

"Just a statement saying you received a cash payment of twenty dollars per horse."

"And after I massaged the horses, I received another eighty dollars from Wally." She avoided his eyes, concentrating on closing the plastic containers. "I'm not sure if I mentioned that last night."

"No, actually you didn't." He swirled the wine in his glass, holding it up and inspecting the color. "So now you're saying you received a total of one hundred dollars per horse?"

"Yes, that's right." She nodded but the food in her stomach suddenly felt like a brick. "So you see, I can't sign your paper. I'm very sorry about this—your time, the beautiful dinner, the lovely wine—such a waste."

"Not a waste at all, as I do have some other questions." He set his glass down, his expression unreadable under the darkening sky. "You can tell me the town's opinion of Three Brooks."

She tilted her head. Seemed like a reasonable request. Nothing that could hurt Wally or anyone else on staff.

"The previous owners, the Canadians, were hardly ever here," she said slowly. "They left everything up to Wally. He always hired employees from Stillwater and also sponsored a lot of events, like the annual steeplechase. And of course, town horses were treated at a reduced rate. Wally, naturally, is very popular and some people even think he owns the place."

She leaned forward, stacking the leftovers in the bags Burke had brought. "Wally's dad used to run the Center but back then it was more of a lay-up and training facility. Now it's a combination of equine health and conditioning. It's always been a good corporate citizen. Three Brooks has a great relationship with the town."

But Wally's generosity wasn't good for any company's bottom line, and she gulped, fearing Burke's next question.

"You're good friends with Wally?"

She blinked in surprise, staring at Burke through the gloom. Not the financial questions she'd expected. "Really good," she said cautiously. "Everyone likes him."

"Likeable, but he's not a good manager?"

"That's not what I said. He's an excellent manager." She grabbed the bags and twisted in her chair. "Here are the leftovers. Thanks for supper."

He gestured at the half-empty wine bottle "The food can stay but I'm not leaving until the wine is gone."

"It is good wine," she admitted, picking up the bottle, trying to read the label in the dark. "Way better than what's brewing in the still out back."

And that didn't even get a rise out of him. He stared silently across the road to where Peanut grazed contentedly, hardly distinguishable now in the darkening rain. "The receptionist smiled a little more this afternoon," he finally said. "I assume you spoke to her. I appreciate that."

"They're scared of you, Burke. They think you're always mad at something."

"But not you?"

"You've got a little spot on the side of your mouth. Right here." She touched the right side of her lip. "It's a giveaway. You actually smile quite a bit."

"Bullshit. You can't see that."

"Sure I can."

"You'd be a helluva card player."

"I already am. We *have* heard of cards around here."

"Grab a deck and prove it."

She eyed him warily. Probably no harm but there'd been some hot-tempered poker games played on this porch. And way too many fights. In her experience men didn't like to lose, even if they could afford it. She definitely didn't want to piss him off.

"We're not playing for real money." She reluctantly pushed aside the bags and gathered some red and white poker chips. Be nice to take his cash but clearly it would be corporate suicide. He was a guy who expected to win—that was abundantly clear. "How about white chips are a buck, red are five?"

"That'll do," he said but there was a wolfish eagerness to his mouth and when she passed him the deck, his easy handling of the cards showed he was no amateur.

She leaned forward, intrigued at how his lean fingers flew over the cards. Her dad had always said to watch the shuffle.

"Poker. Texas hold 'em," he said. "And to make it more exciting, the winner gets the leftover food, including dessert." He raised an eyebrow as though expecting her to protest, but she'd already checked the dessert and it wasn't one she liked. No, she'd let him win, put him in good humor and maybe he'd forgive her for not signing that paper.

Strangely enough though, he seemed to have already forgiven her.

An hour later, they were still playing and she forgot she was trying to let him win. And that the wine was long gone. "Ah, ha! You were bluffing!" She fanned her cards on the table in triumph. "I hate to take your food like that. You're actually a pretty good player, Burke."

"You're not a bad player yourself, Jenna, but you were lucky tonight." He touched her arm and she stiffened, fumbling with the deck. "How's the shoulder feel?" he asked.

"It's fine." She rose, grabbed the smaller bag and shoved it into his arms. "And because you're such a good loser, you can take the dessert as a consolation prize."

"You must not like Tiramisu?" he said dryly. "I should be relieved. If we were playing for money, you'd be rich."

"You don't seem to mind losing," she said thoughtfully.

"Not at all. I'd like to play again. For small stakes, of course."

"Of course." It was an effort to keep from rubbing her hands in glee. He wouldn't miss fifty dollars here and there, and he wasn't even a poor loser. In fact, he was the most level man she'd ever met—the Internet reports painting him as a ruthless ogre were totally wrong.

It wasn't until his headlights swept over the dark hill that she realized the dinner had been in vain, and her new credentials still hung, unnoticed, on the kitchen wall.

Chapter Seven

"Good morning, Mr. Burke."

The receptionist's smile was forced but it was a huge improvement on her previous mumbled greetings. Jenna clearly had influence over her co-workers and targeting the unofficial leader was always an effective labor strategy.

Soften the leader and the rest came along easily. It kept employment disruption to a minimum. When the occasional staff members were fired—an inevitable occurrence—Burke Industries was already entrenched.

Clearly there was a new buzz to the Center. Aisles were spotless, workers moved with alacrity and soon they'd be ready to treat some classy horses.

Burke shoved his key in the lock and pushed open the office door, scanning the room with a suspicious eye. One drawer was tightly closed; he'd deliberately left it open a quarter inch, and the pen on top of his files now lay at a different angle.

Wally, no doubt. Nothing a locksmith couldn't fix, but it would be a relief when Wally Turner was gone and a new manager installed. Three Brooks was no longer a charity case and deadwood had to be culled. Unfortunately, Wally's termination for just cause had been blown when Jenna refused to sign the statement. Burke sighed. He hated to give a severance package to a thief.

It was clear Wally was skimming profits but that would be difficult to prove. Burke had scrutinized the appointment books and none of the other technicians had received cash, only Jenna. He needed her good will. And her signature.

He scrolled through his phone messages. Three increasingly plaintive ones from Theresa that he'd have to answer sometime but Christ…he rubbed his forehead. Feminine distraction was not what he needed now and besides, it was more fun playing cards with Jenna.

Hell, she was distraction enough. A couple times last night, he'd even forgotten why he was sitting on her cozy porch. Her saucy smile made his brain fog. She'd sucked at her bottom lip and dropped her guard when she was playing cards, so into the game. Damn good at reading him too, although he could have won most of the hands.

The subject line of the next text shoved Jenna from his thoughts: Derby winner struggling in breeding shed. We ready?

He quickly called his cousin. "What horse is it?" he asked, grabbing his pen.

"Mr. Nifty," Edward said. "Chestnut colt that won the Derby and Preakness eight years ago. His offspring have been burning up the track. But confidentially, he's having trouble covering mares, and the owners are desperate. They're hoping it's body soreness. Bad for them but a great opportunity for us.

"Anyway, how are you doing out there in the boonies?" Edward gave an amused chuckle. "Straightening out those hillbillies?"

"It's not so bad," Burke said. "Some mismanagement needs to be worked out. Staff is generally competent."

"Then can you help this horse?"

Burke dragged a reluctant hand over his jaw. He didn't like to be rushed, hadn't reviewed all employee qualifications yet and there was that sticky business with Wally. Still, the public relations benefits of helping a Derby winner would be astronomical.

"Who are the owners?" he asked, stalling for time, uneasy with his gut reaction.

"Ridgeman Racing Stables, that outfit in Kentucky. And they're willing to transfer full payment in advance. The stud is worth millions."

"Worth zilch if he can't breed," Burke said.

"Whatever. They're going to pay someone so it might as well be us. Let's do it. You got special lights and magnets and all that yoga shit."

"Jesus, Edward. It's not yoga." Burke grinned, picturing his citified cousin sitting behind his mahogany desk high in their New York office. Edward was a master negotiator but didn't care much about the workings of the companies. As usual though, his enthusiasm was contagious.

"All right," Burke said, blowing out a sigh. "We'll take the horse for a couple weeks. He'll be our first big client. Be great if it works out." *Not so great if it doesn't.*

He cut the connection and began listing preparations. Sharpen staff, beautify the landscape, check on security. Wouldn't be smart to fire Wally now, although maybe he'd quit on his own. Without just cause, that would be the perfect solution. Staff would be complacent too, especially if pay hikes were pushed through. Money was generally the quickest way to inspire loyalty.

Checking on staff credentials though—tedious job. Best to hire a temp, and quickly.

He called the reception desk, struggling to remember the woman's name, and then remembered Jenna had called her Frances. "I need the number for the local employment center, Frances," he said.

"You looking for grooms?" Her voice had an irritating squeak.

"No," he said. "Secretarial work."

"Don't think there's a place like that…not sure."

"Well, think a little harder. And call me back," he snapped. He'd search it himself, find a landscaping company too. For God's sake, how hard could it be?

Ten minutes later, Jenna burst in.

"Did you have to be so cruel?" She stalked up to his desk, hands on her hips, eyes flashing.

"Don't you have a horse to massage?" he asked, surprised at her temper but secretly appreciative of the distraction.

"Only one, and I'm already finished. We're not booking locals, remember?" She gave a theatrical sigh then seemed to remember her mission. "So why are you replacing Frances? She only looks unhappy because she's overweight. And she did wash the feed room floor yesterday." Jenna splayed her hands over his desk and leaned closer. "I really think you should reconsider. People here are just starting to like you. And that's important in a small community."

He couldn't help it. Her beautiful chest grabbed his attention and he guessed he'd have to invite Theresa down for a sleepover after all. He forced his gaze back to Jenna's face, amazed she could look so damn hot in a T-shirt and faded jeans. This girl was getting more attractive every day.

"I'm not replacing Frances." His voice was husky and he coughed. Christ, he'd be putty in Jenna's hands if she ever guessed how his body reacted.

"I'm not replacing her," he repeated. "I only asked the woman for some help finding office staff. Obviously she jumped to conclusions."

"Use your head, Burke." Jenna rolled her eyes. "Of course, she jumped to conclusions. She's the only employee who's a secretary."

"There might be one less employee," he said, "if you don't show a little more respect."

Her eyes widened and she instantly raised her hands and stepped back. "Sorry. I didn't mean offense." The words were quick and apologetic but he wasn't fooled. She was smiling exactly like she did last night—right before she'd aced his king.

"There's no employment office around here," she added, "but old Mrs. Turnbull can do some typing. Bit of a gossip, but if it's routine stuff...?"

"It's not. More of a sorting." He glanced at the employee files, scowling at the thought of the tedious job.

"Maybe I could help? I don't have many horses booked."

He paused, tempted by her offer. Shouldn't be a problem. Salaries weren't noted in the files, and he merely needed someone to go through and pull credentials. Once they were listed it would be a simple matter to adjust the pay.

"Or maybe Wally could do it," she added helpfully.

He studied her through narrowed lids, wondering if the minx was actually trying to manipulate him. Wally certainly wasn't going to set foot in this office. Ever again.

"Take a seat." He gestured at the small conference table. "You need to cross-reference each category, then insert Three Brooks' employees based on their educational background."

"What about experience?"

"There's another category for that, but it's at a lower pay scale."

"But that's ridiculous." He was surprised by the defensive flush in her cheeks. Clearly, if there was ever a union brewing, she'd be one to watch. "Experience is better than classroom learning," she added.

He thumped the first stack of files on the table. "But we're positioning Three Brooks based on superior employee education. Besides, you don't have to worry. You have a diploma...and a certificate." He paused, searching her face for that guilty flicker. Ah, there it was.

He'd check out her background later, but not yet. At this point he needed her. It was clear Wally and Jenna had a lot of influence, and it would be rash to alienate both employees at the same time.

"Stop breathing down my neck," she said, her blond head already bent over the files. "You make me nervous."

If she only knew. "I'm going to check the oxygen chamber," he said. "I'll bring you a coffee on the way back."

"I prefer tea actually, really hot, with a squeeze of lemon."

He didn't bother to reply.

Jenna whipped through the stack of files, searching for her name. This was perfect. She'd stick her name in the applicable category and there'd be no more worries. It hadn't even been necessary to copy the certificate. Who'd have thought it would be this easy?

She flipped through the stack again, searching for Murphy. 'A to L.' Okay, so he was pulling them in batches. Made sense but she was rather disappointed she couldn't doctor her file today. This wasn't even interesting, nothing about salaries. Only resumes and job responsibilities, stuff she already knew.

A knock sounded and she glanced up.

"What are you doing in here?" Wally asked, his brow rising in that familiar gesture.

"Working on some employee files."

He shook his head in grudging admiration. "Have to hand it to you, Jenna. You can get things done. Does Derek know you didn't finish high school? Don't worry. Your secret's safe with me."

He stepped further into the office. "We'll make sure no one loses their job."

"I already said you paid me a hundred bucks per horse," she said stiffly. "Not sure what else I can do. I don't want to lie to him."

She glanced uneasily at the yellow notepad on the desk. Burke's masculine scrawl was clearly visible, and she knew he wouldn't like Wally poking around his office. His face always tightened when she mentioned Wally's name, almost imperceptible, but his disapproval was evident.

Too late. Wally crossed to the desk and picked up the pad. "Cobblestones? Plant more flowers?" He flipped the pad back on the desk. "Sure, like that will improve our clientele. Listen, Jenna. I want you to get close. According to reports, Burke Industries is ruthless. Six months after a takeover, thirty percent of the staff is gone. Imagine what that would do to this town."

Jenna glanced nervously at the door. "He hasn't fired anyone. Seems very straightforward."

"He's a calculator." Wally's voice rose. "He doesn't think like us. It's the bottom line, nothing else. If he knew the truth about your education, you'd be out on your ass."

Her fingers turned clumsy and sheets of paper fell to the floor.

"Hey, don't worry." Wally's voice softened. "I've got your back. Just keep an eye on him. Keep me posted, okay?"

She stared into his concerned face and slowly nodded, ignoring the traitorous ache deep in her chest.

Chapter Eight

Jenna flinched in dismay as another handful of Peanut's hair stuck to her fingers. "Shit, fellow. What's happening?"

She stopped her massage and stepped back, a lump thickening her throat. At this rate, the pony would be bald in two weeks. She didn't know what kind of weird skin condition he had, but it certainly wasn't improving—even with the best supplements Three Brooks could buy. She couldn't just stand around and watch her pony die though, not when she worked at a wellness center.

She led him across the road for his evening grass, pulled out her phone and called Wally. "Any chance you could leave the door to the Center open tonight?"

"No chance. Burke changed all the locks." Wally gave a disgusted snort. "The only way is through my apartment door. What's wrong? Is Durling's donkey sick again?"

"Actually it's Peanut. His hair's falling out." Her voice caught. "I don't know what to do."

"Hey, no problem." Wally's voice softened. "He can fit through the apartment entrance. Then you can take him down the hall to the therapy rooms. How long do you need?"

"Only twenty minutes in the solarium. I'll wait until Burke drives by and then lead Peanut down the path."

"All right. I'm going to the Hunt Club tonight but will leave a key by the statue. Did Emily get a part-time job yet?"

"She can't, Wally. She's busy with biology. The course is tough. Takes every minute of her time."

"Figures. Should be you up there studying. You're the smart one. Good luck with Peanut."

The line went dead. She lowered her hand and frowned at the phone. She wasn't the smart one; reading was always boring. Even the massage books—a subject she loved—turned monotonous after a few chapters. Sometimes Wally said such stupid things.

Peanut's head lifted and he stared toward the crest of the hill. *Damn.* She didn't want to be caught standing by the side of the road. Burke might think she was waiting for him, wanting his company again. She dropped to the ground, flattening in the tall grass, praying he hadn't spotted her.

The big car braked. "You all right, Jenna?"

"Oh, yes, sure." Breathless, she scrambled to her knees and snatched at some flowers. "Just picking some flowers."

"Dandelions?"

"Of course, ah…for dandelion wine." He'd lowered the window and the distinctive smell of pizza drifted in the breeze. "You don't look like someone who eats pizza," she added, drawing in an appreciative sniff.

He stepped from the car. Dropped a square box on his hood, opened the lid and extracted a generous slice. Looked like cheese and pepperoni, maybe some green peppers and tomatoes. The mozzarella stretched in generous threads. "I love pizza," he said. "Come out of the grass and join me." He propped his hip against the fender and chewed contentedly.

She'd planned to heat the leftovers from last night, but pizza was always tempting. Besides, she and Peanut had a hike scheduled for tonight and that would burn plenty of calories. "You sure know your way to a woman's heart, Burke." She tossed aside the handful of yellow dandelions, brushed her hands on her jeans and stepped out from the grass.

"We might as well sit on your porch," he said, picking up the pizza box and holding it out of her reach.

She groaned but he gave such a teasing wink, she forgave him and gestured at the trailer. "I already said I'm not signing any papers, but you and your pizza are welcome."

She stepped into the kitchen, grabbed two beers and settled beside him on the swing. They munched companionably and if he had any questions, at least he had the decency to let her eat first.

"Okay." She wiped her mouth with a napkin and leaned back in the swing. "What do you need now?"

His expression turned serious and he took a thoughtful swig of his beer. "I'm thinking of bringing in a horse, a big horse. Can our current staff do a competent job?"

"A big horse?" She leaned forward. "What do you mean, like a stakes horse?"

"Like a Derby winner."

"Oh my gosh! Of course we can. I'm going to massage a Derby winner!" She shot her fist in the air. "How did you swing it? Family connections? You own him? What?"

"Hey." He reached over and patted her knee. "We have to keep it low key. A lot of nice mares are booked to this fellow. The owners don't want anyone to know he has issues."

"Issues?" She leaned forward. "Is he shooting blanks? Or just limp?"

Burke winced and she couldn't resist a grin. Men were so sensitive about that sort of thing although it was doubtful he'd ever experienced any trouble in that department. He exuded sexuality. Just sitting with him on the swing was exhilarating.

"He's not interested in the mares," Burke said. "Won't mount. Vets can't see anything wrong with his hind end and extensive testing revealed nothing."

"So we're a last resort?"

"Yes. Lights and the oxygen chamber will probably be a big help. Maybe the pulsing magnetics. What's your opinion of Darlene, the oxygen tech?"

"Her name's Debbie," Jenna said. "And she's discreet, a good operator. All the staff are fine. They're starting to relax, knowing there won't be layoffs. They'll follow your directions, especially since nearly everyone is getting a raise." She stiffened. "So that's why you have me going through the files in such a rush?"

"Yes," he said, not sounding a bit contrite.

"So tomorrow I'll do files M to Z?"

"Thanks for the beer." He rose. "I've got to finish some paperwork. No time for cards. Maybe tomorrow."

He strode down the walkway before she could say that she didn't have time either. She would have refused a card game and certainly didn't exist for his entertainment, even though last night had been fun, and his visits did soothe the sting of yawningly long evenings.

She sighed and took a half-hearted sip of beer. Maybe Emily would answer her text messages and at least ask about Peanut. Besides, there was nothing wrong with solitude.

And she did have plans for tonight. Obviously Burke wasn't lurking around the Center so a visit would be safe. She'd have to be careful though. As Wally warned, Burke was a smooth operator. He hadn't even revealed the name of the Derby horse.

She stepped back inside, wrapped up the remaining pizza—Burke was certainly stocking her fridge—tied her hair back in a ponytail and added a sweatshirt. It was humid and there might be a lot of mosquitoes. A girl had to be prepared.

Jenna paused by the door to Wally's apartment while Peanut waited patiently at her side. If he were curious about their late night hike, he didn't show it. She gave him a reassuring pat, wincing as another tuft of brown hair drifted in the breeze.

Best to be careful when she touched him. Otherwise their path would be marked with a trail of pony hair. Burke was no fool. He also would be less than pleased. She gulped but shoved away her fear. Peanut needed this treatment. Needed it badly.

The eyes of the jockey statue gleamed and she fumbled around the iron base, checking for the key. There it was. Good old Wally. She inserted the key in the lock and pushed the door open. Peanut fit through with inches to spare. His tiny hooves rattled on the concrete, silencing when they reached the thick rubber that lined the aisle.

Two swinging doors and they were in the Center. The rest of the way she knew by memory. It was a little creepy, picking their way through the dark, but Peanut's stoic presence was reassuring.

A horse nickered and Peanut's ears pricked. Poor guy. He was a friendly fellow but his contact with other animals was minimal. She straightened his head and led him into the solar chamber. Pressed a switch. The lights lowered, the sound grating in the dark. A clear light covered both her and the pony.

She eyed the clock, monitoring the time. Larry, the night watchman, checked the building every hour but his routine never varied. Top of the hour, every hour. She should be in and out of the Center with time to spare.

"Hope this works, fellow," she whispered, resisting her impulse to stroke his neck. The floor had been washed at the end of the day, and she didn't want to leave any evidence of their visit or cause any extra work for the technician.

Ping! Both she and Peanut jumped as the timer sounded. Sometimes twenty minutes felt like an hour, and it seemed as though they had both been dozing. She raised the lights, turned off the switch, and Peanut trustingly followed her back down the aisle.

They squeezed through Wally's apartment door and onto the walkway. She replaced the key with a sense of relief. Done.

A truck roared up the drive and her hand tightened around the lead line. Definitely a diesel. Hopefully Wally. But just in case, she tugged Peanut into the shadows, straining to see.

Aw shit, not Wally. Her heart pounded as Larry stopped his truck and stepped out. Not good. He wasn't the smartest guy around but he was methodical. He'd definitely check all the doors, including Wally's apartment. Damn Burke must have changed the times. *Shit, shit, shit!*

But maybe Burke wouldn't freak out. He seemed so tolerant around her, even amused. However, the rational part of her brain knew he couldn't overlook this. She'd have to be fired. He'd expressly forbidden Peanut to set foot in the Center. Had even given what he thought were valid reasons. And maybe they were to him but she loved her little pony.

She choked back a panicky breath, her mind scrambling. Tied Peanut to the doorknob, praying he wouldn't nicker, then tugged off her sweatshirt and tied it around her waist. Sucked in several gulps of air and jogged out, forcing her breath to come in rapid-fire huffs as though she were in the middle of a strenuous run.

Not difficult. Her heart already raced, and a line of sweat trickled between her breasts.

"Hi there, Larry," she called, meeting him between Wally's door and the truck. "I've been jogging every night but haven't seen you around."

"Mr. Burke instructed me to change patrol times. Not much crime around here but it's good to shake things up."

"Yeah. Good idea," she said brightly. *Damn Burke.*

Larry continued toward Wally's apartment but she rushed forward, pausing under the white driveway light and blocked his path. "I jogged by Wally's door and it's secure. You don't have to do this end."

"Thanks, Jenna, but I still have to check," he said. "It's my job to keep everyone safe."

She smiled and widened her eyes. "Yes, and I personally feel much safer, knowing you're around, changing up the schedule. You're so smart. You probably walk another route too…checking different doors first."

"Yes. That's right." He shuffled his feet and glanced toward the far end of the building. "Sometimes I do check the receiving doors first."

She nodded encouragingly. "They're probably the easiest doors to jimmy open." She smiled over her shoulder and edged along the walkway, relieved when he followed her away from Wally's door.

"Maybe I'll see you up here tomorrow night," he called as he veered off the path and followed the walkway along the back of the building.

"Maybe," she said. "What time are you coming?"

"Ten ten, and then again at ten fifty. I can bring you a cold drink, if you want?"

"Oh, I can't drink when I'm running, but it's nice to know you're around. You hurry now and check those side doors. You never know what's out there." She faked a nervous shiver. "You do have a gun, don't you?"

He nodded, patting his bulky holster. "Right here on my hip. And I completed my firearms course and a second update. Mr. Burke was happy to hear that."

"I bet he was," she said dryly. She backed out of the light before pretending to jog away, peeking over her shoulder until the beam of his powerful light disappeared around the building.

She wheeled, retraced her steps through the mantle of darkness and untied Peanut. "You are one smart fellow," she whispered. She couldn't resist giving him a big pat then hustled the obliging pony into the woods, up the path and back to his safe kennel.

Chapter Nine

"Tea? Lemon? Really, sir, you are too kind." Jenna stared in delight as Burke placed a teacup, complete with a slice of fresh lemon, on the table beside her stack of files.

The corner of his mouth lifted in a familiar twitch. "If it makes rebellious employees call me 'sir,' I'll bring fresh lemon every morning."

"Really? But I'm starting to like the name Burke."

"So am I, Jenna." He reached down and flipped through the files, not looking at her. "Actually I have a favor to ask."

"Oh, of course. Hence the tea." She leaned back in her chair, hiding her disappointment with a flippant smile.

"The big horse's owners are flying in next week for a tour of Three Brooks," Burke said. "They're a brother and sister team, but according to my sources the brother makes all the decisions." He dropped a brochure on the table. 'Ridgeman Racing Stables' was splashed in glitzy gold letters across the front.

"Ah," she breathed, staring in admiration at the chestnut with the imperious head pictured on the front cover. "Then the Derby horse must be Mr. Nifty. He's coming here? Oh, my." She lifted both hands, waggling her fingers in anticipation. "I can't wait to touch him."

A low noise sounded and she jerked her head up. Burke was actually laughing, a deep sexy laugh that softened his chiseled jaw and made her forget all about horses. He circled the table, still chuckling. "We do this tour right, you'll be able to touch him all over," he said.

Touch him all over. She swallowed, yanking her gaze off Burke's beautiful mouth, and staring instead at his ridged forearms. But that wasn't wise either. She feared she might lick her lips. It had been a little too long since she'd stopped seeing Colin, and she'd always had a thing for muscles. Probably a natural fixation developed from working with big horses. Completely understandable.

She cleared her throat. "So you want me to help take the owners around? No problem. I've done quite a few tours."

"Yes, that's what the receptionist said." When he turned around, his smile had been replaced with a customary scowl. "I'm not exactly sure what Frances does behind that counter besides crossword puzzles. I expected she could look after some tours. We may have to make a position adjustment."

There was no doubt what he meant. "She's fine," Jenna said quickly. "Just a little set in her ways. She keeps the feed room clean and the staff washroom. Beside, I always do the tours with Wally. Usually I look after technical questions and he looks after the business side."

"Really? Wally doesn't know the technical side?"

There it was again and she took a hasty sip of tea. First a threat to Frances and now obvious disapproval of Wally. All in thirty seconds. Burke was so damn attractive, she sometimes forgot he was also dangerous. Big mistake. She set her cup on the table, hiding her slight tremor.

"Of course, Wally knows the technical side," she said. "But it's just the way we did things. He's great with people. And smart. You might want to consider using him for the tour. After all, he'll need to build a relationship with Nifty's people."

Burke stepped closer and abruptly dropped three green files in front of her. One 'N' and two 'M's.' 'Murphy, Jenna' included. She couldn't believe her luck.

"You want me to work on these now?" she asked, trying not to stare at her name. "And once I check everyone's certificates, their salaries are adjusted?" She kept her voice neutral, almost bored. This was way too easy.

"Not quite. Anyone you find eligible for a pay hike, based on educational qualifications, will then sign a document testifying validity. Employees are automatically terminated for falsehood, so it provides us with recourse…in the event action is required."

She swallowed a lump the size of her fist but crossed her arms and shrugged, pretending the topic was all rather amusing. "Terminated? What a ridiculous word. Why don't you just say fired? And nobody's going to fake something so easily checked. Gosh, don't you trust us?"

He turned, crossed to the large window, and studied the workmen. Silent. If he were trying to intimidate her, it worked.

She forced a disdainful sniff and flipped open a file but couldn't resist a cautious peek. He still stared out the window, his broad back to her. Everyone had an outlet, and it was obvious construction was his. That fresh piney smell showed he'd been working with wood again. His hard hat had been tossed on the corner chair, the battered white hat that had been so misleading on his first day.

Sometimes she wished he were a simple laborer. A saw whirred from outside and someone laughed, but it seemed like hours since anyone in this office had spoken. He hadn't answered her question, and it was painfully apparent he *didn't* trust them.

"Why didn't you just go into the construction industry?" she asked quietly, unable to remain silent.

"My family would have been appalled."

"You like this instead?" She gestured at the files in frustration. "Searching for weak links, entrapping employees, firing well-meaning staff? Frances and Wally are good people."

He spun from the window and stalked toward the door, his voice clipped. "Better get to work. This isn't efficient use of company time."

The door closed behind him with a controlled click. Heck, he didn't even slam doors. She picked up her tea, trying to warm her cold hands, trying to ignore the fact she'd just been given a very clear warning.

It would be risky to sign a paper, but it was too late to back out now. Besides she and Em needed that eighteen-percent raise and since she was stuck in Burke's office, laboring over boring files, there should be some type of reimbursement. Or at least that's what she tried to tell herself.

She dropped her head in her hands and sighed, wishing Burke wasn't her boss, wishing she wasn't grade-eleven stupid and wishing the expensive lemon didn't leave such a bitter aftertaste.

Jenna patted the chestnut gelding on the neck and nodded at the handler, pleased with his progress. "Guess he's returning to the track tomorrow. Is he scheduled for the saltwater spa?"

"Going there now." The wiry man holding the gelding paused, his gaze darting to the floor then back to her face. "Jenna, I was wondering if you'd ask Mr. Burke if...well, I was hoping you'd ask if we could take a break at ten? You know, we might need to use the bathroom, have a smoke, and, well it'd be nice to have a regular break."

"Just take it, Jim." She shook her head in exasperation. This was the third time today someone had asked her to approach Burke. "He's actually very reasonable as long as you do your work. Besides, you never worried about smoke breaks before."

"With Wally, we just took them when we wanted." Jim had the grace to flush. "It never really mattered."

"Well, I'm afraid those days are over." She gave a rueful smile. "This place is going to be quite busy."

"Wally said if we banded together, we might be able to force Mr. Burke to re-install him as manager."

"Wally said that?" She shook her head at the ridiculous notion Burke could be forced to do anything. "Where is Wally anyway?"

"Out back, doing inventory. A little pissed about it too."

Of course. Wally wasn't accustomed to grunt work. She nodded, pushed open the swinging door and walked down the aisle past the reception area.

"What's another word for superfluous?" Frances asked, poking her head up from her crossword puzzle. "Nine letters."

"Redundant." Jenna paused. "Maybe you should spend less time with your puzzles and work at the computer a bit more. Sweep twice a day instead of once." Annoyance darkened Frances's round face. "Just until Burke goes," Jenna added. "Just to be safe."

"But I smile at him now. And I answer the phone."

"But it hardly rings." Jenna softened her voice, trying to be tactful. Frances could be quite spiteful if annoyed; conversely the woman's feelings were easily bruised. "Everyone uses cell phones now. I'll continue to do the tours but why don't you tell Burke you'd be happy to do some of his typing?"

"Maybe." But Frances flounced back in her seat, clearly resentful. "By the way, I saw your sister's boyfriend on Facebook," she added snidely. "They seem to be having a good time. Take a look."

Jenna leaned over the counter. Emily's face flashed on the screen followed by a black sports car. A skinny, nondescript guy leaned against the fender, one arm around Em's shoulder, his other hand splayed over...her breast. The self-satisfied leer on his weasel face was nauseating.

"Are there any other pictures?" Jenna asked, but it was an effort to work the question past her tight throat. "And can you tell me where this was taken?"

"A little town somewhere. Look at the cheap motels. Good grief. Aren't you Facebook friends with your sister?"

Jenna shook her head. She barely went on Facebook; her ancient computer was much too slow.

"I can see why." Frances snickered. "There're some raunchy pictures here. Maybe you should sweep the feed room first. Then I'll let you see them. All I can say is your sister deserves her reputation."

Jenna lunged over the counter. Grabbed a pen and rammed it into Frances's hand. "Watch your mouth. Now write your password down. Or else I'll have my buddy Burke kick your useless ass out that door."

Frances shrank back, the chair squeaking in protest. "I didn't mean it. And I shouldn't have said that about Emily. You're both skinny and pretty and you've both been nice to me. I'm sorry." Fear blanched her face as she scribbled down her code. "Please don't tell him to fire me. I've worked here for fifteen years. I deserve this job."

Jenna snorted and grabbed the paper, checking that she could decipher Frances's scrawl. It was convenient Frances thought Jenna could control Burke—that everyone seemed to think it—but Frances was a gullible fool.

She shook her head in disgust and swung around. The blood drained from her face. Burke stood in the doorway, arms crossed, expression carved in granite.

"Hi." She forced a flippant smile. "Guess we sorted out who will type your papers."

She sauntered toward the door. He probably hadn't heard. Oh, please, God. She prayed he hadn't heard. But he didn't step back and she reluctantly stopped, lifted her head and met his hooded gaze.

"I'm heading into town to meet with the hay suppliers." He glanced over her head at Frances. "We'll discuss this incident later."

"Perfect." She raised her voice so Frances would be sure to hear. "Drop by the usual time. I'll chill the beer. Make some of my special cornbread." She added a tight smile before brushing past him and escaping.

At least, Burke hadn't given her away in front of Frances. Time enough to face the music later. But obviously he'd heard something. What had she said? 'I'll have my buddy Burke kick your lazy ass out the door?'

Well, lots of people referred to others as buddy. It wasn't her fault if Frances misunderstood. Jenna hadn't specifically said Burke would do what she wanted. She'd merely inferred it. People had to be so careful with words now; it was such a shame. Surely Burke would understand that?

She rechecked the password, tucked the paper safely in her pocket and circled around the building. Her thoughts shot back to Emily. God, what the hell was her sister doing in Philadelphia?

Voices grew louder. Wally leaned against some hay bales, a clipboard tucked under his arm, while two stable hands called down numbers. "Hey, take a break, guys," he called when he spotted Jenna. "What are you doing out here? You in the dog house too?"

"I've got another horse to massage," she said. "But I just talked to Jim and I don't think it's wise to stir everyone up. Burke isn't going to like it, and...certain jobs might already be in jeopardy."

"Screw him." Wally's voice rose. "He's looking to push me out and I'm not rolling. There's already talk in town he doesn't belong. Doesn't understand the area. Our hay supplier promised to raise his price."

Jenna dropped onto a bale, shaking her head. "But Wally, how is that going to help Three Brooks? I can tell you exactly what Burke will do. He'll find another supplier out of town. Your friend will lose an important contract, our profitability drops, and Burke will be pissed. You don't want to piss him off."

"He doesn't scare me. And if I'm fired, I'll hit Burke Industries with a wrongful dismissal suit. Even if I lose, the publicity will have to hurt."

Jenna pulled out a piece of hay and chewed glumly on the stalk. "If you want your old job back, you're going to have to earn it. Everyone else has stepped up. Come on, Wally. You can too."

"Just stick close to him," Wally said. "Let me know what he's doing. Although maybe you won't find that too big a chore." Something ugly stained his voice and she jerked her head up.

"By the way, how was Peanut's visit to the solarium?" he added. "Want me to keep a key by the statue so you can continue treatments?"

Jenna rose and this time couldn't meet his gaze. Her breath felt jerky, as though she were being sucked into a vortex completely out of her control. "That would be great," she muttered. She tossed aside the mangled stalk of hay and walked away.

Chapter Ten

Jenna powered up her ancient computer, groaning as it struggled to connect to the Internet. What a shitty day. She fingered her phone, hating the thought of the hefty bill, but agonizing more about Em's pictures, about Wally's future and that she'd been rather mean to lazy, old Frances.

"Five more minutes and you're junked," she snapped at the monitor. She checked the oven before striding outside to see Peanut.

He chewed steadily at the grass, not moving as she inspected his skin. No worse than yesterday. Maybe even better? At least, his hair had stopped falling out. He still looked a bit like a Chihuahua, a giant hairless Chihuahua. "We'll go for another walk tonight," she promised, patting his neck and hurrying back to the trailer.

Dammit. She hated rushing around for a man, although the cornbread did smell delicious. If *he* didn't come, she'd keep a loaf and take the other to old Mrs. Parker.

But she needed a confidence boost. She slipped on a clingy top, swiped on some mascara and lipstick, brushed her hair and waited on the swing.

Not long. Burke's car rolled into her driveway promptly at six thirty.

He sauntered toward the porch with that confident walk, almost a swagger, but on him it looked good. Besides, he had plenty of reason to strut. Money, education, good family.

He paused. His eyes narrowed on her tight top before drifting over her breasts and lingering on the inch of skin that rimmed her hip-hugging black pants. His appraisal was bold and assessing, a thorough almost predatory scan that made her nipples tighten.

He didn't sit and she didn't invite him. "Looked like a bit of a tussle in the reception area today," he finally said. "Not the kind of impression we want to create."

She shrugged, aware the gesture would pull his attention back to her breasts, maybe make him forget about the bawling out she truly deserved. "Frances and I were just horsing around. Nothing important."

He didn't answer right away and she hoped he was distracted. Glanced up but the intensity of his gaze was almost scary. She jerked her head away and jammed on her sunglasses even though the porch was shaded. His silent, smoldering appraisal left her flustered, and it was clear he wouldn't be diverted like the security guard. Amazingly, she was the one unbalanced.

She clasped her arms over her chest and shivered, wishing she could hide, wishing she'd worn something different. He was way too much man for this ploy, and unlike Emily, she wasn't very skilled at the game. In fact, her pulse kicked like a captured bird in a fist.

Still, he said nothing.

"All right, so we were arguing." She scrambled to fill the silence. "Frances said something about my sister and I lost my temper. I'm sorry…not for getting mad at Frances but for losing it at work." She blew out a regretful breath. "I'm very sorry."

"Is that cornbread I smell?"

She nodded but he'd already opened the screen door and disappeared into the trailer, giving her a chance to steady her breathing. A moment later, he reappeared with a plate of warm bread, two beers and her old grey sweater.

"You look cold. Put this on."

She slipped the sweater on, buttoning it almost to the top, unable to meet his knowing gaze. The swing shifted as he sat beside her.

"Did you hear what I said to Frances?" she whispered.

"I believe you threatened to kick her useless ass out the door." His chuckle surprised her. "Jesus, Jenna. If I'd said that, we'd be in court. Something Burke Industries doesn't want. Never let anyone push your buttons."

"Emily's not my button." She jerked forward. "Not at all."

He raised an eyebrow and she forced herself to lean back. Sucked in a breath and sagged against the seat. "Okay, maybe a little. But I've always looked after her. Mom had cancer. Dad was gone. She's my little sister." Her voice cracked and she coughed, surprised by the quaver in her voice. "Now she's gone, has posted strange pictures on Facebook and my computer won't work."

"You really want to see those pictures?"

"Of course. I need to know what she's up to. She can be a little…impulsive."

He tapped the screen on his phone then pressed it into her hand. "There's the Internet. Go ahead."

She stared at his phone, reluctant to pull out Frances's password. "It might cost a bit," she said.

"It's covered." His smile was oddly gentle. "And I owe you for the work you did on the files."

"Maybe instead," she sucked in a hopeful breath, "you could pay me by letting Peanut have some infrared treatments?"

"No. That animal doesn't even look like a member of the equine species. Doubt his shots are up to date either. Are they?"

She kept her head averted, staring at the confusing buttons on his touch screen phone. Burke had thoughtfully brought up the Facebook login; he actually was kind in a tough sort of way, and the thought of sneaking Peanut back into the Center tonight seemed ungrateful. She'd feel much better if he gave permission.

"Of course, his shots aren't up to date," she said slowly. "But he isn't exposed to anything alone on this hill." And she couldn't ask Colin to come, and the only other vet was out of her price range.

"Exactly. He hasn't been needled in a while." Burke spoke with smug authority. "We have to keep the good horses safe."

"But Peanut's my good horse, and he's sick and needs h-help." She swallowed her pride, prepared to grovel for her pony, but the painful lump in her throat turned her words awkward. "If he had a flu shot and a Coggins test, could he come? I'll work the light treatments off at the full price."

"Forget it, Jenna. I don't want that mangy pony around. People shouldn't have animals they can't afford."

Something stung her eyes and she blinked in despair, grateful for her sunglasses. Squeezed his phone, staring straight ahead as Peanut chewed contentedly at the grass—at the Three Brooks' grass. She couldn't even afford good second-cut hay, the fine hay that was easier to chew.

Her phone rang and she leaped up, grateful for the chance to escape. "Excuse me." She dropped his phone on the swing and pushed open the screen door. Grabbed her cell, praying it was Em. Slumped in disappointment when she recognized Wally's number.

"Hi, there," she said.

"Are you bringing Peanut by the Center tonight? There's some aloe body wash I found while doing inventory. Might help the little guy. I'll stick it out for you. And maybe you want to stop by the apartment for a tea or something?"

"I'd like that." The painful band around her chest loosened a notch. "Um, thanks. I'll see you later."

She stepped back outside but walked to the steps, urging her company off the porch, firmly but politely, the way her mother had taught.

Burke rose immediately, the empty seat swinging behind him. "Busy?" He scooped up his cell, his face inscrutable. "I need this but you can use it tomorrow. Thanks for the bread."

She nodded, waiting until he descended the wooden steps and slid into his car. She wheeled and walked back into the trailer. Poked at her computer, not surprised it still hadn't connected to Facebook. Maybe it didn't matter. Wally had a computer and he was always kind, even to mangy ponies.

Besides, Wally's company was safer. His thoughtless comments only annoyed her; they didn't rip her heart out like Burke's.

She changed quickly, pulling on jogging shorts and a comfortable shirt, and even grabbed a water bottle for good measure. If Larry expected to see a jogger on his security rounds, that's exactly what he'd see.

Burke stared at another prospectus then tossed it aside in boredom. He crossed to the huge French windows and stared up the hill. Dark now and he couldn't see the reflection of any lights. Other than Jenna's trailer, there was nothing else on the road. Only the two of them.

Damn, he was restless. Three businesses to evaluate and for the last hour he'd been staring at a jumble of numbers, numbers that turned into legs, breasts and hair. A shaft of heat shot through him and he paced back to the table.

Sex. He couldn't get it off his mind. Maybe he should let Theresa fly down for a visit, although admittedly it wasn't her he was picturing right now.

It had always been apparent Jenna had a smoking hot body, but tonight, in that tight top, those low pants, she reeked of sex. And he wanted some of it.

Rationally, he knew it wasn't smart—generally he didn't dip his pen in company ink—but he hadn't signed up to be a monk either.

He stroked his chin, turning clinical now, searching for solutions. One option would be to fire her, provide a generous severance—hell, give her anything she wanted—then bonk her brains out.

Unfortunately, he liked her. Liked her a lot. Sitting on that porch, enjoying a beer, had turned into the highlight of his day. Damn good poker player too, and it was hard to find someone who didn't irritate the crap out of him. Besides, she was one of the few friendly faces around and they were getting fewer by the minute.

Much fewer.

The town seemed to be aligning against Burke Industries. Ironically as more suppliers raised prices, forcing him to buy elsewhere, the notion that Burke wasn't supportive of locals would grow.

It was a problem he'd faced before, and the solution was generally simple. Find a few well-respected people and lure them onside. Like sheep, the rest would follow. Then it would be possible to cull Three Brooks of deadwood—deadwood like that subversive Wally Turner.

He grabbed his wallet and headed for his car. Despite his aversion to the Hunt Club and its snobbish clientele, it was the only establishment that catered to the elite citizens of Stillwater.

And he needed their support.

Jenna froze as Burke's car crunched past. Headlights swept the road, narrowly missing her and Peanut standing at the top of the narrow path. Obviously he was in a hurry, going fast, driving much too recklessly on a road known to have a loose pony.

Asshole. Gathering her resentment like a cloak, she clucked at Peanut and continued down the wooded trail. She never used a flashlight on the path, disliking the way it blinded her in the dark. When she was little, her mom had said to put a hand on Peanut's withers and he'd guide her through the trees, even in the darkest of nights.

He did that now, his tiny hooves almost silent as he descended the path. He walked eagerly, as though sharing her belief that the infrared treatment might help. Or maybe he was just eager to see the other horses. She fought a pang of regret. He didn't get out much, not like he used to, and he was such a sociable guy. No doubt he was lonely too.

Wally had conveniently left the door unlocked and she and Peanut slipped into the hallway, through the swinging doors and into the Center's solarium.

The pony stood unmoving under the lights and she peered closer, inspecting his skin, relieved the hair had stopped falling out in such distressing clumps. Something moved and she jumped. Relaxed when she saw it was Wally.

He dropped a bulky bag on the floor. "Here's some old shampoo and aloe rinses, also some of that tea tree stuff and eucalyptus. Found it during inventory. It won't be used so take all you want." He gave a wry shrug. "Best not let the big guy know though."

The big guy. Until a week ago, Wally had been the big guy. Now he was regulated to stock boy. No wonder he was a tad bitter.

She gave a grateful smile. "Thanks. I really appreciate it. Things aren't going that great for Peanut..." Her voice trailed off and she fussed with the pony's ragged mane.

"Don't worry." Wally's voice softened. "You'll be amazed at what the infrared can do. And maybe he's a little depressed. Stick him in a stall afterward and let him see the other horses. That

might perk him up. Ponies are like people. They get lonely too."
He gave them both a reassuring smile and headed down the aisle.
"I'll find some special hay for him," he called.

It was comforting to see Wally back in control. Animal care
was his passion. She slid a hand into her pocket and pulled out the
paper with Frances's password. She'd intended to ask if she could
use his computer but now hesitated. Wally had been one of her
mother's best friends. If the pictures were awful, he'd be horrified.
He had enough worries of his own and he already felt she spoiled
Em. Best to wait until she checked them first.

Ping. The timer sounded and she stuck the paper back in her
pocket and raised the lights. Peanut turned, as though aware the
session was over and pulled her toward the stall area. He could be
amazingly strong when he wanted to go somewhere. Clearly Wally
was right—her little pony was lonely.

She led him into the main section and down the aisle. Horses
thrust heads over their doors, curious about this newest arrival.
There weren't many occupied stalls now, certainly no local horses,
and she doubted many of these gorgeous Thoroughbreds had ever
seen anything like Peanut.

Peanut didn't care. He bounced down the aisle, confident as
ever, not worrying that he barely rose above their knees. And that
he was unwelcome. *Take that, Burke.*

She closed the pony in a spacious stall, noting the huge water
bucket Wally had thoughtfully lowered to suit Peanut's height, then
climbed the narrow steps to his apartment.

"Hot tea or a drink?" Wally asked.

"Tea, please." She wandered around the living room, checking
the deserted driveway through the window, suddenly uneasy.
"Does Burke ever drop by here late at night?"

"He hasn't yet." Wally joined her, rattling the ice cubes in his
glass as they both stared out the darkened window. "You think
he'd mind your little pony?"

"I know he would."

Wally turned back to the wailing kettle. "Another one of our
secrets then," he said.

Chapter Eleven

Burke tossed his hard hat on the corner chair and scanned his office. Nothing seemed to be touched. He picked up a protractor and measured the corners of the files. Each paper matched the angle from yesterday. Perfect. After the locksmith's visit, he finally had some security.

He strode over to the employee files and saw that Jenna had completed the lists and someone, probably that lazy receptionist, had typed the statements. They all appeared to be signed, sealed and delivered. Looked like about half the staff qualified for raises. That should boost morale.

He paced back to the window and stared at the new storage building, flexing his hand as he watched a worker expertly pound a nail. There was a small cost overrun but not much. Everything was looking good.

As though on cue, a parade of mismatched vehicles zoomed into the lower employee lot. He didn't have to check his watch. Obviously it was eight am. They were all very careful not to arrive a second too soon.

Jenna sauntered up the walkway, hips swinging, hair blowing in the breeze. He noted every damn construction worker stopped to stare. One bold fellow he knew only as Terry, even grabbed his thermos and chased after her, mouth flapping until she stopped and turned around.

Dammit. Burke Industries didn't tolerate sexual harassment.

He charged from his office, not even bothering to lock the door. Strode down the long aisle, around the corner and rammed open the heavy door. *Bump.*

Hot liquid splashed his fingers. "Damn!" It hurt like hell and he swore again, watching uncomprehendingly as Jenna's blue eyes darkened with pain, then lowered to stare at her arm, now soaked with scalding liquid.

Aw, shit. He scooped her up and rushed to the bathroom. A nameless girl leaned against the sink, carefully applying mascara. "Out," he snapped. Leaned past and jerked on the tap, tugging Jenna's arm beneath a cold spray of water. She whimpered, struggled for a second but soon stopped resisting.

"I'm so sorry, sweetheart," he murmured, pressing his face against her hair, trying to absorb her trembles. "Don't move. Ten minutes and then we'll see, okay?"

Her face was pale in the mirror, her teeth gritted. He clamped his eyes shut, overwhelmed with regret. "I'm so sorry, Jenna," he repeated, keeping his arms wrapped around her.

"It wasn't your fault," she said.

But he knew it was, knew he wouldn't have reacted like that for anyone else. He took a deep breath and opened his eyes, staring at her arm, trying to assess the burn through the flowing water. Christ, his skin hurt and only a few drops had reached him. That idiot must have had boiling water in his thermos. And lemons? He remembered seeing a wizened slice of lemon on the ground at her feet.

She shifted and he loosened his hold, surprised at her tiny wrists. She acted so tough, so confident, had sauntered up the walkway like she owned it and now she was fighting not to cry. Fresh remorse tore at his gut.

The door opened and the receptionist stuck a cautious head in. "Anything I can do?"

"Grab our first aid kit," he said. "I'm taking her to the hospital."

She nodded and the door swung shut. He moved his hand over Jenna's elbow, tilting her arm. "We better get that ring off, in case there's swelling." He managed to turn her hand, saw the reddened skin on the inside of her fingers and paused. "Maybe they should take it off at the hospital."

"No." She jerked in protest. "They'll cut it off. And it was my mom's."

He gulped, studying her skin beneath the flowing water. The inside of her hand and fingers were damaged along with her wrist. Pulling off the ring would hurt like hell. No way could he inflict that kind of pain.

"Please." Her eyes gripped his through the mirror and he saw the shimmer of tears, recognized their stark plea. "Please, Burke. Just pull it off."

He swallowed again. "Shut your eyes," he said gruffly. He reached for her hand, not wanting to see her expression. The ring twisted beneath his fingers and he tugged, felt her wince and paused.

"It's okay," she said. "Not bad at all."

But she squeezed his arm with her left hand, her grip tightening as he worked the ring over her damaged skin. Round and round he tugged, seemed an endless number of times until finally it passed over her knuckle. He checked her pinched face in the mirror, but her eyes remained tightly closed and for that he was grateful.

"Got it," he finally said, his voice husky. "I'm going to turn this water off now. We'll wrap your hand and go to the hospital."

The door opened and the receptionist tiptoed in, gauze in both hands as she craned to see Jenna's injuries. "I couldn't find a first aid kit but here's some sterile horse wrap."

Damn incompetent Wally. Burke's mouth tightened. "Well, that gives you something to do today."

The receptionist stared, her round face blank with confusion.

"Order some first aid kits," he snapped.

Jenna squeezed his wrist, forcing a wan smile. "Thanks for bringing the gauze, Frances. That was smart of you...to check the horse supplies."

Real genius, Burke thought. But Jenna was shivering and for her sake, he tempered his sarcasm. "Thank you, Francis. Go and call the hospital. Tell them we're coming."

He ripped open a gauze sheet and wrapped the burn, noting Jenna's eyes, the wide irises stark against the vivid blue. Scooped her up and carried her from the bathroom.

"I can walk," she said. But her voice was reedy and she didn't protest again, silent even as he deposited her in the passenger seat and clipped her belt.

The hospital was nineteen miles away on a hilly country road. He made it in fifteen minutes, relieved it was next to the Hunt Club, one of the few landmarks he knew.

He gently lifted Jenna and rushed into the lobby, stopping in front of a nurse brandishing a clipboard. "She needs to see a doctor," he said. "Which way?"

"Sorry, sir. She has to go through triage first." Her eyes flickered to a swinging door with the word 'Emergency' in red letters.

Ignoring her protest, he barged through the restricted doors with a silent Jenna cradled in his arms.

"Is that the burn patient?" A doctor with a long face and grave eyes stepped forward. He pulled back a green curtain. "Just put her on the bed here and I'll take a look." He gently removed the gauze. "Cold water treatment?"

"Fifteen minutes," Burke said.

"Good. We'll be about an hour. You can wait outside or leave your number with the desk." The doctor gestured at a bald orderly, and Jenna and the bed were rolled away, seemingly in competent hands.

"Sir?" The nurse with the clipboard had followed him, quivering with disapproval. "We have some paperwork that needs completing. It should have been done first."

"Just call the receptionist at Three Brooks. It was a work injury." He pressed a business card into her hand. "And give me a call when she's ready to be picked up. I gotta go."

He stalked outside, desperate to escape the cloying smells, the strained faces, the way Jenna had looked, helpless and alone on that rolling white bed. Damn, he needed a strong coffee.

He wiped the back of his sweaty neck, feeling oddly unbalanced and desperate to regroup. Perhaps he shouldn't have said it was a work injury. That would create more paperwork, maybe impact the Center when the town's good will was critical.

He walked up the walkway to the Hunt Club's wooden door where a tasteful brass sign proclaimed: Members & Guests Only. Three Brooks, of course, had a charter membership, and it was apparent from Wally's expense statements that the man frequented the place. Burke suspected Wally also used it as a meeting place to stir up the townsfolk.

The hay man yesterday wouldn't even meet Burke's eyes when asked to justify the abrupt price jump, but the gold Hunt Club decal on his windshield revealed plenty. Fortunately the type of people that frequented ostentatious places like this were usually swayed by power and money. And Burke had both.

A willowy brunette with dark eyes and a white smile rushed forward. "Glad to see you again. Will you be joining Mr. Winfield's breakfast meeting?"

"No, just a coffee and I'd like a window table." Burke guessed Leo Winfield would spot him soon enough. On the two previous occasions Burke had visited the club, Leo had made it clear any owner of Three Brooks was welcome in the town clique, despite Wally's negative politicking.

But it was best to make Leo come to him. And Burke definitely didn't want to be dragged into any ritual breakfast meetings, no matter how big an honor it was considered. He settled at the gleaming table and pulled out his phone.

A plate of smoked salmon and some sort of waffle wraps were placed in front of him, and he hid his irritation. What part of 'just a coffee' had been unclear?

He pressed Edward's number and stared out the window, glad it overlooked a pristine garden rather than the ugly hospital. He didn't want to think of Jenna and her scalded arm. Jesus Christ.

"Hello, Derek." Edward sounded preoccupied when he finally answered. "What's up? You finish evaluating those companies?"

"Not yet, and I'd like to shove back that Derby horse's visit."

"Why? Thought the Center was ready to go?"

"Just lost my only masseuse, for a few weeks at least."

"So, hire another. They must be a dime a dozen. Don't all girls learn a little massage on the side?"

A coffee magically appeared, and Burke swallowed his annoyance along with a gulp of delicious black coffee. "I've never seen a girl get results like she does," he said mildly. "It's weird, almost a cross between massage and chiro."

"Damn, I want her."

"Too bad. She's mine." Burke glanced over his shoulder, somewhat surprised Leo Winfield hadn't accosted him yet. He'd deliberately picked a visible table and didn't want to hang around here all morning.

"Fine for you," Edward said. "When you want a woman, you just give her that look and she takes off her clothes. Some of us have to work much harder."

Burke sipped his coffee, already bored and only half listening. Leo rushed across the floor with his tweed jacket, silk hunt tie and fawning smile. Perfect. Burke cut off Edward's rant about women; his cousin was on his third wife and understandably bitter. "I'll finish up my portion of the evaluations by the weekend," he said. "But find out if the Ridgeman horse can be postponed. It's better to wait."

"Can't you find another masseuse?" Edward asked. "We worked hard for that contact. They're desperate to get their big boy covering mares again. Stud fee is a hundred thousand bucks. Imagine how many bookings they'll lose if word leaks the stud's a dud?"

Burke crunched some quick calculations and blew out a sigh. "All right. I'll hire some more staff." He cut the connection and nodded at Leo, trying not to stiffen as the man touched him on the shoulder with a too-familiar hand.

"Glad to see you back, Derek," Leo said. "We come here every morning, talk about the town's problems, hash over business. More deals are made in this club than in my office."

"Good to know," Burke said. "Because I'm looking for a new hay supplier."

"Oh? Wally's friend can't help? He grows the best horse hay around."

"Apparently he doesn't grow it for me." Burke watched Leo's face, noting the lack of surprise, the complacency in the man's grey eyes. Leo already knew. "Luckily I have your support," Burke added smoothly. "You did say you more or less ran this town?"

"Yes, but unofficially, of course." Leo pursed his lips in thought. "I might be able to put in a good word. However, folks around here are a mite standoffish. They haven't seen much of you. Might be a good idea if you attended some community functions. Let everyone know you're not an ogre."

Burke raised an eyebrow.

"Not that you're an ogre, of course, but they know and respect Wally. He didn't lay off anyone in ten years. Helps the town in a lot of ways. Even sponsors the local steeplechase. Since you pulled the Center's support for that, the entire valley is crushed."

"I don't recall pulling any specific sponsorships." Burke took a thoughtful sip of coffee remembering he *had* slapped a moratorium on all unnecessary spending.

"A lot of folks are also disappointed they can't take their animals to Jenna Murphy," Leo continued. "But I guess having the clinic off limits isn't a big problem since she'll see them on weekends."

"Jenna treats horses on weekends?"

"Sure. Her mother did the same. Horses, hounds, whatever. Everyone loves her." Leo gave a suggestive leer. "Damn good looking woman. Fine ass but no smarts on the business end."

Burke leaned back, crossing his arms and scowling.

Leo gave a nervous cough. "Of course, not everyone can make money, not like us. That's what I'm talking about here, business minds. And I'll take care of your hay situation. Heard you hired a local construction company. At least that's beneficial for industry." Leo was almost babbling now. "My daughter said the new building was almost finished."

Burke glanced at his watch. Soon be time to pick up Jenna. Maybe he wouldn't wait for a call from the hospital. Leo showed no inclination to quit talking, and they'd already discussed everything on Burke's agenda. Leo's support—if he really had it— along with a little more community work might be enough to nullify Wally's backstabbing.

"Who's your daughter?" Burke asked absently, draining his cup.

"Kathryn," Leo said. "Remember? I said she was coming by. Dropped off her resume last week. Has a degree from the new facility in Kentucky."

"Yes, that's right." Burke nodded, remembering the girl. Exactly what he needed right now, especially if she were Leo's daughter. "Impressive credentials," he added. "I've actually been planning to give her a call. We'd love to have Kathryn join our staff. I'd like her to start on Monday."

Leo grinned and pumped Burke's hand. "Well, that's excellent. Exactly the kind of support this town recognizes." He beamed and gestured for more coffee.

Burke rose quickly and initialed the bill. "I have to go. See you at the next community event. Appreciate your help with the hay." He left Leo puffing out his chest and strode from the club, more than satisfied with events.

Always leave the other guys believing they had negotiated the better deal. And let them feel their support was essential. Leo might sort out the Center's hay glitch, and in the process Burke would find out how much influence the man really had.

Having Leo's daughter on staff should cement the man's support. Besides Jenna needed some time off, and this new masseuse would fill that gap nicely. A public relations appearance at the next community function should smooth out any remaining bumps.

Wally was digging himself a very deep hole.

Burke shoved open the hospital door and approached the desk, still thinking of Wally, still frowning. "Is Jenna Murphy ready yet?" he asked.

The nurse's face darkened with disapproval. She shot a pointed glance at the score of people crammed in the waiting room. Leo's ogre comment flashed in Burke's mind, and he forced a smile.

"I know you're very busy," he added, "and I appreciate your work with Jenna's file. Can you tell me if she's ready…" He scanned the nurse's nametag. "Anna?"

"Well, um," Anna straightened, clutching the clipboard against her chest and a red stain crept up her neck. "I…I'll certainly check for you."

"That would be great. Appreciate it." He gave another polite smile, and she rushed off in her thick-soled white shoes

He pulled out his phone and checked his messages. Smiled triumphantly at the email from the hay man confirming a contract frozen at last year's prices.

Fast work, indeed. Leo obviously had plenty of clout and hiring his daughter had been an excellent move, a small price to pay for stability.

The nurse rushed back, her face still flushed. "She'll be right out. They're finding a wheelchair."

"A wheelchair?" Burke frowned. "Are you sure you have the right girl? Mine had a hand injury."

"It's the pain medication, sir."

"I see." He stiffened as an orderly opened the swinging doors, pushing an ancient wheelchair. Jenna's head lolled to the side and her eyelids drooped. A bulky white bandage covered her right arm, hand to elbow.

He strode toward Jenna and the long-faced doctor who'd materialized by her side. "She's okay, right?" Burke asked, appalled at her drowsiness. "Maybe it's best if she stays the night?"

The doctor shook his head and held up a fistful of papers. "Everything's fine. Prescription for pain pills. Start in four hours. Also directions for some hand exercises and basic info on burns.

"It's important to keep the skin from tightening," he went on, "although she shouldn't apply much pressure. Damage was reduced because of the cold-water application. However, there's still a risk of scarring. Some good creams are on the market. If she's careful, especially the first week, there should be no residual damage."

Burke gulped, pocketing the material and bending toward Jenna. "Hey, Jenna. Feeling better?"

She opened her eyes, tried to focus, but her lids almost immediately shut again.

"She's had some morphine," the doctor said with a slight smile. "Be sure to give her a couple pain pills in four hours. She'll be hurting then, but for now she's not feeling a thing."

Burke nodded then rushed out and moved his car to the front entrance. He swooped around to open the passenger door while the attendant bumped the wheelchair to the curb. "Easy," he snapped, reaching past the bald man to ease Jenna from the chair.

"Just putting you in the car, Jenna," Burke said, but she seemed oblivious to her surroundings. He tilted the passenger seat so her head wouldn't loll, slid into the car and headed south.

Her eyes remained closed the entire trip.

He turned into her driveway, pausing to stare in consternation at her trailer. Damn. He had no key. It wouldn't be hard to kick in the flimsy door although he doubted she'd be pleased. Probably she had a key in her purse but that was back at the Center.

No, he paused, remembering she hadn't been carrying anything as she sauntered from the parking lot. Those hips and arms had been swinging—exactly what had caused this mishap in the first place. When she was by the Center's door, she'd only been holding the tea.

She must have stuck the keys in her pocket.

He leaned over, sliding his hand over her left leg, feeling for a bulge. Nothing. He ran his hand over her other leg and around her hip, patting her pockets.

"I can't believe you're trying to feel me up." Her voice was so weak he could barely hear. "Asshole."

He jerked back, bumping his elbow on the steering wheel. "No. I'm just looking for your house keys." But her eyes had already closed. Perfect. Now all she'd remember was that he'd groped her. Which he hadn't, not all—not even close.

He hadn't noticed the firmness of her ass, the curve of her hip, her enticing smell. Hadn't made one single move, not even over the last few days when it had been increasingly hard to keep his hands in his pockets.

He reached over and shook her shoulder. No reaction. Wiggled her head, her left arm. Still indignant, he lightly slapped her cheek.

"What the hell...stop bothering me, Burke." Her words jumbled, like she had gum in her mouth, but at least she was awake, her eyes a frosty blue.

"Jenna, I was *not* feeling you up. I'm trying to find your keys."

"Not locked," she muttered. Her lids slipped shut again.

"Your door's not locked?" He jerked from the car and stalked up the steps. Pushed open the screen door and turned the knob. Shook his head as the inner door swung open. Probably nothing to steal, but from a security standpoint an unlocked door was rather foolish.

He returned to the car and unclipped her belt. Didn't try to wake her, just swung her in his arms, still feeling aggrieved. Goddammit, he *hadn't* been feeling her up.

He tramped down the narrow hallway, over the uneven floor, looking for a bedroom. The first one was frilly and pink, with a lingering hint of cheap perfume, and the girl in the picture had garish makeup. Definitely the little sister. He backed out, careful to keep Jenna's bandaged arm from hitting the wall.

There were only two other rooms: a tiny bathroom with a green shower curtain and a smaller bedroom with a blue bedspread and the smell of fresh flowers. He laid her on the bed, stepped back and folded his arms. There. All done. Finished.

He could get back to work now. Had already lost half of a day. But maybe he should cover her up first, although she probably wouldn't be comfortable if it turned too hot. Forecast was for sunny, seventy-five degrees. No air conditioning in this ancient trailer so it probably boiled in the afternoon.

He tilted his head, oddly uncertain. Maybe it would be best to cover her with one sheet. She only wore jeans and a T-shirt, and her shirt had drifted up, exposing her flat belly. The sight of that smooth skin made him scowl. Short T-shirts would have to be banned at the Center. He could see the hint of her navel, enough to make any man ogle. No wonder Terry had been serving her tea, probably hoping to soften her up. Ask her out.

He edged closer. Looked like there was a hint of blue on her hip too. Some sort of tiny tattoo, but it was half covered by her jeans. What the hell was it? A butterfly maybe? He stepped around the bed but the different angle didn't help. Maybe it was a butterfly. Could be anything really but suddenly it was important to know.

She shivered, rolled to her side and her bandaged arm knocked the headboard. At her shocked gasp of pain, he leaped forward. "Lie on your back, Jenna. Keep your arm still." Her eyes were wide open now and she gulped but nodded. He pulled the sheet up and tucked it tightly around her, watching her face.

"I'll be back in a few hours with some pain pills, okay." He paused, trying to think what she might need. "Maybe some chicken soup?"

"That would be nice," she whispered, her voice scratchy. "Did your mom give you chicken soup when you were sick?"

"My mother wasn't the type to make soup."

"We were lucky." She gave a wan smile. "My mom made us chicken soup when we were sick."

"Then you were very lucky." He reached out and awkwardly patted her hair. "Don't worry about anything. Try to sleep, and I'm sorry."

"Sorry for trying to feel me up?"

"I was not. I told you…"

But she closed her eyes, her lips tilted in a teasing smile, and went to sleep.

Chapter Twelve

Pain jerked Jenna from a muddle of disjointed dreams. She sat up, struggling against the sheet that was tucked so tightly it felt like a straitjacket. Her hand and arm throbbed, a sharp knifing pain that made her stomach roil and left her cursing.

Terry had promised the tea was hot, made just the way she liked it. Heck. She should have been more careful. Had never expected the door to swing open so violently. At eight am, people were supposed to be rushing *into* the building, not out. If it had been anyone else but the owner, she would have chewed him off a strip.

Clearly though, Burke felt bad. She figured the blame was fifty-fifty even though she'd never suggest it was even partially his fault. He already was very apologetic, a rare occurrence for a man such as him.

She just had to figure a way to get through the next couple of weeks. Each massage would take twice as long—she'd only be able to use one hand—but since the Center was only accepting fancy clients now, the work shouldn't be a problem. Lately, she only had three horses a day anyway, not counting the neighborhood animals on the weekend. They might be tough to look after but she didn't want to disappoint anyone; some of them were planning to ride at the Stillwater Fair, part of the annual steeplechase festivities.

And it would be a good incentive to strengthen her left hand. She'd always thought it would be helpful to be ambidextrous. Now was her chance to learn. If only it didn't hurt quite so much.

She eased from the bed, pausing to lean against the wall, briefly amazed that burn victims—real patients with third degree burns—could be so stoic. It was tempting to remove the bandage and check her skin, but she didn't think she was prepared for the sight. Maybe tomorrow.

The floor tilted as she staggered down the hall, and she dropped gratefully into a kitchen chair. They must have given her some powerful drugs. Her tongue was thick, her mouth cottony, and she craved a drink. But walking the five feet to the sink suddenly seemed like a marathon.

She laid her head on the table, feeling weak, vulnerable and alone. Closed her eyes, trying to fight her exhaustion.

"Jenna. You asleep?"

She straightened, blinking, and was swept with an odd rush of relief at the sight of Burke. "Hi." Her voice cracked and she tried again. "Hi." The second time it sounded much better, not quite normal, but much better. "I must have fallen asleep," she said.

His arms were loaded and he dropped the bags on the kitchen table, his gaze on her face as he pulled out a case of water. He lifted a bottle, cracked open the top and moved to the cupboard. Found the glasses on the first try.

He had a good memory, she noted, trying to sit straight and not slump. And she was perfectly fine. It would be no problem working tomorrow. She'd show him.

"Here," he said.

She automatically reached for the water glass with her right hand then paused in dismay. He scowled and she switched to her left. "I got it, thanks," she said and drank the entire glass.

"Save room for soup," he said, turning away.

He was pissed about something and she squared her shoulders, wishing she had more energy. She should tell him it was all right to go but conversely didn't want him to leave. Her hand burned, the pain escalating with each endless minute, and even though she rarely cried, her eyes felt oddly itchy.

The smell of soup abruptly overpowered the hot airless kitchen, and her stomach lurched with nausea.

He pressed a spoon in her left hand, his face dark and unsmiling. "Eat," he snapped, shoving a plastic container in front of her.

"I think maybe later," she managed, trying not to breathe, trying to avert her nose from the steaming soup. God, the smell clogged her nose, her throat—she feared she'd vomit.

"It's five o'clock. You haven't eaten since breakfast. Eat while it's warm."

"I…" She shivered, fighting the overwhelming pain in her arm and the horrible feeling she might throw up. He looked angry. He'd obviously taken the time to send someone for groceries and he had driven her to the hospital and even though he was acting like a bully, she wanted to please. Her mother had probably felt this exact same way, every time her dad picked a fight.

A tear pricked the corner of her eye. She tried to wipe at it, but her bandage was too bulky, and it slid down her cheek. Oh, God, he saw. She reached up with her left arm but was trembling too much—

"Damn." His face darkened and he turned and walked out, slamming the screen door behind him.

She wiped at her face and rose, unsteadily. Her hand gripped the edge of the table, and then he was there again.

"I'm sorry, honey. The doctor said to give you these pills. Here." He twisted the cap off a vial and shook out some blue tablets. "Take two. Maybe even three." He stuck them in her mouth and waved a bottle of water by her face. "Drink."

She was shivering so much that he missed her mouth. Water dribbled down her chin, but he brushed it away with a gentle knuckle.

"I can do a much better job of taking care of you." His voice roughened. "Really I can." He scooped her up, his body so big and healthy and comforting, she just wanted to burrow close.

And then they were on the bed and he'd pulled the sheet around them. "It'll get better. I promise." His breath was warm and minty on her forehead. "Those pills will kick in, probably about fifteen minutes. Not long."

They must have already kicked in because she felt much better. Her arm no longer throbbed with the same intensity. His hand splayed beneath her hair, rubbing the back of her neck. She hadn't dropped her defenses in a long time but she liked his touch, the feel of his chest. Sighing, she closed her eyes and surrendered to a bone-deep exhaustion.

Someone was talking and she cranked her eyes open. The room was dark. A fat moon gleamed yellow through the narrow window. Her arm hurt but not the excruciating pain from the morning, or had it been the afternoon? Details blurred. She remembered the doctor's needle though, that wonderful needle and the rush of relief.

Burke had been wonderful too, driving to the hospital, staying with her, giving her water...holding her. Her cheeks flamed, and she jerked her head sideways, checking her bed. Empty, thank God. He must be in the kitchen, talking on the phone.

She rose and went to the bathroom. Struggled to brush her teeth and hair, awkward with one hand. Walked down the hall.

He greeted her with a smile, his gaze scanning her arm, but he continued talking on his phone. "Okay. We'll show them the facility. See what happens." Cutting the connection, he uncoiled from the chair.

"Pain pills first, I think," he said. "Then how about some soup?"

"Okay," she said, oddly shy, even though this was her kitchen. "Wish I could have another needle like the one the hospital gave. But really, I'm feeling much better now. Thanks...for everything."

He passed her two blue tablets and a bottle of water, his expression inscrutable. She couldn't imagine paying good money for bottled water—their tap water was fine and actually tasted better—but she obediently drank and swallowed the pills.

Her stomach lurched and she realized she was hungry. Peanut would be too. She twisted, peering out the kitchen window at the dark kennel. Her pony was probably wondering where she was. He'd been loose for an hour of grass early this morning but his supper was definitely late.

"I let the pony out," Burke said. "He's eating grass now."

"Oh." She turned in surprise. "That was sweet of you."

"Remember how sweet I am after I beat you in poker." He pressed the microwave buttons. "You can eat the soup outside."

She realized what he was doing half an hour later, when he kept insisting she flex her fingers over the cards. "But that hurts," she said. "I'll just use my good hand."

"You will not. And keep wiggling those fingers. They need the exercise."

She huffed and muttered and complained but then won the next two hands and was so delighted she forgot she was playing under protest. "I won all the water," she said. "What else can we play for? I know you're secretly angling for Peanut, but he's off limits."

Burke gave a mock shudder then grinned, not his lip twitch but a nice smile, the kind that made her heart flutter. "We'll play for questions and answers. Honest answers."

"Okay." She leaned forward, concentrating on her cards, determined not to be distracted. She'd love the opportunity to question him and so far, was feeling rather lucky. After that, maybe the stakes could be pumped up to some real money. Burke sometimes made rash card moves, and it would be easy to capitalize.

The first hand was a cinch and she leaned back, studying him thoughtfully. She already knew he had an engineering degree as well as a masters in business management, but when she saw him like this, relaxed and smiling, he seemed to have unknown depths. "If you could do anything with your life, anything at all, what would you like to do?" she asked.

"Build my own house."

Shit. She'd wasted her question. That answer had been obvious, considering all the time he spent working on the construction site. "That's not what I meant to ask."

He raised an amused eyebrow. "Too late. Deal and use your right hand."

She sniffed but dealt the cards, only fumbling two that he politely ignored. It appeared she had the next hand safely won and she was already preparing a good question, but he got lucky with two aces.

"What do you want?" He pushed her water glass closer, his dark eyes enigmatic.

"Is that your question?" she asked. "Because that's almost the same as my first one and in this version of the game, repeats aren't allowed." She'd already learned he was a marshmallow about letting her make up ridiculous rules.

"Maybe you just don't know the answer." His watchful gaze didn't leave her face. "Everyone should know what they want."

"Certainly, I know the answer." She wiggled in the swing, trying to get more comfortable. "But there're a number of things I want, and then it would be more than one question." She wanted Emily to earn her degree, wanted Peanut to get better and she wanted to be able to help animals stay healthy.

"Come on," he said. "Don't think. Just say the first thing that jumps into your head."

I don't want to be like my mother. She jerked forward, her bandaged hand slamming the water glass. Pain seared. Water spilled over the table, drenching her thigh. Burke snagged her upturned glass, his eyes narrowing on her gritted teeth. "Maybe that's enough for one night," he said. "I'll check on you tomorrow."

"Not necessary." She picked up the soggy cards, trying to save them before they were ruined. "I'll see you at work."

"Jenna, you're not working tomorrow. You're off for a while. At least a week."

"But I can massage with my left hand. It will take longer but I can still do it."

"Wouldn't be much of a massage. And it wouldn't look good for the Center either."

She sank back in the swing, staring at him, too stunned to speak. She'd used all her sick leave when she'd helped Emily move to Philadelphia. On short-term disability, she'd be down to sixty percent of her pay. Even with her ill-gained raise, that wouldn't cover Emily's monthly living expenses, let alone her own.

"I'll wear a long-sleeved shirt," she finally managed, trying to keep the desperation from her voice. "No one will see. And really, I can do my job. One time, I broke my wrist and Wally let me—"

"Wally isn't in charge anymore." He rose, picked up the wet cards and ruthlessly tossed them into the garbage. "I am."

"But you need me. We have horses booked and Nifty's coming soon."

"We're fine. I already hired another masseuse. She starts Monday."

Her mouth opened and she slumped in the swing, dumbstruck. He'd replaced her, didn't need her, hadn't even told her. She struggled to speak but a brick of pain clogged her throat.

"I'll put the pony in and fill his water." He rumpled her hair. "Get some sleep. Don't forget to take another pill."

He strode down the steps, leaving her reeling from shock, despair and the sharp pain left by his massive blindside.

Chapter Thirteen

"Collect call from Emily Murphy," the operator's voice said. "Do you accept the charges?"

"Yes." Jenna rose from the kitchen table and pressed the phone tightly against her left ear.

"Good morning," Emily said. "I know you wanted me to text, not call, but we haven't spoken for a while."

"Oh, Em, I miss you." Jenna stepped onto the porch, breathing in the fresh morning air. The sun was still low and already the trailer was unbearably hot. "I thought maybe you were...away?"

"Nope, nose to the books, constantly. That's one of the reasons I called. These textbooks are expensive. I've been going to the library to study, but it would be much better if I could buy them. You wouldn't know, of course, but books can cost about two hundred dollars."

Jenna sank on the swing. "Two hundred dollars?" Her voice squeaked.

"And that's just for one book," Emily said. "The profs assign outside reading. Scholarships are available, bursaries based on need too, but they're impossible to get without the extra reading."

"Do you think you could get one of those?"

"Maybe. If I had the books."

"I'll see what money I can scrape together." Jenna averted her gaze from her injured arm.

"Send it as soon as you can," Emily said. "I'll text a reminder."

"Okay. And there's some good news. The solarium is really helping Peanut's coat—" But Em had hung up.

Jenna swore at the rudeness of the dial tone. Emily needed a kick in the ass. *Maybe I should drive over.* She started to punch Em's number back in then stiffened at the sound of a car.

Aw, shit. Burke. She stared in dismay at her shorts and strapless top—clothes intended to beat the heat but definitely not to wear in public. Groaning, she rose and ducked back into the kitchen. The car crested the hill and wheeled into her driveway.

She didn't want him to see her dressed like this. Didn't want to see him at all. She still ached from his meanness and doubted she could be civil—even though she had to be. But Wally would never have put anyone on disability, had always worried about employees having enough money for groceries.

She tiptoed back into her bedroom and silently eased the door shut. Heard two hard knocks then the slam of the screen door. *Thump.* Another smaller *thud.* The door slammed again and an engine purred. She peeked out the window, relieved to see his car disappear over the hill.

She left the bedroom and walked cautiously back down the hall. A grocery bag sat on the kitchen table along with a black leather case. She peeked in the bag: more soup, whole wheat rolls, two packs of playing cards, beer, three gold-colored jars of fancy skin cream and a year's supply of sterile white bandages.

The leather case was small and obviously not food. She tugged open the zipper and blinked in amazement. Oh, gosh, an Iphone! She scrolled quickly through the apps—everything a person could want, and more. A breeze blew through the screen door, rustling a sheet of paper lying on the counter. She snatched it up and studied his bold scrawl.

Phone is on the Burke account, full features. Use your right hand. (Be helpful if you would research Lorna and David Ridgeman of Ridgeman Racing Stables, the couple coming next week.)

Okay, so it sounded like she was still expected to do the tour, but more importantly he'd left her a fully featured phone. She skipped around the table, needing to tell someone.

Called Emily but cut the connection before the call went

through. *Not cool.* Probably she shouldn't use the company phone for personal calls. Email was okay though. That was free along with Skype and Facebook.

Facebook. She rushed back to her bedroom and retrieved Frances's password.

Logged in quickly. Friend list, Emily Murphy. Scrolled across the screen and stared in dismay. Holy shit. Somehow Emily had found time to post four hundred and two pictures.

A wide range of pictures. Pictures of laughing faces, drunken faces, leering faces. Pictures of blue pools and tiny rooms and trendy bars. Pictures of beach volleyball and impossibly small bikinis. Yes, indeed. It looked like Em was having a very good time at college. Of course, this could be happening on weekends. Em had said the spring session was lot easier.

Steadying her breathing, she logged onto her Facebook account with its grand total of three friends—Wally, Colin and Mrs. Parker.

Tapped a friend request to Emily. That should flush her out. If she was goofing off instead of studying, Em would find an excuse not to friend her. But, damn, if she were goofing around, all their scrimping and saving had been wasted.

Jenna chewed her fingernails and stared at the screen.

Two minutes later: friend request accepted. And a message.

Okay, that was fast. She'd been holding her breath but took a relieved gulp as she read Em's message. 'Check out Trevor's cool car. Meeting parents soon. They have a pool!'

Jenna scanned the pictures, trying not to blanch. She did *not* like this boyfriend. He had a shifty look she didn't trust and when he wasn't leering for the camera, he had his hands draped suggestively over Emily.

She sighed, trying to lighten up. Maybe she was a teensy bit jealous that Em was having such fun, that she was working toward her degree, that she was moving toward a better life. But it would have been much simpler if her sister had applied to the local college. Cheaper too. Easy admissions. Only a thirty-minute drive and a heap of money could be saved by living at home.

She pressed Wally's number, needing the reassurance of a friendly voice.

"Good morning. Wally Turner speaking."

"Hey, Wally," she said. "Why so formal? It's only me."

"The display said Burke Industries. Jesus, Jenna. I left three messages yesterday, and one time Burke answered your phone. What the hell was he doing there? Acted like he'd moved in."

Jenna squeezed her eyes shut, shaking her head at the accusation in Wally's voice. Men were such idiots. "Well, I'm fine. I burned my wrist yesterday and can't work for a few weeks. But thanks for asking."

"Calm down. I was going to ask about your hand next. But you have to come in, if only to pretend to work. All your sick days were used moving Emily. Or maybe you can help tally some of the inventory. At least, show your face for half an hour each day."

"Oh, Wally." She gave a hysterical laugh. "You make it sound so easy. I wish you were still the boss."

"What's wrong?" He paused and his breathing turned heavy. "No way. You mean that bastard stuck you on long-term?"

"He doesn't believe I can do the job right now. But it's only for a little while." She swallowed, slowing her words, surprised by her need to defend Burke. "And he did buy some groceries. And left me this neat phone."

Wally snorted. "He just doesn't want you to sue. Their rep for not being employee friendly isn't helped by your accident, especially since I heard it was his fault. Damn ruthless people. They have their tentacles everywhere. My hay guy already signed a new contract with Burke, even though he promised to jack prices.

"Why don't you sue him, Jenna?" Wally added. "Might get a fair chunk of change. Maybe not have to work for a while. Pay for a year of Em's tuition."

Jenna stared blankly at the tips of her pale fingers poking from the bandage. So that's why Burke had encouraged her to use her right hand. Playing cards, leaving the fancy phone. He was afraid she'd have residual damage. Good God, and she'd thought he was being nice.

"I'm not suing anyone, Wally. I like to work. And it was as much my fault as his." Her voice came out flat and resigned. "Do you know who he hired?"

"He hired someone? To replace you? Aw, Jenna, I'm so sorry."

The genuine sympathy in Wally's voice made her throat tighten. "It's only for a little while," she said quickly. "I just wondered who it was."

"Don't know. Look, I've got to go. He's here now, only about thirty feet away. Giving me one of those dark looks."

The phone went dead. It was obvious who Wally was talking about. She hoped she hadn't landed him in any more trouble with Burke. She retreated to the cooler porch and stared blankly across the road. Peanut grazed contentedly, probably surprised he was getting extra time to eat. Didn't realize she wasn't going anywhere. Not today. Not for a while.

Damn. At least she could make good use of her time. She eyed the wooden ladder by the deserted chicken coop. Probably a good day to inspect the roof. If the shingles weren't too bad, she could postpone repairs and wait for Emily to come home. Between the two of them, they'd get it done.

She dragged the old ladder to the side of the trailer. Struggled to prop it on the uneven grass. It was hard climbing with one hand and damn hot, but she managed, though she moved slower than usual.

She edged along the roof, inspecting the worn shingles and staying low. The roof over the bedrooms wasn't too bad. That section had been recently patched, but the part above the kitchen needed immediate repair. There was some roofing left at the Center's construction site. Maybe she could ask the friendly guy, Terry, if she could buy the leftovers. She wouldn't need much, about twelve square feet, and they generally discarded it anyway.

Of course, Burke might not like that. She'd have to paint it a different color so he wouldn't guess the source, and good paint was expensive.

Christ, Burke was becoming a major pain in the ass.

Frustrated, she banged the top of the ladder then jerked in dismay as it wobbled, slid sideways and toppled to the grass.

Burke crossed his arms, waiting impatiently for Wally to finish his phone call. The man had been on his cell all morning, probably trying to whip up more trouble. It wasn't going to work. With Leo Winfield's support, Burke would soon have the town in his pocket.

A few publicity appearances for the locals and any lingering hostility toward the Center would disappear.

Perhaps it had been rash to cut off the visits for local horses. He should have waited a month or two before clamping down.

Wally closed his phone and raised an inquiring eyebrow. "What do you need…boss?"

His tone edged on insolence and Burke scowled. He'd merely intended to give Wally a heads-up about the Ridgeman stud, but the man definitely needed an attitude adjustment. Needed to have his chain yanked.

"We have cobblestones scheduled for installation tomorrow," Burke said, "as well as flowerbeds by the front entrance. You'll need to supervise."

"But tomorrow's Saturday."

Burke gave a tight smile. "That's right."

"But I was planning to attend the steeplechase. So folks can see Three Brooks still supports this town."

"No problem. I'll handle it."

Wally's mouth flattened. "Fine, then. Where are the stones going?"

"In the courtyard, by the visitors' parking lot."

"I always thought cobblestones would look nice there," Wally nodded reluctantly, "but could never justify the expense."

The man seemed to truly care for the Center and Burke softened. "We may have a Derby winner coming. His connections are checking out the place next week. Staff might have a big horse to pamper."

"What about Jenna?"

"What about her?" Burke squared his shoulders.

"Heard she's off work for a bit. She's got a special touch with a horse. I think we need her around…and she needs us."

"I'll look after staffing. And the employees."

"Good to know. And I'll look after the rocks and flowers." Wally gave a sardonic salute and walked away, shoulders stiff with resentment.

Burke's eyes narrowed. If he could only prove the stealing, Wally would be gone within the hour. And the man's inference that he wasn't looking after staff stung. Yesterday, he'd spent most of the day with Jenna. Had enjoyed it even. Liked looking after her.

He glanced at his watch, wondering if she were awake yet. Probably still asleep, especially if she'd popped those pills, but it was important to keep flexing her fingers. Yeah, probably time to check on her progress.

Smiling, he headed for the parking lot.

When he pulled in the driveway, she wasn't in sight but the ugly pony chomped grass by the side of the road. The little guy even surprised him with a friendly nicker when he walked past.

Something moved on the roof. Jenna? A flash of bare leg. He jerked to a stop and adjusted his sunglasses. "What the hell are you doing up there?" he called.

"Just checking the roof. Seeing what needs to be patched. Thanks for the great phone, by the way."

He nodded, not really interested, too busy craning his neck trying to see what she wore. Didn't seem to be much. "Come on down and make me a coffee," he finally said.

"Well," she blew out a resigned sigh, "I'm actually a bit stuck."

"Where's your ladder?"

She gestured at the side of the trailer and he circled to where a wooden contraption lay on the patchy grass.

"It fell when I was starting to climb down, so if you could just lean it back against the roof, I'd be grateful."

"Lucky you weren't hurt. It wouldn't help your wrist…" His words trailed off. Oh, wow. Her tanned legs were long and bare, and she wore either a tiny pair of pink shorts or else, please God, some slinky, scanty underwear.

He shoved his sunglasses higher on his nose, straining to see. Definitely shorts—but tiny shorts she filled out perfectly. Great legs too, which he'd already surmised, but it was a treat to see them free of the customary jeans. Hard to look away. He didn't even try and instead blew out an appreciative whistle. "How grateful would you be," he asked softly, his hand pausing over the ladder.

"Not grateful enough for sex," she said. "And don't be rude."

"I wasn't thinking of sex." *Liar.* "But I do need you to accompany me to the local steeplechase tomorrow."

She uncrossed her arms and peered down, seeming to relax a notch. "I always go to that anyway. Wally presents the trophy."

"Not tomorrow he isn't. And I need someone to introduce me."

"That's not fair." Her voice thickened with resentment. "I'm not healthy enough to go to work but okay to work on weekends?"

"That's right. And I need a local with me. Someone who the people like."

"What about the person you hired for my job?" She slapped at a mosquito, the sound unusually sharp in the still air.

"She doesn't start until Monday. So unfortunately, I need you."

"You're such a smooth talker." Her lips tightened. "I'm coming down now. But can you turn around, please. It's hot and I'm not dressed for company."

"But someone needs to hold this rather wobbly ladder." He propped it against the side of the trailer but couldn't keep the chuckle from his voice. "I promise to catch you if you fall."

Her head appeared over the edge of the roof. She wasn't wearing a bra and the outline of her nipples was visible beneath the white tube top. Her breasts were bigger than he'd originally thought, firm and pretty as hell. He stared in blunt appreciation. Maybe he'd wiggle the ladder a bit, cause some convenient tipsiness. Maybe she really would fall.

Her gaze flickered as though reading his mind, and she stared at him for a long moment. "It looks so high from up here," she finally said, crossing her arms. "Are you sure it's steady?"

He dragged his eyes off her breasts and back to her face. "Absolutely. Look." He stepped on the first rung, hoping the rotten wood would hold his weight, keen to get closer. He hadn't seen a tube top in years but had always thought they were the brainchild of a very smart man.

She gave a helpless shrug. "It is scary though. I'd feel better if you held it at the top. That's where it slid earlier, when I tried to turn around and couldn't hold on with my right hand."

"I'll come up," he said, his voice husky. He'd been looking forward to checking out her ass and legs as she climbed down, but the view from the top carried its own advantages. Besides, a man always had to be gallant, and gallantry was much easier when the woman looked like Jenna.

He climbed quickly, placing his feet on the far outside of the rungs. The ladder had to be a hundred years old, maybe more, and she looked relieved when he reached the top.

"Be sure to hold it tight," she whispered as she slipped past. Her breasts flashed but she descended quickly, amazingly nimble for a one-handed woman. He couldn't see down her top, not at that speed, but it was still entertaining. He was disappointed when she reached the ground and her breasts stopped bouncing. He pulled his gaze away, turned to follow—

Thud. The ladder toppled to the ground. She glanced up, her coy smile replaced with a mutinous expression. "Did anybody ever tell you that you're mean and rude and—" Her chest heaved as she searched for the right word.

"Annoyed," he added but he wasn't, not really. He stared down, careful now to keep his gaze on her face. He *had* been ogling and it was already clear she didn't like to be cornered. But yesterday he'd had her in his arms, and he'd assumed they'd made some sort of progress.

However, the resentment in her voice was laced with something even more confusing—genuine hurt.

"I *can* massage horses and I *can* do my job," she was saying. "Look!" She waved her arm, fluttering the tips of her fingers. "And by Monday, I'll be even better and there was no...n-need to put me on short-term. Or hire a replacement. And I hate it that you have to buy me food." She spun away. "I'll get dressed," she muttered. "Then put the ladder back."

He groaned then crossed to the front of the roof, hung onto the edge with his hands, and dropped lightly to the ground by the porch.

She walked around the corner of the trailer, swiping at her face. Froze when she saw him, her eyes as wide as a startled deer.

"Maybe you better explain what short-term is," he said mildly. He lowered himself on the step, trying to appear less threatening but careful to remain between her and the screen door.

She averted her head, wiping furiously at her face, pretending to look at Peanut, anywhere but at him. "Short term means sixty-percent salary. And maybe I should be but," her voice cracked, "it just makes things a bit hard right now—"

"Oh, sweetheart." He swooped across the walk and wrapped his arms around her. "I didn't know that. Don't worry. I'll fix it." She didn't move, standing so stiffly he slipped his hand around the back of her neck, remembering she liked that, and rubbed until she marginally relaxed.

"I just want you to heal," he added. "The company doesn't want to cause any hardship."

"And that's another thing." She tilted her head, her eyes wide and concerned. "This…thing we have. It's uncomfortable because you're my boss. I like you. I like playing cards with you. But it's definitely not a good idea to have sex."

"Probably not." He matched her solemn expression, refraining from mentioning she was wrapped in his arms, half naked, something he'd learned was always an excellent step toward sexual relations. And he definitely wasn't going to be the first to move away. In fact, he subtly shifted so that her breasts nudged against his chest, camouflaging the action with a reassuring neck rub.

"Did you take your pills today?" He splayed his left hand over her hip, discreetly checking out her curves, over the spot where he guessed her tattoo was.

"Sure did, ten already."

He jerked back. She sidestepped and waltzed up the steps, so smoothly he realized it had been a ploy. Escape from his arms without hurting his feelings. The screen door slammed behind her sculpted legs, and he chuckled. This was going to be fun. Like taking over a particularly resistant company.

He wandered to the porch and stretched out on the swing. The shade was nice, the breeze fresh; it really was a pleasant place. He whipped off seventeen emails, fifteen texts and called Edward.

"Things will be stable here by the end of the month," Burke said, "so you can slot me in for another job."

"Good. We'll make more money off the Ridgeman stud than that Center made in three months." His cousin loved turning big profits, and Burke could picture Edward rubbing his hands in glee.

"Yeah," Burke said, "and it's a simple operation. With a good manager, not much can go wrong. Although I might drop in and conduct periodic checks."

"Why the hell would you want to go back there?" Edward groaned. "Let me guess. You got a woman stashed away. Some society chick with fancy horses?"

"Not exactly." Burke watched as the scruffy pony swished his tail and wandered into deeper grass, contentedly seeking a choicer selection.

"Good, because Theresa misses you." Edward's voice carried a trace of warning. "And her family has important connections. Wouldn't hurt to give her a call, stroke her a bit."

The screen door squeaked and Jenna appeared, awkwardly balancing a tray in her left hand. "Got a meeting," Burke said, cutting the connection and rising to his feet.

"Is that what upper management says when they're goofing off?" She lifted an eyebrow, letting him take the tray.

"Pretty much, and you should avoid carrying such hot drinks." He shook his head as he placed the cups on the table. "They're dangerous."

"That was an unusual occurrence. I told Terry I liked boiling tea and he took me literally."

"Who's Terry?" He picked up his coffee mug, careful to keep his voice neutral.

"An old school friend of mine. Works on the construction site." She paused, studying him over her teacup. "I thought if there was some old roofing that wasn't being used, just scrap pieces of course, that Terry could drop by some evening and fix the leaks in my roof."

"Really? You thought there'd be that much scrap?" He injected a deliberate note of incredulity, raising an eyebrow until she flushed and looked away. It wasn't such a big deal but he didn't like the image of Terry pounding on her roof, relaxing on the swing afterward, sipping a cold beer. His beer.

"Guess it's not such a good idea." She plucked at the bandage on her arm, her sigh slightly forlorn.

"I'll fix your roof on Sunday. Forecast is good all weekend."

"Really. That's so nice of you to offer." She beamed such a satisfied smile, he realized he'd been conned. He set his mug on the tray, stretched his arm over her shoulder, and chuckled. "Is Terry really a school friend?" he asked.

"Hardly know him," she said with a mischievous smile.

"Let's keep it that way then." He tucked her into his chest, wishing she hadn't changed from her tiny top and shorts. Clearly, she wanted to move slowly which was fine with him, so long as they were moving. "Did you remember to take your pills?" He slid his hand beneath her hair and began rubbing the back of her neck.

"Just took two." She suppressed a yawn. "They work really well. I'm fine to go back to work though. Not a bit tired."

He smiled but said nothing, just continued massaging her neck, waiting patiently for her eyelids to lower.

Chapter Fourteen

Jenna's eyes flickered. Probably time to wake up and get off the swing, but she was too content to move. Burke was doing something on his phone and occasionally his deep voice sounded above her, crisp and assured. She understood most of the terms but generally concepts of leverage and buy-outs bored her.

His hand dropped to her head, idly stroking the nape of her neck, and she sensed movement of his other hand as it thumbed the phone. His lap was hard but comfortable although she didn't understand how that could be. She did know his hands hadn't once roamed, and on Sunday he was going to fix her roof.

She trusted him, she realized, in that relaxed moment before waking when the mind was crystal clear and ideas zapped like lightening.

It had been a lazy afternoon though. She probably should get Peanut off the grass before he foundered, and she should definitely think of something for supper. Maybe Burke would want to hang around to eat, although she was probably a very boring date—if hanging out on the swing could even be called a date.

Those drugs definitely drained her energy. She didn't know how long she'd napped, but so far this enforced disability had been rather pleasant.

She stretched in contentment, cracked her lids open and stared up into Burke's enigmatic eyes.

"I've got to go back to Three Brooks for a bit," he said softly. His hand slid around her neck and his thumb made her skin tingle. "I'll stick Peanut back in the kennel—he's probably had enough grass—and pick something up for supper. What would you like?"

She blinked, wondering if she'd thought aloud. His thumb moved along her jaw to her cheek, slow and sure, so light she could barely feel it. She tilted her head, automatically leaning into his touch.

"Probably tired of soup." His thumb caressed her upper lip. "Maybe tonight you'll be ready for something a little more…meaty?"

His eyes, his voice, his touch made her body spark with awareness. Shit, even her nipples tingled now and part of her wanted that big hand to drop to her breasts.

It would be disastrous though. She had to keep her wits, what little she had. Unfortunately her traitorous body was sizzling, arguing with her brain, and being scarily insistent. *Pick me up and carry me to the bed.*

And now his other hand traced her collarbone, his thumb still working seductively on her lips. "You can have anything you want," he said, "but you have to tell me."

She hated her weakness, knew sex was a weapon, love was a weapon, and exactly how her father had played her mom. It was important to stay in control here. Or escape before she lost it.

She eased upright, sliding away from his hand. "I don't eat much meat. I'd like to stay with something lighter, maybe sushi."

Disappointment darkened his eyes but she thought he rallied well, better than most men. "Sushi it is then," he said.

She adjusted her cards and glanced at her watch, unable to hide a yawn.

"Am I boring you?" Burke's mouth curved in a tolerant smile.

"No, but raw fish always makes me sleepy."

"I never heard that before."

Neither had she, but she still had to sneak Peanut up to the Center and tomorrow was the annual steeplechase. Always a demanding day. And those pain pills made her sleepy. Probably time to cut back. She fervently wished she didn't have to sneak.

"What about playing for a light treatment for Peanut?" she asked casually, staring at her cards—two Jacks and two nines.

"Jenna, that pony isn't worth the cost of electricity. Besides you lose."

Her eyes widened as he flipped over three Queens. "How did you do that?" She'd been sure she had a winning hand. "Are these cards marked?"

She scanned the deck suspiciously. She'd won the first few games but it seemed whenever she really wanted something, he squeaked through with a win. She definitely wouldn't have agreed to stay off work for a whole week if she hadn't been positive of winning.

At least, payroll had called to confirm full pay while she researched Ridgeman, as though *that* would take more than half an hour.

He stretched his arm over the back of the swing but she scrambled to her feet, avoiding his touch, hurt by his worthless pony comment.

"I'll pick you up in the morning," he said, rising and walking to the steps.

"Okay," she said. "Thanks for dinner."

He didn't even try to kiss her for which she was grateful, although it was rather humbling. He could at least have *tried* to kiss her. But maybe he didn't want to. Maybe he was the kind of guy who only liked to touch women, to massage them, to stroke them. Make them feel good and then leave.

Oh, God, he had her all balled up again.

She sighed as his car eased from the driveway, but she waited several cautious minutes before changing into her jogging outfit and gathering Peanut.

The pony had already missed two days of light therapy; he couldn't miss a third. And it was Burke's fault she had to sneak. The man was infuriating—sometimes incredibly kind, other times so thoughtless it felt like he was snapping an elastic band around her chest.

It was a game to him. A little amusement on the side while he stabilized Three Brooks and searched for more companies to conquer. But that was okay. She could handle it.

She tugged the pony down the dark path, but he was unusually slow. Breathing heavy and labored... She jerked to a stop, chilled by fear. "Okay, buddy, we'll stop and rest. No problem."

He shoved his wheezy nose against her stomach, as though grateful for the break, not even trying to sniff at the ground and snatch something to eat.

"Oh, Peanut." She rubbed his neck, murmuring nonsensical words of love, checking her watch as she counted his respiration rate. High but not critical. He was fine, probably wanted a break. He was a smart pony, just kind of lazy. He was absolutely fine.

But her breath caught in a sob, and she bent down and pressed her damp cheek against his neck. Take care of Emily and Peanut, her mother had said. Yet, lately she'd been doing a piss-poor job of both.

The lights from Three Brooks glimmered through the trees and she swallowed her fear. Wally was great with horses; he'd know what to do. She just had to make sure Peanut arrived there safely.

They stumbled from the tree line, moving achingly slow. Larry's truck was nowhere in sight and she breathed a sigh of relief. Other than Burke, no one knew when the security patrols were. Not any longer. She fought a rush of bitterness.

She checked the base of the statue, searching for the glint of a key. Wally's truck was shoved against the side of the visitors' lot in an obvious show of defiance. Probably not a good idea to wave a red flag in front of Burke, but she shared Wally's frustration.

She unlocked the door and anxiously called his name.

"Jenna? What's wrong?" Wally rushed down the steps, his gaze sweeping her face before narrowing on Peanut. "How long has he been breathing like that?"

"I'm not sure. For the last thirty minutes, at least, maybe more." Regret swept her. She'd been too busy eating sushi and flirting with Burke to even check her beloved pony.

Wally slipped his hand under Peanut's jawbone, taking his pulse then pressed his ear against the pony's belly. "I need to check his temperature first, but has he ever been in the oxygen chamber?"

She shook her head. "Would it help?" she asked brokenly.

"Probably. Come on. Bring him down."

Wally unlocked the door to the oxygen room, strode across the floor and pulled open the heavy metal door to the chamber.

"Lead him in, Jenna, then come out and shut the door. We'll give him forty-five minutes."

Wally turned to the control panel and pressed a green button. "He's too small to look out the window so just stand there so he can see your face. Most horses don't mind the chamber. Some love it, and Peanut is a very smart fellow. In a minute, he'll be breathing a hundred-percent oxygen."

Jenna peered through the window, studying Peanut who merely flicked his tail and stared back with an accepting look in his liquid eyes. She should have been using this years ago when she had easy access. The chamber was great for healing lung tissue and stubborn infections. She'd been crazy not to take full advantage, and now Burke had put this out of reach.

"How's he doing?" Wally asked gently.

"He doesn't mind it at all," she managed.

"Good." Wally gave her a faintly sheepish look. "I have company upstairs. I'll get rid of her and be right back."

"No, please don't, Wally. We're fine. I know how to work this machine."

"I'll be right back, Jenna." Wally said firmly. "Peanut is a special fellow and I want to help. Besides, waiting here all alone is boring." He paused, hand on the doorknob. "You know about the emergency shutoff button? Seals all the oxygen, in case of a leak?"

"Yes, and there's a valve in the other room."

"That's right. Red knob on the side wall." He pushed open the door. "I'll be back soon."

Jenna squared her shoulders and crossed the room. She settled into the chair by the controls, staring at the blinking panel loaded with lights and gauges. It was going to be a long night. Forty-five minutes of oxygen, twenty minutes in the solarium and maybe Peanut should have some magnetic therapy too.

It was critical to get this pony's health turned around, so much harder to straighten animals out when they were aged. Thank God for Wally and his inherent kindness. It wasn't at all necessary that he come back, but part of her was rather relieved.

There was something spooky about the metal chamber and its pressurized environment—the capsule always reminded her of an alien space ship, mysterious and slightly menacing. The red explosive warnings didn't soothe her senses either. When giving a tour, she touched blithely on the dangers of gas under pressure but tried not to worry about it. Tonight, with her pony in the chamber and oxygen filling the slender pipes, she really would appreciate some company.

Chapter Fifteen

Burke turned into the driveway. Peanut lifted his head from the dewy grass, trotted a few steps then gave a playful buck. Little pony was feeling good.

He climbed the porch steps, pausing as Jenna opened the screen door. Damn, she was hot. It had been a long time since he'd had such a visceral reaction to a woman. Maybe it was because he'd never seen her in a dress. A creamy-white sundress that looked simple, but wasn't. Not when it was on her.

"Add a hat and you're ready for the Derby," he said, dragging his gaze to her full pink lips, wishing he could taste them. She rarely wore makeup and that was a damn good thing. It was going to be difficult to keep things as slow as she wanted.

She pirouetted, clearly oblivious to his thoughts, scooped up an elegantly brimmed hat and gave a mischievous smile. "Ah, but the Stillwater Steeplechase is much more fun than the little old Kentucky Derby." Her smile turned rueful as she waved her right arm. "I planned to change the old bandage for a sparkling new one, but couldn't remember if you said thirty-six hours or forty-eight?"

He stepped in. The screen door banged behind him, and he hooked a chair with his foot. "Sit down. It was thirty-six hours and I totally forgot. You were so high from the pain needle it's amazing you remember anything. Where are the bandages and cream?"

"In the bathroom." She made no move to sit, didn't ever do anything he said. "But here's the thing. When I tried peeking to see how it was healing, the bandage was kind of stuck to the skin."

Concern darkened her beautiful face and he guided her gently into the chair. "Don't worry," he said as he walked down the hall and into the bathroom.

It was tiny but comfortable. A pink toothbrush stood in a sparkling clean glass and on the side of the sink lay two tattered horse magazines stamped 'Three Brooks' along with the antibiotic cream and bandages. A fresh breeze sifted through the window, fluttering the curtains, and even from the bathroom, he could survey the sloping valley. A damn nice view, all around.

He washed his hands, smiling at the flowery-smelling soap. Scooped up the bandages and cream and rejoined her in the kitchen.

"You're not going to yank real quick, are you?" she asked, eyeing him warily.

"Jenna, I'm going to make you squeal. Especially since there are company magazines in your bathroom. You're not borrowing supplies again, are you?" He shook his head in mock dismay, dragging the chair closer until his knee touched her thigh. "It's probably easier for me to pull off than you. We could go to the hospital, but the wait might be quite long."

"Pull away then." She gave a resolute nod, held out her arm and averted her head.

He unwrapped the first layer, slowing as he neared the bottom of the bandage. Shit. It definitely was stuck. Really stuck. This was going to hurt. "Maybe we should go to the hospital," he muttered.

"Just do it," she said.

He hesitated, staring at her left hand curled trustingly over his knee, then set his jaw and ripped. He winced but she didn't make a sound.

Oh, shit. He stared in dismay at the blistered skin, wondering if she'd need a skin graft. He fumbled for the ointment, his movements clumsy with regret. The lid clattered sideways onto the linoleum table.

She turned her head questioningly, looking down before he could distract her. "Oh, that's healing great," she said.

"Yeah." His throat had gone dry and he struggled with the container, wishing he'd been the one who'd been burned. "I'm going to rub this on," he added, his voice gruff. "It might hurt."

"This was not your fault, Burke." She smiled at him for a long moment, rich with generosity, but he knew he couldn't forgive himself as easily.

"Don't wiggle," he said, his voice thick with emotion. He slathered on half the container of cream and wrapped the burn, holding her wrist much longer than necessary, willing it to magically heal. "There," he said, trying to match her smile. "The bandage matches your dress. Very nice."

Her arms were tanned and toned and also very nice, and he couldn't resist dragging a finger over the curve of her arm. "Guess we're ready to go," he said, still holding her wrist, intensely aware of the warmth of her leg against his thigh.

"One more thing," he added, not wanting her to move. He slid his hand in his pocket. "I have your ring. Want me put it on your other hand?"

"I can do it. Thanks for saving it." She leaped up, taking the ring and awkwardly sliding it on. "I still have to put Peanut in."

"I'll do it," he said, rising more slowly. She was already halfway out the door. He followed, resigned to watch her flounce across the grass in her sexy white dress and matching sandals. She reminded him of the model in his favorite car commercial, and just as distant.

He propped his hip against his car, waiting as she did that ritual kiss thing on Peanut's forehead. The pony responded with some sort of head press back. He'd prefer to stay here—swing on the porch and talk—rather than join a mob of rowdy villagers. But if he could meet a few influential people, have his appearance duly noted, then maybe he and Jenna could leave early, come back and play cards.

Maybe even engage in something much more pleasurable.

He tilted his sunglasses, watching as she headed back to him, dress swirling around those toned legs…legs absolutely perfect for wrapping around his hips. And one day, she was going to walk right up to him, unzip his pants, slide that saucy mouth over his throbbing dick—

"Quit it," she said, brushing past him.

He grinned and pulled open the passenger door. "You don't practice visualization?"

"This isn't the time for x-rated stuff."

They drove silently for a few minutes. However, sex lingered in his mind, in his gaze, in the car. He kept looking sideways, drinking her in with his eyes. He could tell she was feeling it too, the self-conscious way she wet her lower lip, the subtle shift in her breathing.

"Turn right at the first corner." Her voice was husky.

"When are you going to sleep with me, Jenna?" he blurted, accelerating out of a hairpin turn. "You know it's going to happen."

"Not until the day before you leave."

"What?" He slammed the brake and a trailing pickup swerved past, horn blaring. He ignored the gesturing driver and twisted in the seat. "The day before I leave? That doesn't make any sense."

"Makes sense to me. Go ten more miles on this road then left at the signs."

He scowled, studying her face. She looked perfectly serious although in one aspect, he should be delighted. Up to this point, he really hadn't been sure she *would* sleep with him. Now it seemed she would. And didn't that make him harden with anticipation. "But what if it's good," he scowled, "and we both want more?"

"Oh, it'll be good, Burke." She squared her bare shoulders against the seat. He could see those gorgeous breasts, those perky nipples straining against the fabric of her dress, and a throbbing heat filled his groin.

He jerked his head away, knuckles whitening on the wheel. Damn. This was going to be tough, knowing he was going to have her soon, just not quite yet. "I might forget this conversation," his voice sounded hoarse, "so you might have to remind me before I leave."

She jerked sideways, staring. As though believing he would, could, ever forget. Her nose tilted in a haughty sniff but he caught the slight droop to her shoulders and, as usual, her hint of vulnerability made him cave.

"Actually, I'll be counting the days," he said quickly. "And if this waiting has anything to do with work, I can easily fix that."

"Oh, what would you do?" She twisted again, the seatbelt cupping her left breast. "Fire me?"

"Sure, but I'd give you money." His dragged his attention back to the road. "Plenty of money," he added. "And I'll come back and visit."

"In exchange for the money?"

"It wouldn't be quite like that."

"You're an asshole." She yanked down the sun visor and leaned against the headrest, her face stony as she stared straight ahead.

And that was the problem. She didn't want things, wasn't a bit materialistic. Completely happy with her pony and trailer. He couldn't figure out what motivated her, and it was damn difficult to control people if you didn't understand their motivations. And didn't everyone want things?

"You're complicated," he said, needing the last word. He jammed on the radio, deliberately choosing classical music that he guessed she'd dislike.

He didn't throw out offers like that every day. Besides he was her boss; she really shouldn't be calling him an asshole. She probably needed a little attitude adjustment after enjoying such liberties with Wally. He wouldn't actually fire her. It was clear she loved working with the horses. But he'd make her wonder, put her on edge and maybe then she'd be a little more…accommodating. Women were natural-born conciliators; they didn't like disruption.

He concentrated on driving, enduring endless minutes of a string quartet. Finally he blew out an apologetic sigh and glanced sideways, admitting he was thinking like an asshole. Just like she'd accused him of being.

"I'm sorry…" He stopped talking. Clearly she was a lot less disrupted than he. Her eyes were closed, lashes long and dark against her cheeks. First time he'd seen her with mascara, but it was obvious now. Proud cheekbones. A hint of darkness beneath her eyes, something he hadn't noticed earlier when he'd been so distracted by their vibrant blue.

He softened the music and flipped on his GPS. She looked tired, no doubt affected by the drugs. Kinder to let her sleep.

He found the fairgrounds on his own. She woke forty-five minutes later when a laughing family wandered too close to the car. She jerked her head sideways, then straightened, fumbling with her seatbelt.

He put down his phone, leaned over and unclipped her belt. Switched off the ignition, silencing the whirr of the air conditioner.

"We're here already?" She blinked at the crowded parking lot, obviously fuzzy.

"Maybe you should go to the doctor tomorrow," he said. "Have him check that hand for infection."

"Oh, I'm fine." She covered a wide yawn. "Just not used to drugs. How long have we been here?"

"Not too long." *Almost an hour.* And no Internet connection in this low section of the valley.

"I'm sorry. And you wanted to meet all the important people." She opened her door, stuck out a shapely leg and glanced back. "Thanks very much for letting me sleep. That was thoughtful of you." Her smile was so sincere, it rattled him and he almost forgot his keys in the ignition.

He circled the car and protectively tucked his fingers over her elbow, frowning in dismay at the people swarming the admission gates. It looked like the entire town had gathered, along with some neighborhood dogs. There was even a spotted goat on a leash.

They walked closer. A chubby boy with a ragged haircut stared at him and began to bawl.

"Quit scowling," Jenna whispered. "You're scaring the kids." She shook his hand off her elbow and circled the line of people. He hustled after her, not wanting to be left behind in this circus. Barns to the left, one rickety grandstand dead ahead and scores of campers, trailers and RVs jammed in a rutted field to the right.

He didn't see any box seats but surely if he bought two of the most expensive tickets, they'd be somewhat separated from the riffraff. It appeared they'd be at least twenty minutes getting in. One snaking line, one tiny wicket. Maybe everything would be sold out.

"Maybe there're no more seats," he said hopefully.

"Hey, Jenna!" A paunchy man at the side of the exhibitors' gate stepped forward. He beamed a smile at Jenna and waved them through with a beefy arm. "Margaret will be glad to see you. Wants you to know Snuffers is much better."

"Glad to hear that, Mike," Jenna said.

She grabbed Burke's hand and pulled him past the lineup, through the sagging door of a paint-peeling guardhouse. Blessedly they were free from the racket.

Several white tables were cordoned off in the infield, surrounded by gaily striped umbrellas and a distinctive alcohol banner. Probably Leo Winfield and his cronies. Good. Burke planned to order a large scotch and pray this day ended quickly.

"Are we sitting over there?" He gestured hopefully at the infield.

"No, but you can sit there. I have to go to the barn area. I'm judging the sprint and am already late."

"Quarter horses?" He glanced around, looking for a starting gate but she just winked and headed toward the low ridge of buildings, moving fast in her elegant sandals. A randy teenager ogled her shapely legs and Burke charged forward, slipping his hand around her hip. "I'm coming with you," he said. "I like the sprinters too."

"Jenna. You're here!" A sandy haired boy on a too-big bike pedaled beside them, pumping his legs and crunching gravel as they approached the first barn and a squealing din of noise.

The wails intensified as they rounded the corner. He stopped, too stunned to speak. Must be at least forty kids, muddled in a chaotic group. No—not muddled—grouped in pairs, each child with a leg tied loosely to another.

Jenna gave a wicked smile and stepped forward. The teams silenced except for a little girl who crossed her legs and complained she needed to use the bathroom.

"Good morning, contestants," Jenna called. "We'll start the race in a minute. But this is a special occasion. We have an important judge who likes sprinters. He came all the way from—"

She looked at him and raised an eyebrow, still with that wicked smile, completely unfazed by his ferocious scowl.

"New York," he finally said, blowing out a sigh.

"That's right. We have a special judge this year, all the way from New York."

A boy with a Yankees ball cap jumped up and down but the rest of the kids were silent, even the wiggly girl with the crossed legs.

"So as usual, you'll race along the field and around that little tree." She pointed at a stubby spruce tree a hundred feet away. "Maybe we'll have our new judge stand by the tree."

"But you're always the judge, Jenna. We want you to be our judge," a kid with two missing front teeth called.

"Yeah," another kid screeched, "not some old guy from New York."

"We want Jenna! We want Jenna!" And the little hooligans all started chanting.

Tough crowd but Burke had handled tougher. He stepped forward and raised his hand. "Good morning, contestants. I've been sent by Three Brooks, the sponsor of your big race this year. And to honor this special occasion, there will be two divisions and very, very big prizes. Everyone over eight years old will race first. Winning team gets twenty dollars."

The kids hooted and pumped their fists.

"The next division, the under eights, will race for twenty dollars as well. And everyone who finishes the race receives a free ice cream."

He glanced at the rough grass and then at Jenna's sandals. "We'll wait a few minutes for our junior course judge to get in place." He pointed helpfully at the spruce tree and stared clapping. "Go, Jenna, go."

She scowled and shook her head, but the kids picked up the chant and leaped in delight while the little girl with the crossed legs scooted toward a small brown building.

Jenna smiled and pinched his arm, but the kids kept chanting. "Sonofabitch," she muttered, covering up her finger assault with a cheery wave. She shot him a dark look then picked her way toward the tree, stumbling several times over the rough grass.

The races lasted twenty-six minutes and went off without a hitch.

"Sir? You really want every kid in the race to have a free cone?" the ice cream man asked, dipping his scoop into a murky jar of water.

"That's right," Burke said, keeping his hand on Jenna's elbow. "Just send Three Brooks the bill."

"Sure thing." The man glanced approvingly at the line of kids behind Burke and Jenna. "All these years and Wally Turner never bought the kids ice cream."

Burke felt Jenna stiffen. "Great idea to involve Three Brooks in the kids' race, Jenna," he said dryly. "A bit of a surprise though. You might have warned me. Was it hot out by the tree?"

"It was indeed," she said, not meeting his eyes. "Would you be a darling and get my hat? I seem to have left it on the back seat."

"Tough," he said, still feeling betrayed that she had tried to set him up.

She blew out a sigh, shading her eyes from the bright sun. "I was a little mad at your comments in the car," she admitted. "And if you hadn't been able to handle the children, I would have stepped in." She lifted her head then, her expression solemn. "And you were actually…great. You made a lot of kids happy, and it was smart to split the ages. I never thought of that, not in six years."

Her expression was so rueful, he impulsively touched her cheek. He didn't know why but she turned him into putty. "I'll get your hat if you want it. But please wait for me." He gave a mock shudder. "Please don't leave me alone with this mob."

"I think you do just fine wherever you go," she said quietly.

The sincerity in her voice made him pause. She'd been a good sport about hiking through the long grass, and it wasn't surprising everyone loved her. And he had been an asshole in the car. "Stay in the shade," he said. "You've probably had enough sun."

He turned and headed for the crowded parking lot.

An uneventful walk but without Jenna by his side, he was forced to stand in the admission line for re-entry. By the time he returned to the striped ice cream booth, she was gone. Sighing, he dug in his pocket, searching for his phone.

"Are you Burke?"

A vaguely familiar kid slouched in front of him.

"Jenna said you'd be holding a real pretty hat. Remember me?" the kid added. "I'm Charlie."

Burke nodded cautiously, remembering the freckly kid with the funny-looking mare. "Hi, Charlie. Where is she?"

"With Molly. Come on."

He tailed the nimble kid through the flowing crowd, between some metal struts and along a muddy path beneath the grandstand. They weaved through a litter of half-eaten hotdogs, pop cans and discarded cotton candy. He hoped no one in the stands dropped a drink on their heads but his young guide was savvy, and they emerged from the short cut unscathed.

"Molly needed a little tune-up," Charlie said, gesturing at a motley group of horses. And Jenna.

She gave them a distracted smile but clearly her attention was on the swaybacked mare. Her lips pursed, face set in concentration, as she worked on the horse's left side. Worked both hands over the sacral joint. Granted, her right hand wasn't pushing as hard, but the fingers were thrusting beneath the bandage. Burke slapped her hat against his thigh with disapproval.

She stepped back, nodded and Charlie rushed forward. "Start at the back of the pack," she said. "Give her a chance. I mean it, Charlie."

"Sure will." The kid's head bobbed. "We're going to win this year. You'll be cheering for me, won't you, Jenna?"

"Definitely. As long as you start at the back." Her gaze met Burke's and she gave an apologetic smile. "I had to help the horse," she whispered. "Couldn't wait for you any longer."

"I know." He placed the hat on her head, adjusting the brim so the sun wouldn't reach her nose. "Let's relax now and cheer on Molly."

About twenty horses milled on the straight stretch, mainly kids, but Burke spotted a few men and one lady with bluish-white hair and a pink helmet.

"I first took Peanut in this race when I was four," Jenna said, standing on her toes and straining to see over the rail. "It's more exciting than the steeplechase."

People were definitely milling to see the race, and the grandstand overflowed. Burke propped his arms around Jenna, protecting her wrist from any inadvertent knocks, and stared over her hat.

So far, Charlie was following her instructions, standing three rows back behind a hyper pony and a bored-looking mule. The starter lowered the flag. The pony bolted, the mule refused to move and a fat grey pony wandered to the outer rail, apparently in search of grass. Most of the horses merely shuffled past, turning their heads as though surprised by the burst of applause from the appreciative audience.

But Molly was in a beautiful extended trot and by the time she broke through the front line of horses she'd hit a smooth gallop. Charlie bounced over her neck, hollering and waving at the fans. He crossed the finish line a full length ahead of a blaze-faced Arab.

The kid turned a big circle and trotted back, teeth gleaming whitely through his dirt-smeared face. He leaned over and slapped Jenna's hand, then Burke's, continuing along the row of spectators, smiling and pumping his arm from the back of the unflappable mare.

"That was perfect." Burke grinned, oddly elated. "What does he win?"

"Aren't bragging rights enough?" Jenna asked. "He rode five miles to get here. His mom's fighting cancer. He doesn't have a dad, but right now he's one happy kid. Sometimes that's as good as it gets."

Something in her voice tugged at him and he glanced down, trying to read her expression beneath the wide brim of her hat.

"I suppose you want to go to the infield now?" she asked, averting her head. "That's where the mayor and other people like that sit."

He paused, sensing she wanted to remain here. And it was surprisingly fun rubbing shoulders with the railbirds. But this excursion had always been about contacts, and they needed to be cultivated. "Then that's where I want to be," he said.

She opened her tiny purse and pulled out a gold sponsor pass. "Wally sent this. Just show it to the man in the suit and he'll let you into the tunnel."

"Wait a minute. You're coming with me?"

"I don't have a pass. It's a Chamber of Commerce event. And I need to check on Molly and I promised a few others..." Her voice trailed off, and it was abundantly clear she had no intention of resting her wrist.

He gripped her left arm. "You're not massaging any more horses. We're going to sit down, have a drink and talk to some of these city fathers."

"But it's only open to business owners—business owners and their families."

"You're with me. That was the deal."

"It was never the deal. I said I'd go to the steeplechase, not the infield." Her voice rose. "You can't make me."

If she had smiled then, he might have relented but her outright defiance was frustrating and the only way rebellious employees should ever be handled was firmly. "This is your job today," he snapped. He clamped a hand around her upper arm and propelled her toward the gate.

The man in the dark suit and sunglasses carefully checked the pass then unsnapped the velvet cord, nodding as through granting admission to the White House. Damn pretentious people, Burke thought, but he'd made up his mind and they were going in.

A second man stepped out from the other side of the shadowed tunnel, scanned the gold pass again and shot a curious look at Jenna. "Do you also have a pass?" he asked.

Burke scowled and the guard shut his mouth and stepped back.

A white-jacketed waiter materialized with a tray of champagne. Burke grabbed one, shoving it in Jenna's left hand. "Bring me a Scotch and water, please," he said.

"Right away, sir."

"Derek! Glad you could join us." Leo Winfield shot out from a cluster of suited men. "And who is this stunning young woman? Oh, hello, Jenna." Leo nodded, nostrils flaring slightly and Burke instinctively edged closer to Jenna's side.

Her fluted glass shook as she nodded politely and pressed it to her lips. He could tell she wasn't drinking though, merely hiding behind the bubbles.

"Who are you betting on today, Derek?" Leo asked, pulling his curious gaze off Jenna's bandaged wrist. "Have you picked a winner?"

Charlie and Molly. "Haven't had a chance to check the form yet," Burke said. "Who do you like, Jenna?"

She shot him such a disdainful look, he almost flinched but turned and accepted his Scotch from the attentive waiter. Goddammit. Maybe he shouldn't have dragged her in here. Clearly it was another of those endless functions with pretentious men and fawning women, and besides, her lips were clamped so tightly, they were almost bloodless. He didn't know why she made him lose his mind, but he certainly hated to see her upset. And she obviously wasn't enjoying her champagne.

"Here's a program. Take a look." Leo edged forward, shouldering Jenna to the side. "The three horse has the best breeding and my good friend, George, owns five percent. He knows the uncle of the man who bred last year's Derby winner. Come on. You can meet him."

"Not now," Burke said.

"Well, hello. Look who's here." Kathryn Winfield minced forward, brilliant in a bright red dress and matching hat. "My new boss."

Jenna's hand jerked and champagne sloshed her fingers. Her pained gaze met his, then shuttered as she dipped her head and pretended to take another sip.

"Should I call you Derek or Burke?" Kathryn asked.

"Mr. Burke will work," he said tight-lipped, trying to edge closer to Jenna. Something had hurt her, and that naked pain in her eyes left him unbalanced. But she'd already turned her back, squaring those proud shoulders. A hovering waiter with an obvious eye for pretty ladies passed Jenna a program.

"I'm looking forward to Monday," Kathryn trilled on. "I've always wanted a chance at Three Brooks. The old manager preferred to hire his friends. Regardless of qualifications. Or background." Her sniff was too loud, too disdainful, and Burke edged back a step. He needed to get Jenna a different drink, should have asked her what she wanted instead of just pushing the champagne in her hand. And maybe he should just get her out of here.

Leo grabbed his arm and gave a hearty laugh. "Yes, well, it's an improving Center now. Look, Derek. That's John Simms over there. He runs the local bank. I'll take you to meet him right after this race."

The horses were circling, no gate, only a starter with a red flag. Leo's mouth flapped but Burke stared, not at the horses but at Jenna. Her dress, so gay and jaunty earlier, was now marked with horsehair and a smear of chocolate ice cream, no doubt left by a child's grateful hug. His fingerprints dented her hat, and grass stains covered her sandals. She'd come for the people and animals. He'd come for the money.

Something ached in his chest.

Kathryn's insistent voice jerked at him. "Come say hello to Derek Burke, the new owner of Three Brooks, darling." Kathryn tucked a possessive hand around a man's arm and pulled him closer. "This is Colin McDonald," she said. "He owns a vet clinic." She frowned at the tall red drink in the vet's hand. "A Singapore Sling? Really, Colin?"

"For a good friend," he said evenly. He reached out and shook Burke's hand. "Pleased to meet you. Wally and your staff do wonderful things at the Center and I'm very grateful. Now if you'll excuse me."

He firmly disengaged Kathryn's hand and walked over to Jenna. Pried the champagne glass from her fingers and replaced it with the Sling. Jenna's head tilted. Burke couldn't see her expression, but the naked longing on the vet's face was unmistakable. He jerked his head away, feeling as though he intruded.

Kathryn's eyes narrowed on Jenna's back. Her mouth flattened and she headed toward Colin.

"Kathryn, tell me what horse you like," Burke said quickly, stepping forward and holding out his program.

"My daughter's an expert at picking the good ones." Leo gave another loud chuckle, oblivious to the drama.

Burke forced a smile, nodding attentively as Kathryn began a recital about her expert system of picking winners. He'd dragged Jenna over here and the least he could do was divert this woman.

"Oh, this number six horse I also like," Kathryn went on. She seemed to have forgotten about the vet's defection and enthusiastically summarized the runners' pedigrees. "I massaged him once, and he won his next race. The owner said it was solely because of my work."

The announcer called, "The flag is up!" The crowd roared. Burke grabbed the excuse to escape, easing away from Kathryn to stand on the other side of Jenna. At least she was buffered now. Colin's shrewd eyes met his in a tacit moment of understanding. Jenna, however, didn't look at him.

The horses galloped around the track, leaping over the jumps in madcap fashion, all miraculously staying on their feet. In the end, a pretty mare sprinted from the pack and crossed the finish line, lengths ahead of the other runners.

"That mare was bred to Ridgeman's big stud last year," Colin said, looking at Jenna but politely including Burke in the conversation. "No foal, so she was put back into training. Strange she didn't take. Seems to have a new career with jump racing though."

"She's a pretty mare," Jenna said, her voice rusty. "Same color as Peanut."

"How is the little fellow? I'd be glad to come by—"

Leo rushed over and Burke could no longer hear Colin's quiet words. "You'll be presenting right?" Leo asked. "In place of Wally?"

"No, let someone else do it," Burke said, loath to leave Jenna. "Just mention Three Brooks' name."

"Excellent." Leo hurried around the tables, gesturing importantly at the winner's circle while Burke nursed his Scotch and tried not to brood. He should have listened to Jenna. What a cluster fuck.

The crowd cheered the brave little mare, and the announcer's voice droned on about sponsors and breeding and the history of the race. And then Kathryn Winfield presented the trophy on behalf of Three Brooks, speaking very eloquently about her new massage job at the improved Center.

Beside him, Jenna stiffened but only for a moment because her good friend, the vet, leaned over and coolly advised Burke that he was driving her home. And then they walked out.

Burke walked over to a solitary table, yanked out a chair and sipped his Scotch. Couldn't remember when he'd ever messed up so badly.

Oh hell, and then the Winfield entourage paraded back from the winner's circle and he glanced longingly at the tunnel but it would hurt more to see Jenna slipping into another man's car, so he didn't move.

"Where's Colin?" Kathryn asked, glancing around with narrowed eyes.

Burke ignored her and signaled for another Scotch.

"This is definitely the place to be," Leo said, sinking heavily into a chair. He reached out, grabbing an entire bottle of champagne from a waiter, almost tipping the tray in his exuberance. "I wonder what the poor people are doing now."

Everyone laughed heartily except Burke, who stared at the ice in his glass and wondered if Charlie still celebrated his win or if he'd already started his five-mile trek back home.

"Surprised she had the nerve to come here." Kathryn said, still looking over her shoulder, searching for Colin.

"Who?" Burke asked, his fingers tightening around the glass.

"Jenna Murphy." Kathryn sniffed. "It's just not done. The infield is reserved for business owners. Her family certainly doesn't own a business. Never have, never will. Don't you know? They're trailer trash."

Burke wordlessly pushed back his chair, rose and strode into the dark tunnel. Took the shortcut beneath the grandstand, trudging through a litter of discarded programs, cold fries and soiled napkins. Weaved through the parking lot where patrons picnicked on tailgates, cars honked and girls giggled.

He blocked the racket. Tried to concentrate on his next project—the bankrupt company in Maine or the buyout in California. Tried to think of anything but his most pressing fear.

She might forgive him, but she probably couldn't.

Chapter Sixteen

Jenna groaned and dragged a pillow over her head, muffling the earsplitting racket. Someone pounded on her roof. Oh, God. *He* couldn't possibly have come today, could he? Not after yesterday's humiliation.

She lifted the pillow, pried open her eyes and peered through the crack in the curtains. The sun had poked over the trees but was still very low. Couldn't be more than six, maybe seven. Too damn early. A ragged piece of tile flew past the window onto the ground.

Maybe Burke thought she'd run out and yell for him to stop, a convenient way to avoid his promise to fix her roof. Or maybe he didn't want to work in the midday heat—it was supposed to be blistering hot today. She squeezed her eyes shut, debating. Tell him to get lost and feel good for five minutes, or suck up her pride and get her roof patched?

And what was he using for patching anyway? She rolled over and checked the bedroom clock. Six thirty. She groaned but scrambled out of bed and crept down the hall. Looked like someone had made a delivery. A load of tiling had been dropped only fifteen feet from the trailer. A conservative beige color, rather pretty actually. It would definitely keep the trailer cooler in the summer.

She pressed her nose against the window, straining to read the writing on the boxes. It looked like those fancy tiles that carried a lifetime warranty, rather wasteful since the trailer couldn't possibly last many more years.

A lot of boxes too. She tilted her head, counting. Looked to be enough for the entire roof which would be freaking wonderful.

Of course, she was still very, very cross. She flounced back to bed, surprised to discover the sound of a man working on her roof was quite comforting, a bit like a lullaby. She was even able to fall back to sleep.

The next time she woke, she stretched, totally refreshed.

She dressed carefully, even swiped on some coral lipstick. Walked across the yard, not looking once at the roof. Gave Peanut his morning kiss and led him over to the grass. The rat-tatting stopped for a moment, but not long.

She peeked up but Burke wasn't looking, and it was obvious he'd already made considerable progress. He appeared to be doing the entire roof, hauling off old shingles and replacing with new tile. A shiny aluminum ladder was propped against the side of the trailer, as though her wooden one wasn't good enough.

She sniffed but it was hard to show how huffy she was when he wasn't even looking. She stuck her nose in the air and flounced inside. Made a pot of tea and wandered restlessly around the small trailer. Unfortunately, the sun was now beating down, and the kitchen was airless.

She retreated to the swing with her tea and fancy phone. Called Emily and received a cheery message.

"Come home and see our new roof," Jenna said, trying to sound equally upbeat, but it was early Sunday morning and where was Em? "No more leaks," she added. "Good luck applying for the scholarship. You can do it. Love you."

She cut the connection and wandered back into the kitchen. Sounded as though Burke was working on the left corner, closest to the kennel. He hadn't yet taken a break. Maybe he had a thermos up there, but he wasn't stopping to drink, not long anyway.

Perhaps she should offer him a coffee, or at least water, but he'd been such a prick yesterday. Certain that he knew best. Not earlier in the day though; he'd actually been a good sport earlier. And now it sounded like he was fueled by demons.

She sighed, trying to fan her anger, but she'd never been able to hold a grudge. He definitely had an overdeveloped sense of responsibility, winding himself in knots at her little burn. Frances said the Center doors were now marked 'entrance' and 'exit', and the staff room had been equipped with a new beverage machine, one of those fancy models that made anything one desired.

Kathryn would probably like a machine like that. Jenna scowled and dumped the rest of the tea in the sink.

The hammering stopped. Silence. Something splashed, then a trickling. Good grief. Was he pissing on her roof? She tiptoed down the hall until he was directly above her. It definitely sounded like something dripped.

Maybe the coward was afraid to come down. She certainly wasn't letting him use her bathroom. No way. Not after yesterday. But he could at least have the decency to climb down and go in the woods. Her roof leaked, for heaven's sake.

She huffed but her curiosity was overpowering. She wheeled and headed for the door. Had to go outside anyway; after all, it was time to clean Peanut's kennel. She grabbed the binoculars on the way out.

The pounding didn't slow even when she rattled open the kennel door and yanked the wheelbarrow inside. He was definitely intent on his job, which was the proper thing, considering all she'd endured at the steeplechase.

Out of habit she grabbed a pitchfork but edged to the only window in the kennel. The glass was old and distorted but if she pressed her eye against it, she could see Burke's back. Beige T-shirt with long sleeves. He must be roasting.

Oh, my…it wasn't a shirt.

She hastily wiped a corner of the dusty window with her finger and pressed the binoculars against the glass. Blew out a slow sigh of appreciation. He was bare-chested and those arms she'd noticed earlier weren't the only thing big. He was magnificent and definitely qualified for any beefcake calendar.

She refocused the glasses, moving lower. A smattering of dark hair led into the waistband of his jeans.

Jesus. What was she doing? She dropped the binoculars. If someone spied on her like this, she'd be furious. On the other hand, it was her land, her house, her roof. She hadn't told him to remove his shirt. And he was sort of her employee. People always watched their employees. Certainly Burke did.

She dragged a bale of straw to the window and made herself comfortable. Picked up the glasses and supervised, determined to keep her attention on the roof.

He was doing a good job, only about a quarter of the way through but it was excellent progress. Would he leave at noon and come back tomorrow? It would be horrible if he pulled off all her tiles and then didn't come back until next Sunday. Or didn't come back at all.

He climbed down, his back glistening in the sun. Maybe leaving now? No. His muscles rippled as he hoisted a box of tiles over his shoulder and climbed back up the ladder.

Good. He should keep working. He was really sweating though. Maybe she should take him a towel, even though the sheen on those ridged muscles was wildly attractive. He scooped up a bottle of water. His throat rippled as he took a long swig then raised it over his head and dumped.

Ah, so that explained the splashing noise. Maybe he'd like a big jug of water, even some ice. Heat stroke could be so dangerous. Her mother had always worried, rushing to deliver her dad a chilled beer even after an eye-blackening fight. *Wimpy Mom had never stayed mad either.*

She blew out an agonized sigh and sank back into the straw.

Burke cursed as he hit his thumb, readjusted the hammer and drove in another nail. Damn, it was hot. He swiped his forehead with his arm and opened the last bottle of water.

He'd have to make a run back to his house, grab a sandwich and something more to drink. He was sweating buckets, but this kind of work was always therapeutic, doubly so since it was *her* roof.

He could hear movement in the hall beneath him. The screen door slammed and he paused, praying this time she'd speak, even if it was just to call him an asshole.

"Hey, Burke."

He dropped his hammer, almost tripping as he rushed to the side of the roof.

"Do you want some water or lemonade?"

"Yeah." His voice croaked with relief. Finally. She was speaking.

"Well, which one?" She tilted her head, eyes flashing with impatience.

"Doesn't matter," he said. "I'll come down."

"No!" she said. "Stay there."

"Okay." He sank meekly to his knees, watching as she wheeled around the corner. Her denim shorts almost reached her knees, her faded blue T-shirt was two sizes too big, and if she was trying not to be sexy, it wasn't working.

She returned with a pitcher of clinking ice and lemonade, and a plastic cup. Passed it up to him without a word.

"Thank you," he said.

She wordlessly began to climb down.

"Wait," he said.

She lifted a haughty eyebrow but paused on the ladder.

"The cup will blow away. Wait a sec and I'll give it back." He took his time drinking then quickly refilled his cup, studying her face. In situations like this, it was always important to get the woman talking, but he didn't have a clue what to say.

'Sorry' wouldn't work. She'd look wounded and stalk off, and they'd both feel like shit all over again. Christ, he hated her wounded look.

"There will probably be some tiles left," he said, scrambling to fill the silence. "Maybe enough to do Peanut's kennel."

"Really?" Interest flashed across her face then her expression shuttered. "That'd be nice."

"I'll do it next Sunday."

"This roof looks good," she said grudgingly.

He poured himself another lemonade, wondering where the hell he was going to put it. There was no way she'd let him use her bathroom, and anyway he didn't deserve it.

"The raises are going through this week," he said, trying to hide his desperation. The accountants were going to scream and he didn't give a rat's ass.

She nodded thoughtfully. "I imagine they're retroactive."

"Yes…of course." He paused and wiped the sweat off his forehead. "Ah, when did you imagine they'd be retroactive to?"

She tilted her heat thoughtfully. "Back to the sale date, of course."

"Yes. That's what I thought." He stared blankly at his full glass. "Was there anything else we should talk about?"

"I think Frances deserves a raise," Jenna said. "Even though she doesn't have much education, she's been trying. Even doing a lot more typing."

"Yes. I was thinking that myself." He cleared his throat. "Five percent, I thought?"

"Should be ten."

He nodded. Would have gone fifteen but Jenna was having fun and deserved to turn his screws. He drained a fourth glass, almost bursting his bladder. "I wonder if I could use your bathroom?" he asked meekly.

"All right," she said.

Jenna parked Burke's Audi after a drive to town and swept back into the trailer, carrying a bag of antibiotics for Peanut. It had been rather fortuitous Colin had driven her home last night and lingered to check the pony. 'Low-grade skin infection,' he'd said. 'Drop by and pick up some antibiotics. And use that light therapy at Three Brooks. It works wonders for this type of thing.'

Kind, gentle Colin. Seemed she always pushed the good ones away. She stumbled on the bottom of the step but straightened her thoughts and peered up at the roof.

Burke had materialized at the far corner, scanning his big car, obviously checking for damage. The Audi had been a dream to drive, so loaded the dashboard resembled a small airplane, unlike the simplicity of her battered Neon.

She stepped back a few feet, tilting her head so she could watch his reaction. "Thanks for letting me borrow your car. I haven't been able to drive my standard yet," she waved her wrapped hand just in case he needed a reminder, "but it feels a lot like my Neon. My car takes the bumps a little bit better though. I'll let you drive it sometime. Maybe we should trade for the week."

His eyes flared with panic and the thought of him squeezed into her underpowered rust bucket made her grin. He hadn't said much when she'd delivered a peanut butter and jam sandwich on dry whole wheat bread. Only nodded when she'd stated that the chicken coop needed a roof too, and he had wordlessly tossed down his keys when she'd mentioned a standard shift was hard to handle with one hand. He hadn't even complained about the blaring country music.

But a car swap for an entire week would require some heavy guilt.

She swept into the bathroom, hesitating over her makeup bag. He'd worked tirelessly for her today and seemed to be trying to apologize the only way he knew. But he'd been so dogmatic yesterday, always thinking he knew best. She hated bullies.

He was coming down. She could hear his tread on the roof, then the jangle of the ladder. She resolutely grabbed her makeup.

Two minutes later, she returned to the kitchen and pushed open the screen door. He stood on the porch, mopping his face with his balled up shirt, muscles bunching as he dragged it across his forehead. Her dad had never worked a fraction as hard.

She paused, trying to gather her resentment but it had drained away with the day.

"I'll do Peanut's roof on the next nice evening," he said, "then the chicken coop." His dark eyes swept over her, widening as he noticed her bruised arm.

She immediately regretted her decision. He looked so appalled, and now she was taking this thing too far. "This bruise isn't from yesterday," she said quickly. She dropped on the swing, unbalanced by his stricken gaze.

The porch creaked beneath the tread of his work boots, and he lowered himself beside her.

"Really, it's not from yesterday," she repeated. "You didn't grab me that hard. I'm sorry. I shouldn't have made you think that." She glanced up and spotted the amused twitch of his lip.

"Oh, good. You already knew." She blew out a sigh of relief. He carried his guilt much too heavily, and she already regretted applying the dark makeup to her arm. "How did you know?"

"I grabbed you by the left arm," he said. "That bruise is on the right. Makeup?"

She nodded ruefully.

"So are we about even now?" he asked.

She nodded again.

"Good." He leaned over, tilting her face with a finger. His mouth dipped, surprising her with a kiss, a kiss so tender she moved her lips, searching, wondering if they were even touching.

The sweetest, nicest kiss, a kiss of apology that made her heart dance.

Her left arm lifted, drifting over that damp, rippled chest, exploring what she had admired all day. He was slick and hard and controlled, and she slid her hand around the back of his neck, feeling his hair damp against her fingers.

His tongue slipped into her mouth, and she automatically tilted, her nipples hypersensitive against the fabric of her shirt. His kiss deepened, turning hungry, and she pressed against him, wanting to get closer to that sweaty body.

He pulled back with a frustrated groan and dragged his mouth over her cheek, the cords in his neck taut. "I need a shower, Jenna. But come home with me. Please."

"I need to catch Peanut first."

"I'll look after the pony. Just get in the car."

"Yes but Peanut is hard to—"

"Just get in the car, sweetheart."

He was being bossy again but in a nice way, so she let him tug her to the car. He turned on the air conditioning and tossed his crumpled shirt in the back. "I'll be one minute, max," he said, his voice gruff.

But she knew he'd be much longer than one minute, and he really should learn to listen to her. She sighed as her shirtless hunk of a man rushed toward Peanut.

The pony pricked his ears, watching with curious eyes. He looked more energetic after the oxygen and light therapy, almost mischievous. His tail swished and he sniffed the air, hopeful for carrots.

Burke reached out to grab Peanut's halter, his forearm as thick as the pony's leg, but Peanut whirled at the last second. Trotted deeper into the grass, tail lifting, in no hurry to leave his grazing.

Jenna grinned. Peanut was wily. She'd spent hours chasing the little rascal and it had been a game in itself, playing pony tag. Now she was older, didn't have so much time, and had learned to just stick some carrots in her pocket and whistle. But, of course, Peanut still loved playing tag. And he was only getting warmed up.

She could help, of course, but Burke had insisted she remain in the car. He always thought he knew best. His chest glistened, his skin a much darker shade than it had been this morning, and he made another futile rush for her pony.

It was almost five. The sun was lowering, but it was still hot. He was probably getting irritated. If Peanut were a female, Burke might have better luck but his killer body didn't impress the gelding—not one little bit.

She twisted, watching out the back window as the bright-eyed pony waited until Burke's hand was an inch from the halter. Peanut made another truly devious move, leaving Burke empty-handed once again.

Wow, Peanut was moving great. He looked like he was ten again. She reached for her door handle then paused. Best to wait until Burke asked for help. Maybe next time he wouldn't be quite so authoritative. Besides she was in no hurry for him to have a shower. He looked good out of a suit, all rumpled and sweaty…more like the folks she was used to.

But Burke had already turned away and walked to the edge of the gravel. He reached in his pocket, clearly distracted. Was his phone ringing? Obviously something had made him forget about catching Peanut, forget that they were supposedly in a hurry to get to his house. To his bedroom.

She wiggled impatiently. He'd seemed so eager. Hell, she was eager. Curious even. Guys with such ripped bodies often turned out to be duds in bed. Emily blamed it on steroids, but Burke didn't seem a steroid kind-of-guy. Didn't matter now as he appeared to have forgotten she was waiting; he was totally engrossed with whatever was in his hand.

Even Peanut was curious. He turned and followed Burke with pricked ears. Sidled closer. Paused. Another two steps. He reached out and nudged Burke's pocket.

A big arm flashed. Incredible! Burke had single-handedly caught Peanut.

She wasn't needed after all. She turned and pressed her shoulders against the seat, staring straight ahead while Burke led the captured pony to the kennel.

A minute later, the door opened. Burke slipped into the driver's seat, carrying the smell of male sweat and impatience. "That pony is the devil." He reached over and gave her hand a rueful squeeze. "Just like you. Too damn smart."

"How did you catch him?" she asked.

"Thought the crinkle of plastic might trick him into thinking it was candy."

"Candy? You have candy and you didn't share?"

"Oh, I'll share." He tossed an open condom package on her lap.

She fingered the black package, shaking her head. "You used a condom to catch my pony? That doesn't seem proper. No doubt, you shocked him." She sniffed. "I hope you have another. There's grass on this one."

He grabbed her hand, circling his thumb over her sensitive palm, and stepped on the accelerator. Didn't speak and at the speed the car was going, she was rather relieved.

The stroking of that big thumb was turning her all dewy, and she leaned back, staring at the road as rocks pelted the undercarriage. He was going rather fast with his luxury car. The road wasn't even paved, and earlier she'd driven much slower. His hand moved along her inner wrist. Her nipples tightened and she stopped thinking about gravel and cars. Couldn't deny her attraction to him. He'd affected her from the very first day.

It wasn't a long drive. The Three Brooks' house was only a half mile away; heck, they were already there. The imposing white mansion loomed dead ahead. Burke's hand drifted possessively, and she suddenly wished the drive were much longer. She could feel his raw need but her heart was hammering now, her stomach doing nervous little flips. She'd made a very rash decision in the heat of a kiss.

The car slowed in front of a four-car garage and the door lifted. In they sped. Dark coolness now. Her skin prickled and she glanced sideways, thinking he must be cold without a shirt, but no, he looked totally at ease. She could see the ripped abs, the corded muscle. She gulped.

"The entrance is through there." He leaned over and opened her door. "Have you been here before?"

"A couple times. The Canadians had staff barbecues."

"I see." His expression was enigmatic and he released her hand, stepped out of the car and guided her into the house. They walked down a hall with odd Japanese art and into a marbled foyer.

Ah, yes, she remembered the white marble, the high ceiling, the horse pictures.

"I'm going to have a quick shower," he said. "But first, what can I get you?"

She stared past him, awed by the vast room. It looked so much larger without people in it. Seemed like the previous owners had left almost everything, even the win picture from last year's steeplechase. They'd loved that picture. Had promised to hang it in an honored spot, which they did. Front and center in the huge foyer. She hoped Burke had given them a chance to grab some of their possessions, but guessed he probably hadn't.

"What about a Singapore Sling?" he asked.

She crossed her arms, still staring numbly at the pictures. "I'll just wait until you're finished your shower," she murmured. Only a half mile from home but it seemed as though she'd entered a foreign country. She'd half expected him to tug her into the first bedroom in the hall. Wally had said there were eleven. *I shouldn't have come here.*

"Maybe we'll go out back first," Burke said. His firm hand wrapped around her elbow and they pushed on, through an elegant dining room with a ridiculously long table, into a kitchen gleaming with spotless steel, and onto a small brick patio.

He circled to a portable bar, reached down and returned with two frosty Corona, no glasses. Snapped off the cap with an effortless twist and passed one to her. "I'll be in that little shower." He gestured over his shoulder. "Three minutes max."

He padded around the corner. She heard spraying water and when he returned his head was slickly wet. He wore a light sleeveless shirt and smelled of sandalwood.

He lowered himself into an adjacent chair, picked up his beer and pointed up the hill. "Your place is just up there. Sometimes I can see the glow of your lights. If the trees weren't there, you'd look down on me."

Despite her discomfort, she couldn't help but smile. Her little trailer had the million dollar view. She glanced around the manicured yard, rich with bright flowers and strategically placed shrubbery, but sadly lacking warmth. "Do you like this type of house?" she asked impulsively.

He shrugged. "I move so much, I don't notice houses. It's part of the Three Brooks' property, a convenient place to sleep. We'll put it up for sale soon. The private road was a plus because I'm rather antisocial."

He stated it as irrefutable fact and she didn't argue, even though it wasn't quite true. The scowl and dark eyes could be intimidating but he was also extremely friendly when he chose. And he did have that very charming lip twitch. When she was alone with him, it was easy to forget he was of a different world. An elite world.

She stretched out her legs and loosened her tight arms, determined to relax.

"Your shoulder bothering you?" he asked.

"No, not anymore." Not since she'd been accompanying Peanut under the lights. She took another nervous sip of beer and pretended interest in some bright flowers, wondering when he'd pull her upstairs. Maybe they'd have a couple more drinks and then go up, or maybe they'd do it right here. Or maybe he took his women in a Jacuzzi.

There was a hot tub by the pool, she recalled, although this side of the house was unfamiliar. The tiny secret alcove seemed built for kitchen staff. She could feel his scrutiny. Wished she'd grabbed her sunglasses, even though their chairs were shaded. Maybe if it was dark, maybe if the house weren't so imposing, maybe if she had a lot more to drink. Shit, she shouldn't have come here. Not yet.

She jumped when he abruptly leaned forward and picked up a deck of cards. "I think a wild woman like you needs a little excitement," he said.

Wild? He thought she was wild? But cards were good. Cards might get rid of that queasy feeling in her stomach, the sick feeling that always hit when she knew she was going to do something foolhardy. Maybe if they played a couple hands, drank a bunch of beer, then by the time they moved to the bedroom she wouldn't feel like she was making such a bone-headed mistake.

She forced a smile, watching the cards blur between his deft fingers. "What are we playing for?" Her voice squeaked, so she drank another inch of beer.

He fanned the deck over the table. "One card, ace high. If you lose, you take off your clothes, put them on the chair and walk upstairs. First bedroom on the right."

"And if I lose," he said, not looking at her, "I give you a back rub and cook you dinner. Then drive you home."

Shit. She gulped, knowing she needed to win, needed a graceful way to escape. She uncrossed her legs and edged forward, staring at the cards. Peeked up. Checked his mouth. Not a whisper of a smile, only an odd expression on his face—uncertain maybe, although she doubted a man like him was ever uncertain.

She stared back at the cards, fingering them, forgetting her nervousness. She'd always been lucky at cards. She trailed her finger over the table, not sure now what she wanted. *An ace?* Slowly flipped it over. A four. Her breath leaked out in a whoosh. Part dismay, part anticipation.

He studied the remaining cards for a pregnant moment, his hand hovering over the end then purposefully moved past and selected the second card in. She held her breath, silently admitting she did want to sleep with him. But it would be humiliating to take her clothes off and climb upstairs naked. And her pride made it impossible to admit they'd made a mistake, and now she just wanted to go home.

She'd have to face him in the office too. When he was dressed in an intimidating suit, sitting in his big chair, wielding all that power. This had been so rash, especially since he wasn't leaving for at least another week. Her throat was desert dry, and her stomach flipped panicky summersaults.

He turned his card over. A two. Oh, my God, a two!

"Aw, shucks. You win," he said. "Come get your massage, sweetheart." He opened his arms, and she leaped onto his lap, hiding her tiny twinge of regret.

He draped her against him, his sure hand moving over her back. "Who taught you to love cards?"

"My father. He took me around with him. Let me join their poker games as long as I didn't drop my cards. That made him really mad."

"How old were you?"

"Eight," she admitted. Usually she didn't speak of her father but with her cheek tucked against Burke's solid shoulder, she felt separated from her sketchy childhood.

"No wonder you have a mean shuffle," he said.

And that was his only reaction—no shock, no disgust, not even a slight recoil. Her tension slowly eased and she let her fingers trail over his arm. After seeing him work all day, his body was like an old friend, familiar yet fascinating. Free to touch without any commitment, only a massage and dinner. Perfect. She slid her hand beneath his shirt and skimmed her fingers over his chest.

"You worked awfully hard today," she whispered. "And I appreciate it. I'm rather shocked you were able to finish the entire roof."

"When I was nine, I built a two-story tree house with a tile roof and a very cool rope ladder." His mouth curved in memory.

She didn't know why people thought he scowled when it was obvious he smiled all the time. "Your parents must have been very proud," she said.

"They were horrified. Sent me to private school so I could learn proper skills."

"Parents can be so stupid." She reached up and pressed an impulsive kiss against his cheek. Didn't like to think about him being hurt and didn't want to talk about parents. Not any longer. She just wanted to snuggle in and savor his closeness.

He seemed to understand. He tucked her head back under his chin and continued his gentle massage.

"And this is where the game ends." Jenna leaned over her cue stick, lined up her last shot and sank the eight ball with authority. She smiled mischievously and pocketed his twenty-dollar bill.

"You hustled me!" Burke shook his head in disbelief. Cards, ping pong, darts, now pool. He hadn't stepped foot in the games room until tonight. Couldn't remember the last time he had so much fun.

But she'd misrepresented her skill with a cue stick, hidden it even, and that definitely warranted punishment. He circled the table, planted his arms and pinned her against the wall. She was still laughing, her beautiful face flushed with victory, but graciously tilted her mouth, accepting his quick congratulatory kiss.

And he had to keep it quick. The evening had been an exercise in restraint but definitely exhilarating. Yet it would pay off in spades. She was no longer jumpy, accepted his touch almost everywhere. He purposely brushed his knuckles over her breast as he reached over and extracted the cue stick from her hand, then flattened his palm over her rear and tugged her closer.

She pressed in willingly, even wrapped her arms around his neck and gave the nicest hug. He loved her hugs, the sweet way she had of pressing her face against his chest. So affectionate, like a spooky kitten just learning to trust. It would be impossible to sleep beside her and not make love, but she wasn't ready. Not quite yet.

Something wasn't right. He could sense it, a whisper of reserve—as though she were holding back. It pricked at him, like a missed business detail that seemed unimportant but ended up as the deal buster.

He raised his thumb to palm her breast, heard her sleepy sigh and quickly adjusted his arms. "It's almost midnight," he said. "I'll drive you home. The Ridgeman people are coming tomorrow. You still okay to help with the tour?"

"Of course."

"Good. I'll pick you up. But you'll have to get up earlier than usual. I'll be by at six."

"Really?" She paused, wetting her lower lip. "Well then, maybe we could do something a little different."

Her smile was slightly wicked and heat shot to his groin. She was going to stay overnight after all. Thank God. He wanted this woman, badly. Wanted to spread her legs, leave his mark, possess her.

"You could drive my car," she added.

"What?" His voice croaked with disappointment.

"We'll switch cars." She smiled brightly. "*You* don't have a sore hand so you can drive my standard. I'll come along later, in your car."

His mouth flattened in horror. Her Neon was so rusty, he'd probably fall through the floor. No goddamn way. "Or I could come just drive back and pick you up at eight thirty," he said quickly.

"That is such a good idea." She kissed his cheek.

He sighed at her slick maneuvering. Of course there was no reason to drag her in at six am other than he wanted her company. But he wasn't in the habit of considering others, usually set his agenda and barged forward. Obstacles were shoved aside or flattened.

And with Three Brooks, the only remaining obstacle was Wally. Get rid of Wally, hire a new manager—a pragmatic, professional one—and move on to his next project. And in between, enjoy Jenna, who was certainly making this backwater town a very pleasant place to be.

Chapter Seventeen

Jenna fed Peanut a piece of carrot then gave his shoulder a quick scratch and guided him back to the kennel. "Enough grass for now, my man. I actually have to work today."

She strode back to the trailer. Twenty minutes to change and add a dab of makeup. Her heart was pounding a little too quickly, but it wasn't because Burke was coming. She had this relationship totally under control.

Hugging herself, she bounced down the hall. He was fun and exciting and surprisingly nice. Not nice like Colin but nice in a different way. Hard and soft at the same time, an iron hand in a velvet glove. She shook her head, uncomfortable with the analogy.

Gloves always came off.

Didn't matter though. She needed to indulge in a man once in a while, and Burke was this year's indulgence. He was leaving in a week or so. It was perfect.

She pressed her speed dial, surprised when her sister answered. "Good morning, Em. Glad I reached you. How are things?"

"Fine." Sleep crusted Emily's voice. "But I'm really tired."

"Don't you have classes today?"

"Yeah, but we're not doing much. And the material is so stupid. Why are you calling anyway? I thought we were supposed to text."

"I have been texting. You haven't been answering. Besides, they gave me a work phone with unlimited calling, Internet and everything." She gave a happy skip, remembering Burke's statement that she could call anywhere in North America. "And I wanted to tell you that Peanut is getting better. His hair is growing back, he has more energy—"

"That's great, really great." Emily's voice faltered for a moment. "Sis, I want to come home."

"Come home? You mean for the weekend?"

"No...I mean for good. Maybe Wally would give me my summer job back. It was fun grooming and hanging out. I miss everyone, even mean old Frances."

Jenna's legs wobbled. She sank into the kitchen chair, gripping the small phone, struggling to hear Emily's voice over the painful roaring in her ears. "But we paid all that money," she finally managed. "Borrowed, scraped. You're doing so well—"

"I'm failing."

Failing. And probably Trevor had just dumped her. Jenna squeezed her eyes shut, biting back her despair. Wouldn't do any good to yell. Emily always molded her life around her current boyfriend, tended to fall apart when left alone. That fatal gene ran deep.

"Trevor and I broke up," Emily said. "He hooked up with this girl with a big nose, someone he met golfing. If only we could have afforded lessons. If I'd gone golfing with him, it never would have happened."

Jenna's throat clamped so tightly she couldn't speak.

"So, would you talk to Wally?" Emily went on. "See about getting me a job? You're his top employee."

"I told you before," Jenna said, "he's not the manager now."

"Right, well the new guy then. Can you talk to the new guy?"

The new guy's car rolled into the driveway, crunching gravel under its gleaming tires and casting a long shadow.

"I have to go." Jenna muttered, wiping at her eyes. "I'll call you tonight. But go to your classes. Don't be rash. And don't let Trevor tank your life."

She closed the phone and rushed into the bathroom. Damn cheap mascara. She rubbed the black off her cheeks, added a quick touch-up and hurried back down the hall.

When she opened the screen door, Burke stood beside the hood of his car, texting. A beautifully cut grey jacket emphasized his broad shoulders. She paused for a moment, sucking in her breath, gathering her equilibrium. He looked like a high-powered businessman, not her sweaty, bare-chested roofer. She much preferred the sweaty roofer.

He stepped around the car and pulled open the passenger door, then abruptly put away his phone, concerned eyes narrowing on her face. "Is Peanut okay?"

"He's in the kennel," she said quietly, still a little off kilter. "I never let him loose when I'm not home."

He nodded but shot her another assessing stare. Then slid behind the wheel, backed out and whipped over the hill in a ricochet of gravel.

When he pulled into the Center's parking lot, his attention had returned to the screen of his phone.

"I'll see you inside," he said. "The Ridgemans won't arrive for their tour for another hour." He gave a distracted smile before dipping his head back over the phone. "Sorry, but this California company wants to play hardball."

And he looked delighted about that. Just another little challenge he'd sort out before lunch. She fingered the handle of the door, fighting her melancholy, thinking of Emily as she studied Burke. He was capable, too capable, and it was incredible he could take care of so many things yet always remain in control. She had trouble with an aging pony and an immature sister.

"What do you do," she asked, "if it doesn't go the way you plan?"

"Find their weakness," he said, not looking up from the screen. "Exploit it. If that doesn't work, we walk away. You always have to be prepared to walk."

"Of course." She sighed and slipped from the car. That kind of policy might work for Burke and company, but it wasn't going to help with Emily. You can't walk away from someone you love.

She jammed her hands in her pockets and trudged up the walkway. Em was always a drama queen. Maybe she just wanted an excuse to come home. Maybe she was temporarily homesick and would feel better next week. God, she prayed Em was joking.

The construction crew called their usual greetings. Terry rushed out and pushed a wheelbarrow off the sidewalk so she could pass.

"How's your hand today, Jenna?" His concerned gaze swept over her gauze wrap and then shot back to Burke's car.

"It's fine," she said. "That spill was pretty clumsy of me."

"No, it was my fault. You said the hotter the better so…well." He gave a rueful shrug. "The job's almost finished here. Another week at the most. Can I give you a call sometime?"

"I'm sorry, but I have a boyfriend."

"Figures. But if you just want to get together for lunch or a…tea, that'd be good too." He glanced past her, yanked his tool belt higher, winked and turned away.

Burke stalked up the walkway, scowling at Terry's back. "Was that the idiot with the boiling water? What did he want?"

"He was just saying how nice it was that you helped with the building," Jenna said dryly "They're finishing early because of the six am start."

Burke's lip twitched. "Sorry. I'm out of line. Let's go inside and you can try our fancy tea maker." He stood back and opened the door, now marked with a gleaming white 'Entrance' sign.

"Hi, Jenna." Frances poked her head up from behind the reception desk. "I didn't know you were coming in today. That bitch Kathryn Winfield is here, telling everyone she's taking over your job. Thank God it's not true—" She ducked her head, flushing, as Burke stepped inside and closed the door.

Jenna's smile froze on her face. She'd forgotten all about Kathryn, had even hoped Burke might relent and agree he didn't need a second masseuse. At least not Kathryn, whose lifetime goal had always been to make Jenna's life miserable.

Burke apparently was clueless as to Kathryn's animosity to anyone not of her social ilk. "Where's Kathryn now?" he asked, pausing to flip through the incoming mail.

"Checking out the massage room," Frances squeaked.

"Tell her to come to my office. And Jenna, please join us. Bring me a coffee when you come."

She stared mutely, fighting her ache of betrayal. Maybe they needed another masseuse while she was hurt but once Kathryn had a toehold, she'd never leave. Leo Winfield was too powerful. Even Wally's good friend had buckled under Leo's influence.

And Burke was obsessive about secondary education. He was constantly printing directives about staff qualifications and new requirements. Kathryn would immediately rank above Jenna, in both salary and authority. Work would be intolerable.

Frances kept her head down, engrossed with the blank page of her appointment book. Burke picked up a couple letters and strode down the hall.

Frances peered over the counter, waiting until he was out of earshot. "I feel like quitting," she muttered.

"Me too," Jenna said, but of course they couldn't. Jobs were as scarce as hens' teeth. Even the influential Leo Winfield's daughter had been unemployed for two months.

"I wish Wally was still the manager." Frances slammed the appointment book shut. "This is what happens when outsiders try to run things. They just don't understand how things work."

Jenna nodded, her throat too thick to speak. She wouldn't be able to drink a drop of tea, no matter how good it tasted from the pricey new machine. First Emily, now this—on a day that had started out with such promise.

Frances rose. "Guess I'll tell Her Highness to go on down to Mr. Burke's office. And you better hurry and get the man his coffee."

Jenna squared her shoulders and detoured to the staff room, making small talk, fielding greetings, but too devastated for more than polite replies. Yes, she was fine. No, she wasn't fired and yes, she'd be back in a week or two despite what Kathryn had said.

The new beverage machine was definitely deluxe with an array of choices. Hot chocolate, coffee, tea, cappuccino. Press a button and make a selection. It even had a button for adding lemon, which last week would have left her ecstatic. Now she was filled with despair, her fingers oddly clumsy. It was clear she'd soon become adept with the buttons though, now that she was relegated to coffee girl. Unless she was horrible at getting it right.

She shoved Burke's cup under the spout and impulsively added a dash of lemon, then four more generous squirts.

Sucked in a resolute breath and walked to his office.

The door was shut and she knocked quietly. Heard his deep 'come in.' He always sounded impatient and here she was, a little errand girl reduced to delivering coffee. Kathryn would love it.

Her longtime nemesis was seated in front of his desk, signing employee forms. Burke leaned against the wall by the conference table. He immediately walked behind the desk and pulled out his chair.

"Sit here, Jenna."

She paused, so surprised coffee sloshed against the rim of the cup. He quickly pried it from her hand as though afraid of another burn. "I was just explaining Kathryn's duties," he added.

Jenna sat, warily eyeing both Kathryn and Burke. It was rather empowering to sit in his massive chair with its buttery leather. Even Wally had never let her sit here. She gave the chair an exploratory twist, surprised at how easily it swiveled.

Terry and the boys were loading long boxes in a white pickup and if she turned another six inches to the right, she could see the new flowerbeds. A chair like this probably cost more than her fridge but it certainly was comfortable, certainly could swing—she grounded her feet, stopping its motion.

This was a serious meeting. Kathryn had the education and Leo's backing. But Jenna had more experience. Maybe Burke would place them on the same level. *Please, just don't make Kathryn my boss.*

Kathryn's cheeks were oddly flushed and Jenna straightened, trying to portray cool confidence. Her movement triggered something in the chair. It rose six inches. The armrests extended and a lumbar extension soothed her lower spine. She hid the widening of her eyes but definitely was taller. If she looked straight ahead, her gaze was over Kathryn's head. Wow. She felt tall, important, invincible.

"Kathryn, if you're finished with the documents," Burke said, "you can take them to Frances. She's your immediate supervisor, then Jenna. We all pitch in around here so just do whatever they tell you. Your job description includes cleaning some stalls," his face was impassive, "and the staff bathroom."

Kathryn's cheeks flamed a brighter shade of pink. "I have a degree. I don't clean toilets."

Burke scowled and crossed his arms, the material tightening dangerously. "You'll do whatever they say. Now take those papers to Frances. She'll let you know what's on your list for today."

Kathryn grabbed the papers, fumbled with an errant sheet and rushed from the office, the click of her heels oddly subdued.

Jenna stared at the door then closed her mouth and looked at Burke. Couldn't speak. Could only stare with heartfelt gratitude.

"I don't think she'll stay long," he said wryly, picking up his cup. "I should have talked to Wally before hiring her. Staff synergy isn't my strength."

"Thank you." Jenna swallowed twice, wetting her throat. "Kathryn and I have never been friends."

"No, and with her family, I'm sure it's been tough."

She nodded, appreciating his brevity yet the empathy in his voice made her heart kick against her ribs.

"If you're finished playing in my chair," he added, "I'm going to sit down, enjoy my coffee and make some calls."

She scrambled from the chair, crossed the room and removed the cup from his hand. "Since you've so masterfully handled our first staff dissension, I'd like to bring you another cup. A...fresher one."

He raised an amused eyebrow. "And perhaps one that's a little less bitter?"

"Absolutely," she said.

"Any candidates for a new manager?" Edward asked, from his office in New York. "When are we free of this Wally Turner?"

"Still trying to force him to quit." Burke adjusted the phone against his ear. "Can't prove his theft and politically it wouldn't be wise to fire him. Stillwater is a tight town."

Edward gave an impatient sigh. "Someone must know something. We're not there to coddle."

"I'm working with someone now. She's starting to trust me, but they're all inconveniently loyal."

"You talk to Theresa yet?"

"Yes, I did. Not that it's any of your business." Burke jotted a reminder on his yellow pad. Theresa hadn't been happy but he'd send her a necklace, a tastefully expensive one, along with his very best wishes. Women were always soothed if they walked away with a blue Tiffany box. Perhaps he'd order one for Jenna as well. Two necklaces, he scribbled.

He swiveled his chair, watching Wally through the window. The man grinned and gestured again, pointing out the new flowers and cobblestones to Jenna. Wally always seemed more animated when she was around.

Interesting.

"I might have found Wally's little weakness," Burke said into the phone.

"Good. Because the quicker you find a manager," Edward said, "the quicker you can leave that hick town."

"I'm not in that big of a hurry," Burke said, and cut the connection.

He turned in his chair, watching as Wally and Jenna re-entered the building. Waited one minute then called Frances. "Please tell Wally to come see me," he said. It was always good to send for employees; it made them feel vulnerable, and vulnerable people made mistakes.

Wally walked in ten minutes later.

"Good work over the weekend," Burke said. "The courtyard looks nice. Just in time for our visitors today."

Wally looked blank. If Jenna had told him about the Ridgeman visit, he hid it well.

"Have a seat, Wally."

Wally pushed the chair further from the desk and sat.

"As you know, we're changing our target market," Burke said, "and our strategy. Better employees, better horses, higher fees. No more locals dropping by the back door. Some of our employees have been lax about that."

Wally held his gaze for a long moment, eyes impassive, but a muscle twitched on the side of the man's jaw.

"I'm thinking of Leo Winfield's girl," Burke continued, watching Wally's face. "Thinking of moving her to head masseuse."

"Oh, God!" Wally jerked forward, his composure gone. "You can't do it. A move like that would kill Jenna."

Bingo. Burke leaned back in his chair, careful to keep his expression impassive.

"I mean you can do it, but it wouldn't be good for employee morale." Wally's words came out in a rush. "Kathryn Winfield is jealous of any pretty girl but especially bitter toward Jenna. Carried a grudge since eighth grade when Jenna won the science fair, the 4-H leadership award and was voted May Queen all on the same day. And it's only worsened with time."

"Oh?" Burke raised an eyebrow. "Jenna has a nimble brain and is definitely spunky, but everyone seems to look up to her. She's very likeable."

"You bet. She has a huge heart. But Kathryn won't accept being second best. And really, who would want Kathryn if they could have Jenna?"

Burke's lip twitched. Wally was actually very astute, full of information too, but the man was backing into a yawning crevasse. "So is there a specific problem between the two girls now?" Burke asked as he scrawled a memo on his legal pad.

"The new vet. He moved here hoping to get closer to Jenna, but she doesn't want anything permanent. Now he occasionally dates Kathryn but it drives her crazy, always having to settle for Jenna's leftovers."

Wally shifted, lowering his voice and edging his chair closer to the desk. "Look, if you hire Kathryn, Jenna will be gone in a few months. And then she'd be in a real pickle. She's sacrificed everything for her younger sister. Three Brooks owes her more than that."

"Indeed," Burke said dryly. "I like to think employees owe the company rather than the other way around. But if you're adamant, we can certainly reach an agreement."

He ripped his newly composed memo off the pad and slid the paper across the desk. "Sign and date this, Wally, and I'll ensure Kathryn Winfield never bothers Jenna again."

Please accept this letter of resignation effective immediately. I agree to vacate the Three Brooks Apartment by the end of the month and hereby waive any right to legal counsel as well as any past and future claims against Three Brooks Inc.   Wally Turner

Wally's throat moved convulsively.

"Of course, these details are confidential," Burke added, averting his gaze, "and if I hear you've engaged in any behavior derogatory to Three Brooks, Jenna's employment here would certainly turn fragile."

"You sonofabitch!"

Burke faked a dismissive shrug and pulled the paper back. "Not a big deal to me if Jenna stays or goes. I'm sure there are other jobs around. Maybe that vet would hire her."

"She wouldn't accept a job from him! Independence means more to her than anyone I know. That's why—"

Wally dropped his face in his hands, and for a moment Burke experienced a rare spike of pity. However, the man was a thief and a liar, something he never tolerated.

Wally raised his head, eyes defeated as he stared at Burke. A moment later, he yanked back the paper and signed his name in a ragged scrawl. "You can stick this job up your ass," he said, rising so fast the chair toppled. He jerked from the office, the back of his neck a mottled red.

Burke picked up the signed memo, studying it with grim satisfaction. He planned to get rid of Kathryn Winfield anyway but this had turned out to be a bonus, a goddamn wonderful, unexpected bonus.

Chapter Eighteen

"And this is our hyperbaric oxygen therapy." Jenna gestured at the airtight chamber. "It gives a hundred percent oxygen in a pressurized environment and provides the horse with an amazing boost.

"Oxygen is excellent for healing open wounds and for treating stubborn infections," she went on. "It also helps heal lung tissue. A few treatments of about fifty minutes will show immediate benefits."

David Ridgeman stepped closer, finally registering some interest as he studied the interior and exterior of the chamber. He turned to the large blinking console. "Is that thing complicated to work?' he asked.

"Somewhat." Jenna smiled at Debbie alert in the control chair. "But our experienced technicians are well trained in the procedure. The green button starts the oxygen flow. The horse is free to move in the chamber, and the door can only be opened from the outside. Monitors allow us to watch the patient and they can also see out the window. We've even had a horse so relaxed, he lay down—"

"Where are the tanks?" David interrupted, staring up at the ceiling valves. "Okay, I see," he muttered, taking out his phone and snapping some pictures. "Then the oxygen tanks are on this side. I assume you have holding stalls in the area?"

"Yes, of course," Jenna said. "The main barn area is down the aisle and through the door to the left. We also have three stalls adjoining the oxygen chamber. They're especially helpful if an animal has severe mobility or breathing issues."

"Show me the stalls please."

"Certainly." Jenna nodded her thanks to Debbie, glancing over her shoulder at Burke and Lorna Ridgeman who lingered on the other side of the room. Lorna was clearly disinterested in the Center's holistic features, and it seemed that the decision to send their stud to Three Brooks would be entirely up to her brother.

Lorna reached up with a manicured hand and tapped Burke's upper arm. His dark head politely inclined as he listened to another of her mundane comments. Jenna let the door swing shut behind her. Obviously David was the decision maker, and if he wanted to see the holding stalls, they could be included in the tour.

"The stalls are over here," Jenna gestured, "just on the other side of the oxygen chamber."

"Nice big stalls," David said, stopping beside her and nodding approvingly. "Perfect for a stud."

"There are no windows though," Jenna said, "and we use them only as holding stalls." *Or for little ponies making a midnight trek.*

"But Nifty gets upset and kicks the walls if other horses are too close." David crossed his arms, his voice hardening. "For safety purposes, I'd like him stabled here. Would that be a problem?"

"Certainly not," Jenna said quickly. "We'll put in a mineral lick and have it ready for him. When will he ship in?"

"As soon as possible." David gave a satisfied nod. "I'm very impressed with the facility and what you offer. I'd like some more material with complete specs though. But first, let's find the other two and we can make arrangements to meet for dinner."

Jenna's shoulders relaxed. David had been hard to read, very controlled, sometimes abrupt, and at one point she'd even thought his interest was feigned. "We also have a one-mile dirt track and a seven-eighth artificial surface," she said, "so horses can be kept in training. It's an option that mainly appeals to our long-term clients."

"Yes, Derek mentioned that on the phone. Nifty is used to controlled exercise so a few laps every morning would do him good. He can be ridden out or ponied."

"Okay." Jenna gestured at the door. "We can go out the back door and check the oval. Meet with some of the riders and Wally Turner, our in-house expert. He'll establish an exercise schedule in conjunction with our treatment."

She paused, not certain where Wally was. Hadn't seen him since his enthusiastic display of the landscape additions earlier in the day.

David glanced at his watch. "The track isn't important. I'd prefer to go back to the hotel and meet you later for dinner."

Jenna let the inner door swing shut, hiding her surprise. Owners and trainers were usually anal about footing. In her experience, they always wanted to inspect the track and give detailed instructions to the rider.

Burke and Lorna stepped out of the oxygen room. Burke nodded at something Lorna said, but his mouth was taut with tension. From the moment the Ridgemans had arrived, it had been clear David was in charge. However, Lorna had latched onto Burke with single-minded zeal, and it had been up to Jenna to close the deal. For a man who needed to be in control, it must have been frustrating to be relegated to the clinging sister.

Jenna shot Burke a reassuring smile, and his mouth immediately relaxed.

"Would you like to meet some of our exercise riders, David?" Burke asked, easing away from Lorna. "Two of them graduated from the California Jockey School."

David shrugged. "Not necessary. Jenna has answered all my questions beautifully. As long as our horse can have this stall right here—which she assures will be no problem—we'll ship our stud this week."

"Very good," Burke said, his face impassive. "There are some forms we can review in my office."

"Which we can do just as easily over dinner," David said, clearly eager to leave. "We hope you and Jenna will join us later. Perhaps you can suggest a suitable restaurant?"

"We can go to the Hunt Club," Burke said. "I'll pick you up at eight."

"Perfect," David said. "Let's go, Lorna."

The door closed behind them and Burke turned to Jenna, his face creased in a grateful smile. "Great job, Jenna. We did it. Thank you."

She shrugged. "I didn't really do anything. He wasn't interested in many of the applications, only the oxygen chamber. Rather strange."

"Doesn't matter. We got the business. Thanks for stepping up." His smile deepened. "Let's celebrate. Ask Frances to order in a bunch of doughnuts or cake for the staff. Whatever you think. This is the first time the Center has been entrusted with a Derby winner. I'll grab your tea."

She nodded, flushed from his compliments. Sometimes he was so thoughtful. Everyone would be delighted to enjoy a rare treat, and her boss was even serving the tea. A simple gesture but it meant a lot. And he'd intended it to mean a lot.

She floated to the reception desk and shared the news.

"Mr. Burke wants to celebrate? Awesome!" Frances pumped her fist. "I think cinnamon buns would be best. Those big ones with extra icing. And maybe a fruit plate for the riders. But first I need to thank you, Jenna."

Gratitude colored Frances's face. "Mr. Burke is giving me a ten-percent raise. Said you praised my typing skills. And all raises are retroactive to April. He's a great manager. I mean Wally was good but Mr. Burke is better."

Jenna shuffled her feet, slightly uneasy. Burke had tightened his grip on employee loyalty and was clearly a master tactician. He'd even swayed the kids in the three-legged race, and children were always a tough sell.

"Kathryn Winfield sure didn't look very happy." Frances snickered, oblivious to Jenna's discomfort. "She decided she'd rather work somewhere else, thank God. Mr. Burke walked her out the door himself."

"That's strange. I thought she was going to try the job for a while." Jenna leaned over the counter, frowning. In the office, Kathryn had signed all the papers as though she intended to stay, at least for a while. Burke must have come down on her later, even harder.

At least he was focusing that unrelenting will on other people and not on her. She shivered, abruptly eager for a fortifying cup of tea. "I'll see you later, Frances." She turned and walked down the hall to Burke's office.

"Come in," he called at her light knock. He pushed his drawer shut and rounded the desk, pulling out a chair at the conference table. Carefully slid over her cup of tea and sat down in the chair beside her.

"Careful," he said. "It's hot. I think we need to turn the temperature down on that machine." His gaze narrowed on her bandage. "Did you make a doctor's appointment?"

"This afternoon. If you can't drive me, I'll ask Wally."

"No, I'll drive you," he said quickly, his gaze flickering over her arm. "Thanks for coming in today and showing David around. Sorry you had to do the bulk of the work but he was obviously pleased." He paused. "You heard him mention dinner?"

"Yes." Her hand tightened around the hot cup.

"Then you'll come?"

"I'd rather not." The thought of sitting in the pretentious Hunt Club, making small talk with David while Burke pretended to listen to Lorna was unappealing. And Leo Winfield and his cronies would be there, and Leo was always hostile, no doubt influenced by Kathryn.

"But I need you." Burke's voice lowered and though he didn't move, his shoulders seemed to shift closer. "We both agree David is more comfortable with you, right?"

She nodded.

"And the Center will benefit from his horse, correct?"

She nodded again.

"And you realize the most strategic moves are usually made outside the office?" His voice turned husky.

"Yes." She nodded, feeling like a puppet.

"Then you realize you have to come. You have to help this horse. If they don't sign the contract, Nifty is the loser."

She nodded again, almost helplessly, then realized what he was doing and jerked her head up. "But I don't belong in places like that. You saw how it was at the races. And this time Colin won't be there to help."

A muscle ticked in Burke's jaw. "Sweetheart, there's not going to be a repeat of that. I'll have your back. Surely you know that?"

She wrapped both hands around her cup, absorbing its warmth, wishing she could be beamed up and dropped somewhere else. Maybe at college with Em. She shouldn't care about snubs from people like Leo and Kathryn. Had worked hard to develop a thick skin, but it still hurt. Maybe if she had a degree, she wouldn't have such a fragile sense of self-worth.

Burke must have sensed her weakening. "Pass me your phone."

She slowly pushed it over, watching as he programmed in a number.

"If you want to leave the club," he said, concentrating on the phone, "you walk in the bathroom and call me. Anytime. I promise we'll leave immediately."

"Even if you have to push Lorna off your lap?" she asked. "And risk losing the Ridgeman horse?"

"Even if," he said.

Jenna paused outside the waiting room and carefully inspected her bare arm. It was ugly and mottled and blistered, but the doctor had recommended no more bandaging. Let the air touch it. She opened and closed her fist. The skin stretched but there was no searing pain. Burke had been right. Playing cards and using the phone had been great exercise.

The doctor's visit had been reassuring—protect from the sun, apply lots of cream and there'd be no need for skin grafts. However, she would have preferred to keep her wrist wrapped. Looking at the pink skin made her slightly nauseated. She left the doctor's office and stepped onto the sidewalk.

Burke's car was still parked by the curb, powerful, sleek and patient. At her approach, he unfolded from the driver's seat, his gaze flickering over her wrist. She pressed it against her side, trying to hide the ugly skin, and slid into the passenger seat.

He lowered himself back behind the wheel. "Do you need to go anywhere else? Drugstore maybe?"

"No, everything's good. No more bandaging. And the doctor doesn't think there'll be any scarring."

Burke's hands relaxed over the wheel. He didn't seem at all repulsed by her flawed skin. "Did he suggest anything else? Physio maybe?"

"No." Her gaze drifted over the leather steering wheel, the sleek dashboard. God, she loved this car. "But he did say driving would help," she added solemnly. "Not a standard, of course, but an automatic. An automatic just like this."

Burke's lip twitched. "I suppose the car should be black?"

"Black cars are the most therapeutic of all."

Two hours later, she was still driving. Burke had relaxed enough to stop giving directions but not enough to pull out his phone, although perhaps he was too busy having fun. She smiled at him, no longer conscious of her ugly burn. Especially since he didn't seem to notice.

"And that ridge is where we all went parking," she gestured, continuing the impromptu tour, "before the summer cottages were built. One memorable night, my mom sent Wally to drag me home. I was mortified, especially since Kathryn Winfield was in the next car."

"You've known Wally a long time?"

"Oh sure, he's like an uncle. He helped a lot, especially when Mom was sick. Do you want to open the sunroof and go on the highway for one last spin?" Burke looked distracted, so she reached over and touched his arm. "Or maybe you need to go back to the office?"

He turned to her then, giving his rare, deep smile. "I choose sunroof and highway. I certainly don't want to go back yet. But put on the four-way flashers and stay under forty."

She laughed with delight and gunned it.

Chapter Nineteen

Jenna twisted, studying her reflection in the mirror. The black skirt was nice, but the blouse was much too dowdy. It was, however, the only one with long sleeves. She didn't want to shock David and Lorna with the sight of her damaged skin. Be nice if she had something a little sexier though, something cut low in the front, maybe even lower in the back.

The type of clothes Em wore.

She hurried into her sister's room and scanned the closet, crammed full of clothes even though Em had taken six bulging suitcases to college. So many clothes, some still with price tags. Oh, gosh. Jenna's hand lingered over a hanger. This top was the perfect little number, if only it fit. Emily was a little bigger in the hips, smaller in the boobs, but maybe…

She tugged it on and stared in delight. Not bad, not bad at all. If she kept the palm of her hand down, no one would even notice the burn. She lingered for a moment, studying her reflection, then added a simple silver necklace and matching earrings. Checked the clock. Burke would be here soon. He wouldn't make the Ridgemans wait. She swapped her leather purse for a sleek clutch and tossed in her phone.

A black car crunched into the driveway, familiar and confident, as though it knew the way. Not surprising since she'd been spending most of her days with Burke. She brushed aside a needle of worry. He'd be going soon and she was merely having some fun. It wouldn't bother her in the least when he left.

She slipped on her heels and walked out to join him. "Remember your promise." She dipped her hand in her purse and waved the phone.

He remained by the car, silent, wearing his designer suit as if it was made for him, which of course, it probably was. And he was looking at her oddly. Suddenly her cute little clothes felt gauche. Maybe she wasn't dressed appropriately after all.

"You look beautiful," he finally said. He swung open the passenger door with a flourish. "May I catch a pony, shingle a roof, slay a dragon? Anything, my lady."

His compliment sounded genuine and did so much toward restoring her confidence, she impulsively rose on her toes and kissed him. He'd turned still so she lingered, sliding her lips over his mouth, absorbing his lips, the angle of his jaw, the spicy smell of his aftershave. Slid her mouth over his top lip then the bottom, exploring, enjoying, thanking.

Stepped back with a grateful smile.

He'd flattened his palms against the car, eyes half shut then slowly widened them. "You make me dizzy, Jen." His voice was gruff. "Please kiss me like that at the end of the night."

She slipped past him into the car, slightly embarrassed.

He didn't say much while they drove, just held her hand, dragging his thumb over her palm and releasing it only when they pulled in front of the hotel.

"Fill me in on your research before I go in. Anything important I should know about these two?"

She groaned. Of course. He'd asked her to do that when he gave her the phone. "I forgot," she admitted. "I'm so sorry."

He gave her a long look and released her hand. "Don't worry. David will probably stare at you and Lorna will natter at me. We'll eat fast and escape, okay? Be right back."

He left the car slanted in front of the hotel, two feet from the curb, completely disregarding the 'no parking' sign. However, no one seemed to bother the nice vehicles. Or maybe the car had simply absorbed some of his natural assurance.

The hotel door closed behind him. Five minutes later, he strode from the lobby with Lorna Ridgeman clinging to his arm and David sauntering behind them.

"I'm starving," Lorna said, as she slid into the car. "Wasn't sure if we'd walk or drive. Oh, hello, Janet," she said, sounding less than pleased that there was another woman in the front seat.

"Jenna. Her name is Jenna," Burke said, closing Lorna's door and slipping back behind the wheel. He glanced at Jenna. "Did you bring a jacket, honey?"

Honey? Jenna's eyes widened in confusion, and she shook her head. He'd been totally professional this afternoon, always contained in the office. Now though, he stretched his ridged arm across the back of the seat, his fingers stroking her shoulder.

Lorna turned remarkably silent.

"The Hunt Club's not far." Burke glanced at Lorna in the rearview mirror. "Four minutes. We could walk, Lorna, if you prefer."

Still exceedingly polite, Jenna thought. Lorna could find no fault with Burke's manners although he'd certainly made it clear he wasn't available.

"I walked enough this afternoon," Lorna said. "So you're employed at the Center, Jenna? Is that your job, giving little tours?"

"I massage the horses too." She turned politely in her seat but Lorna's frown seemed locked on the back of Burke's arm and the way it rested on Jenna's shoulder.

"Massage," Lorna said, with a pointed laugh. "How…interesting. Do you do people too, or just horses? I've had a sore neck for ages."

"Here we are," Burke said, pulling into a prime parking spot by the door. He stepped back and opened Lorna's door.

"Looks wonderful." She tucked her arm around Burke's as she admired the grandiose entrance. "I was rather afraid there wouldn't be any suitable place to eat. You should have seen what the hotel served for lunch."

"Really," Burke said. "I stayed there my first night in town and had an excellent meal." He turned and looped his right arm around Jenna's waist. "Watch the step, ladies." He disengaged Lorna's hand to open the door, nodding for the Ridgemans to precede him, but kept Jenna at his side, his hand splayed around her waist.

If she were supposed to be an employee, he was really overdoing it. She hoped no one from work was here. Burke sure didn't act like this in the office, and Lorna didn't seem at all pleased.

Clearly the Ridgeman contract was signed or he wouldn't have risked losing Nifty. Still, it was reassuring to have his protection.

"Good evening, Mr. Burke," the hostess chirped brightly. "We have your window table ready. Follow me, please."

Jenna slipped into her chair, smiling at the wiry teenager who rushed to fill her water glass. "Thank you, Brian."

She glanced at Burke. "This is Brian, Charlie's older brother. Brian owned Molly before he gave the horse to his brother."

"I remember Molly," Burke said, with a hint of a smile.

"I'd prefer my water room temperature with no ice." Lorna leaned forward, eager to join the conversation. "And two twists of lime."

"Certainly, ma'am." But Brian lingered, bending down between Burke and Jenna. "I'd like to thank you both," he said. "Sure appreciate how you helped Molly. Three Brooks really made a difference. Charlie is still grinning."

Jenna peeked at Burke, hoping he wouldn't belittle the race or announce that local horses were no longer welcome at the Center. Brian was so proud of his little brother, so proud of Molly. The mare might be homely but she had a huge heart, and regular massage kept her comfortable. It was too bad Burke didn't understand.

"It was an entertaining race," Burke said. "And when Molly needs another massage, I'm sure we can work something out."

Lorna gave an impatient sigh and Brian immediately straightened. "I'll get your special water right away, ma'am." But he gave Burke a grateful smile before striding away.

"Derek, what race is that waiter talking about?" Lorna asked.

"A local turf race, hotly contested," Burke said. "A most enjoyable day." He seemed to understand Lorna craved the limelight and smoothly added, "I saw the Derby this year. Two of the entries were sired by your stud. You own a remarkable horse. Who was the genius who crossed Barkeeper with Nifty's Lass?"

David puffed out his chest. "That was me. Unusual cross but I liked Lass for her speed, and of course, Barkeeper was bred for the classics. Everyone thought it was my father's idea, but I knew those two would produce a winner. Nifty is now the leading sire of two-year-olds. We have mares booked for the next three years."

Both Lorna and David were delighted to spew endlessly about Ridgeman's success and whenever their boasting slowed, Burke drew them out with another question.

Jenna cut another piece of her tender steak, rather surprised the meal had been so enjoyable and that the time had passed so quickly. She only had to smile and occasionally widen her eyes to show her interest. Burke was a master at this game, and it was almost amusing to relax and listen while he controlled the conversation.

"And after Dad died in the fire," Lorna was saying, "David took over the entire operation. But I'm sure you've heard enough about our tragedy?"

Burke glanced at Jenna with such disapproval she fumbled with her fork. She'd witnessed his annoyance turned on others, but it was rather disconcerting to have it directed at her.

"I remember hearing something about a fire," Burke said, looking back at Lorna.

"Five years ago. Horrible time," David said. "We lost our father and seven horses. Ironically, Ridgeman Racing experienced its greatest success over the last few years. With me at the helm."

Lorna picked at her plate and said nothing.

"Indeed, life does go on." David raised his wine glass. "And now we have a Derby winner who's a proven sire. What a way to make money. It doesn't get any better than that."

"Well, perhaps Dad and the dead horses wouldn't agree," Lorna said, rising and scraping back her chair. "Excuse me. Derek, can you show me where the bathroom is?"

"Certainly." Burke rose immediately and escorted her around the corner.

David shrugged. "Guess it's just us, Jenna. Here's to keeping our stud healthy." He raised his glass, his gaze following Lorna. Red drops splattered over the tablecloth as he clumsily tapped his glass against hers.

How much wine had David and Lorna consumed, Jenna wondered. Hard to judge as the waiter kept their glasses full after conferring about grapes and vintage. Beer was much simpler. However, David was clearly inebriated.

"Oops, sorry, my dear," he said. "I spilled wine on your hand." His eyes narrowed and he abruptly grabbed her fingers. "My goodness, what happened here?"

"Just a little burn." She politely attempted to free her hand.

"Doesn't look little." His grip tightened. "Does it hurt?"

Jenna yelped at the unexpected pressure.

"Burns can be so painful," David added, checking her expression. He twisted her palm, still gripping her hand. "Imagine how much my father hurt? Burnt to the bone with horses screaming around him. I heard them, you know. Unforgettable. The smell of flesh is like no other.

"*She* doesn't like to talk about it." His eyes had an faraway glitter now, and he no longer seemed to see her. She tugged at her hand, trying to free his grip but only hurt herself in the attempt.

"Are you full, Jenna?" Burke asked, materializing by the table. He sat down and David abruptly released her fingers.

She nodded and jammed her throbbing hand into her lap. She wasn't full but her appetite had completely disappeared. She glared at David, trying to imitate Burke's dark scowl. However, the man didn't even notice. He cut into his barbecued salmon, stabbing at the crispy skin with renewed vigor.

"I had the trout here last week," Burke said, glancing curiously from David to Jenna. "Delicious. Freshest fish I've ever had. Want to try my bass, honey?"

"No, thanks." She shook her head, keeping her hands buried in the napkin on her lap.

"Hey," he murmured. "You're pale. What's wrong?"

"Not a thing." *But your psycho client deliberately manhandled my burn.* She knew Burke wouldn't tolerate abuse. Not to his staff…not to her. He'd have a very strong reaction which would definitely result in David sending Nifty elsewhere. And that would hurt the Center, the employees and the town. Burke needed Nifty. They all did.

She forced a smile and picked up her water glass.

"So," David said, dismissing Jenna and looking at Burke, "I talked to our shipper and Nifty will arrive on Wednesday. I have every confidence Three Brooks will be able to help." David took a last bite of blackened salmon and tossed his napkin on the table, acting as though the bizarre incident with Jenna had never happened.

"Now where is my primping sister?" He twisted, peering toward the back of the room. "Women take forever in the bathroom." He gave a condescending smirk, and even Burke had the gall to nod in agreement.

Jenna inched her chair further from the table, putting more distance between her and David. She could have been safe at home, relaxing on her swing, watching Peanut graze. Instead she was stuck with these hoity-toity people and their weird hang-ups, forced to act as though every word they uttered was golden. It would have been more fun to share beer and pepperoni with Wally and talk about horses. Even better to be playing cards with Burke and talking about...anything.

And that was the real problem. She balled her napkin in despair. Lately she hadn't been thinking of anyone but him. Her loyal pony hadn't had any light therapy for two days, she'd forgotten about the Ridgeman research and she'd brushed off her troubled sister who clearly needed a good heart-to-heart. She'd dropped everything and everyone for a man, just like her mom. Silly, selfish, stupid.

She wanted to lean down and bang her forehead on the luxurious tablecloth. And wouldn't that just shock the hell out of her sophisticated dinner companions.

Although Burke would probably remain fairly cool. She peered sideways, watching as he enjoyed his bass. He was comfortable with anyone, anything, anywhere. Heck, she'd thought him a construction worker when they'd first met.

She wished he *were* a construction worker.

He must have sensed her scrutiny and slanted a deep smile, the type he seemed to reserve for her, and her frustration fizzled. It wasn't that bad being here. If she were home before eleven, she'd still have time to call Em, still have time to lead Peanut down the hill, still have time for everything she should be doing. And she was also going to dig out everything she possibly could on the Ridgemans, especially David.

A halo of perfume announced Lorna's return. She swept around the table and settled back into her chair. Her eyes and lipstick had brightened, and she spoke animatedly about meeting an Alpha Delta Pi from university days.

"And who's your alma mater, Derek?" she asked, briefly pausing for breath.

"Yale."

"And yours?"

Silence. Jenna jerked her attention back to the conversation, realizing that for the first time that evening, Lorna was addressing her.

"Riverview College," Jenna said, scrambling to remember the institution on her certificates. Or was it Riverbend? She hadn't used the local college, afraid it would be too easy to check.

"Oh, I've heard of Riverview." Lorna waved a dismissive hand. "That's good. I suspect some people in this town barely finished high school."

"Really?" Jenna gave an exaggerated gasp but at Burke's warning squeeze she clamped her mouth and concentrated on her wine. The night was almost over. Thank God.

"Well, maybe not the people in *this* club." Lorna glanced around as though suspicious of undereducated patrons. "But I must admit David and I were reassured to learn Three Brooks only hires qualified staff. Nifty is the foundation of Ridgeman. He deserves the best."

"Of course," Burke said, keeping a warning hand on Jenna's knee. "That's part of the Center's mandate. Jenna, do you need to use the phone?"

"No." She flashed a brittle smile. "Everything's just peachy."

Burke initialed the bill and rose. He reached down to pull out Jenna's chair, but she'd already slid out the other side. It hadn't been such a bad evening. She'd done her job, smiled and nodded, but at some point over dinner she'd drifted off to another place, completely shutting him out.

Her eyes suddenly sparked with genuine emotion and he glanced over his shoulder, catching the busboy's respectful salute. She definitely loved this town. And they loved her.

"Derek!" Leo pushed past a waiter and rushed to their table. He pumped Burke's hand, beaming his delight. "What an opportunity you created for Kathryn. Your friends in England offered her the masseuse job. When she returns from such an elite stable, she'll be able to land a job anywhere in the country."

He glanced curiously at Lorna and David. Burke introduced them and they immediately began gabbing like long-lost friends. Except for Jenna who edged toward the door.

Burke touched her elbow and winked. "A little patience, honey. One more minute." He stepped back, stunned by her look of utter despair.

"Kathryn's going to England?" she whispered brokenly. "Aren't there better, more deserving employees you could have recommended? What is it with you people?"

He dropped his arm, fighting his annoyance. It wasn't his habit to explain business dealings, but this arrangement had fulfilled his agreement to Wally without angering Leo. He certainly hadn't intended to slight anyone, but frankly he didn't much care.

He glanced at the door, his face uncomfortably hot. He hadn't done anything wrong. At least he'd disposed of Kathryn. Jenna was simply being difficult. He swiped his warm forehead. The hell with waiting for the Ridgemans; he needed air.

He stalked to the door, paused and glanced over his shoulder just as David helpfully reached out for Jenna's hand. She swung her arm back in a vicious elbow. Burke jerked in shock. If he hadn't been watching, he wouldn't have believed it but aw, hell. The Ridgeman deal would be tits up now.

But David only smiled, shrugging it off with baffling blandness.

The drive back to the hotel was weird. David chatted brightly, seemingly energized and in a far more gregarious mood than during the tour. Lorna struggled to calculate the calories in her meal while Jenna sat in rigid silence, left hand balled in a defensive fist.

Burke stopped in front of the hotel and walked Lorna and David to the lobby. "I'll let you know when the horse arrives," he said. "Thanks for entrusting Nifty to us."

He slipped back into the car, studying Jenna in the darkness. "Want to tell me what that elbow was about?" he asked, with fake amiability. "I assumed you'd know how to behave with clients."

"Guess you assumed wrong." Her voice sounded weary. "Is that why you won't give me a reference for a job in England?"

He jabbed at the ignition button, his jaw clamping. The engine roared to life. "Someone like you wouldn't want to go to England," he said.

"You're right. People like me should stay and work the rest of their life in a little West Virginia town. I've never even been on a plane."

He'd only meant it was apparent she loved her home but the raw yearning in her voice yanked at him, and his annoyance dissipated like smoke. "I'll take you to England whenever you want," he said quietly. He turned the car in the opposite direction of Three Brooks and headed toward the highway.

"Where are we going?" She shot him a suspicious look.

"Just for a drive, some cleansing air." He swallowed, his breath escaping in a ragged sigh. "I didn't intend to slight you. I really thought you'd be happy if the Winfield girl were far away."

"But she'll come back in six months, maybe a year. With her new credentials, she'll land a job at the Center and make everyone miserable. And Colin will be lonely again. Poor Colin."

Burke groaned. Gravel rattled against the underside of the car as he swerved onto the shoulder of the road and dropped his forehead against the steering wheel. It was impossible to look after a woman who worried about half the people in town, and it was wearing him down. "I've never met a lady so hard to please," he muttered. *Or for whom I've tried half as hard.* But he didn't want her to know that.

"I wanted to pound my head on the table earlier tonight," she whispered.

At least she sounded amused now and not filled with that aching hurt that twisted the very center of his chest. "Then let's console each other," he said. He unclipped her seatbelt and tugged her close.

She resisted but only for a moment then rested her head against his shoulder in that trusting way that always turned him to butter. She smelled of flowers and freshness and suddenly everything was simple again. It was much easier to talk like this, when she couldn't get all remote and huffy.

"I didn't think it went all that bad tonight," he said cautiously. "Getting the Ridgeman horse is exactly what the Center needs…but, honey, we can't be jabbing owners in the stomach. No matter how irritating they are."

She'd stiffened but really couldn't move. He had her arms wrapped beneath his, her head tucked against his chest. Yeah, it was a pretty good position.

"You think I'd just elbow him for no reason?"

She sounded wounded but he'd seen her leap over the reception desk at Frances in defense of her sister, and the incident with David had to be addressed. "I just think you might do things a little differently around here…and I don't want it to happen again."

He tilted her chin and tried to kiss her—to prove how understanding and forgiving he really was—but she jerked her head away. "Please take me home now," she said, sliding to the far side of the car.

She hardly spoke the rest of the way home but pain emanated from her in waves, and he realized that somehow he'd offended her. Again.

He parked in the driveway but she opened her door before he'd even turned off the engine. "Good night," she said, and ran lightly up the steps.

He sighed, lingering long after she was safely inside and the porch light clicked off. She fought when mad but ran away when hurt, and it was damn frustrating. He always believed in knowing when it was best to throw down your cards and cut your losses. She wasn't exactly high maintenance, but she was unlike any woman he'd ever slept with.

And he hadn't even slept with her.

He gave an indignant grunt and backed from the driveway. The closest they'd come to making love was the day he shingled her roof. He should have done things differently then and perhaps slipped past all this prickliness.

Of course, she had a couple more roofs that needed repair. He brightened and grabbed his phone, keen now to check tomorrow's weather forecast.

Chapter Twenty

The sound of a hammer jerked Jenna from a deep sleep. Rubbing her eyes, she peered out the bedroom window. Early morning and Burke was pounding again, this time on top of the kennel. Poor Peanut would likely have a heart attack.

She pulled on a T-shirt and shorts and rushed out, the screen door slamming behind her. Peanut lifted his head, gave a welcoming nicker and shoved his nose back into the dewy grass. Okay, so Burke had let Peanut out first. That was good...rather thoughtful actually.

She hadn't expected him to really fix the old kennel, but only a fool would turn down a helping hand. She slipped back inside and made a cup of tea and a big pot of coffee.

Ten minutes later, she walked over with two steaming cups and stared up suspiciously. "What is it you want today, Burke?" Luckily he had his shirt on, although those brawny arms were probably enough to quicken any woman's pulse.

He walked to the side of the roof, grinned down and her heart flip-flopped. He could rip her insides out with his blunt comments, but that endearing grin sucked her in every time. She hated lying to him. And she was falling deeper. *I hope he leaves soon.*

"What do I want?" he repeated, still grinning. "How about supper tonight? I'm pretty lonely in your little town, sweetheart."

He climbed down the shiny ladder and she had a chance to discreetly admire those broad shoulders, his muscled forearms. No need for him to be lonely—anywhere—although it would kill her to see him flirt with someone else.

The admission left her agitated and she shoved the cup toward his chest, almost sloshing coffee over her toes.

"Whoa. Remember the tea." He grabbed the mug, then stilled, staring at her hand. "What happened? Your blisters are ripped." He studied her fingers, an odd expression on his face. "How the hell did that happen?"

His voice had hardened with such fierce protectiveness, she knew she'd been right to not speak about David. She rose impulsively on her toes and distracted him with a quick kiss. "I gave Peanut a long massage last night," she said.

"You stayed up after I drove you home?"

She nodded and glanced guiltily at Peanut. He'd had a late night session in the oxygen chamber as well as under the infrared lights. But Wally hadn't been around and it had been a lonely, almost spooky visit. "He looks great, doesn't he," she said. "Guess the antibiotics are really working."

"He looks good but no more massages." Burke still frowned at her hand. "If you're coming back to work next week, we need you healthy. We also need you able to massage the Ridgeman horse. Otherwise," he paused for effect, "we'll hire someone else."

He was such a manipulator. But she only rolled her eyes and let him guide her to a flat rock by the kennel.

"Sit." He pulled her onto his lap. "And tell me what you're cooking for supper." His words were bossy, but his tone was nothing but hopeful.

"Trout, I think," she said, watching his face. She was an expert at pan-fried trout, but he was probably used to some very fancy meals.

"Trout's my favorite," he said quickly. "I'll buy it, you cook it."

"No need. There's plenty in the brook. The Canadians stocked the upper lake but didn't fish it much so the trout are thriving. I actually go there once a week."

"Ah, ha. So you've been pilfering my fish."

"Just a few meals, boss." She placed her tea on the ground and snuggled into his chest. It was so much easier to relax with him when he was out of a suit, out of his office, away from work. Right now, she could pretend he was a normal guy. Heck, he even acted normal. Last night's stiffness was gone, and everything was so simple. So easy.

He seemed to feel it too. He set his mug down and tilted her chin, drinking in her face. "You know how I feel about stealing," he said gruffly. "This definitely calls for some sort of punishment." His head dipped, blotting the sun. His lips were gentle at first then more insistent as his tongue slipped inside her mouth, exploring, until she turned completely in his lap and wrapped her hands around his neck.

Minutes later he pulled away, his breathing ragged. "Honey, you're killing me. I'm going to finish the shed tomorrow then rip the shingles off and do it all over again. If that's what makes you sweet and cuddly, consider me your personal roofer."

"There's something very attractive about a man with a hammer," she admitted. "And much more my type."

"Good to know. And now I'm going to follow you down to the brook and supervise this fishing operation."

"Only if you've finished the roof," she said.

"Damn, look at that monster." Burke whooped as he pulled in another olive-brown fish, its silvery speckles glinting under the sun. This was the most fun he had in years, so much so, that he'd confiscated Jenna's fishing rod after the first trout and hadn't yet returned it.

She was a stickler about size though. "Sorry," she said. "A quarter inch too small. You'll have to throw it back."

"Too small. This is the biggest yet." He whirled in time to catch her grin and splashed her with a handful of water. "Four is probably enough though, right?"

"Why don't we catch a couple more and we'll take some to Mrs. Parker. She always appreciates fresh fish."

"Great idea. Bait my hook, honey," he teased. He had no idea who Mrs. Parker was, but he definitely wanted to keep fishing. He loved the little squeals Jenna made when he pretended to drop a worm down her shirt.

He stuck another worm on the hook, chuckling when she averted her head from its helpless twisting. "For a country girl, you're quite a sissy. What would you have done if I wasn't here?"

"Bait my hook with hot dogs." She idly chewed a blade of grass and studied the row of fish lying at her feet. "By the way, how much longer do you think you'll be here?"

"That depends." He cast the line across the brook toward the shade of a big tree where the fish had been biting all morning. She wandered up and he pulled her in front of him and stuck the rod in her hand. "You bring the next one in, hotshot."

As expected, she turned her attention to the water, let out a little more line and forgot her question. He had an interview late this afternoon for Wally's position. As soon as a good manager was in place, he'd be ready to move on. Although it would be nice to see the Ridgeman stud before he left. And Jenna—he didn't know what to do about her.

He nuzzled the back of her neck. "Think I'll do some work on your porch and then drive up to the Center around three. Come back around six for supper. That sound okay?"

She'd already hooked her fish and was reeling it in. "Sure," she said, expertly guiding the line past the deadfall in the middle of the brook.

"It might rain tonight," he added, watching her face, "so I better sleep at your place. Watch the roof for leaks."

"It's supposed to be nice for the next three days," she said. "Wow, look at this guy!"

At least she hadn't said no. He kept his arms around her, even letting her catch the last fish, although his arms twitched to take possession of the rod. Damn, this was fun.

"Thanks for sharing this spot, Jen." He rested his chin on the top of her silky head, listening as water bubbled merrily down the brook. "I thought the Canadians were idiots, but maybe they knew what they were doing."

"They weren't idiots. They were very nice people. And maybe they'd like some of their stuff returned, including those horse pictures in the hall."

"Okay," he said quickly, hearing the indignation in her voice. "I can do that. Crappy at management but they sure made a nice fishing hole."

"Not everyone manages like you," she said.

"Fortunately. Because mismanaged companies offer a lot of opportunity."

"But how do you pick?" she asked. "Why buy Three Brooks?"

"We look for undervalued companies in a growth industry. Make some strategic changes. Place appropriately minded managers at the top and move on."

"Appropriately minded?" She was stroking her fingers over his forearm, and he liked her gentle touch. Didn't want to think about work right now.

"Usually the corporate personality has to change," he said absently. "New management is better equipped for the tough decisions. You cold?" He tightened his arms, feeling her shiver even though the morning sun was comfortably warm.

She didn't speak for a moment. "It's nice to have met you," she finally said, "but I have to admit I preferred the Canadians' policies. And you're scaring me, because it sounds like you're definitely getting rid of Wally."

He debated the best way to change the subject, maybe even wave a worm in her face, but surprised himself with the truth. "Wally gave his notice yesterday, Jenna," he said gently. "We'll have a new manager in there soon."

She twisted in his arms, her eyes widening. "But why would he quit? Isn't it standard to give a month's pay for every year of service? And where will he live?" Her voice turned pensive. "Maybe I better clean out Em's room."

"You will not." His jaw clenched, and the words came out much too clipped.

"Of course I will." She rammed her hands on her hips and stepped back. "He's a family friend who's suddenly out of a job. So unless you can think of a better idea..."

Burke blinked, appalled at the idea of Wally ensconced on Jenna's swing. "Maybe he can stay another month in the apartment."

"At least three," she said, her face mutinous.

"But we need his place for the new manager. We don't want to pay for a motel." He dragged a hand over his jaw. "And Wally quit on his own. Obviously he doesn't want the apartment."

Her eyes narrowed with suspicion.

"Okay," he said quickly, turning away. "We'll go back to your house and I'll call about the legalities and insurance issues but hell, Jenna, this won't be easy."

A half hour later, he closed his phone and leaned his head on the swing. She pushed open the screen door, watchful as a cat, so he stretched out and closed his eyes. "Think I'll have a nap," he said. "Wake me at three."

She squeezed onto the swing, sweetening the air with a hint of cinnamon and apple. "But what did your legal people say about Wally?" she asked.

He cracked open an eyelid, trying to keep his lip from twitching. She was a natural at negotiations and had even learned the lingo. "My people said your people could stay, four months max."

He'd added an extra month, hoping to please her. It worked. Her face sparkled with delight and she wrapped her arms around his neck. "You're very kind even though you try hard not to be."

"I'm not kind at all," he said, feeling his throat constrict. "Just tired. You're wearing me out, sweetheart." He pulled her down, tucking her alongside him. "Stay right here and don't move. Unless you have something in the oven." He gave a hopeful sniff.

"Apple cobbler. But it's not in the oven yet."

"I love apple cobbler." He blew out a contented sigh, pulled her head into his shoulder and fell asleep.

He wasn't sure what woke him, maybe an ingrained alarm clock. She was still asleep beside him, fingers over his chest and head tucked trustingly against his shoulder. A light breeze rocked the swing and a hawk circled in the cloudless sky. He'd never felt so serene. Or happy.

A man could live like this, work from home, travel when necessary but keep the trips brief. He checked his watch, dropped a reluctant kiss on her forehead then eased her back onto the swing, so smoothly she didn't wake.

He grabbed a sports jacket from the back seat of his car, tugged it on and headed to the Center.

"Your three o'clock appointment is here, Mr. Burke." Frances stopped typing and gave a bright smile. "Would you like me to bring some coffee?"

"No thanks, Frances. I'll get it."

He found Ben Vickers in the waiting room and led him into his office, mentally reviewing the man's background. Vickers would be perfect for the Center: tough, knowledgeable and experienced.

He knew horses, knew the industry and had been a key force in settling a labor dispute two years earlier.

He had some good ideas too which Burke noted with interest.

"We'll follow all the horses we treat," Vickers went on. "Insert congratulations in the *Racing Form* and industry publications. It may not be the Center's treatment that propels them to a win, but we can certainly create that impression."

Burke nodded, flipping through the man's comprehensive resume. Education, experience, networks. All excellent. His last position included an impressive man-hour ratio. But this couldn't be right. "Each masseuse handled eight horses per day?" Burke asked, staring at the number.

Vickers gave a smug nod. "One masseuse, eight horses. And technicians were ultimately responsible for production shortfalls."

"One person can massage eight horses?" Burke frowned. "In one day?"

"Of course. Admittedly it's demanding work so we preferred to replace staff every year, before being hit with repetitive strain injuries. I'm not convinced of the benefits of massage, but owners and horses love it. And there're always plenty of workers to fill the positions."

Burke pushed the resume aside and rose. "Thanks for dropping by. I'll give you a call if you make the short list."

Vickers frowned. "Thought I was on the short list?"

"Not anymore," Burke snapped.

He was still scowling, staring through the window as Vickers gunned his pickup past the new building and out of the parking lot. There must be someone else in Stillwater, someone with good managerial skills, someone who cared about animals and staff. Someone a little…softer.

He called Frances on the intercom. "How many vets in town?"

"Three," she said. "The Center uses Hillcrest Vet run by Paul Johnston."

"What about the other two?"

"One only does small animals," Frances said, "and Colin MacDonald never does any Three Brooks' work."

"Give me Colin's number."

Burke jotted down the vet's number then glanced through his mail. Some invoices, a purple handwritten envelope and a couriered jewelry box. Good, that meant Theresa had already received her kiss-off present, and he had a spare necklace ready for gifting.

And not one piece of the usual hate mail, thanks to Leo and Jenna's influence.

He opened the purple envelope and grinned at the picture. Beautiful crayon colors of children running in a green field, a white stick figure with matching shoes smiling by a blue tree and another darker stick figure standing by the finish line.

'Thanks for the ice Cream' was underlined in pink and surrounded by a generous row of smiley faces and purple sparkly hearts. Signed, Sophie.

He didn't know who Sophie was—maybe the little girl who Jenna had boosted onto his shoulders—but it was the nicest piece of mail he'd ever received.

He folded the picture and carefully slipped it into his wallet then called the number Frances had provided.

Colin MacDonald's clinic was easy to find, on the main highway with a receiving barn for horses and a large graveled turnaround for stock trailers. A small metal sign stated: 'Closed on Sundays. Emergencies only.'

Dogs yipped as he walked into the reception area, a cat scurried between his feet and a little boy protectively cradled a black and white rabbit.

"That way," a harried receptionist said, pointing down the hall to an open door.

Colin didn't rise or offer to shake his hand, just stared with anxious eyes over a desk littered with drug samples. "You said this was important. Is Jenna sick?"

"Not to my knowledge," Burke said, sitting down on an uncomfortable, high-backed chair. "Looks like you're working hard. What do you put in? Twelve-hour days, six days a week? Probably net a hundred thousand annually with no chance for growth unless you hire another vet."

"I'm very busy," Colin said, "so if you have a point, please get to it."

"Three Brooks needs a manager. Someone honest and reliable, someone who knows horses and cares about the employees. I'd like you to apply for that position."

"What about Wally?"

"Wally's given his notice." Burke cast an approving eye over Colin's degrees, the elite university and the magna cum laude distinction. Yes, this man would be ideal.

"Any other staff changes?" Colin's voice had turned gruff.

"None so far and I'd like to keep it that way."

"Then thanks for your offer," Colin said, "but I decline." He nodded at the door. "I'm sure you can find your way out."

"Salary would start at one twenty with full benefits and an apartment in four months' time." Burke leaned forward, studying the man's face, certain he'd spotted a flash of interest. "Imagine. No more working nights, no weekends. No more animals dying on your operating table. No need to tell a bawling kid that Rover's really gone to heaven."

Colin's eyes shuttered. "You really are a ruthless son of a bitch. Now get out."

"Fine." Burke rose, then paused. He wasn't the type to flog a dead horse but this man interested him, and it was obvious the vet would take care of Jenna. "What would you need?" he asked. "If there's someone on staff that's unsuitable, possibly we could make an adjustment."

Colin opened his desk drawer, deliberately laying out three gleaming surgical knives. "You neglected to do your research on this one, pal. I wish you luck, I really do. Now I'm afraid Rover needs me."

Burke inclined his head and walked out.

Chapter Twenty-One

"I'm coming home for good," Emily said. "No way you can change my mind."

Unless Trevor asks you to stay, Jenna thought, sinking into the closest kitchen chair. "There are no jobs around here," she said frantically. "Even Kathryn Winfield is moving away."

"Really? I heard she was seeing Colin. He must have been hard up for a woman—or else Leo influenced him."

"No one influences Colin."

"You did," Emily said.

Jenna rubbed her temple, fighting a rush of guilt. "Just remember Wally is no longer in charge at the Center. You won't be able to work there." Gravel shifted as a black car pulled into the driveway. "Someone's here for supper," she added. "I'll call tomorrow. Please write your exams. Don't waste the entire semester."

She started to close the phone on Emily's plaintive whine then froze. *What am I doing?* Her sister was more important than Burke. "It's okay, Em," she said quickly. "We can talk now. Tell me about Trevor."

"Don't bother," Emily snapped. "Go make supper. Obviously you're very hungry." The connection switched to an angry dial tone.

Jenna dropped the accusing phone then glanced through the screen. Burke sauntered up the steps, a bag dangling from his right hand. He must have come directly from his meetings and wore a dark sports jacket, white shirt, loosened tie. Had her father even owned a tie?

People like Burke didn't belong here, didn't belong in this trailer, didn't belong with her.

She forced a smile and opened the door but he was bored and slumming—looking for a spot of entertainment in Hicksville—and she suddenly viewed his presence with a bone-deep resentment.

"I dropped the fish off at your neighbor's." He paused, studying her stiff face. "Mrs. Parker said thanks and wants you to drop by for tea this Sunday." He spoke so slowly, so carefully, her eyes pricked. She knew he must be confused but she couldn't hide her despair. He simply didn't belong here.

"And I'll be right back," he added. He pivoted and walked out the door.

Probably leaving and the hollow place in her chest ached but, of course, she wanted him to leave, the sooner the better. She rose and yanked out the frying pan. Feed him quickly, then call Emily. If he didn't come back, she'd have fish for lunch tomorrow.

The screen door opened and he stepped back in. She stared, her hand squeezing the frying pan. He'd pulled on his hard hat along with a faded T-shirt, ripped over one big shoulder. A rugged tool belt hung around his lean hips, loaded with every size hammer imaginable. Even his face was smudged.

"Did you put dirt on your cheek?" she asked.

"A little." His grin was slightly sheepish.

"Damn. You sure know how to please a woman." Her lips quivered, turning into a reluctant smile. How could she ever resent a man like this?

"You are the dangest little lady."

He even had the hillbilly lingo, albeit delivered with a snooty New York accent. His muscled laborer's body moved further into her kitchen, and he opened the cupboard door. He removed two glasses and deftly uncorked the wine.

"We'll eat later," he said. "But first, you and I are getting drunk."

Burke refilled both glasses and settled her back against his chest, dragging his mouth over her forehead.

"And then what happened?" she asked.

"Another fight, another expulsion. I wasn't good at making friends but I did learn how to fight."

She squeezed his hand, appalled his parents wouldn't let him attend public school. *Parents can be so dumb.*

She stared across the driveway, picturing her mother hurrying across the gravel, worn dress flapping, dropping Emily to hug their father. Sucked in once again by a cocky smile, token promises, and another bottle of cheap champagne.

Her hand tightened around Burke's fingers. "I never cared much for my father either," she admitted. Maybe a few times. Like when he'd sat up all night with a colicing Peanut and the weekend he'd tossed her cheating boyfriend into the lake. "It didn't matter though," she added. "My mom cared enough for all of us."

"Love makes people do strange things," Burke said. She felt his scrutiny but he must have sensed she didn't enjoy parent talk. His hand slid comfortingly over her arm. "Your shoulder seems better," he added.

"Doesn't hurt at all. Probably the time off helped." *And the sessions with Peanut under the infrared lights.* She sighed, wishing the wine hadn't left her melancholy. She hated sneaking, wanted to tell the truth, but they were getting along so well. She liked seeing him happy.

"Before I go, I'm setting up a Policy and Procedures Manual," he said. "And no more than two horses will ever be massaged in one day."

"Really?" She gaped, remembering all the times her muscles had ached after working on too many big, and sometimes uncooperative, animals. "That's so thoughtful. We'll be deluged with resumes." She peered through the gloom, trying to see his expression. "Did you hire a new manager yet?" Her tongue tripped slightly from the wine.

"Talked to a couple candidates. Then I thought it'd be preferable to have a vet in that position. Give the operation a little more credibility. What's your opinion of Colin MacDonald?"

The hollow place in her chest caved. She drew in a deep breath and averted her head. "He's kind, honest, loves animals and is very good looking. He has the smartest Australian Shepherd I've ever seen and makes a mean Singapore Sling."

"Entirely unsuitable then." Burke's arms tightened. "I gather you two have some history."

The pain in her chest spread. "We met in another town," she said quietly, "and it was perfect, seeing each other once a month. He thought it would be better if his practice were closer. We should have kept it casual but he wouldn't listen.

"He'd be a great m-manager," she continued, her voice cracking. "And he deserves it." She placed her glass on the table, feeling like her chest was imploding. "But we can't work together. I'll leave."

"You're not going anywhere." He scooped her up, pressing her against his chest, so tightly she could hear the thudding of his heart. "But you have the damnedest knack for making people care."

"I don't want that though." She pressed her knuckles against her cheek. "I don't want to love anyone. Don't want to turn into my mother. That's why it's good you're leaving soon. You *are* leaving soon, right?"

He tilted her chin, staring for a long moment. A slight frown wrinkled the skin on his forehead. "I think I understand now," he finally said.

His gaze settled on her mouth, and his expression changed, his eyes darkening. He reached up, caressing her lip with a touch so tender she could barely feel it. "I am leaving. Very soon. Now may I come inside?"

"Yes," she whispered, shivering slightly from the touch of his thumb.

He uncoiled, tugging her off the swing. Pulled open the screen door and walked her into the kitchen. Reached over and clicked off the oven, and the intensity of his gaze turned her warm all over.

His right hand stroked the curve of her jaw, so gently she trembled with wanting. He slid his other hand under her shirt, his fingers warm against her skin. She wet her lips and swallowed, but it was still difficult to breathe.

"Jenna," he murmured, cradling her face, staring with such intensity her breathing turned ragged. And then he shifted, his mouth brushing hers, moving slowly. She could feel the tip of his tongue and pressed forward, her senses whirling.

She rose on her tiptoes, wanting more of his teasing touch. Looped her arms around his head and urged him closer. His head abruptly slanted, his mouth hot and heavy now, until she lost herself in the kissing.

Somehow her bra released. He worked the T-shirt over her head, until she was bare breasted, his mouth and hands covering her with raw urgency.

She curled one hand through his hair even as he backed her to the wall and lowered his mouth over her breast. He stopped way too soon and she clung to his neck, breathless and wobbly.

He scooped her up and strode down the hall and into her bedroom. Springs creaked as he dropped her on the bed and yanked at his belt. His jeans dropped to the floor. He was gorgeous, big and clearly ready. She drew in a shivery sigh. Hoped he wasn't going to be too fast; it had been a long time since Colin.

His hands closed around her ankles and he pulled her to the edge of the bed. Tugged her jeans over her hips, clearly in a hurry. Hooked a thumb over her panties, eyes darkening with appreciation as he slipped them off.

He stroked her with a knowing finger. She jerked with impatience, trying to reach him, but he flattened his palm over her stomach, holding her in place. His warm mouth circled her navel then swooped lower.

She protested, but weakly. Aw, shit. She couldn't stand it. It felt so good and it had been way too long. She shattered in seconds, boneless, unable to move. "Thanks," she whispered, "but you shouldn't have done that. Now I just want to sleep."

"I don't think so." His chuckle sounded slightly wicked in the dark. He adjusted her against the pillow, cradling her head until she opened her eyes.

He kissed her then, deeply and intimately, doing such erotic things to her mouth, to her breasts, that she started tingling all over again. His palms were slightly calloused and moved over her body with deft assurance, finding all her hot spots, showing her new ones.

When his clever hand finally moved between her legs, she arched from the bed, afraid she was going to climax again but wanting it so badly, she gripped his damp shoulders and marveled at his control.

She reached down and stroked him. He sucked in a sharp breath and groped around the floor, fumbled with the pocket of his jeans. He rolled on a condom and nudged her thighs apart, staring with possessive eyes as he angled her hips to receive him. One hard thrust.

And even though she was wet and so very ready, she stiffened in discomfort. He paused, propping his elbows by her head, reassuring her with a deep kiss even as he reached down and stroked her with that wonderful hand, creating a pulsing pool of need.

She automatically widened her legs. He thrust further, lodged deeper, still stroking with his hand until a primitive urgency replaced the ache. Craving him now, she wrapped her legs around his hips until they moved with the rhythm of long-time lovers.

It was good and it had been so long. She tried to be silent, pressing her teeth against his shoulder and gripping his ridged back. His body tightened, one last deep thrust, and she couldn't stifle her moan.

She collapsed on the bed, unable to move, scarcely able to breathe, somewhat surprised that he had the energy to pull her close. He tucked the sheet around her and slid his hand to the back of her neck.

"That had to be better for me than you," she managed, still boneless.

"Not a chance." He kissed her so reverently, her heart lurched but continued to rub her neck, coaxing her closer until she settled into his chest, totally pliant while he cupped her breast and explored her body all over again.

"This was all great but I'm rather sleepy," she said, keeping her eyelids shut. "Guess I'll see you tomorrow."

He chuckled but continued his possessive sweep of her body as though memorizing her curves, silent, not bothering her too much. She wasn't used to sharing a bed but this wasn't too bad. She snuggled a tiny bit closer. He wasn't asking any questions and she loved his woodsy smell. Besides, his slow hands made her feel all protected and a little…aroused.

She obligingly parted her thighs, exhausted but curious and his fingers felt so good, his touch so tantalizing. She stopped thinking and minutes later groaned as another climax swept her.

She opened her eyes and stared, half dazed. But the room was dark, his expression hidden, her body and brain too lethargic. The most she could manage was to plant a grateful kiss on his chest. "You can stay overnight if you want," she whispered, then immediately wanted to retract the offer. He was too much of a dealmaker not to pounce, and her defenses had melted somewhere along with her multiple orgasms.

"Three nights," he said.

She pulled back an inch, too drained to escape to her side of the bed. Still, no man had slept overnight before. Emily had been a built-in chaperone, and a pretend boyfriend in the next town kept most men away. Burke, though, rammed like a runaway freight train.

"Three nights and I make breakfast. Plus," he added, lazily thumbing her nipple, "I'll even cook the fish tonight."

Her stomach rumbled. She'd forgotten all about the trout along with the apple cobbler in the oven. And now breakfast? Bacon and eggs had been a rarity since Emily left for college. "What kind of breakfast are we talking?" she asked. "Continental?"

"So suspicious." He chuckled and slid his hand beneath her hair until she'd settled back against his chest. Such a nice chest too. She traced the contours with her fingers, drifting lower, unable to resist some exploration of her own.

"All right," she murmured, "but you also put Peanut in for the night and cut up his carrots."

"Peanut's top of my list," he said.

Chapter Twenty-Two

Jenna clearly had no idea how sexy she was in her little shorts and white T-shirt, hair slightly tousled, one slim leg folded beneath her. Burke resolutely lifted his gaze to her face and slipped another piece of crisp bacon on her plate.

"Thanks," she said. "It's great you can cook too."

"Too?" He raised an eyebrow, trying to keep it light, but he hadn't been able to get enough last night. Even now, it was hard to keep his hands off her. Jenna's quick blush and accompanying wiggle on the swing made his body jerk to attention. Unfortunately, she didn't seem to share his fascination. She'd been trying to get rid of him for the last half hour.

"You probably have to go to the Center," she said, averting her gaze. "I can find a mug so you can take the coffee with you."

"Actually it's nice not to be bothered by staff," he said. "I'll do some work from here, if you don't mind."

"All right."

The words were carefully neutral. However, her mouth tightened and if her eagerness to be alone hadn't flattened his ego, it would have been funny. But this wasn't funny; it was damn frustrating. "I also want you to research some things for me," he said.

That got her attention and she leaned forward, so close he caught a hint of her flowery shampoo. "Of course," she said, still clearly contrite about her earlier oversight. "What would you like me to check?"

What could she check? He dragged a hand over his jaw. Something that would keep her by his side for several hours. "Just the stud fee increase over the last year…no, over the last five years. You also neglected the background check on Lorna and David, even though you had the entire week off. That fire was a shocker." He injected a hint of censure in his voice—people were always more pliable when off balance.

"I'm so sorry." Her eyes darkened with regret. "I'll start work on the Ridgemans right away."

Ah-ha. He had her now. He stretched his arm across the back of the swing, unable to resist fingering a tendril of her silky hair. "No need to rush," he said. "Relax and have another cup of tea first."

Jenna stared blankly at her phone. 'David Ridgeman, widowed,' but the rest of the words turned to black squiggles. Despite her best intentions, Burke was getting to her. She'd never been so intensely aware of a man's movements—his frown when he read something that displeased him, his bold scrawl when he made notations, the absent-minded way he stroked her hair.

He was a generous lover, a fabulous lover, and it seemed that her body had implanted the memory and now leaped to his faintest touch.

'David Ridgeman, widowed,' she read again, trying to make her brain work, trying to be like Burke who never had the least trouble concentrating. He'd been jotting notations for the last half hour, completely at ease, while she struggled with what had happened last night.

Just sex but it always seemed to arouse her needy feelings. And this time she couldn't bolt. He was always around, always anticipating; it was impossible to lock her defenses into place. Too bad he wouldn't leave today, just fly away to another job before she was sucked in too deep.

After last night, she wouldn't need sex for another year, maybe three. She sighed and leaned into him, not intending to cuddle but somehow he'd found the spot, that nagging shoulder soreness, and his hand felt so good. He cradled her against his chest with no pause of that swiftly moving pen, though he obligingly continued rubbing.

She hoped her little sigh of contentment had been inaudible. It was nice lounging around with a man—usually she bolted long before breakfast but it was difficult to leave when she was already home. His touch was soothing too, although surely he'd scold if she didn't snap out of her daze and finish the research.

Or maybe not?

His fingers drifted along her inner arm, her shoulder, along the curve of her collarbone. He wasn't even doing anything, his touch so light it was surprising she felt it. But she did feel it, every single stroke, and her nerves quivered beneath her skin.

She looked into his dark eyes, unable to move as that slow finger moved along her body, tracing her with such tenderness she wanted to cry.

"Don't fight things so much, honey," he said. "Everything will be okay."

But it won't. A lump balled in her throat as he tucked a strand of hair behind her ear. She wasn't like a normal woman. She should be ecstatic to spend time with such a wonderful man. Instead she was terrified.

"I have to go to the Center now," he said quietly. "Why don't you come with me?"

"No." Her voice rose. "I have to finish this research." And he was too magnetic, too overpowering. She needed to be alone, needed to reclaim her independence.

"Okay." He shuffled his papers and slipped them into his briefcase. "Guess you can see Nifty tomorrow."

"He's here?" She scrambled to her feet. "But of course, I'll come with you. Please wait a sec."

He grinned and she rushed into the trailer. Changed into jeans, pulled on her worn boots and stuffed a pair of thin leather gloves into her pocket. He was waiting in the car when she scrambled into the passenger's seat.

"Looks like you're planning to massage," he said, his eyes narrowing on the gloves.

"Just a quickie." She jammed the gloves deeper into her pocket, wishing he wasn't quite so observant. "I want to see how he feels in the hind end. With a glove, the blisters won't bother me at all." He looked so skeptical, she laughed. "He's a Derby winner.

Of course, I'm planning a massage. But I'll do all the Ridgeman and stud fee research first."

"You can work on that in my office," he said.

"Okay." She jammed on her seatbelt, eager to see Nifty, then realized she'd just agreed to another intensive day in his company…along with the next two nights. Her chest kicked with an equal portion of dread and longing. It would be much wiser to hang out in the staff room, away from Burke.

"We should probably get Nifty out to loosen up after his trip," Burke said, as he backed the car from the driveway. "Want to go over to the track with me? See how he moves?"

"Oh, yes. That would be great." She bounced in the seat, forgetting her reservations. She loved watching morning gallops but it ate up a lot of work time, and Wally had never approved of staff hanging around the oval. She stiffened, realizing she hadn't talked to Wally since he'd turned in his resignation. "Does Wally know Nifty's here?" she asked.

Burke stepped on the accelerator and the car sped up. "He's not a Three Brooks employee anymore."

"Of course. But this is a very famous horse, and I'm sure Wally wants to see him." She picked up her phone.

"I'd really prefer that you didn't call him." Burke's voice was silky smooth, but there was no mistaking its ring of command. "At least on company time," he added with a tight smile.

His smile was the clincher and she pocketed her phone. Besides, she'd rather speak with Wally when Burke wasn't within earshot. It seemed strange Wally would quit when he'd been so determined to hang on. And she wanted to know all the details.

They pulled alongside a gleaming silver trailer parked by the receiving doors. The ramp was down and the trailer was empty, except for a bored driver lounging behind the wheel. Clearly, the groom had already unloaded the horse.

"Did you ever see Nifty before?" She unbuckled her seatbelt, waiting for Burke to park, almost quivering with excitement.

"I was at Churchill the day he won the Derby. His stud value skyrocketed so they retired him early. He's a walking bank machine and deserves the best of care."

She bit her lower lip, her enthusiasm flattened. Nifty was a star and to Burke, it was all about book value. Beloved animals like

Peanut and Molly were worthless so didn't rate the Center's care. The stark economics of his world were depressing—and rather chilling.

"Top care. Absolutely," she muttered, gripping the door handle. "I'll lay down my life for him."

Burke reached over, covering her hand with his. "No need. Save that for me. Or at least three nights of it," he added softly. "And start thinking about what you want this evening."

Her gaze cut to his mouth and she gulped, no longer thinking of Nifty. "You mean, like…to eat?"

"Of course. What did you think I meant?"

His lip twitched and she blushed, but the pressure of his hand was so intimate, she couldn't help but remember what they'd been doing a few short hours ago. What they'd probably be doing again tonight.

He finally pushed the door open. She scrambled out, grateful for the cooling breeze, determined to steer her thoughts back to Nifty. And away from sex. This was turning way too intense. It would be wise to make up some excuse, to snuff out these feelings before it went any further. Conversely, if he were leaving soon she'd have no worries anyway.

She blew out a sigh of indecision and circled to the front of the car. "Are you interviewing any more managers today? When exactly are you leaving?"

He closed the driver's door, seemingly preoccupied with some data on his phone. "The groom is called Tank," he said, "although I guess you know that from your research this morning?"

"Yes, he's been with the horse for six years and three months."

Burke smiled. "Very good. Now let's go meet Tank and Nifty."

He always changed the subject when he didn't want to answer her questions, but at least he didn't lie. Besides, she was keen to see this big horse. Nodding, she followed him inside.

Tank was short and wiry and lingered around Nifty's stall as though on guard. "I was told to put my horse here. But there's not a single window." His brown eyes flashed with disapproval.

"Mr. Ridgeman requested this stall," Burke said. "He thought Nifty would be less agitated."

Tank snorted. "Nifty's never agitated. Some food, a mare and he's happy."

Jenna pressed her face against the mesh, studying the stud. Chestnut with a blaze. Three white feet. Standing square, appeared beautifully balanced and already eating hay as though unperturbed with his new home.

He raised his head and approached the screen. Sniffed her hand curiously, his eyes large and luminous, then moved over to the door and nudged Tank. Turned back to his hay and resumed chewing. Calm, composed, confident.

"What a cool horse," she said.

"He's Mr. Cool," Tank said. "But I still don't understand why he had to come here."

"We'll get him feeling better," Burke said. "Get his sex life back on track."

"There's nothing wrong with his sex life. It's much better than mine." Tank shook his head. "You'll get him out every day?"

Burke checked his notes. "Jog a couple miles a day but watch for stiffness in the hind."

"I haven't noticed any stiffness." Tank frowned, obviously unhappy with his orders to leave. "But I will miss him. He likes his peppermints and a carrot or two." He looked at Jenna, obviously realizing Burke wasn't the type to feed a horse peppermints. "Will you give him his treats for me?"

"Of course," Jenna said. "We'll take good care of him."

Tank sighed and gave Nifty an affectionate pat. "Then I'm taking some vacation. *Hasta luego.*"

He shuffled out the door, hands in his frayed pockets, not once looking back. Nifty charged to the front of the stall with an ear-splitting neigh but Tank had disappeared.

Nifty called again, his nostrils flaring a bright pink. "He'd probably be happier closer to the other horses," Jenna said. "Especially his first days away from Tank."

"He'll settle." Burke had already turned and gestured for Nifty's new groom to bring another hay net.

But Jenna lingered by the stall as Nifty circled, rustling the straw in obvious agitation. He was the only horse in this wing and with his trusted groom gone, the stud was definitely upset. The only person around was the technician attending the oxygen chamber. Clearly Nifty wasn't accustomed to solitary confinement. David Ridgeman was an idiot.

Her gaze cut back to Burke. "Couldn't we move him to the main wing? The Ridgemans probably won't be visiting for a while."

Burke's scowl was quick and disapproving. "This stall was already discussed. They want the horse alone. I'm surprised you'd even suggest a switch. It was an integral part of the agreement. Non-negotiable."

His rebuke stung. He was so inflexible. If he gave his word, it was good but any deviation was considered an absolute betrayal. Not a good person to lie to. She rubbed her arms, trying to ward off the sudden chill.

Burke's voice softened. "We'll get him out for some exercise later this morning. That'll help him relax and we can see what his problems are. Who's our top pony rider?"

"Wally is the best one to ask," she said, still gripping her arms.

"But I'm asking you."

"Guess it would be Terry and his quarter horse gelding," she muttered.

"All right. They can pony Nifty." His voice softened. "Jenna, the Ridgemans own this horse. If they want us to paint him pink, we'll do it. Never forget who calls the shots."

"Yes, boss," she said. "But we could at least make sure the paint is non-toxic."

His mouth flickered for a moment, resigned but amused. "Okay. Check the Internet for pictures. See if they had any toys in his stall. We can't move him but maybe we can make it more like home."

She smiled, relieved he could compromise even if it was minimal.

"My office is locked but here's an extra set of keys," he added. "You can use my computer this week." He reached in his pocket and tossed her a jangle of keys, his voice lowering. "Password is bluechip649."

Regret flattened her smile. His trust wasn't given lightly. "Thank you," she said. But her voice wobbled and she averted her head, unable to meet his gaze.

Chapter Twenty-Three

The information on Ridgeman was extensive and much easier to read on Burke's large computer screen than on her phone. The facility had certainly been plagued with bad luck.

The tragic fire that killed David Ridgeman Sr., along with seven valuable Thoroughbreds, was only the first of a rash of incidents. In the past year alone, a prize broodmare had broken a leg, David had lost his wife in a car crash, and Lorna had been in and out of two pricey rehab clinics.

Nifty was their major moneymaker, raking in a hundred thousand dollars per live foal and covering two mares a day. Ridgeman capitalized on the horse's popularity by sending him to Australia for the southern hemisphere breeding season. Jenna shook her head in dismay. No doubt, the stud was exhausted; they treated him like a sex machine.

An image of Burke's hard body flashed in her head and she permitted herself a brief moment of indulgence. Damn, he'd been good. She peeked over her shoulder. He tilted in his chair, feet propped on his desk, talking to someone called Edward while they debated which company they should 'fix' next.

Poor unsuspecting company didn't stand a chance.

She turned back to the screen and clicked another Ridgeman link. Pictures of the property, the paddocks, the barns. And there it was—Nifty's stall. No rubber balls or toys but a mineral lick on the wall and three airy windows. And it was in view of at least two other horses. Strange. The stall he occupied at the Center was the exact opposite of his longtime home.

Her neck tingled. She glanced back over her shoulder. Burke had finished his call and now stared with hooded eyes. "Find anything?" he asked.

She swallowed, still off balanced by his trust, guiltily aware she didn't deserve it. "No toys but the website says Nifty loves company." She drew in a deep breath. "Especially playful ponies with sweet dispositions."

Burke crossed his arms, and it was hard not to be distracted by his rippling muscles. She lifted her gaze and locked it on his face. "I'd be happy to lend Peanut as a companion for Nifty. Wouldn't even charge anything except a few solar sessions." Her words came in a rush now, but it was clear she couldn't sneak Peanut in any longer. Couldn't stand to deceive Burke that way. But her pony needed help. "Please," she added, hating the way her voice cracked.

"I'm working on something for the pony, but he's definitely not going in the stall next to Nifty. The little guy is looking better anyway."

That's because I've been bringing him up here. She turned away, struggling with despair, wishing she didn't have to tiptoe like a thief in the night. She couldn't do that any longer. But she couldn't stand back and watch Peanut die either.

Burke's chair moved. Seconds later, his hands flattened over the table, his heat covering her as he leaned down and studied the screen. "Is that the stall?" he asked. "Wonder why they insisted on the horse being alone?"

"Because David likes to hurt," she said, remembering the look on the man's face when he squeezed her hand, his obvious pleasure at causing pain.

Burke's warm breath fanned her neck. If she turned her head, she sensed his mouth would cover hers. *But he won't help my pony.* She squared her shoulders and stared stubbornly at the screen.

"Likes to hurt? That's ridiculous." Burke straightened and stalked toward the door, his frustration obvious. "I'm going over to the track to watch Nifty. You're welcome to come if you want."

"I want." She rose from the chair and trailed him to the car.

He opened the passenger door then circled the car and slid behind the wheel. Slipped on his dark sunglasses and wordlessly nosed the vehicle from the lot.

They climbed the steps to the balcony in front of the viewing stand. Nifty trotted past, head high, escorted by Terry and his muscular gelding.

"Looks good to me," Burke said, finally breaking the stiff silence. "Sounder than a lot of horses still racing."

Jenna shaded her eyes from the sun, straining to see. Nifty trotted perfectly, stepping underneath with a long, even stride— happy, healthy, eager. Only two other horses were on the track this late, both galloping with riders, and he tracked them with pricked ears, as though keen to race again.

"Well-behaved fellow," Burke added. "With that smooth action, I can see why he's in demand as a stud. Apparently he's booked for the next couple years."

"And a season in Australia, according to industry reports," she said, still watching Nifty. "I wouldn't be surprised if they tried to boost his mares from two to three a day."

"Not a good idea. His sperm count might suffer. The last thing Ridgeman wants is impotence."

"Yes, that's the last thing anyone would want." She couldn't resist a mischievous smile and glanced up, checking his expression, wondering if he was quiet because she'd avoided his kiss. But that top lip twitched and the wind ruffled his thick hair. He looked relaxed again, almost boyish. Obviously he enjoyed life outside office walls. Little wonder he grabbed a hammer whenever possible.

He even smelled as if he'd been working with wood again, and she moved a step closer, drawing in another appreciative sniff. "I thought the construction was finished?"

"I'm working on the interior now," he said.

"But isn't that an open building for storage?"

"That was the original intent. Sometimes in this job," he slipped his arm around her waist and gave a gentle squeeze, "a man has to be flexible."

She smiled, unable to remain annoyed despite his stubborn refusal to let Peanut into the Center. "You're the least flexible person I know. And Terry and Nifty are getting closer. You'd better move your arm so he doesn't see."

"What does it matter? I'll be gone soon."

"Really?" Her smile deepened. "You found a manager?"

"Seems so. Talked to a good candidate on the phone." He looked at her, his expression hidden by the dark sunglasses. "It really makes you happy I'm leaving?"

"Well, I'll certainly miss you," she said, "especially the first couple of weeks. But maybe you'd come back every spring and visit?" A weekend a year would be perfect. She'd love to keep in touch with him. She was so delighted by the prospect she tilted on her toes, brushing his mouth with an excited kiss. "There's a long weekend in May," she went on. "I'll put in now for vacation."

He remained motionless for a second, completely still behind the dark sunglasses. Then his arms tightened and he backpedaled her into the deserted viewing building. Yanked off his sunglasses and lowered his head. The kiss was hard, almost punishing, but when she tried to pull away, his mouth softened. Turned persuasive.

He really was a tremendous kisser and it was very private in the cool room. She linked her arms around his neck and twined against him. Already his hand was on her breast, thumbing her nipple, creating ripples of sensation. He tilted her against the wooded wall and pulled her shirt up. When his warm mouth replaced his hand, she went a little crazy.

She wrapped her calf around his leg and arched against the bulge in his jeans. He slipped his hand between her legs, his fingers moving over the denim, but not enough, not near enough, and she groaned with frustration. It was scary how quickly he'd aroused her.

He abruptly pulled away, yanked down her shirt and coolly replaced his sunglasses. "I'm rather busy now. Guess we'll finish this next May." He strode from the building and back onto the balcony.

She stared at his back, stunned and disbelieving. Fumbled with her bra, listening as he calmly called directions to Terry. And now they were discussing the weather. She pressed her hands to her cheeks trying to soothe the heat. Half horniness, half humiliation. She'd never felt so cheap. God, what a prick.

She stumbled past him, head averted as she fled down the narrow steps. The Center wasn't too far. Half a mile, max. She'd walk back. No way was she getting in his car. Never, ever again.

A vehicle slowed and she jerked around. Not Burke but a green security truck. If she hadn't been so shattered, she would have recognized the distinctive diesel engine.

"Hi, Jenna." Larry stuck his smiling head out the window. "Too hot to jog? Want a drive to the Center?"

"Yes, thanks." She climbed into the cab, struggling to act normal. "But could you drop me off at my place instead? I'm not working this week."

"No problem. It's not on my route but won't take long. And I want to thank you for reminding Mr. Burke about my firearms update. Getting a raise, can hardly believe it." His phone buzzed and he picked it up, his smile fading as he listened to the caller.

A brown clipboard lay on the seat between them. Larry was absorbed with his call so she tilted the board and scanned his schedule. Night checks this week were every hour, on the hour. Good to know.

She was going to bring Peanut up and stand him under the lights, in the oxygen tank and maybe even in the saltwater spa—and she wasn't going to feel an ounce of guilt. Not anymore. Larry shot her a curious glance, and she eased the clipboard back on the seat.

"Yes, certainly, sir," he finally said and hung up.

His knuckles whitened around the wheel and his Adam's apple moved convulsively, but he didn't look at her again. Seemed embarrassed by her presence.

"So, how's your day going?" she asked, trying to help him relax. She checked her shirt, wondering if things were a little askew. That would explain his discomfort but no, Burke had replaced everything he'd handled. *Asshole.*

Larry turned to the right and headed up the hill. Rocks pelted the bottom of the truck. She leaned forward, eyeing the pothole on the second curve, the deceptive hole that had already cost her two mufflers. Of course, they were in a rugged truck but still...

"Better slow down, Larry," she said. "The road's rough. Big pothole coming up."

He didn't slow. The truck's right wheel slammed the hole, bouncing her several inches off the seat. "Oops, well that's the spot. And there's my place." Her voice rose. "Better slow down a little."

He still didn't speak. If anything his speed increased as they topped the crest of the hill. "Larry! You know where I live. What are you doing?" And then she knew.

She twisted. A powerful black car loomed behind them. "What the hell did he tell you to do?"

"Drive to his house and not let you jump out."

"I'm not going to jump out, Larry. That would be stupid." Her hand crept to the door handle. *Click.* The locks dropped.

"Sorry, Jenna. He said you might try that."

Her jaws clenched as the truck roared down the road, only slowing when they approached the huge Three Brooks' mansion. Larry stopped at the top of the drive, scanning his side view mirror, clearly upset with his orders. "This doesn't seem right. Making you come here." His throat convulsed. "Guess if you're really scared, you don't have to get out."

"No." She shook her head, somewhat mollified by his concern. But Burke expected Larry's total obedience, and security jobs weren't plentiful. "It's okay," she said quickly. "Mr. Burke just wanted a meeting. I misunderstood the time."

She faked a nonchalant wave and stepped out, keeping a smile pasted until Larry's truck disappeared. Burke's car door slammed. She wheeled to face him, hands fisted, fury stoked with humiliation. "You're truly a professional prick. Bet you wouldn't treat your rich friends like that."

"I've never cared enough to treat anyone like that," he said.

She turned and strode up the driveway, head high. If he touched her, she'd plug him in his arrogant nose. But he caught her in three strides, clamped her arms at her sides, and she was reduced to impotent jerks.

Her father had taught her the head-butt move, to be used only in dire situations, but this seemed to qualify. She snapped her head up. However, he clearly was adept at street fighting and blocked it easily.

She was hogtied and helpless and the knowledge was infuriating. She wasn't going to cry, wasn't going to swear, but he'd have to let go of her sometime and when he did, she was going to kill him. She quivered with impotent rage, her fury escalating as she waited for the moment he'd relax that steely grip.

Swearing, he carried her around the side of the house, past the flowers, the fountain and the patio chairs.

He released her—she had one second of shocked comprehension—then hit the cold, bracing water. She went under cursing. Came up choking. The sonofabitch just stood by the edge of the pool.

He'd thrown her in the shallow end and she sputtered to her feet, arms and legs flailing, clumsy in her drenched clothes. Oh, no, her phone! She fumbled for her pocket, struggling to rescue it. Finally. Held the phone above the water, staring in horror at the display. But it was black, dead and dripping. Her phones calls to Em were finished.

She pressed it to her chest, her heart as broken as her phone. Water streamed over her face, but she was too defeated to push back her bedraggled hair. A wrecked phone at the worst possible time, now, when Emily needed her. Her shoulders drooped, and despite her best efforts an aching sob leaked out.

Something splashed. A moment later his big arms wrapped around her. "Don't cry, honey. Please don't cry."

But her anger had wilted, leaving her vulnerable, and the only thing she could do was cry—wracking sobs that tore at her chest, hurt her lungs and made it difficult to breathe. And she didn't understand him, not one tiny bit.

It was several minutes before she even managed to speak. "Why'd you do that…that m-mean thing in the viewing room?"

He was silent for a long time. When he finally spoke, his voice was so quiet she could barely hear. "Because I want you. And you don't want me."

"And that technique's been working for you?" She gave a hysterical sob and hiccupped.

He remained silent, and she was too drained to manage more words. His hand lifted, brushing her wet hair off her face but other than that they didn't move, didn't speak. He only held her in the clear water as though he'd never let go.

The sun was high and warming, rather pleasant really, and even though her shirt stuck to her chest it was already drying over her shoulders. She looked up, saw his bleak expression—so at odds with his usual control—and her natural compassion surged.

"I'm not trying to be difficult," she whispered, "but I've always known, have always said, relationships aren't good for me. That was never what we were about."

"I know, sweetheart. I'm sorry." He slipped his hand beneath her hair and cradled her, pressing her head tighter against his beating heart.

She swallowed, aching for both of them. "Mom didn't care much for anyone except my father," she said haltingly, her mouth pressed against his wet shirt. "But he made her less of a person, not more. Love can be so destructive. I remember the fists...taking Em and hiding with Peanut in the kennel. She should have left him." Her voice cracked, and she was glad he couldn't see her face. "She shouldn't have done that to us. To her."

"How old is Em?"

She glanced up. Burke's voice sounded rusty but it was the first time he'd shown much interest in Emily, and her chest gave its usual bump of pride. "Twenty. She's in Philadelphia taking her science degree. Finally, a Murphy will have some education."

"But you've done some studying."

His voice had sharpened and, too late, she realized her mistake. That was another problem with Burke; he was just too damn quick.

She wiggled from his arms, trying to distract him. Skimmed her hands over the top of the water, watching as it swirled around their bodies. His shoulders were completely dry and she splashed some water. "Hardly fair," she said, with forced gaiety. "I'm completely soaked, and your hair isn't even wet." She shook her head in disbelief. "I still can't believe you threw me in. Wish I was strong enough to return the favor."

He stared at her for a moment then abruptly sank beneath the surface. She edged forward, searching for his dark shape. He rose behind her, head sleek as a seal's.

"Now we're even," he said.

"Not quite." She dunked his head back down, realizing the extent of his remorse when he let her hold him under for five, ten, twenty seconds. Shit. She lifted her hand, allowing him to surface.

"You can hold me under much longer," he said, "if it makes you feel better." Rivulets streamed down his bleak face.

"Really?" She tilted her head. "How much longer? After all, I feel pretty bad." But she never could hold anger very long and hated to cause sadness in others. "How about you swim to the end and back?" she asked brightly. "Underwater. And doing the dog paddle."

"It's been a long time since I've done the dog paddle." A trace of amusement glimmered in his face. "Never was very good at it."

"Really." She stuck her nose in the air with exaggerated haughtiness, relieved to see a hint of a smile. "I was champion dog paddler of the entire county."

"The entire county?" And now he actually did smile. "Impressive qualifications, indeed. Perhaps a race is in order?"

"Definitely," she said. "To the end and back."

It took a minute to remove their boots. They both tried to cheat and grab a head start, but she was faster. Won again in the breaststroke although he beat her in the sidestroke race, and when she saw his effortless crawl, she merely grabbed his leg and let him drag her the length of the pool.

"You definitely won that one," she said, struggling to reach the bottom with the tips of her toes. Couldn't quite touch so gripped his shoulders, needing time to catch her breath. "Looks like you have an Olympic-caliber crawl, Burke." She tried not to pant because his breathing seemed unaffected, and he had definitely swam further. "I need to rest for a second but well done," she managed, still huffing.

"And you're definitely the dog paddle star, sweetie." He pulled her close, obligingly providing a convenient rest spot.

She tucked against her favorite part of his chest, letting him support her, and when her legs kept floating up, wrapped them around his thighs. "It's hard to swim in clothes, isn't it?" She closed her eyes, letting the sun warm her face. "It's also hard to stay mad," she added in a whisper.

His arms tightened but he didn't say a word and she was glad. For now, this was the perfect combination of sun, water, man. She blew out a sigh, accepting that her anger and hurt had dissolved. "How long can you stand here?" she asked.

"Long as you want." He paused and she could almost feel him thinking. "But you're not getting in my car with those wet clothes."

"You'd make me walk home after nearly drowning me in your pool?"

He grinned. "Only solution is to let them dry in the sun. Won't take long." He tugged off her T-shirt, ignoring her weak protest, and tossed the soggy ball onto a pool chair. Slid his hand behind her back and unclipped her bra with such skill, she experienced a prick of jealousy thinking of all those other women.

"There, much better." He tilted her so that water lapped around her breasts. Rather erotic although the sun seemed to make her skin itch, especially her nipples, and she half wished he'd use that big hand, his mouth, or even his teeth.

But he just lingered over her face, his lips brushing her cheek, then moving along her neck, agonizingly slow. At least kiss me, she thought, obligingly tilting her head. But no, his mouth had already wandered to her ear and while that was nice, fine in fact, her nipples were really tingling now and surely he noticed how they stuck from the water. It was scary how he could turn her on so quickly. Like earlier today.

She peered at him suspiciously. "You're not going to start something, and then, ah…leave me hanging again, are you?"

"No."

But he continued to nuzzle her neck and now—she wasn't sure how he did it—her entire body quivered, craving his attention. "Burke," she said, trying to twist to her feet, wanting now to move along to his bed. "I'm a little afraid of sunburn here."

"As well you should be." His hand obligingly moved to her breast, making her shiver under its lazy touch. "Is that better?"

"Much." She closed her eyes, feeling wanton and wicked as he caressed her. "Although the sun's very strong. I should soon cover up—"

"Let me," he murmured, his breath fanning her skin. "But hold still. This is delicate work. And I like to do it just right." His teeth closed around her nipple, and the intense pleasure almost jerked her from the water.

She groaned. He was definitely doing it right but he was working a little slow, and she wiggled with impatience.

"We better get your jeans off," he said. "Unsnap them, sweetie."

She reached down, lowered her zipper and tried to wiggle out. He wasn't much help, too busy concentrating on her breasts but she wasn't about to complain. Definitely didn't want him distracted. She finally kicked off her jeans and panties, locked her bare legs around him, and reached for his belt.

He stilled her hand, setting it back on his shoulder. "You're going to have an orgasm in a minute, but you're not running off afterwards. You're sleeping here with me. Okay?"

"Okay." She yanked her hand back down and fumbled at his buckle.

"You'll sleep here and I'll drive you home in the morning, and then we'll go on a little trip," he said. "Agreed?"

"Sheesh, Burke. Quit talking." She locked her lips on his mouth. Shouldn't have because he seemed to forget what he was doing and wrapped both arms around her, and now she couldn't even reach his belt.

But he was such a good kisser, so intense, so deep, so thorough. She shivered with pleasure as his tongue mated with hers and she lost herself in the kiss. Was barely aware when his nimble hand drifted between her legs and sent her spinning into orgasm.

She opened her eyes. He was breathing hard but then again, so was she. "You're very generous," she whispered, halfheartedly reaching for his bulging erection. He stopped her hand and she was relieved, much too drained of energy.

He grinned at her languor, the tiny lines around his eyes crinkling. He looked totally happy now, almost boyish, and she was glad. Her arm felt heavy but she reached up and tenderly touched his cheek. "If you let me go now, I believe I'd drown."

"But I'm not letting you go, Jenna." He kissed her forehead and carried her up the steps and out of the pool.

"Wait." It had all been very nice but now she stiffened, realizing he was fully clothed while she wore nothing at all. "My jeans are at the bottom of the pool."

"I know where your jeans are." His smile was rather wicked. "But you need to warm up."

She glanced over his shoulder at the sun, trying to calculate the time. She really should go home soon. Check on Peanut. Figure out a way to call Em.

"Stop thinking," he said. He pressed a button by the Jacuzzi. Water churned.

He padded down the steps. Hot bubbles wrapped around her like an old friend, hiding her nudity, a reassuring development especially since he was fully clothed. And wasn't having the other person naked a standard interrogation practice? She tugged at his shirt. "Play fair here," she said.

He chuckled but let her unbutton his shirt and pull it off before maneuvering her back onto his lap. Since he was being so agreeable and the water so soothing, she stopped thinking, tucked her head against his chest and let herself relax.

"This is my favorite spot," she said drowsily, unthinking.

"The Jacuzzi?"

"No, this spot on your chest. It's comfortable. I can hear your heartbeat. It feels safe."

"And I love you being there, Jenna," he whispered, his words strangely solemn.

She tried to remain still, but the odd note in his voice made her uneasy. "How long before my clothes are dry?" she asked, wondering if he would dive down and retrieve her jeans or if she'd have to.

"Don't worry. I'll look after them."

She knew she should protest, insist on getting dressed and away from there, away from him, but she'd agreed not to run off and besides he wasn't talking anymore. In fact, he was rubbing her shoulder, something she always loved, and the thought of hauling on wet clothes and leaving wasn't nearly as appealing.

"You sure Peanut was fine?" Jenna asked as she bit into her pizza, looking small and lovable in his over-sized bathrobe.

"He was fine, relieved you stayed here actually. We had some important guy time. He even told me a few secrets."

"Really?" She sniffed as though bored, but her cheeks turned slightly pink.

"Surprising things," Burke added, studying her face. Yes. He definitely spotted some discomfort. Even guilt. What the hell had she been up to? She dropped her half-eaten slice of pizza on the plate and reached for her wine glass.

"Of course," he went on, playing a hunch, "I've taken several horse telepathy courses so it simplifies communication. And Peanut is an excellent subject. Wants you to know he prefers cut-up apples, not those old carrots. He also confided about what you've been doing."

She leaned back in her chair, eyes wide, wine forgotten. Definitely a guilty stain in her gorgeous cheeks, and there was simply no way he could let this go. He blanked his face, drilling her with his eyes.

"I'm always truthful with you, Jenna." *Except about Wally.* He shoved aside his regret. "And I expect you to be honest as well." He scowled for added effect, but it was tough because he was much too distracted by her horrified expression.

A moment later she dropped her head and he could no longer see her face, but, ah shit, her shoulders quivered, and he wished he'd just let her keep her little secrets. He hated to see her upset. "Peanut didn't tell me much," he added quickly. "Nothing private, you understand."

She peered up, giggling, eyes moist with laughter. "Horse telepathy. You! For ten seconds there, I actually believed you."

He pushed his chair closer and scooped her onto his lap. "Ten seconds? That's all? Thought I was keeping a pretty straight face."

"You have that little twitch right here." Still laughing, she kissed the left side of his mouth. "Big giveaway, every time. It always was there, even when we first met. Remember that day?"

"Certainly," he said wryly. "You were robbing me blind, and I helped carry the contraband to your car."

"Now that I know you better, I'm surprised you didn't fire me on the spot. Why not?"

"Maybe I hoped to get lucky." He reached across the table and snagged his beer, needing something to occupy his hands.

"No, you're not like that. What was it? Tell me." She snuggled into his chest. Christ, she was impossible to resist when she did that.

"You were loyal to Wally," he said slowly. "Companies with loyal employees survive even when business gets tough."

"Sheesh, that's not romantic at all." She winkled her nose. "I would have made up something much better."

But the truth would scare her, he thought bleakly. He'd been intrigued from the moment she'd accused him of line butting. And now she was cuddled on his lap, so open and affectionate it was hard to believe she was still fighting this. He didn't have much time either, and the gut-wrenching feeling it wasn't going to work out simply wouldn't go away.

"Hey," she said, "you're cracking my ribs."

"Sorry." He loosened his arms and took a sip of beer.

"I can't believe you convinced them to deliver a pizza way out here," she said brightly. "Want another piece?"

It was obvious she was trying to cheer him up—she had a generous heart. However, it didn't belong to him and he had the perverse need to sulk. To have her fuss over him like she cared. So he only shook his head and scowled.

She just tucked her head back against his chest, completely unfazed. "Life sucks sometimes," she said. "What was the worst day you had when you were a kid?"

He didn't need to think. "I wanted to go home for Christmas, and my parents sent me to ski camp." He immediately felt ashamed. She'd probably never even had the chance to ski.

"Wish I'd been there." She pressed a kiss against the base of his throat, a balm to his frustration. "It would have been fun skiing with you, or at least trying."

"I'd enjoy doing anything with you, sweetheart." He rose, lifting her to her feet. "But for now, let's just go to bed." He grabbed her hand and pulled her away from the table.

She followed him trustingly, out of the kitchen and across the cold floor of the lobby, up the winding stairs and into his bedroom.

"I haven't been in all the bedrooms yet," he said, glancing out the window. "But this is the one I sleep in, closest to your hill. I can see your lights from here."

"Really?" She peered out the window, looking vaguely troubled. "So you can see if I'm up late?"

"Have you been carousing without me, sweetheart?"

She shook her head but he spotted a guilty flush. Ms. Jenna Murphy was definitely not a simple woman but at least she was here, in his bedroom. And sometimes an occasion should simply be enjoyed.

He turned from the window and traced a finger over the top of her bathrobe. "Time to return this, Jen," he said.

Her hands slipped to the knotted sash, and she gave him one of her rebel-angel smiles. "But you're still wearing quite a few clothes, even though I've been trying to get them off all day. Something we should work on? Some shyness with women, maybe?"

"Definitely some issues," he said. "My buckle's been sticking around other women ever since I came here. Ever since I met you."

She tilted her head, as though not quite understanding what he was saying. "It didn't stick before?"

"Never had this kind of problem," he said.

She reached down, skimming her fingers over his belt, tracing his outline, then cupped him. He swallowed but didn't move from the window.

"I'm not sure why your buckle wouldn't open earlier." She kneeled down. "Maybe I'll have another go at it."

She obviously didn't want to talk, and suddenly neither did he. He hadn't wanted to make love in a pool or hot tub, places where he'd enjoyed sex with so many women on so many other occasions. But as her fingers glided over his zipper, it no longer mattered where they were. If he didn't drive into her soon, he was going to explode.

He tried to yank his zipper down but she pushed his hand away. "This is delicate work and like you in the pool, I need to do it just right." Her smile was wicked, her soft breath tantalizingly close to his jeans.

He splayed his hands against the wall and tried to think of Edward and their last phone call—not what she was doing, so damn slow with his zipper. Edward was always in a hurry, always eager to move on but he wanted a good manager, wanted to make sure she'd be okay.

His mind blanked as her hand drifted along his length, cupping him, and he couldn't wait another second.

He twisted away and scooped her up, glad he had a condom close. Kicked off his tangled jeans and dropped her on the bed. Yanked her bathrobe apart and pried open her legs with raw urgency. Almost too urgent but she was wet and ready. He pushed in, groaning with pleasure.

She tensed but he already knew her buttons and rolled her nipple between his thumb and forefinger, waiting until she quivered and widened her legs. Drove deeper. Her body fit him perfectly now, molding around his and moving in perfect accord.

He kissed her fiercely, possessively, wanted it to last but he'd been under such taut restraint. Pumped faster, unable to slow. Found her breast with his mouth and angled her higher, driving harder, until she arched against him and their cries blended in mutual release.

Chapter Twenty-Four

Jenna woke alone in Burke's huge bed amid a tangle of sheets and the lingering smell of passion. She propped herself up on an elbow. The previous owners hadn't been given much time to pack. There was still a Canadian flag draped in one corner. She hadn't noticed that last night. Of course, there had been a lot she'd overlooked last night.

She flopped back on the bed. Burke was a wonderful lover and knew her body intimately. An erotic spot behind her knee, that area on the arch of her foot, her sensitive breasts—she'd never realized they were hot-wired to her orgasms. A man didn't achieve that kind of thoroughness without paying attention to a lot of women.

Which was good, because they both knew this thing was short-lived. He might get a little sulky but only because he was accustomed to calling the shots. She thrust aside the covers and stepped onto the hard marble floor, flinching at the cold beneath her feet.

Strange how rich folk always chose marble and slate. Those surfaces were unforgiving. If you were knocked down, it'd be tough to pick yourself up. Probably left plenty of bruises too.

She rubbed her arms and walked around the cool room, searching for the errant bathrobe. Couldn't find it anywhere. Not under the bed, not hanging in the enormous bathroom and not in the walk-in closet. Plenty of suits though. She scanned the hangers. Scary power suits carrying private labels and the smell of money.

She backed out quickly. Yesterday Burke had worn jeans and a shirt, and it was easy to forget he was grossly rich. She wanted no part of that life. Meanwhile she didn't have a thing to wear.

She sensed a presence and somehow knew he was there. She turned, resisting the urge to cover her nakedness with an ineffectual arm. He'd paused in the doorway, looking so ruggedly handsome in a simple black T-shirt, her breath stalled.

"Hi," she managed.

His gaze swept her with such honest appreciation, her self-consciousness faded. If anyone knew her body, this man did.

"What are your plans today," he asked, his gaze now locked on her face.

"Um, tea, shower, massage Nifty."

"Okay. After that, would you like to fly to Atlantic City? Visit a casino. Have a little fun."

She remembered him mentioning a trip and stiffened in a blend of fascination and fear. Edged back a step, shaking her head.

"Could make a few dollars," he added, "to put toward your sister's tuition."

Her automatic refusal stalled in her throat. She tilted her head, swept with a rush of interest. "Is it easy to make money?"

"No, but it's always a good time."

Her gaze shot to the closet and his intimidating wardrobe. "I don't have anything to wear," she murmured.

"We'll look after that later. Besides, you always look beautiful." He glanced longingly at the bed, his voice turning husky. "Honey, you better get dressed, or I'm not going to make it in to work."

"I'm trying to," she said wryly, "but the last time I saw my clothes they were at the bottom of the pool."

His boyish smile tugged at her heart. "I forgot." He strode into the closet, then emerged with a white T-shirt. "Slip this on for now and come have your tea. Your clothes are in the dryer."

The shirt only reached mid-thigh and was probably transparent. However, she felt more composed even partially clothed, and followed him to the patio. He'd obviously been working for a while. Sheets of paper were stacked by a silver coffee pot.

"Can I help with anything?" she asked.

He was intensely private with his work, and she was surprised when he slid over a thin file. "I need to decide on one of these companies. My cousin, Edward, is pushing for a decision. Wants me to leave right away."

She nodded and stared at the file, surprised by the tightening of her chest. Of course he was leaving. She knew that. Wanted that. She scanned the summaries: a hotel in Boston, a health resort in Maine or a pharmaceutical company in California. "I think the Boston or Maine companies would be best," she finally said.

"Why?" His dark eyes didn't leave her face.

"Because they're service industries, like Three Brooks, and they seem to fit your experience."

"I see." His voice turned clipped.

"And they're also pretty close." She played with the corner of the file, not looking at him, folding it back and forth and mangling its crease. "Maybe you could visit the Center when you're flying past. Check on our progress."

"I don't do that. My role is to streamline processes, establish competent management. Unless specific arrangements are made with…specific people, there's no going back. Ever."

She stared at the sheet, a lump tightening in her throat. Could feel the intensity of his gaze but didn't want to look at him. Couldn't.

"Then that's unfortunate," she said.

The plane leveled in the air. Jenna gripped her armrests, trying not to appear gauche but secretly thrilled. This was so cool. First class too. She peeked at Burke who stretched in the seat beside her. He'd already opened his laptop and now scrutinized numbers on a black and red spreadsheet.

She checked the company name: Edge Technology, probably the pharmaceutical company in California. He'd withdrawn a notch since this morning, in fact hadn't even kissed her. Which was fine since he'd had his mouth all over her last night. Sometimes men pouted like babies.

Even Colin had acted as if she'd carved his heart out, but she'd always been honest. Heck, girls needed sex too. Burke should be happy there were no strings attached.

It might not be a very good time in Atlantic City though. She hoped he wouldn't ignore her. He glanced up, caught her eye and winked, then bent back over his numbers, but his reassuring gesture turned her chest fuzzy.

She adjusted her seatbelt then played with the entertainment system, but there didn't seem to be any sound. Leaned forward and looked out the window. Thick clouds blocked her view.

"Anything from the bar, madam?" A flight attendant removed her empty teacup and carefully set down a napkin and some giant cashews.

"Red wine, please," she said. Service was excellent and had started before the plane even left the ground. She was so excited, she considered ordering a double rum and coke, but probably gambling while drinking wasn't the smartest plan.

Burke ordered beer, a brand with a moose head on it, but remained absorbed with the numbers on his computer screen. She leaned back, then tilted forward again, studying every detail of the plane. Some of the other passengers were talking. If she had the aisle seat, she could have made conversation with the friendly gentleman in the polo shirt.

"I'll be finished soon. Need these numbers for a meeting tomorrow," Burke said. "Then I'll have the rest of the day. And night."

The implicit promise in his voice made her stomach kick. The plan was to catch a morning flight tomorrow and be back at the Center by noon. She had no idea where they were staying, but Frances had promised to feed Peanut. Jenna would have preferred Wally. Unfortunately, no one had seen him for days.

Concern for Wally tempered her excitement and she picked up a cashew, rolling it idly between her fingers.

Burke shot her another glance, turned his shoulder to the friendly man across the aisle, and closed his laptop with a decisive click. "What's on your mind?"

She flushed. "Nothing really."

He raised an eyebrow.

"Just wondering where Wally's gone," she admitted. "Would you have kept him as the manager if he hadn't quit?"

"No," he said.

"But if you can't hire someone else?" His tanned throat rippled as he sipped his beer, distracting her, and she had the crazy urge to lean forward and press her mouth against his neck. She'd always loved his throat, right from the very first day.

"Edward's found someone," Burke said. "Competent lady. I talked with her at length on the phone. She's arriving tomorrow. She'll stay at a motel until Wally's apartment is vacant."

"Oh, I didn't realize you'd found someone." She jerked her head away, breaking the cashew into four tiny pieces. "You never told me you'd hired a manager."

"Why would I? That's not your area of expertise," he said.

Not her area of expertise. A flush warmed her cheeks and she twisted toward the window. His blunt comments always cut deep—always knocked her off balance. She knew she was only a bedmate, something they both wanted, but he didn't have to remind her. No need to belittle.

She stared at the clouds, needing a moment to hide her pain. The only thing she still controlled, and something that clearly irritated him, was that she wanted him to leave. He wanted her to beg him to stay, for some reason wanted to strip her last bit of pride. And that was absolutely not going to happen.

When she turned back to him, her voice was level. "Of course, hiring a manager isn't my area of expertise, but I thought you'd tell me, simply to share the good news. And I'd be happy to drive you to the airport when you go…see you off."

He smiled wryly but she failed to see the humor. He'd barged into her world, turned it upside down, made her feel things she didn't want to feel. Had provided a taste of a sweeter, more complete life. Probably why he'd suggested this little jaunt, although she wasn't sure he could be that calculating. He just wanted some entertainment.

Still, give anyone half a chocolate and they'd be hooked, eager for more. Burke knew that. Heck, she knew that. Her economics teacher had taught it back in grade eleven, and she'd been preaching it to her sister for years. She blew out a worried sigh, not sure now if Em would even pass her economics.

"We'll buy a new phone when we land," he said quietly. "So you can keep in touch with your sister."

Her chest squeezed, and she fingered her wineglass. She'd never been around anyone who was so attuned to her thoughts.

"And there are some stores in the hotel where you can do a little shopping," he added. "In case you have hostess or tour duties at the Center. I also want you to get something to wear tonight."

She stiffened and a drop of wine spotted the top of her thumb. *He doesn't like the way I dress?* "No need," she muttered, trying to steady her shaking hand.

"I want to," he said, in a tone that brooked no argument.

Three hours later, she stood numbly in the dressing room of a designer boutique, watching as the saleslady rushed in with another cocktail dress, shoes and an exorbitantly priced bra.

"That outfit is stunning but you definitely need these shoes," the lady said. "Then there's the negligee, the underwear and those other things he sent—"

"No, please. That's enough," Jenna said. "I'm finished. Just put my old clothes in a bag."

"Are you sure? He told me to bring in all these other things." The lady paused, looking disappointed before shrugging and turning away.

Jenna stared in the elegant mirror, barely recognizing herself. The dress was cut very low and with the fancy bra, she felt exposed. The material also showcased her curves much more intimately than anything she'd ever owned.

She stepped out, walking cautiously on unfamiliar stilettos. Burke lounged in a wide chair, tapping on his laptop, but clearly sensed her presence. He glanced up, then leaped to his feet, grabbing the laptop before it slammed to the floor.

"Isn't she stunning?" the saleslady asked, fluttering around Jenna.

"She's always stunning," he said, pulling out a credit card.

Jenna gave him a wobbly smile. Maybe he didn't totally hate her jeans. She was still shocked at the ridiculous prices and stunned by his insistence that she buy all these clothes as well as another phone. She never understood his motives but didn't want to spend the evening arguing with him.

He picked up the laptop and plastic bags. "Ready?"

And that was it. His hand rested on her elbow as he guided her back to the hotel, through a vast atrium with dark glass and water bubbling over rocks. A valet accompanied them to a private elevator, and when she stepped out, she was in a large penthouse. An elevator—direct to their room, definitely very secure, definitely very cool. Definitely different.

Her eyes widened as she wandered through the living room, past the Persian rug, the wide-screen TV, the smell of freshly cut flowers. "Wow," she murmured. "A person could get used to this."

"I hope so," he said.

She spun around, flustered, still awed by the huge suite. They had to be sharing it with someone. Maybe they were meeting his cousin, this Edward guy he always talked to. "I notice there are two bedrooms," she said cautiously. "The second?"

"Won't be used."

He crossed the room, wrapped her in his arms and gave a reassuring kiss. "Let's go down to the poker rooms and make you some money."

It took her an hour to relax and stop gawking but there were so many players, so much pulsing energy, and the atmosphere was infectious. She couldn't concentrate on her cards and glanced again at Burke who sat completely stone faced, with a pile of colorful chips stacked in front of him.

And she was way out of her element. Sitting on the porch, laughing and teasing with him, was fun. This was not. The money sliding back and forth was scary. She counted her chips. If she lost this hand, a thousand dollars of his money would be flushed down the drain.

Why had he chosen such an expensive game? No limit hold 'em, and she was barely holding her own. She turned over her crappy cards and gathered her remaining chips. "I'm out," she said, rising from the table.

"Me too," Burke said, and the other players looked relieved.

"What is it, sweetheart?" he asked quietly, his eyes concerned.

"Sorry. Guess I'm too cautious to be a real gambler. I couldn't stand the thought of losing all that money."

"You were doing great."

She shook her head. "No, I wasn't. I started losing after that guy with the cowboy hat and aviators joined in. And every time the dealer took my chips, I wanted to smack his hand."

Burke chuckled. "You'd have me barred from my favorite casino. You just need a change of pace. Come on."

He led her from the poker room, around a cluster of tables and to the front of a buzzing room where the action appeared even more clogged. "Blackjack, five dollar table. Pure fun." He sorted their chips. "We'll both play with a hundred dollars and leave when we're finished. At the end of the night, we'll still have almost ten thousand. Could have been more though." He glanced back at the poker rooms with a trace of wistfulness.

She remembered the rapid check-in, and the man in the tuxedo who'd greeted him by name. "You come here a lot?" she asked slowly. "You're a big player?"

"Competent. But you gave me unusual luck tonight." He shrugged off her question. "Now about blackjack. Have you played much?"

"Only on the computer."

"Perfect."

She couldn't lose. The stone-faced dealer turned her card over, revealing another twenty-one. Burke pushed a purple chip in front of her and calmly sipped his beer.

She didn't want to know what the purple color was but sensed everyone watched with heightened interest. The man on her right fingered his cards then reached over and grabbed her arm. "Can I rub you a little and borrow some of that shit-hot luck?" he asked.

Burke's eyes narrowed to dangerous slits, and the man quickly removed his hand.

The dealer flipped over his last card and shrugged. Twenty-two. Jenna stared in disbelief as he shoved a pile of markers in front of her.

"I think Blackjack is your game." Burke grinned and passed her a plastic container. "But it's two in the morning. Tip the dealer and let's go."

She jerked in disbelief. It had been ten o'clock the last time she'd checked but the friendly people, the wine, the winning—it had all been totally exhilarating. "I didn't spend all the hundred?"

"Jenna, you made about nine. Now go cash in." He pushed her gently toward the cashier.

She watched in delight as the machine flipped out bills. Nine hundred and eight dollars. That should buy Emily a few books, winter hay for Peanut, maybe even fix the exhaust on the Neon. But a hundred dollars belonged to Burke.

Holy shit. He'd moved to a special teller and the machine spewed money. Big money. The cashier said something and he grimaced, signed some papers, and turned back to Jenna. "Don't want to screw up your income tax so I cashed in your poker chips. You made about six thousand."

She stared at his wad of money. "Not mine," she said slowly. "I didn't do well at poker. That's yours."

He tugged her toward the elevator, inserted his room card and the elevator smoothly lifted. "Hard to say who won what," he finally said.

But his eyes flickered and she entered their suite, aware he was lying. The big money was his. She'd barely broke even at poker, wasn't half the player he was, if that.

She walked into the bedroom, past the mirrored wall and sank onto the edge of the massive bed. All those times she'd beaten him at cards, he couldn't have been trying. Even when they'd been playing for sex.

He walked in behind her. Silent. Watchful.

"You said you were always honest," she said slowly, "so tell me. The first night at your house, when you pulled a three—

"It was a two," he said.

"Did you cheat?"

He sank down beside her, crossing his arms. "That was a while ago. What does it matter?"

"But I don't understand." She scanned his face. "We were playing for sex and you deliberately lost?"

He shrugged, looking oddly embarrassed. "You didn't seem comfortable. I thought you needed more time."

She squeezed her eyes shut and leaned forward, resting her head against his shoulder. "That was a really nice thing to do. But I don't understand how you can be so good at cards?"

"I play a bit. A lot actually," he admitted.

"Damn." She gave a broken laugh. "There go our card games."

He slipped a hand under her hair, rubbing the nape of her neck. "What's bothering you about all this?"

"I can't take your winnings. I understand now what you're trying to do and it's very generous of you—incredibly generous—but I can't accept it. The clothes and phone are already too much. Anything else will make me feel cheap. God knows I usually feel like that." She raised her head, blinking against the sting in her eyes. "I do appreciate this trip though and I, well, I think you're wonderful."

Sighing, he pulled her onto his lap. "You're one frustrating woman, and I'm pretty much out of options here. Can't bribe you, can't impress you, can't seduce you."

"Well, I'm not sure about that last one." She gave a wobbly smile. "I don't see why you couldn't come back and visit me once in a while. Not just in the spring, but maybe a little more often." Her words came in a rush, as if they'd been circling for a while, scrambling over each other and longing to escape.

"Like every six months?" His voice flattened.

"Yes, sure. That would be perfect." She nodded eagerly, glad he was finally willing to consider that option. "We could fish, you could beat me in cards, I'd let you chase my pony, maybe do some roofing, which by the way still needs—

He pressed a finger against her mouth. "Jen, that won't work for me."

An ache squeezed her chest. She wanted him to stay, craved his company, could barely think of anyone else. Emily, Wally, Peanut—they were all on her periphery now. Was this how her mother had felt, feelings so centered on a man they'd turned destructive?

She'd always thought her mother weak but her father had been a smart and relentless charmer. Probably her mom had been powerless. Had fallen too deeply in love and then simply let him yank her chain.

She squeezed her eyes shut for a moment. "But that's all that will work for me," she said brokenly. "That's all I can give."

His face was stony, shadowed by the elegant bedside light. "We better get some sleep," he said. "It's an early flight."

She nodded and rose, but this luxurious suite now seemed like a waste. They'd barely spent an hour in it. She walked woodenly into the huge bathroom, past the fancy Jacuzzi surrounded by strawberries and champagne.

I should have taken some pictures. Something to look at when he was gone and life had jolted back to normal. But her phone was too new, and it would take time to figure it out. In the meantime, he'd spent a lot of money—the trip, the phone, the clothes; he'd probably expect some damn good sex. A band tightened painfully around her chest.

She removed the tags from the negligee and walked back into the bedroom, self-conscious in the scanty silk. It looked fine but was clearly designed for seduction, and she was relieved he was still in the dining room.

She slipped between the cool sheets. Listened as he rustled some papers then walked into the bathroom. He seemed to be taking a long time, and despite her ambivalence about this pricey excursion, she couldn't stop a shiver of anticipation. Couldn't deny her feelings.

She didn't understand why he was so averse to visiting. Maybe they could try monthly visits. See how that worked. But an image of her forlorn face counting down days in a calendar, waiting for his next overnighter, left her gripping the sheets in panic.

He walked back into the bedroom. The room darkened, and the mattress shifted as he sank onto the bed. She turned to him, waiting. It was a huge bed. She couldn't even feel his body heat. She scooted a couple inches closer, waiting for his big arm to tug her close.

"Good night, Jenna," he said.

"Good night," she said automatically, but shock jerked her rigid. His breathing was deep and even but dauntingly far away, and hurt balled in her throat.

She had a pesky itch behind her eyes but refused to move. In a moment, she'd fall asleep too. She wasn't at all bothered by this rejection. And it wasn't a rejection, not really. They were both tired. Possibly he didn't realize it was one of their last nights together, that the countdown had begun.

But her eyes really itched now and she couldn't stand it. She eased her hand up and wiped her face, surprised by the wetness on her cheek Blinking, she stared at the dark ceiling, determined not to move her arm again, determined to fall asleep.

But the more she tried, the more sleep wouldn't come.

Chapter Twenty-Five

"Time to get up."

She cracked her eyes open and sat up, blinking away the confusion. It had been a horrible sleep. The mattress was too hard, the pillows too soft and Burke hadn't touched her all night.

"Sleep well?" He stood beside the bed, knotting his tie.

"Great, thanks." She stretched and pushed back the sheets. His eyes flickered over her negligee and she gave a tentative smile, wary of his new coolness. In the early days, she'd have been flippant but now, when she cared, uncertainty had set in. A fragile dependency that she didn't like. "Is that bacon I smell?" she asked, scrambling for safe ground.

"It is. And there's tea and lemon on the table." His voice was cool. "But get changed first."

"Of course," she said numbly. She'd be more confident in her clothes anyway, much better than being half-dressed. And they could linger over breakfast and maybe regain their easy relationship.

He paused in the doorway. "I ate earlier. Have a meeting now but I'll be back in half an hour. Then we'll take a limo to the airport."

Her cautious smile froze and she could only manage a nod as he grabbed his laptop, walked toward the door and pushed the button.

"Have a good meeting," she said, but the elevator arrived, the door slid open and he didn't seem to hear.

*

Burke studied the most recent figures Edward had supplied. Labor unrest and poor management but a great product. Looked like California would be his next stop. Definitely a hostile environment but one that suited his mood perfectly.

He glanced sideways. Jenna stared out the plane window, her face solemn. She was tearing him up, and he wanted to shake her. And *that* wouldn't advance his cause. Preferably, he'd like to shake her parents.

She turned, eyeing him so cautiously, his restraint crumbled. He slid his arm over her shoulders and pulled her close. "I don't want to let this thing we have go," he whispered. "But I will, if that's what you want. I'm not going to push you. No worries." He kissed the top of her silky hair, sucking in her fresh fragrance. "You okay to drive to work on Monday?"

She gave him such a big smile, his chest thumped. "My hand's pretty good now," she said. "I'll be fine."

"You want to massage Nifty this afternoon?"

"Yes. He felt good yesterday. I didn't find any problem areas." She straightened and it was clear her thoughts were locked on the horse. "Don't you think that's odd? Nothing showing up in the massage? Usually I feel something. Is it possible the Ridgemans are exaggerating?"

"And why would they do that?" His shoulder felt cold and empty, and he wished she'd lean back against him and stop thinking about work. Maybe she'd let him come back once a month, at least for a start.

"I'm not sure," she said. "But some of the research suggests they're struggling financially. And Colin knows of two mares Nifty covered last year that didn't produce foals."

"You were talking to Colin MacDonald? About confidential company business?" A muscle ticked on the side of Burke's jaw. That damn vet was going to be around after he left, just waiting to pick up the pieces. The man would probably wait another decade for Jenna. Only a fool would do that—a fool or a very patient man.

He rubbed his tight knuckles. "Surely you have some understanding of client confidentiality," he muttered. "And your job is to give massages, not question owner finances or why they sent their horses."

"I know my job." She raised a stubborn chin. "But I thought *yours* might be to check some facts with your contacts. And I didn't reveal anything to Colin. I just wanted to talk to you about Nifty's owners."

"You better get used to discussing this stuff with the new manager." His mouth tightened with frustration. He wanted to talk about *them*. Not work, not Nifty and definitely not the lovesick vet. "I'm already busy with my next project," he muttered. One she was urging him to take.

"Of course." She inclined her head and turned away.

"Jenna," he stopped, afraid of what he might say. He'd completely botched this. His control was splintering and any minute, he'd be begging at her feet.

It was a relief when the plane landed and he was back in his car, in control of something again. Anything. He gripped the steering wheel and pressed his foot on the accelerator, relieved when the Audi responded.

"I'm meeting the new manager this afternoon," he said. "Not much time to spare but we can stop at your house on the way. You can change and then massage Nifty."

He parked in her driveway and waited while she changed into a pair of jeans and T-shirt. He liked that she was always so fast but, dammit, she grew more beautiful every day. His melancholy grew as she rushed to the kennel and checked on Peanut. At least she'd be happy about what he'd built for her pony.

The passenger door opened. She slid back into the car and thrust something on his lap. "Here's a little something so you won't forget us."

He stared down at the compact photo album. Remained silent for a moment before flipping it open, knowing he'd never forget her. Slowly, he scanned the pictures. Everything was there, almost from his very first day. Pictures of the Center, pounding studs at the construction site, all the staff waving, even Wally. And, of course, steeplechase day.

"Who's the kid on my shoulders?" he asked, fighting the constriction in his throat. "I think she sent me a letter."

"That's little Sophie and there's Charlie slapping your hand after he won."

"This is great." His voice sounded odd. "I didn't see you taking all these pictures."

"Phones are good that way," she said.

"You even have one of me sweating on your roof."

"My personal favorite," she said, and the sadness in her voice made his heart squeeze..

He coughed, struggling with his reaction. "Thank you, Jenna," he finally managed. "This is one of the most thoughtful things anyone's ever given me." He fumbled in the console for the necklace, knowing expensive jewelry wouldn't mean much, not to her, but at least it was something. He wanted to give her something.

He pulled out the Tiffany box, silently thanking the sales clerk for decorating it with pretty white ribbon, and pressed it into her hand.

She opened the lid, cautiously lifted the necklace, watching as it glittered beneath the hard sun. "Thank you. It's beautiful." Her eyes narrowed. "But who's Theresa?"

Damn! His hand whitened around the steering wheel. "I'm sorry. The store must have mixed up the two necklaces."

"So she has one that says my name?" Jenna's voice cracked.

"Actually I didn't have your name on it."

She closed the box then, her throat moving in curious little bobs that seemed linked to his own convulsing throat. *Aw, shit.*

"Smart," she said. "Leave your options open. Have to hand it to you, Burke. You really know how to make people feel special." Her voice flattened. "My father did that once. Gave my mom a bracelet with someone else's name on it. Of course, he'd stolen it. You didn't steal this, right?" She forced a smile but her lips quivered, tiny trembles that tore at his chest.

He plucked the box from her hand. "I'll sort this out."

"No problem. It's the thought that counts." Her voice quavered and he reached toward her, but she pushed his arm away. "Let's get going. You have a manager waiting."

"Jenna, please." His chest was so tight, it was hard to breathe. "Theresa is an old friend, a past friend. I didn't mean to hurt you."

"No one ever does," she said.

*

Jenna trailed her hands over Nifty's back and hindquarters, feeling for any soreness, watching his reaction. His ears flicked but he remained remarkably quiet, showing no pain, nothing that would account for his problems in the breeding shed.

If in fact, he really did have a problem.

Tank didn't think Nifty had any physical difficulties, and no one knew a horse better than his groom. Of course if the stud's sperm count were low, that would be an entirely different problem. He could physically do the deed, just couldn't accomplish the desired result. It would be disastrous for the Ridgemans to lose Nifty's services.

She tried to remember exactly what David had said, but her mind kept sneaking to Burke. Damn him. She'd let him worm his way into her heart, a place she always kept tightly sealed, and *wham*.

Without warning, the door swung open and Nifty spooked, knocking her sideways. She straightened, trying to soothe him.

"Please knock when you enter," she said over her shoulder.

"I forgot," Burke said, his voice deep, impersonal and not a bit apologetic. "Jenna, this is Barb Schmidt. Barb, this is Jenna Murphy, our talented masseuse. Jenna has a therapeutic massage diploma as well as an equine certificate."

Jenna nodded a greeting, not looking at Burke, trying to ignore her gut wrenching guilt at the lies he'd repeated. It was much easier to concentrate on the new manager and her beautifully cut suit, her perfect hair, her gleaming white teeth.

"Excellent." Those teeth flashed again as the new manager smiled up at Burke. "Proper credentials are another aspect of the Center that I'm extremely enthused about. Derek, I'm thrilled the staff are all qualified, at least to acceptable standards. Are you working on your degree part-time, Jenna?"

Jenna's fingers pressed a little harder into Nifty's hindquarters, and he swished his tail in warning. "Not right now," she said.

"Well, I understand there's a college very close. And increasing staff qualifications will strengthen the magnificent job Derek has started here." Barb beamed another ingratiating smile at the man by her side. "I'm thrilled to be part of Burke Industries."

"It does have its perks," Jenna muttered, ignoring Burke's sharp glance.

"So this area is dedicated to massage but restricted to two horses a day." Barb frowned as though confused. "Two massages will leave you with a lot of extra time. But we'll pull together. Jenna. Find enough work to keep all the team busy, even if it means mucking out stalls."

Nifty's tail swished again and Jenna pulled her hands back, forcing her fingers to lighten. But she resented Wally's replacement: this woman with her fawning smile, her irritating eagerness and most of all her troublesome college reference.

She wished the Canadians hadn't sold, wished everything had stayed the same, wished Wally was still the manager. She shot a look at Burke, but he wore a bored expression even though Barb was literally hopping on her heels trying to capture his attention.

"A good scrubbing, that's what this room needs." Barb continued her prattle, glancing around the room. "And what do you think of a coat of paint, Derek? Something to brighten the place, maybe varying shades of red. I see what you mean about how the last manager let things slide."

Jenna clamped her mouth shut, but somehow the words leaked out. "Wally was a good manager," she said. "The horses always left with a bounce in their step, and he was brilliant at analyzing their problems. Compassionate too. Never turned anyone away. He also knew horses have trouble seeing certain colors, such as red."

Oh, no. What am I doing? She sucked in a breath, her hands freezing over Nifty's back. And she wished for a long stick to pull back the color comment. "Of course, it's difficult to know what colors they really distinguish," she added, forcing an agreeable nod. "Actually red is a brilliant idea, Barb." But now she only sounded sarcastic, even though she hadn't intended to knock Barb. Not really. Well, maybe a little.

Barb's smile pinched and she crossed her arms, glancing at Burke as though searching for direction.

"I'm sure Jenna and all the staff here will support you in whatever decisions you make," Burke said. "We'll visit the oxygen room now. It's one of the Center's more effective applications."

Ouch. Jenna winced and dropped her forehead against Nifty's rump, drawing comfort from his solid bulk. His tail swished and she quickly stepped away, because, although the stallion was being extremely cooperative, he was still a stud and she didn't want to push his tolerance. He could kick her chest in as effortlessly as Burke.

She led Nifty back to his lonely stall, guilty at his disappointed expression. "I'll bring you some company tonight, fellow," she promised, slipping him a peppermint. "The friendliest pony in the world."

She trudged down the hall and paused at the reception desk. "So, did you meet the new manager? What do you think?"

"I dunno." Frances moved a stack of papers to the side of the desk, concealing her crossword puzzle. "But there will never be anyone like Wally."

"I've been calling and he never answers. Have you seen him lately?"

"No. Not his truck either. I'm surprised he quit," Frances said. "Three Brooks was all he cared about. Wish things had stayed the same. Horses like Nifty create too much work. I had to order special feed and the phone hasn't stopped ringing. An insurance company even wants to come next week and run some tests. Do you think the new manager will make me give tours?"

Jenna shrugged, her gaze shooting to the door of the oxygen chamber. Burke and Barb might emerge soon. Probably best if Barb didn't catch them gabbing. Their new boss was already forming opinions, and on Monday she'd be the head honcho. Peanut's access to the solar panels would be severely restricted.

"I'm going to check Wally's apartment and then walk home," Jenna said absently. "Better put your crossword puzzles away for a while. See you Monday."

She pushed through the swinging doors and rapped on the door to Wally's apartment. Tried the knob but the door was locked. Stepped outside and checked the corner of the statue—the key to the Center's outer door glinted back at her. You're the best, Wally, she thought. She'd bring Peanut up tonight for one last visit.

She pivoted and crossed the new cobblestones. It was different walking across the uneven surface but the changes made a huge impact. Flowers brightened the drive, the shrubs were perfect and Three Brooks looked like a facility that really did cater to expensive horses.

Movement flashed. She glanced up, certain a curtain had moved in Wally's apartment. She pulled out her cell phone and pressed his number, but only heard a recording. "I know you're in there, buddy," she said. "Thanks for leaving the key. Peanut and I will be up tonight."

She paused, uncomfortable. Wally had always been the guy to dole out favors, and she understood pride. "And," her words came in a rush, "I know you have the apartment for another four months but if you need a place to stay after that, or if you want to move out now, I'd love to have you."

She shoved the phone in her pocket and followed the wooded path to her trailer. If she weren't always rushing in the morning, she'd walk to work. She loved the smells, the air, the land. Loved helping animals.

Didn't want to move.

She scooped up a rock and drove it at an oak tree, then a second and a third, throwing harder until the rocks hit with a satisfying *thwack*. Her job was secure. Had to be. Barb had no reason to check her qualifications, no reason to wonder why she wasn't working toward her degree. Everything was fine.

But she was tense when she reached the trailer. Her phone chirped. She checked the display, Burke. Her heart raced even faster, and she answered slowly.

"Meet me in the parking lot," he said, his voice clipped. "I'll drive you home and later we can take Barb for dinner."

"I already walked home. And thanks for the invite tonight but I'm busy."

"Jenna," his voice deepened with impatience, "it would be good for your job security if you accompany us tonight."

Her hand tightened around the phone. "You think the only reason Barb would keep me is because of your influence?"

"She might feel more favorably toward you, especially after your disrespect today. However, I don't interfere with decisions at such a low level."

Low level. He had such a way with words. She climbed up her porch steps and sank into the swing. "I didn't intend to be disrespectful," she said quietly. "But she should know horses have a limited color range. It's hard not to speak out if she's wrong about something."

"Barb's a good manager. Edward highly recommends her. She'll keep the Center in the black, but her type expects a certain amount of deference." Papers shuffled in the background. "I'll pick you up at seven. We have reservations at the Club."

The thought of enduring another long night at the Hunt Club, nodding brightly while Barb prattled to Burke, was nauseating. Besides, Peanut needed a trip to the Center—before Barb locked the doors—and Jenna wasn't going to let a man derail anymore of her plans. She knew better.

"Sorry," she said. "I'm busy tonight. But your warning is appreciated. As a *low-level* employee, I'll try to be more respectful. Maybe your friend, Theresa, can accompany you."

She cut the connection and called Emily. She hadn't given her sister much support over the last few weeks, too enamored with Burke to worry about the really important people in her life. She shook her head in disgust.

"Hi, sis." Em sounded subdued, devoid of her usual bravado. "Can your green machine handle another trip out here?"

"Of course," Jenna said. "She's a little loud but running great. Want me to come visit?" Just the thing to help her forget about Burke. "It'll have to be a weekend though. We have a new manager and my vacation is used up."

Em's breathing sounded ragged. Finally she spoke. "Don't yell, sis, but I'm moving home. I don't want to hang out here anymore. I'm failing most of my courses anyway."

Jenna's knees buckled and she dropped onto the swing. "Do you get any money back when you fail?" she squeaked.

"No, but it was a good learning experience." Emily's voice quickened. "It wasn't a waste. Not a bit."

Jenna's left temple throbbed. Not a waste? She'd sacrificed so much, gone to such lengths. Now she was stuck with a heap of lies, a fake diploma and increasingly shaky employment. Her head pounded so hard, it hurt.

"Come on," Em said. "You don't know what it's like. You're the one that wants a degree. You pushed this on me."

"I'd love for someone to push that opportunity on me."

"Well, you go to college then," Emily snapped. "But I'm finished here. Let me know when you're coming."

A dial tone buzzed. Jenna clung to the phone for another anguished moment, but Emily was gone.

Chapter Twenty-Six

"I don't think Barb has the right management style for the position here." Burke turned up the speaker phone and resumed stacking files on the dining room table. "She seems somewhat inflexible."

"You're calling someone that?" Edward chuckled. "Besides, we owe her family a favor. And let's not forget they have important contacts in Virginia. The final decision is up to you, of course, but last week you were eager to move on."

"You're right," Burke muttered, scanning the pile of files. He'd put most of them through the paper shredder. No need to drag them on a plane. "One other thing," he said. "Have you heard any rumors about the Ridgeman stud and his potency? Specifically how many mares had live foals this year? Staff here think he's healthy—that there're no physical reasons why he can't cover a mare. Frankly, we can't understand why they sent him."

"Don't know anything about that. Maybe he doesn't have the energy to nail two mares a day?" Edward snickered. "What a life. Wish I were a horse."

Burke stared through the patio window at the pool shimmering beneath the setting sun, blocking Edward's rant about the deplorable lack of pussy. He wished Jenna were lounging here now, naked or clothed, but at least here. Without her, dinner at the Club would be yawningly boring. He was tempted to cancel. And what the hell was so important that she didn't want to spend their last night together?

She'd written him off.

The realization drained him and he dropped the files on the table, knowing he was going to let her. When you love someone, you tried to give them everything they wanted—and she wanted him gone.

A kernel of resentment tightened in his gut. He switched his attention back to Edward, nodding agreement with every single complaint his cousin uttered about women.

Jenna jerked around at the quiet knock on her door. Seven o'clock and she half expected Burke to stop on the way to town, to plead for her company tonight.

Plead? She gave her head a shake. Who was she kidding? Burke wouldn't plead. And he wouldn't knock quietly. She walked to the door, straining to identify the dark shape through her meshed screen.

Wally! She pushed open the door, horrified by his unkempt shirt, the sour smell of liquor, his defeated expression.

"Sit on the swing," she said quickly. "I'll make some coffee."

"Rum would be better." Wally burped. "Ran out of liquor. Only a few beer left."

"Oh, Wally." She sat down beside him, scanning the driveway but it was empty of everything but her little Neon. "How did you get here?"

"Walked. Asshole took my company truck. Can't even get to the liquor store." He squeezed his eyes shut, his expression pained. "Been sitting in the apartment for a few days now. Fifty years old and I only know horses. What the hell will I do?"

"Why did you quit? I thought your plan was to hold out for severance."

"Yeah, well," Wally's eyes shifted to the left. "Plans change." He jerked to his feet as Burke's car rose over the ridge. "Aw, damn. He sees me."

"It's all right. You no longer work for Three Books. What can he do?" She gave Wally's knee a reassuring pat and urged him back down on the swing. Drunks always had odd reactions. "He's just stopping for a second, probably to see if I changed my mind about dinner."

She walked down the steps to his car, her mouth going dry at the sight of Burke, unbearably handsome in a crisp white shirt and dark dinner jacket.

"What's he doing here?" Burke gestured disdainfully at Wally.

She stiffened. "Visiting. He's my friend. And now that he's stripped of the company truck, I'm the only house within walking range."

"He should have thought of that before he misused company assets." Burke's scowl deepened. "I won't tolerate dishonesty."

She opened her mouth to explain that Wally had only been trying to help the locals but knew it was useless. Burke saw everything in black and white. "I'm sure you'll outline all your likes and dislikes to Barb tonight." She crossed her arms and stepped back. "Have a nice night."

"I might drop back later. If you're home?"

"No!" She heard her telltale note of panic and calmed her voice. "I'm busy with Wally tonight."

"I see," he said. "Then enjoy your evening." He backed out of the driveway and sped over the ridge, a cloud of dust spiraling after his car.

She forced a nonchalant smile and climbed back up the steps. Wally had straightened on the swing as though Burke's visit had injected him with a new level of sobriety. "What did *he* want?"

"Just checking if I was coming for dinner."

"Dinner?" Wally's eyes narrowed. "You two hang out like that? You're...close?"

Jenna couldn't hide her blush.

"Oh, fuck me." Wally's face twisted and he laughed with a bitter note she didn't understand. "Goddammit. Sonofabitch played us both."

"You're not making sense."

"He said if I didn't quit, he'd replace you with Kathryn. And fire you if I said anything. So I signed his damn paper."

Jenna's legs wobbled. She dropped like a rock onto the swing, staring at Wally in disbelief. "Fire me?" Her voice quavered. "He threatened to fire me? And you gave it all up? Oh, Wally–"

"It's all right, Jenna. Bastard outplayed me. He eats people like us for breakfast."

Jenna choked back a hysterical sob. Dear Wally, always so loyal. And damn that Burke. Would he have fired her? Maybe. Of course, now she was likely to lose her job anyway, not this week or next, but down the road. Barb would wonder why she wasn't taking courses. Would check her credentials and discover they were all a pack of lies.

Wally's sacrifice had been in vain. He'd even signed a stupid document. Just like she'd signed one confirming her education. If only those papers could be destroyed.

"There may be a way to fix this," she said slowly, "if we can get into his office."

"Impossible." Wally shook his head. "The locks were changed a few weeks ago. I've already tried."

"But he gave me a set of keys. They're still in my pocket."

Wally jerked around, stared for a moment, then embraced her with a clumsy hug. "You're as loyal as your mom but as smart as your dad. And I mean that as the sincerest compliment."

"I don't want to be like either of them," Jenna said, swept with unbearable sadness. She'd actually believed Burke, believed he was beginning to care. Her mouth quivered with disgust. The Murphy women were such suckers.

"The security checks are on the hour this week," she added. "I'll bring Peanut up as soon as it's dark, ten minutes after nine. Put him under the lights and afterwards check the files. Meet you up there."

"How do you know when Larry patrols? Asshole Burke shuffled the times."

"When I was in Larry's truck, I checked his schedule."

"See what I mean. You're as smart as your dad."

"Who died in prison," she said.

Chapter Twenty-Seven

Nifty stretched his thick neck over the stall door and sniffed at Peanut, clearly delighted to have company. Jenna glanced over her shoulder at the long and lonely aisle. What kind of sadistic idiot would want a horse kept in isolation?

During the day, the oxygen technologist was around but she wasn't much company, not for a gregarious horse.

Nifty quickly decided Peanut was no threat to his masculine superiority and nipped the pony on the neck. Undeterred, Peanut nipped back, and the two played an energetic game of tag until Peanut tired and turned to his hay. Yes, the valuable Thoroughbred stud and the two-dollar pony were now best of friends. *Screw you, Burke.*

She picked up her phone and called Wally. "I'm here. Meet you in front of Burke's office."

The hall was dark but Jenna knew the route blindfolded. So did Wally, and she jumped when he silently materialized from the shadows.

"We'll keep the lights out and use my flashlight," he said, "just in case Larry drives past." He shone it on the gleaming lock then glanced back at Jenna. "Come on. Hurry up."

Jenna inserted the key, ignoring the awful knot in her stomach. The key stuck and she glanced over her shoulder at Wally. "Maybe this isn't the right key after all," she said.

He reached up and jiggled it. *Click.* The door swung open.

"Bingo." He rushed past her and into the office, panning his light over the filing cabinet. "Employee stuff used to be in the middle drawer."

"Guess I better take a sheet from my file too," she said, following him to the cabinet. "I signed a form, claiming I have more than eleventh grade."

"What a surprise," a cold voice spoke behind them.

Jenna's heart slammed. She swung around. A lamp switched on and she blinked under its stark light.

Burke uncoiled from the corner chair. "Thick as thieves, I see." Disgust darkened his face. "You both sicken me. Step outside, Wally, where we can discuss this awkward break and enter."

He removed his dinner jacket and rolled up his sleeves. She gulped, her breath escaping in painful jerks. His forearms had never looked so massive. Or deadly. She edged in front of Wally. "It's not a break and enter," she said. "Not if I have a key."

"Oh. You're a lawyer now? Perhaps took a course…back in what…grade eleven?" He snorted with such disdain she flinched. "I'll deal with you after."

"But this wasn't W-Wally's idea." Her voice squeaked. "It was mine." She glanced back, appalled to see Wally laying down his flashlight and flexing his knuckles. "You can't fight. Please don't." She couldn't hide her panic. "Someone will get hurt!"

"That's the general idea," Burke snapped.

She swung around. "Please, Wally. Don't go outside." She splayed her fingers over his rigid arm. "Remember Dad. Don't fight. Please, don't."

A muscle ticked in Wally's jaw and she sensed he wavered. "It won't prove anything," she added, clutching him with shaking arms. She felt his stiffness, his own need for satisfaction, but a moment later he slumped and she knew she'd won.

"Thank you," she whispered. Burke wouldn't fight in the office; he was too controlled. And too lethal.

"We'll sign and do whatever you want," she said, keeping her eyes and arms on Wally, not looking over her shoulder. "We'll just go away—" Her voice broke.

She sensed Burke's frustration, his raw fury, but didn't dare look. Couldn't bear to see the contempt in his cold eyes. A long moment. Then heavy footsteps, the door slammed and the air in the office felt safe again.

"It would have been okay." Wally squeezed her shoulder, his voice strained. "People don't usually die in a fistfight. That was bad luck for your father."

"Bad luck for the other guy too. Dad punched the life out of him."

"I think Burke just wanted to have a couple swings. Wanted the satisfaction. Can't blame him really."

"Men." Jenna shook her head, her voice breaking. "So what do we do now?" They both turned, momentarily silent as Burke's car streaked from the lower lot, headlights slashing the window.

"We'll go upstairs and drink the last of my beer," Wally said. "On Monday, let's hope all you receive is a pink slip. Pray he doesn't press charges. But he's a hard man."

They trudged up the steps to Wally's apartment. Cardboard boxes littered the hardwood floor, and a library of dog-eared equine books was stacked on the table.

Wally shoved a beer in her hand. "Only two left. Drank everything else. The glasses are already packed up, I'm afraid."

"You were allowed to stay here another four months, Wally," Jenna said, taking the bottle, shocked to see her hand still trembled. She couldn't shake the image of Burke's cold eyes.

"Obviously I'll have to move out now. But I'll find another job. No problem."

Jenna's throat tightened. Without a reference and blackballed by the powerful Burke family, Wally might have considerable problems. As would she. "What did you do with all that cash from the massages?" she asked quietly.

"Paid for the surgery for the Tutty horse. Remember Copper Duke...also the Fraelic mare."

Jenna squeezed her eyes shut. Two expensive surgeries. No wonder Burke despised Wally. The Canadians had ignored all the help Wally gave struggling owners. Overlooked the free services the Center provided. But Burke called it stealing. The reason didn't matter. He didn't condone thieves or liars. And he considered her to be both.

"I'm sorry. You tried to help everyone, and it turned out to be such a disaster. You lost your severance because of me." She blew out a ragged sigh. "Emily is quitting college," she admitted.

Wally shrugged. "Not surprised."

"She was doing well until her boyfriend dumped her. That messed her up."

"You blame everything on men." Wally's voice turned dry. "Emily is just spoiled."

Jenna automatically shook her head then stopped and blew out another sigh. "Guess she lied about how well she was doing."

"And you can't blame that on the boyfriend." Wally propped his legs on a bulging box and leaned against the sofa. "Wonder if the new manager will put the sofa by the other window. I always liked the view of the gallop track."

"Don't know." Jenna swallowed, relieved he'd changed the subject. Wally was ever empathetic. "Expect she'll want the walls painted though. Think she favors red."

"Red? Good grief." Wally forced a carefree laugh. "Glad I'm moving."

Jenna managed a weak smile but set down her unwanted beer. "Larry is due for his security check. I'm going to gather Peanut and get out of here once his truck leaves. Tomorrow I'll come up with my car and we can move your stuff to my place." She hesitated. "Don't drink any more, okay?"

"Nah, I'm done. Take the flashlight, kid. Larry won't see a thing."

"I'm okay. Don't need one on the path." She impulsively reached over and kissed his cheek. "You're the best friend I ever had. The best friend Mom ever had too."

He smiled. But it was flat and humorless, and her heart twisted. "See you tomorrow," she added, slipping out the door.

She padded down the dark hall, pausing when she heard Larry's diesel. Stayed motionless while he checked the locks. At least, Burke didn't know she'd been sneaking Peanut in for free sessions. He'd only despise her more.

Larry's pickup rumbled off and she continued toward the oxygen wing. Nifty stuck his head over the stall door, eyes bright and content. Obviously he enjoyed having company in the next stall. Of course, other than Burke, who didn't like Peanut?

She couldn't even see her pony and had to press close to the door and peer down. Peanut lifted his head, stalks falling from his mouth, then turned back to the expensive hay as though keen to finish.

"Okay, fellow. Eat up. We won't be back here again." She stepped into his stall and ran her hands over his shiny coat. So much improved. Peanut would be an excellent testimonial for Three Brooks if only his treatment hadn't been so furtive.

Snap. She stiffened at the sound of breaking metal. A door? Not Wally. The noise came from the receiving doors at the other end. Burke? Shit. She dropped into the straw, pressing against the wooden wall. If he didn't look over the door, maybe he wouldn't spot Peanut.

Two people, masculine voices. Her chest thumped and she pressed deeper into the prickly straw. Burke? Back with the police? Was he having them arrested?

She hadn't really believed he'd press charges. Thought he'd be content to fire her. But he'd definitely view Peanut's presence as an added betrayal. He'd really hate her then. Probably would involve the police.

Despairing, she slumped in the straw, trying to gather an excuse. But oh, God, she was so screwed.

"Is this the horse?" someone asked, an unfamiliar voice, low and rough.

Police? She knew many of the officers. They'd visited often when her father was binging, but she couldn't place this voice, not at all.

"Yeah. Useless fucker's shooting blanks."

Jenna's nails curled into her palms. David Ridgeman— unmistakable. But they'd already moved away. Something clicked, then a grinding noise, a mere twenty feet away.

"Explosion will hide the break-in." David's laugh was thick with satisfaction. "Can't have another accident on my property."

Oh, God! Horror chilled her. Her breath jammed in her throat and she couldn't move, was grateful she was already on the floor. The oxygen chamber? An explosion would kill Nifty. No wonder David had wanted the horse stabled in this part of the building.

She groped for her phone, fingers so stiff she could barely tug it from her pocket. 911 or was it 411? Her mind blanked. She pressed a familiar speed dial number, and Wally answered on the second ring.

"David Ridgeman and a man are here," she whispered. "Think they're planning to kill Nifty."

"Can't hear you, Jenna. Speak up."

"They're trying to blow up the oxygen chamber. Get help please," she hissed. "Call Larry or someone." The sawing stopped and she abruptly ended the call.

"Wait. I heard something." David Ridgeman's voice moved closer. She stared at her phone, trembling with horror, blocking the illumination with her hand. If she turned it off, did it chime? It was so new, she didn't know. Was it on vibrate or ring? She couldn't remember that either.

Don't call back, Wally. Please, please, please, don't call me back.

"It's okay. Let's get that oxygen turned on. We'll light this place up." David's voice quivered with excitement.

Powerful lights flicked on. "Hey!"

She slumped with relief at Wally's indignant holler. He was here. Everything would be okay. Even the bright aisle lights made her feel safer.

"This is a restricted area," Wally said, his voice hard and authoritative. "Who let you people in—"

"Shut up," Crude Voice said. *Thump.* A grunt of pain.

"Don't shoot him." David Ridgeman's voice turned urgent. "They'll notice a bullet."

"What do we do?"

"Stick him in the oxygen chamber," David said.

"What the hell—" Wally's voice thinned with shock, and Jenna jammed her hand over her mouth, flinching at the scuffling sounds. Then silence, horrible silence.

She dropped back into the straw, her hand trembling. Pressed 911 and whispered frantically into the phone.

The operator's calm voice was reassuring. "Stay on the line," the voice said. "We'll have help there soon."

"How soon?" Jenna whispered.

"Very soon. Just stay on the line."

She almost choked on her panic. If they were driving from town it would take at least fifteen minutes. Not fast enough. Once oxygen released, the chamber filled quickly. Burke was closer. She cut the connection, pressed his number but it rang endlessly. Oh, God, maybe he was too furious to take her call.

She hunched in the straw, hands shaking. Were they opening a valve now? Setting some sort of incendiary device?

There was no time. The oxygen supply had to be cut. She inched the door open and crept down the hall, willing her trembling legs to obey.

David and a shorter man in a dark shirt leaned over the control panel, but the jimmied door was wide open. No way could she pass without being seen.

Impossible.

The gap was too wide, too visible, her legs too wobbly. They'd spot her. She wanted to slink outside, hide in the dark and wait for help. She'd heard enough burn stories. Seen too many pictures of gas explosions. Horrible, horrible pictures.

Wally's white face pressed against the window of the oxygen chamber. His gaze caught hers, and he abruptly banged on the thick glass. Both men swiveled toward the chamber, and she bolted across the opening and down the hall.

Oh, God. She couldn't believe she'd done it. *Thank you, Wally.* But her breathing was so ragged she was afraid they'd hear. She stumbled through the door of the control room, her gaze scrabbling for the master valve. Where the hell was it? She'd always listened to the safety talks but never imagined she'd have to use the information.

But there it was. Definitely the safety valve. She tugged at the red knob on the left wall then wrenched it desperately to the right. It moved one inch, three, then was completely buried. Done!

She pushed a chair in front of the conspicuous knob and crawled beneath the table, shaking with fear and adrenaline, unable to move another step. Pressed against the cold wall, her breath escaping in terrified pants.

Had she turned it off in time? She didn't want to sit here, didn't want to die, but couldn't desert Wally or Peanut or Nifty. *Ring.* Oh, damn. Her phone. Startlingly loud. Way too loud. She grabbed it, frantically scrambling for the mute button. *Oh, God! Burke.*

A hand yanked her wrist, twisting until the phone clattered to the floor.

"What the hell? Someone else is in here," Crude Voice grumbled, kicking the table back and dragging her out. "You said the place would be empty."

David loomed in the doorway. His eyes narrowed then gleamed with satisfaction. "Good. It's just the massage girl. She knows how this works. Bring her here."

She tried to scramble away but the man yanked her arm behind her back, so high she thought it would break. A helpless whimper squeezed from her throat.

He shoved her into the oxygen room.

"We had pressure for a moment but it disappeared," David said, checking his watch. "Turn it on, Jenna. And hurry."

She swallowed, tried to speak, but her throat was too constricted. "It's…the green button," she finally managed, staring at the controls, not wanting to look into David's glittering eyes. "It takes a while. Pressure will build in about fifteen minutes."

The gun was on the table, on the other side of the control panel. Fifteen feet away. She tried not to stare, but the man's grip had loosened. Maybe she could grab it.

"That's not what you said on the tour. Or what was written on the spec sheet." David's hand shot out, squeezing her arm in frustration. "What did you do, bitch!"

His hand tightened and she winced. He gave a spiteful smile and squeezed her wrist harder. "Still a little tender, I see."

She raised her knee, tried to kick, but the man behind wrapped her legs with his, cranking her left arm higher. A hairy forearm banded around her chest. Rancid breath fanned her face.

"Good. Hold her still. Listen to the squeal." David wrapped his fingers around her hand and pressed. *Crack.* Something shattered, the pain so intense it ripped away her cries. She jerked in agony but the man behind yanked her up. She retched, almost throwing up. David's face blurred, and helpless thumps sounded from the chamber.

"She'll talk soon. Has to." David's voice rose with excitement. "I'll break the other wrist. Then she can join—"

His body abruptly lifted, jerking in the air like a marionette. She was released so quickly, she crashed against the table and instinctively extended her hand. White-hot pain lanced her arm, and she gave an involuntary cry.

She glimpsed Burke, face contorted with fury, almost unrecognizable. He grabbed Crude Voice, smashed him in the face then tossed him aside like garbage. Turned back to David and yanked the man to his feet. Gripped the front of his shirt with a big fist. *Thud, thud, thud.*

Red covered David's nose, his jaw and splattered Burke's fist. A cracking noise replaced the thud. But still Burke hammered, holding David like a punching bag.

Crude Voice rose, clutching his jaw, looking much smaller now. His eyes scuttled to Burke who resembled a maddened mobster. The man turned and fled.

Burke kept striking. Hammering. Crushing. He was going to kill David.

"He's not worth it," she yelled. She lurched forward, trying to grab Burke's piston arm. Something smashed her head, driving her against the metal chamber. Pain knifed.

She fought to remain conscious, struggled to listen to Burke's frantic voice, then Wally's. But waves kept crashing, carrying shards of agony, and finally it was easier to let the darkness cover her.

Chapter Twenty-Eight

Someone groaned. Jenna tried to pry her eyes open—to check who was hurt, but her eyelids were too heavy. Impossible to lift them.

"She needs more medication. Jesus Christ, can't you give her something."

Wally's voice. Her head hurt. Her hand was a jumbled mass of screaming nerves. More groans and she realized she was the one making that awful noise. Tried to stop her whimpers but the pain was excruciating.

"It's too soon," another voice said.

"Give her more. Now." Burke's voice, hard and inflexible.

Who would argue with that? A little prick in her thigh, barely noticeable, and minutes later a welcome relief swept her away.

She turned her head, opened her eyes and blinked at the man slouched in the chair. Wally leaned forward with a huge smile. "Hey, kid."

"Hi." Her voice croaked. "Could I have a drink?"

"Sure." He turned but someone else moved, and a plastic straw pressed between her lips. She tried to suck but it was difficult. Her tongue felt thick, swollen, and water spilled down the side of her mouth. A gentle finger wiped it away. She looked up and saw Burke.

"Is everything all right," she asked, "at the Center?"

He nodded. "Both arrested. Everything's fine. Don't talk."

"What's wrong with me?"

"You had surgery on your broken hand, and your face has a few…knocks."

"Oh," she said and fell back to sleep.

Jenna stared in dismay at the bulky white bandage swathing her right hand. "How long?"

"Six weeks," Burke said, "Approximately."

"And my face?"

He pivoted and turned his back, studying the array of colorful flowers beneath the window. "It'll heal."

He couldn't stand to look at her. A thief, a liar and ugly. She'd checked the mirror, had seen her battered cheek, her blackened eye. She'd always found her mother's bruises repellent so understood his reaction. However, his open aversion rubbed another raw spot deep in her chest.

"Was Lorna involved too?" she asked, struggling to fill the silence.

"No, she was devastated. Especially since police are re-opening the investigation into her father's death." He plucked a leaf off a plant, studying it beneath his fingers.

"What will happen to Nifty?" Jenna asked.

"Guess they'll give him some time off. Ridgeman had him insured for millions but that value would have plummeted after they tested his semen. To David, he was worth more dead than alive."

"David enjoyed causing pain." Her voice buckled.

"God, I'm sorry, Jenna." Burke jerked around, his mouth flat. "You never liked David. And that night at the Club, your hand…did he hurt you?" His voice roughened. "That's why you hit him. You should have told me. I would have dealt with him."

"But you already did. I remember you hitting him." Her fingers automatically lifted to her bruised cheek, but his face filled with such revulsion she averted her face. Tried to hide it in the pillow but the pressure hurt too much, and she gave up. There was simply no way to hide, not in this tiny hospital room, not from his sharp eyes. "When are you leaving?" she asked.

"Not sure."

Her throat tightened. She didn't know what was wrong but felt exposed in the stark bed. She wanted to be alone, alone to sleep and heal and sleep some more. The door opened and Wally sauntered in.

"Hey, good! You're awake." He bounced toward the bed, utterly normal. Didn't seem to have any problem looking at her messed-up face, and his easy presence filled her with relief. Thank, God, he was safe.

"Oh, Wally." Her breath escaped in a flood of emotion. "They were…going to b-burn us up. I wanted to run away."

"But you didn't. You saved my life." He squeezed her shoulder, and his voice caught. "Always so loyal. So brave."

She clutched his fingers with her left hand, trying to stop the shaking. "I didn't feel brave. I felt like a coward. When he was squeezing…I almost told him where the button was."

Wally's eyes looked moist. "He's a sadist and a pyromaniac. He won't be able to hurt anyone again."

"I never liked him. Should have listened to Colin. He knew there was something strange about Nifty—"

The door clicked shut. She twisted, saw Burke had walked out and was hit with a fresh spasm of pain. "He won't even l-look at me."

"He feels responsible. But you'll be better soon. And he's arranged for a car to pick up Emily and bring her home. She'll take care of you until that hand is healed."

"Am I f-fired?"

Wally chuckled and refilled her water glass. "Honey, you're a hero. You could ask Burke for anything and he'd give it to you."

"I just want him to leave." Her voice shook. "I don't want him around…not looking at me."

"Are you sure?" Wally asked. "Because it sounds like he's planning to stay for a while."

"I'm sure."

"And you want me to tell him that?"

"I do," she said.

"Sit down." Burke leaned back in his chair, staring at Wally over his steepled fingers. "I'd like you to remain as manager of Three Brooks."

Wally's eyes flickered with surprise. He hesitated a moment then leaned forward, shaking his head. "Is this some misguided sense of guilt because I stumbled upon a couple of criminals trying to blow up your Center? Because severance would be enough. Jenna was the brave one—"

"Shut up." Burke grabbed a pen and jotted down another notation. "Because of your past waste of company funds, an independent accountant will keep all financial records. There will be frequent audits. And if I have to come back for any reason— any reason whatsoever—heads will roll. Understand?"

He waited for Wally's nod then added, "You'll be receiving good horses now, stakes horses. Just keep the company in the black. Keep the place orderly and…look after her."

Comprehension swept Wally's face and Burke shoved his list across the desk. Didn't want to see the empathy in the older man's eyes.

"The new storage building will be the local receiving barn," Burke said. "Staff can work with those animals on a gratuitous basis, one day a week. But keep them stalled separately from our paying clients. Make sure their Coggins and vaccines are current." He cleared his throat. "Twenty-five percent of Center profits will be earmarked for your humanitarian urges."

Wally jerked forward, his face creasing with delight.

"Not a penny more, Wally," Burke said quickly but felt his lip twitch. The town would be in fine shape with twenty-five percent, and everyone would work like hell to raise profits. It would be a win-win situation.

"Three Brooks will also sponsor one employee for annual educational leave," he added, "with full salary and all costs covered. The first recipient will be Jenna." He grabbed his coffee mug, irritated at how his throat tightened whenever he said her name. "Run it however you want, but I suggest a committee for future scholarship selection—you, Jenna and maybe that vet in town."

"Colin MacDonald?"

"Yeah. That's the guy." Burke's mouth clamped.

"I imagine you want progress reports on the…first recipient?"

Burke slammed his pen on the desk. "I don't want anything. Just look after her. I'm finished."

"She can't help the way she is. For Christ's sake, she saw her father beat someone to death. He abused them all—"

"I'd never hit her." Burke jerked forward, then slumped back in the chair. *He had hit her.* "I didn't know it was her." He squeezed his eyes shut, chest aching. "Thought it was that other bastard. Now she cringes when I walk into the room." He forced a negligent shrug, hating for anyone to see his pain, especially this lucky prick, Wally, who clearly held a special spot in her heart.

He scowled, unable to resist one last warning. "Don't screw this up, Wally. I don't want to have to come back. Now get out."

Wally picked up the list and rose, then slowly extended his hand. "I'll always take care of her."

"I know you will," Burke said. And he shook Wally's hand.

Chapter Twenty-Nine

"I made some awesome chicken soup." The screen door slammed as Emily sauntered onto the porch, balancing a dripping spoon over a napkin. "Taste it."

"I'm not hungry right now." Jenna forced a smile. "But thanks. It smells great," she added, seeing her sister's pout.

Emily stuck the spoon in her own mouth, then gave it an impatient wave. "What's wrong with you? I'm not used to being the responsible one and I don't like it. Honestly, sis, you look horrible."

Jenna stared across the field at Peanut. She couldn't bear to see the gleaming new tiles on top of both the kennel and chicken coop. Burke's guilt must have run deep. He'd finished the roofing when she was in the hospital, his good-bye present. A much better gift than jewelry—and something he knew she'd appreciate.

A warm tear trickled down her cheek. She reached up and swiped it away.

"Good God." Emily sighed and dropped onto the swing. "Don't be such a baby. You have everything you ever wanted." She held up her fingers, ticking them off. "In the fall, you start your science degree. You massage at Three Brooks only when you feel like it. Hell, Wally dotes on you. Our trailer has a new roof and you'll never, ever have to rely on a man. Just like you said you wouldn't.

"Which actually is a very good thing, because you look like shit." Emily wrinkled her nose. "Maybe I should take that scholarship instead of you. Maybe I could stick out college if I lived here and commuted."

Jenna closed her eyes, ignoring her sister's prattle. It was nice having her home, but sometimes solitude was preferable. And sleep. Lately she craved sleep.

"Oh, here comes the big boss now. Talk to him for me, Jenna. He never liked me much."

Jenna forced her eyes open, watching as Wally stepped from his truck. He was such a kind man, often just sitting beside her in undemanding silence. Neither of them spoke much about that horrifying night, but Wally was clearly grateful. On the other hand, if she hadn't called him, he would have remained safe in his apartment.

The chamber would have exploded, killing Nifty and Peanut, but that would have been the extent. It seemed bizarre now, unreal; Burke, almost like a dream.

"Good afternoon, ladies. Oh, Jenna." Wally's voice sharpened as he twisted accusingly toward Emily. "Can't you feed her better than this?"

Emily shrugged. "I can't make her eat. And I already told her she looks like shit."

Wally lowered himself onto the swing "You're getting too thin, Jenna. I can't let you go back to work like this. Does your face still hurt?"

"No." Her hand swept to her cheek. She blew out a tremulous sigh. "*He* didn't mean to hit me. I know he didn't mean to hit me and well… I miss him." Her words were soft but so stark, even Emily silenced. Jenna's eyes clung to Wally's face. "It's been a month. Do you think he'll come back?"

"No," Wally said.

"But wouldn't he come back if you called him?" she asked. "Maybe if the Center had a problem?"

"He's not coming back, Jenna." Wally shuddered. "And I'm not calling him. You told him to go. Live with it."

A vice tightened around her chest. "Sometimes you think you want something and you get it, and then you realize it's not what you wanted at all."

"I'd do a lot for you," Wally said, "but I'm not calling Burke. He's scary."

Sometimes, but not always, she thought. Sure, maybe when he was pulverizing someone who deserved it but usually he was…quite nice. And sometimes he said thoughtless things but he always *did* the right thing. Her gaze drifted to the newly tiled roof.

"Oh, for Christ's sake. How scary is one man?" Emily pulled out her cell phone. "What's his number?"

Jenna stiffened. A wide-eyed Wally scrambled to his feet.

"Never mind." Emily laid down her phone and picked up Jenna's. "You have the free calling package. What's his name? Derek Burke? It's right here on your speed dial." She pressed some numbers and jammed the phone in Jenna's horrified hand. "It's ringing, sis."

Jenna numbly held the phone against her ear. Two rings.

"Burke," he said.

"Hi, it's Jenna." She twisted away from her two craning spectators.

"Hi, Jenna. How are you feeling?" His voice was crisp and confident and such an intense longing swept her, she could scarcely breathe.

"Fine…um, I have the splint off my hand. And I wanted to thank you for fixing the roof. And for the scholarship."

"No need. So you're okay? Hand's good?"

"Fine," she said. "Are you in California now?"

"Yes."

"Good. Okay, well, I just wanted to thank you. And um—"

"What?"

He sounded bored and she gripped the phone, picturing the impatient look in his eyes, the hard thrust of his jaw.

"Good luck out there and um….well, goodbye," she said feebly.

"Goodbye to you too." He spoke with such finality, she wasn't surprised when a dial tone replaced his voice.

"God, sis, you suck." Emily rolled her eyes and pulled the phone from Jenna's limp hand.

"But I wasn't ready to call," Jenna said. "I was nervous. It was impossible to think."

"He didn't say anything about me, did he?" Wally shoved his hands in his pockets and paced across the porch. "He doesn't think the Center is having any problems?"

"You two are such chicken shits." Emily stalked inside the trailer and the screen door slammed.

"He didn't sound like he really wanted to talk," Jenna said miserably.

"He's not a big talker," Wally said.

"He used to talk a lot to me."

"Used to, Jenna. Think he's moved on. Best you do too."

"I guess." She swallowed, trying to work her words around the big lump in her throat. "It's best not to depend on someone, isn't it? But do you think Mom was happy? With my father?"

"He was the only man she ever loved."

Wally's voice sounded strained and she twisted, scanning his face. She'd always wondered why he never married. Couldn't remember a time when he hadn't been around. "You were more than friends?" Her eyes widened. "You loved her too?"

He shrugged and rumpled her hair. "We can't always choose who we love, kiddo. But I don't think your mom regretted anything."

"I used to despise her. How he hit her. Us. How she'd never leave. Couldn't understand it."

"Me neither," Wally said.

"Hi, Jenna. Glad you're back. Gosh, what kind of diet are you on?" Frances shoved aside her crossword puzzle. "Does Wally know you're here?"

"My first day back isn't for a few more weeks, but Wally wanted me to drop by and see something."

"Oh, right." Frances grinned. "Go around to the new building. Wally's out there."

"The new building? You mean the storage shed?" Jenna shrugged and walked outside. It was strange to be back, especially with Burke gone. The Center seemed dull, lifeless, as if a spark had been extinguished.

She walked along the cobblestones toward the storage shed. He'd built much of the new building with his own hands, had helped the construction crew every morning and toward the end had turned it into his own, personal project. 'Working on some special touches,' he'd said with a crooked grin, always smelling of that lovely, fresh pine. God, she missed his smile, missed his company. Missed him.

So what if he thought her a liar, a thief. She should have faced his disappointment, apologized, begged him to stay. Emily was right; she was a chicken shit.

She pushed open the door and jerked to a stop. This was no storage shed. Nine spacious stalls lined the right-hand side and the middle one even had a special door, low enough so a tiny pony could stretch out his neck. Peanut: the sign read.

Wally stepped forward, grinning. "Burke thought you could do your massage on the left side. Horses can use the Center's side door if they need other therapy. But these stalls are reserved for locals. And of course, Peanut is the guest of honor."

Jenna struggled to breathe, too stunned to speak.

Wally cocked his head, frowning at her reaction. "This is a good thing. Now you can bring Peanut up any time, permission guaranteed. Locals are welcome too, as long as they're stabled in this building. Fridays are free. Jesus, Jenna, we thought you'd be happy."

"We? You mean you and Burke?" Her voice sounded rusty. "But when did he build Peanut's stall? Was it before or after the break-in?"

"He'd been working on it for weeks." Wally shrugged. "But what does it matter?"

"Then it wasn't guilt." Jenna's heart leaped. "Not if it was before the break-in." Although that meant he'd built the stalls before he caught her in his office. Before he'd looked at her with such contempt.

Shit, her head hurt and she didn't know what to think. She sank down on a hay bale. "This is great, it really is. But why did he do it?"

Wally rolled his eyes. "Yeah, like I'm going to ask him those kinds of questions. I assume he changed his mind about helping local horses. Maybe hanging out with you helped."

"But why did he hire you back as manager?"

Wally scuffed his toe over the rubber lining the aisle, then slowly lifted his head. "Because he wanted to make sure you were okay. And he knows I care."

A blazing joy burst in her chest, lifting her to her feet. "Then he doesn't hate me for going into his office. And it's not guilt either. Does he call you regularly?"

"No. In fact, he doesn't want to hear anything from me. He's washed his hands of Three Brooks."

Jenna circled Wally, unable to remain still. "I just need an excuse to call him. Some question, some problem, something."

"Goddammit, Jenna." Wally's face blanched. "Don't pretend I can't manage this place. He said heads would roll if he comes back. And I believe him. He's not the type to waffle. I think he made up his mind to go, and, well, he's gone."

"But look what he did." She waved at the stalls. "For the community, for Peanut, for me. I have to thank him. It's the least I can do. Oh, Wally, thank you!" She gave him a heartfelt hug, turned and hurried out the door.

Ten minutes later, Jenna paced the porch, palming her phone and frowning at a hovering Emily. "It would be nice if you gave me a little privacy."

"Are you kidding?" Em snorted. "My big sister actually chasing a man. I want to hear this. Before you always tried to get rid of them—once you had your fill of their studly bodies, of course."

"It wasn't quite like that," Jenna said primly.

Emily hooted. "It was exactly like that. And what do you want from this Burke guy? You called him once to say thanks. Now you're thanking him again? He's going to think you're a nitwit."

Jenna fingered her phone. *What do I want?* She wanted him sitting on the swing, teasing her, kissing her, arguing with her. She did not want him far away in sunny California.

Emily's voice lowered. "What do you want from him, Jenna? If it's just sex, Colin or that new accountant—any number of men—would be happy to provide it."

Jenna sank down on the swing, gripping her phone. "I'm not really sure." She gulped. "I think I love him. But I don't want to."

Emily squeezed Jenna's shoulder. "It's not such a big deal. Your world isn't going to collapse if you love him. He won't beat you. Doesn't seem to want to control you. Just wants to make you happy. I'd kill for a man like that. What's the problem?"

"He thinks I'm a liar and a thief." Jenna's voice broke. "He caught Wally and me sneaking into his office. He was so disgusted. Couldn't even look at me in the hospital. I'm afraid—"

"So, maybe he doesn't want you anymore." Em shrugged. "But maybe he does. Find out so you can kick this funk. I'm going to visit with Peanut. Just call and get it done. And good luck."

Jenna watched as Emily walked across the driveway. Peanut sidled away, as though anticipating a game. Em paused and Peanut circled back, then pressed his tiny head against her stomach. If only Burke were half as easy.

She stared down at her hand where the phone sat like a twenty-pound weight. Sucked in a breath and pressed his autodial before she could wimp out.

"The number you dialed is disconnected," a recording said.

The phone clattered on the planked floor. She rose and stumbled into the trailer. Stood in the middle of the kitchen, staring at the wall, hands pressed to her hot cheeks. *Jerk, prick, asshole.* Well, that certainly clarified things. Wally was right. Burke didn't want contact, had written her off as emphatically as one of his non-performing companies.

Her fake diplomas stared mockingly from the wall. No doubt he despised her for that too. Grade eleven. The look of horror on his face had been priceless. He probably didn't want to associate with someone who wasn't an Alpha Delta Pi—someone who wasn't even a high school grad.

She yanked the certificates off the wall and dumped them into the garbage. Felt a tiny bit better. Besides, in four years she'd have a real degree to hang on the wall, to hang anywhere she wanted.

And he was making that happen. Helping her earn something she'd always secretly wanted. But how had he known? She sighed and plugged in the tea kettle.

Ten minutes later, her sister strolled back into the trailer. "Well? What did he say?"

"Phone number's changed," Jenna said flatly. "It's over. Nothing more I can do." A clock ticked in the kitchen, emphasizing the abrupt quiet.

Emily groaned. "My God. I can't believe this is you talking. Is this the same girl who stormed into the principal's office when I was suspended? The one who studied six subjects so she could tutor me in my college entrance exams? The only person in the county who dared stand up to Dad?"

"Well, that's the sister I love—not this sniveling coward who sits in the kitchen, waiting for her man to wander home." Emily's lip curled. "You're just like Mom."

Jenna jerked to her feet. "You don't know what you're saying. I'm nothing like Mom—and Burke is nothing like our father."

"Exactly. So he's not going to come crawling back, is he?"

"No." Jenna's voice broke. "But he's in California. And I can't call him anymore."

"Well, we can always find a phone number." Emily swept outside, returning with Jenna's phone clutched in her hand. "What's the name of his company?"

"Burke Industries."

"And what do they do?" Emily asked, her thumb scrolling over the screen. "Buy, manage companies?"

"I guess." Jenna leaned forward, staring at the phone with a flicker of hope. "I think he was going to LA."

"Damn." Emily's eyes narrowed. "Look at this. These people are grossly rich. Is this him?" She turned the phone toward Jenna, her voice rising in disbelief. "Are you a complete and utter moron?"

Jenna stared at Burke's handsome face, unable to pull her gaze off his picture. "I'll call that number tomorrow," she muttered.

"Stop thinking like an idiot," Emily said. "We're calling now. You don't let guys like this wander around loose. Believe me, he won't stay loose for long."

Emily pressed a number. "Derek Burke, please," she said in such a crisp, confident voice, even Jenna straightened. "This is Jenna Murphy calling. Yes, I'll hold." She winked and shoved the phone against Jenna's ear.

Jenna grabbed the phone, trying to steady her breathing. *I was wrong. Please come back. I miss you.* That should do for now. And once he was back, she'd let him know how she really felt.

"I'm sorry." The secretary's voice sounded slightly apologetic. "Mr. Burke isn't available. Would you like to be transferred to Employee Relations?"

"No, thank you," Jenna managed, and cut the connection

"Remind me not to leave you alone ever again." Emily dropped her head in her hands, groaning. "My one shot at a rich brother-in-law, and you totally screw up."

"He's an asshole." Jenna rose and circled the kitchen table. "I can't believe he wouldn't talk to me."

Emily peered up from behind her splayed fingers. "How much do you figure he's worth?"

"I don't know. But he's really normal. Likes playing cards and fishing and building stuff. He never worried about money although he's very generous."

"*Generous!*" Emily dropped her head and wailed, a theatrical sound that almost made Jenna smile. Almost.

"Well," Emily jerked upright. "There's only one thing left to do."

"Text him?"

"God, no! Fly out there. Wrap your arms around him and don't let go. You need to latch onto this guy. If not for you, then do it for me."

"Sure. Fly to California? That would cost a fortune. And we still have your college bills."

Emily had the grace to look ashamed but not enough to be sidetracked. "You have to go out there. The only thing that matters is you love him, and he doesn't know it."

Jenna wrung her hands. "But I'm not sure how *he* feels. He never said he loved me. He had other girlfriends, he didn't care enough to come back and visit, and now he's changed his phone number. What does that mean?"

"It means he's looking for another woman to take your place, and we have to hurry." Em leaped up and grabbed her phone. "But you can't go looking so awful. The weight loss is good. It gives you a mysterious look and you have such gorgeous cheekbones. But my God, your hair. You need a sexier cut. I can do your highlights and nails, but we need someone who's a wizard with hair."

Jenna's mouth dropped. She'd never seen her sister so focused on anyone but her current boyfriend and the latest trends. Yet Em was already on the phone, making a hair appointment at the most expensive salon in town—for her.

The haircut, of course, was as far as it would go. She'd never had a fancy cut before, and the prospect was rather appealing. But to fly, uninvited, to California. She wouldn't have a paycheck for another two weeks, and she certainly wasn't going to blow it on a flight across the country to talk to a man who'd walked away. Not only walked away but was incommunicado.

Em hung up the phone. "Perfect. They don't usually work on Monday but when I said your name, the owner promised to open. She wants you to know her grandfather's donkey is doing great. You're booked Monday at nine so we'll check for noon flights. Now show me your hands."

Jenna obediently held out her hands.

"God, they're awful." Emily's scowl was almost as dark as Burke's. "The skin is rough from the burn, your hand is still swollen and your nails are a mess."

"I need them short for massage." Jenna smiled, quite enjoying this unusual attention from her sister. It was fun not to have their usual arguments. Just girl talk. Who'd ever thought she'd be worrying about something as insignificant as nails? She'd skipped that stage of life, leaping from frightened child to protective sister to pseudo mom.

Emily seemed to have grown up a lot while she was away. Maybe the money hadn't been such a waste.

"It's okay." Em still frowned at Jenna's flawed fingers. "One of my roommates had nails like this, and I know how to make them utterly gorgeous. The polish lasts for ages." Her laugh was slightly wicked. "The color lasts in eyebrows too. Did I ever tell you about Trevor? You should have seen what Karen and I did to that sneaky jerk the night he passed out."

Chapter Thirty

The screen door slammed. Jenna turned sleepy eyes toward the bedroom clock. Six am. Where the hell was Emily going so early?

A car started with a familiar backfire, and Jenna smothered her irritation. Em should have asked to borrow the Neon first. Oh, well. They'd had a wonderful time last night. Laughed, cried and giggled without a single argument. Her sister's selfishness seemed to have been left at college or at least tucked away in a bottom drawer. Last night, Em had displayed the wit and intelligence of their father along with the loyalty and charm of their Mom.

After all, their parents had some good qualities. Maybe she and Emily had inherited the best, instead of the worst. Be nice to believe.

She lifted her right hand, admiring her elegant fingers. Emily was a genius with nails too. It was great having her home.

Now the only person missing was Burke. She rolled over, scanning the empty side of her bed. Maybe she could pretend he'd slept there but had left early for a meeting. If she could convince herself he was still around, the aching hollow in her chest might disappear. She punched the pillow and made a head dent. There. Looked real.

But she slumped back, pinching her eyes tight, no longer able to contain her despair. He was gone, really gone. He'd tried so hard, been so kind and she'd been a coward. No wonder he didn't want contact.

Not with a forger, a thief, a liar—someone who sneaked around with their pony, misrepresented her education and broke into his office to steal files. That last rash move had surely snuffed out any love he might have had.

No doubt, he was out jewelry shopping for Theresa or some other lady smart enough to understand how wonderful he was. A tear wobbled down her cheek but she didn't wipe it away. That was the best thing about being alone. One could indulge in a cleansing cry.

Besides, life was great. Everything was exactly as she'd always dreamed. Emily was home, her massage job was secure and in the fall she'd be taking college courses. She hadn't wanted a man before and certainly didn't need one now. Life would be safe, controlled…loveless.

Her breath escaped in a shuddering sigh, and the bed shook from the force of her sobs.

"Good afternoon, Jenna." Wally paused on the porch step, his eyes widening in appreciation. "Wow. You look different."

"Emily gave me some makeup tips last night. I tried to copy her technique." And hide her red eyes. Her crying bout had been long, intense and she hoped, cathartic.

"Well," he cleared his throat, still staring, "you look really nice. Where's your car?"

"Not sure." She hid her irritation. "Em left early this morning. Don't know where she went."

"Typical." Wally snorted. "You've sacrificed everything for your sister, but it's time to cut her loose. Let her make her own way. She's no longer a helpless kid."

"But when you love someone, mistakes don't matter. You always want to help." Jenna sighed and straightened on the swing. "Do you believe that, Wally? Like Mom. No matter what my father did, she always loved him."

"Yeah." Wally shuffled his feet.

"Do you think men can feel like that too? Maybe forgive a little?"

"Some men can." His eyes narrowed. "You're talking about Burke now, aren't you?"

"Want coffee?" She rose abruptly. "Or a beer? Maybe you better choose beer because we don't have any milk. And I don't have a car to drive to the store."

Wally didn't move. His kind eyes filled with empathy. "Maybe you better just call him, Jenna. Get this over with."

"I tried but his number doesn't work, and I can't get past the secretary." She stepped forward and grabbed Wally's hand. "Can you give me his private number? Please?"

"Sorry, kid. Don't have it. I'm not a member of his privileged circle."

"Emily has this crazy idea I should fly out to California."

Wally grunted. "And she's some kind of relationship guru? She's crazier than all of us. Look, clearly Burke has moved on—"

They both turned as Jenna's car sped over the ridge and jerked into the driveway. Hangers draped the back seat and lurched crazily from the Neon's abrupt stop.

Wally groaned with fresh disdain. "Looks like she bought more clothes. Is she even looking for a job?"

"She's only been home a month, and she can't help it. She loves clothes." Jenna's defense was quick and automatic although she stared in dismay at the hangers. Em didn't have a job and only piss-poor prospects. She really shouldn't be out shopping.

Wally rubbed his chin. "Maybe she should drop by the Center and apply for the tour guide position. We've got some fancy Thoroughbreds booked and lots of town interest. The seventh grade kids from Stillwater are visiting tomorrow. Frances doesn't want anything to do with tours so I'm screening job applicants now."

"That would be great." Jenna shot Wally a look of profound gratitude. "She'd be good at that, and a job would keep her out of the stores. She has enough clothes to last a lifetime."

"And you have none," Wally said.

Emily stepped from Jenna's car with an armful of clothes, wilted hair and a triumphant smile. "Busy day at the flea market," she called. "I had more customers than the rest of the tables put together. But no way was I selling these blouses for five bucks."

She trudged up the steps and tossed a wad of money on the table. "Flying money for California, sis. Now I'm going to my room to cry."

Jenna stared in stunned silence at the mound of wrinkled bills. Scads of bills—tens, twenties, even a few fifties.

Wally stared for a moment, as stunned as Jenna. "She sold her clothes? Well, I'll be damned." He leaned forward and started counting. "Looks like you have to find Burke now. And once she finishes crying, tell her she has that guide job. No interview necessary."

"You look beautiful." Em gave Jenna's hair an approving nod as passengers shuffled through airport security. "Call as soon as you talk to Burke. And if he wants to buy me a present, one of those Corvette convertibles would be entirely appropriate.

"Seriously," she went on, "no matter how it goes, at least you tried. He's lucky to have your love." She reached out and wrapped Jenna in a fierce hug. "I take you for granted sometimes, but you're the best sister anyone could have. Now before you see him, remember to change into that little outfit with the sexy cream blouse. And put the lip gloss on over the coral base."

Jenna's upper lip trembled. "Right. And don't you forget to cut up Peanut's carrots. He chokes if..." She couldn't finish, could only give her beloved sister a misty smile. "I w-wish you were coming with me, Em. There's a good chance this could end badly, and now you don't even have any clothes."

"I just want everything back to normal," Emily's smile was slightly sheepish, "so my sister can return to doting on wonderful me. And even if this visit doesn't work out, selling my clothes wasn't a waste. At least you'll have tried."

"You don't think it will work?" Jenna stiffened. "Wally thinks that too, doesn't he?"

Emily shook her head, so quickly it was clear she and Wally had talked. "He just said Burke has a tough reputation. But that's related to business." Em's laugh sounded forced. "You're not business. I'm sure he's different with personal affairs."

"But I'm not so sure he's different at all."

"Just get close to him," Emily said. "Make him think with the part of his brain that isn't business."

"But what side is that?" Jenna flattened her palm against the knot of panic pinching her stomach. "Is it the right or left? I don't know anything about that. Did you learn that in college?"

Emily gently pushed her toward the gate. "Just get on the plane. Most men would stare and not hear a word you're saying anyway. Besides, you've always known how to handle a guy."

"But I can only handle them when it doesn't matter." Jenna's voice cracked. "And this matters. He matters so much—"

Emily shoved her into the moving line and Jenna stumbled forward, her eyes hanging onto her sister until Em was no longer in sight.

It wasn't nearly as much fun flying alone. Nor was it as much fun flying economy. The man on Jenna's right made several persistent attempts, but she was too tense for conversation. There was a good possibility she was risking hotel and airfare, along with her fragile heart.

Wally had confirmed Burke Industries now controlled Edge Technology in California, and that Derek Burke was the acting manager. The office address was close to the LA Airport but what if he wasn't there? She had enough money for two nights' stay, a couple cheap meals and some taxi fare. Wally had pressed a credit card in her hand for emergency purposes, but his concerned expression hadn't been reassuring.

"Be careful, Jenna. LA isn't like Stillwater," he'd said.

She controlled a shudder and stared out the tiny window. At least she was seeing the country unfold. It was a clear day. That had to be a good omen.

The plane landed in LA exactly on schedule. Another good omen.

She watched and waited as the luggage carousel creaked in slow circles. A woman shouldered her aside to snag a bulging black suitcase covered with red stickers, and all around her, passengers grabbed bags, hugged friends and squealed at relatives. Eventually only a sprinkle of people remained.

She stepped back, checking the carousel number. Definitely she was in the right place and quite definitely, her bag wasn't.

The disinterested man in the baggage booth stamped her claim form and placed it on a towering stack. "We expect the bags to arrive within forty-eight hours."

"But that's two days—"

"Next," he called.

She drifted toward an exit, clutching her purse, slightly dazed as people rushed past. Everyone seemed to know exactly where they were going, everyone but her. The last airport she'd visited had been much nicer, much friendlier. Not nearly so intimidating. Of course, Burke had been by her side, and no one would dare lose his luggage. *I wonder what he's doing now.*

Soon she'd know.

His office address meant nothing, simply a blur of numbers, but the taxi driver nodded and ushered her into the back seat, then zoomed away from the queue of yellow cabs. Jenna stared out the window at the backlog of traffic, the chaotic side streets, the looming office towers.

How can he stand it here? It would be hard to find any nails to pound in this place; she doubted he'd be wearing a hard hat when she finally saw him.

"Here you go, lady."

She paid the taxi driver too many of her precious bills, feeling a bit forsaken when he sped away in a rush of gas fumes. Burke's building shimmered beneath the sun. It appeared to be made of dark glass and towered over many of its rivals. People rushed in and out, slender women and chiseled men, good-looking people with officious-looking briefcases, golden skin and haughty expressions.

She stared up, shielding her eyes. Did he actually run this thing? Three Brooks seemed small now, a tiny blip of enterprise, not very important at all except to the horses and town. But whatever they did in this ostentatious building, they couldn't be helping animals. She set her shoulders and pushed open a thick glass door.

Her face immediately cooled as she stepped into the air-conditioned lobby. To reach the elevators, she had to pass between a cascading fountain and an imposing security desk.

A guy in a stained ball cap, delivery bag flapping, rushed past and almost knocked her into the bubbling water as he charged

toward a swiftly closing elevator. The man at the reception desk
ignored him and smiled at Jenna. "May I help you, miss?"

"Yes. Can you tell me what floor Derek Burke, Edge
Technology, is on?"

The man's attention shifted to a big screen then back to her
face. "Edge has many floors but it's restricted access. You'll need
an appointment."

She faked a confident smile. "Can you call Mr. Burke? Tell
him Jenna Murphy is here to see him."

"Just a moment, please," he said. She leaned forward,
following his gaze, reading quickly. Derek Burke, floor fifty. So he
was on the top. She eased back, waiting as the man lifted his
receiver and addressed someone named Miss Higgins. His gaze
flickered over Jenna twice before hanging up.

"I'm sorry." He leaned back in his chair. "Mr. Burke is out of
the office. You'll need to call this number and make an
appointment." He handed her a card.

"But how long is he out of the office?" Her voice squeaked as
she took the phone number. "Not for more than a few days, I
hope?"

The guard's smile faded to a tight line. "As Miss Higgins
suggests, you'll have to make an appointment." He looked past her,
nodding at a man in a light sports jacket and silk tie.

Dismissed, she jerked back, cold with panic. She couldn't
afford to stay for more than two days. Was he gone or just out of
the office for an hour or two? And was he really out? Wally always
told Frances to say he was out when he didn't have time for
visitors.

She glanced wistfully at the elevators. Looked like all deliveries
were routed to the sixth floor. But Burke's floor was on the top,
and she couldn't even see that elevator. The guard's eyebrows
narrowed in clear warning and she turned away, stepping back into
the bright sunshine.

Now what?

She could check in at her budget hotel but her best bet was to
see Burke now, while her only clothes were still relatively clean.
Emily would have a fit if she knew her wardrobe plans for Jenna
had already been scuttled.

"This is for traveling. This is for your first meet," her sister had said with breezy confidence. "After that, it won't matter what you wear."

Yeah, right. Jenna snorted. Maybe tea would help. And she'd have a good vantage point from the little coffee shop across from the office tower.

"We don't have lemon but we have fifty flavors of coffee and boba milk tea," the waitress said, gesturing at an overhead chalkboard.

"Just plain hot tea, please," Jenna said, staring at the confusion of items.

She sat in the only remaining chair by the window, intent on the people scurrying into Burke's building. 'Out of the office.' Maybe that meant he was at a lunch meeting and would be back soon.

Please, please, please, make him come back soon. Her body hummed with anticipation, her nose pressed against the glass. Another delivery guy swooped in on a shiny bike, muscled legs pumping as he hunched over his handlebars. Not a whole lot of people coming or going now. Mid-afternoon lull?

She sipped her tea, watching the office door and eyeing the creeping hands of the wall clock, but even so, she almost missed him. Oh, thank you, God. It was him, walking toward the building. Something twisted in her chest, and for a moment she stopped breathing.

Dark pants, white shirt, loosened tie. He looked so good she simply stared, drinking in the sight. His hair was longer and he seemed relaxed, even smiling at something his companion said. Not a lip twitch but an actual smile.

Odd.

She pressed her nose further against the window and studied his companion, a woman whose pretty coral suit seemed a tad too tight for office work. And those ridiculous heels. Be interesting to see how she managed the concrete steps.

Ah, ha. Not well. She bobbled on her right heel. Burke's hand shot out, such a familiar, protective gesture that Jenna jerked back, spilling her cold tea. She leaped up, swiping at the brown blotch, frantically staring over her shoulder but the pair disappeared into the building.

Oh, shit. She sank back, squeezing her eyes in despair. He didn't give away smiles, not those kind. In fact, he'd never even looked at another woman—not the entire time he'd been with her—not even when women flirted outrageously.

She sat numbly while people laughed and joked and came and went. What a wasted trip. Clearly people like her didn't belong with people like him. She'd been delusional. Thank God he hadn't seen her. She was too sick to move. Could only sit in a heartbroken daze.

A teenager with baggy pants pushed a broom around her feet. "We're closing in ten minutes."

Jenna glanced numbly at the wall. Seven o'clock already. Unbelievable. One thing about California, time passed quickly.

She stumbled from the coffee shop, glaring at the snooty office building. Silent now. No visitors for the security guard to turn away. Burke and his lady friend could have all the privacy they needed.

Hopefully they wouldn't see her. Probably he'd left through another door. No doubt he had underground parking, a secure place for his fancy car, or SUV, or whatever model he drove now. She glanced down the alley. On the left side of the building, a small sign marked a parking entrance. Not that she cared anymore. Absolutely not.

Her hotel was only a ten-minute walk, an ugly concrete walk past aloof pedestrians and a shriveled lady who smiled gratefully when Jenna dropped some change in her plastic container. The air stunk, and Jenna's ears rang from the blaring horns of a wall of Hummers, Jaguars and Escalades.

She arrived at her hotel, tired, dirty and desolate. Stopped in front of the reception desk crammed into a tiny but spotless foyer. "Did my luggage arrive?" she asked with a spark of hope. A shower and clean clothes might loosen the hammy fist stuck in the middle of her chest.

"Sorry. Nothing for you. Sometimes it takes days." The hotel clerk flipped a dark braid over her shoulder, studying Jenna's stained blouse with outright sympathy. "But we have toiletry items. There's also a tourist shop next door that sells T-shirts."

"Thanks." Jenna forced a smile and accepted her room card. This mission was over anyway. She couldn't get to Burke and even if she did, she couldn't possibly appear in a tacky T-shirt. Not when he was surrounded by beautiful babes in even more beautiful suits.

She stepped into her cramped room and flopped on the bed. With the time change, Emily would be asleep so thankfully, it was too late to call. Tomorrow would be early enough to admit the trip was a total bust.

Chapter Thirty-One

A phone chirped in Jenna's ear. She bumped the bedside clock as she groped in the dark for her cell.

"Good morning," Emily whispered. "Is he right beside you? Don't talk. Just say 'yes' and hang up. I couldn't sleep all night wondering."

Jenna squeezed her eyes shut. She couldn't sleep all night either, but there had been no wondering involved. "It's five o'clock in the morning here, Em. And it's not easy to get into his building. Also, I think he's seeing someone else."

Silence for which Jenna was grateful. She kept her eyes squeezed tight, reluctant to face another pissy California day.

"You need a kick in the ass." The vehemence in Emily's voice bumped Jenna wide awake. "Not so easy to get into his building! Since when has anything ever been easy? And so what if he's seeing someone else? Didn't you go out for dinner with Colin just last week?"

"That was different," Jenna said. "Wally was there too, and we were discussing the company scholarship." And it hadn't been fun. She hated seeing the longing in Colin's eyes, realized now how horrible it was to love someone who didn't love you back—the most desolate, awful, bleakest feeling in the entire world.

"Did Burke kiss this woman?"

"No, but he smiled and touched her elbow." Jenna's voice trailed off in fresh misery.

"If you were that close, why didn't you rush up and say hi?"

"I looked awful." She didn't want to admit the sight of Burke smiling at someone else had slammed her in the gut. "Plus the airline lost my luggage, and I spilled tea on my blouse."

"You whine more than me," Emily snapped. "Do you love him?"

"Yes."

"Then you better dig deep because if you're anything like Mom, he's the only man for you. Hell, you fight tooth and nail for everyone else—me, Wally, Peanut, friends, even strangers—yet when it's for your own happiness you turn into a jellyfish. Come on, Jenna. At least find out. Otherwise, you'll wonder the rest of your life. You'll sit alone on the trailer porch, shriveled up on our ancient swing, a lonesome loser, never—"

"Okay, Em. You can shut up now. I get the picture."

"I'll call you later," Emily said, her voice threatening.

Jenna sighed. Her little sister was turning downright bossy. However, it was rather comforting to know there was another adult in the family. Not that Em was right. Of course, there were other men in the world she could love. Other men whose company she'd enjoy. Men who could control their temper, who wouldn't yell and smash and hit and go on drunken binges that lasted for weeks.

Colin, for example. Although he didn't make her heart jump with a single look, couldn't arouse her with the sound of his voice, the touch of his finger—not like Burke.

Thank God, she'd fallen in love with a good man.

Unlike her poor mother. No wonder, she'd been torn. Jenna gripped the sheets, her usual bitterness tempered with fresh empathy. It couldn't have been easy. Her father had been a charming bastard—smart, handsome but selfish. However, he had loved them. There was no doubt, he'd loved them.

And for the first time in her life, she prayed to her parents. *Please, Mom. Please, Dad. If you can, please help me out here.*

"Derek Burke, please," Jenna said crisply, checking the bedside clock, even though she'd been staring at it for the past three hours. Eight am. Finally, they were answering their phones.

"One moment, please," the friendly voice said.

A nanosecond later. *Click*. "Derek Burke's office. May I help you?"

This voice was cool and efficient, not quite as welcoming as the first. Maybe it belonged to the woman in the coral suit? Was this Miss Higgins? "I'd like to speak to Derek, please," Jenna said.

"And who may I say is calling?"

"Jenna, Jenna Murphy."

"One moment please," the voice said.

Jenna's knuckles whitened around the phone. In the hall outside, a cleaning trolley rattled past. Someone laughed and muted conversation drifted through the thin door. She swallowed but her heart wedged in her throat.

She paced to the window and back. Two minutes. Paced some more. Felt like an hour. He must have someone in his office, was trying to get rid of him—or her—so he could talk. Another minute dragged.

"Ms. Murphy?"

Jenna stiffened. The cool voice again, no emotion.

"Mr. Burke wants you to know Impact Management now handles Three Brooks. This is the phone number. They'll be glad to help you out." She recited a number then paused. "Did you write that down?"

"Yes, thanks. Good bye." Jenna said, her voice scratchy. She fumbled and the phone tumbled to the carpet. *Shit, shit, shit*. This was worse than she'd thought. But Burke didn't know she was so close. Couldn't know. Of course, he'd want to meet once he knew she was in LA.

She leaned over and snatched up the phone, trying to control her burgeoning panic.

Another call. Same friendly initial voice, same cool second voice.

"This is Jenna Murphy again." She spoke quickly, hating the note of desperation in her voice. "Please tell Burke I'm in the city and hope to see him today."

"Ms. Murphy, I'm afraid *Mr.* Burke is extremely busy. He'll be out of the office for an extended period. Impact Management is handling all queries. Now have a good day."

This time Jenna didn't drop the phone, could only stare at it with growing incredulity. He didn't care enough to see her. She couldn't imagine being so cruel. Or so blunt. Clearly, with him, it was all or nothing. And right now she was nothing. A piece of trailer fluff he'd enjoyed and forgotten.

Or was trying to forget. Oh, God, she prayed he hadn't forgotten.

She grabbed her purse and rocketed from the room. Found a tourist shop just outside the hotel entrance, with racks and racks of T-shirts, shirts of every color, size and slogan. She picked a tiny peach one that read 'Private Deliveries' and bought a ball cap to match. Tight black biker shorts. The flip-flops didn't fit her outfit but they were only three dollars, and she doubted the security guard would be looking at her feet.

She detoured to her friendly hotel desk clerk. "Do you have a large envelope?" she asked, nodding with approval as the receptionist produced an officious Fed-Ex envelope.

"Sorry but your luggage hasn't arrived yet." The dark-eyed receptionist gave an apologetic shrug. "Maybe this afternoon."

"It doesn't matter now," Jenna said. She wasn't going to sit around any longer. In fact, she was looking forward to showing Burke just how piss-poor his security actually was.

She pulled on her new clothes and checked her reflection in the bathroom mirror. All the delivery people yesterday had worn shorts and T-shirts, not quite as tight as what she had on, but she needed some confidence. And she did look rather…good.

Emily would groan if she saw the ball cap that hid her fancy new haircut, but her cheeks looked nice. A little lipstick, then Em's glossy stuff, and she was ready.

She stuffed some blank hotel stationery in the Fed-Ex envelope and headed toward Burke's office. The streets were crowded but people seemed friendlier today, streaming by with loose-hipped walks and in-line skates. Now that she knew where she was going, what she was doing, she felt invigorated. Now she had something to think about rather than worrying about Burke's reaction. She could almost smile.

"Excuse me. Can you tell me how to get to the Herbalife building?" a slim lady asked.

"Sorry. I'm not—" Jenna glanced up and spotted the sign on top of a towering building. "Look. It's right over there." She pointed helpfully.

"Thank you so much. You delivery people always know your directions." The lady nodded her thanks and rushed off.

Jenna smiled, her steps lightening. Maybe she was a bit of a con, like her dad, but she felt alive this morning. Alive and ready to battle.

The first step was to wait for another delivery person. She lingered in the shade of Burke's building, beneath an island of palm trees, out of sight of the security guard. Missed the first guy, a blue-haired man in baggy shorts, ears plugged with music, who approached from the opposite side. His mailbag swung as he bounded through the doors.

Twenty minutes later, another guy swooped in on a silver bike. She edged behind him while he locked his wheels to a metal rack. Stayed five feet from his hip as he lightly ran up the steps and into the cool lobby. He jogged past the spraying waterfall, the imposing security desk and directly to the elevator with Jenna tight on his heels.

Open elevator. Please open now. But the overhead numbers flashed six. She flicked her envelope with an air of impatience, copying her companion's attitude. Even copied his slight panting. Obviously, this delivery business was strenuous work.

She felt the guard's scrutiny, but he didn't holler a challenge. Didn't demand any credentials. And then more visitors entered and the elevator doors slid open. She leaped forward with alacrity.

She and the deliveryman were the only two on the elevator. "Do all Edge deliveries go to six?" she asked. "My package is for the top floor."

The man grunted and adjusted his bulky bag. "They're anal about security here so we leave everything at six. And it takes forever to get signatures. I was here first, right?"

"Yes," she said, "you were first."

The elevator eased to a stop and the doors parted. She gulped. Now that she was in Burke territory, her palms felt sticky, her face hot. This floor was more opulent, with a gleaming desk and a bored-looking receptionist who didn't even look up as she stamped another delivery. Two loaded mail carts sat to the right of the desk.

Jenna glanced over her shoulder. Five elevators but only one went all the way to the top. There it was, floor fifty. Probably needed a security card, just like at the casino. Not good.

A girl with black pants and a distracted smile wandered past and stopped by the first cart. She checked the envelopes, then wheeled the cart toward the elevator servicing floors seven to twenty. The receptionist was preoccupied with date and time stamping and didn't raise her head.

Jenna edged back, studying the girl on the elevator. Damn. The girl inserted a plastic card before the elevator moved. Jenna sucked in a breath, checking for signs to the bathroom. She might have to hide out for a while. Figure out a plan B.

A man with a sparse goatee and pink tie emerged from behind a door and strode to the last elevator, a manila file and white security card tucked in his hand. She didn't stop to think, just grabbed the remaining mail cart and pushed after him, the back of her neck prickling as she listened for the receptionist's alarmed shout.

But nothing, just the steady thumping of an officious stamp and then soft classical music filled the elevator.

"Executive floor?" the man asked. He slipped his plastic card into the slot.

Jenna nodded. "Yes, please." She opened her fingers, trying to relax her grip on the cart. This floor would be toughest. Worse, she didn't know what direction to turn when the elevator stopped. No doubt, there'd be four corner offices but it was hard to bluff her way when she didn't know which way she needed to go.

"Just a word of warning," the man said, his eyes narrowing.

Damn. Her damp fingers tightened around the handle.

"Mr. Burke and I sent a memo about the dress code. Shorts weren't on it." His eyes lingered on her legs.

"That's why he wants to see me now." She managed a sheepish smile. "Can you direct me to his office?"

"Certainly."

The elevator doors opened and they stepped off, unloading directly in front of a razor-eyed lady sipping from a dainty blue and white cup.

"Morning, Sue," the man said, wheeling to his right. Jenna gave Sue a breezy smile trying to hide her awe at the expanse of windows, the impressive view, the tasteful art. She gripped the cart tighter, squeezing the handle like an old friend, as she maneuvered it past an exotic-looking plant. Her heart rate stabilized slightly once they turned the corner and disappeared from Sue's sight.

The man paused by an open door. "Mr. Burke's office is at the end of the hall. You'll have to check in with Donna first." His gaze drifted back over Jenna's legs, and he shook his head. "Good luck," he added.

"Thanks." But Jenna's voice cracked. "Is he in his office now?"

"Yeah, saw him this morning." The man paused. "You *do* have an appointment?"

"Of course." She tried not to shake. Oh, God, he was here. In a short minute, she'd see him.

She clamped her mouth and began pushing, building up speed and careening down the hall. Donna was on the phone and seemed disinterested in the arrival of the mail cart, at least not until Jenna rolled past and rapped on Burke's door.

"Yes." His impatient voice sounded and Jenna shoved the door open even as Donna yelled, "Stop!"

Jenna rammed the cart in and closed the door, watching Burke's face. A slight flare of his nostrils but nothing. He leaned back in his chair and crossed his arms, a slightly bored expression on his face. His cheeks looked leaner, almost cruel. She swallowed and wet her throat.

"What are you doing in LA, Jenna?"

Okay, so maybe he hadn't known she was here. Her hope spiked. Maybe he'd have seen her if Donna had even bothered to give a proper message. "You mean in LA or this office?" she asked.

His phone buzzed and he picked it up. "It's all right, Donna. Low threat. It's just a..." his gaze flickered over Jenna, "an ex-employee." He pressed a button and leaned back in his chair. "You seem to have a proclivity for breaking into offices." He scowled at the cart and its stack of assorted envelopes. "You do realize mail theft is a federal offense?"

The brick in her throat made it tough to breathe. This wasn't going at all the way she'd expected, or hoped. She didn't even know what 'proclivity' meant but from the disapproving look on his face, it wasn't anything very good.

"What do you want?" he added, picking up a gold pen and returning his attention to a legal-sized notepad.

Words balled in her throat. She'd naively thought he'd be thrilled to see her. Had hoped he'd sweep her into his arms, making talking unnecessary. She edged a step closer to his desk, keeping a grip on the cart, needing it to prop up her shaky legs.

"I miss you," she said. "And you left so quickly, we didn't really sort things out."

"The scholarship, Wally, the new barn, my—" He shook his head in disgust, uncoiling so forcefully his chair slammed against the wall. *Bump!*

Something beeped.

"Security's on the way," he said tonelessly. "Can't stop them. We're on an alert because of some labor unrest." He tossed a wad of bills on the desk, turned and stared out the spotless window. "I don't want you to have any hardship, but I don't want to hear from you again. Take the money and go."

"But I m-miss you and I wanted to thank you personally."

"No thanks are necessary. Just go, Jenna."

He didn't turn around, but his shoulders were stiff and unrelenting. He wouldn't even look at her—Burke—who always faced everything head on. He must really despise her. The realization was staggering. She pried her fingers from the cart and fumbled for the door, shoving it open through a blur of tears.

All this way. She'd come all this way to tell him she loved him and couldn't even get close. *Get close*, Em had said.

She paused, pulled the door shut and turned back. If not for the abrupt slump of his proud shoulders, she doubted she'd have summoned the nerve.

She slipped around the massive desk and wrapped her arms around his waist. It was hard to press her head against his chest, not with his arms crossed over them like steel protectors. But she tried anyway. "I can't just leave," she whispered brokenly. "You see, we Murphy women have a big problem. Once we love someone, it's forever. And I wanted to tell you that. And I'm sorry for sneaking into your office. So sorry about all my other …proclivities. And for lying about my education. I'll go now, but I'll always love you."

He moved then, quick as a panther. One arm banded around her. The other tilted her face, his dark eyes almost frantic. "Pardon?"

"I'm sorry." She gulped. "And I love you."

His hand flattened over the back of her head, knocking off her cap as he pressed her into his thudding heart, his mouth moving over her hair, her face, her neck, moving as if he couldn't get enough.

"Even though I hit you?" he finally asked, his voice ragged. "You flinched in the hospital. Wanted me gone." He tilted her chin, scanned her face, his throat jerking convulsively. "I'm no better than your father."

She shook her head and tried to press back into his chest but he kept his hand on her jaw, still staring intently at her face. "You're saying, I hope, that we can see each other more than once a year?"

"I want to see you every minute of the day," she said. "It just took a while to admit—"

His mouth lowered over hers in a hungry kiss, and it was impossible to talk and cry and kiss at the same time, but the kissing prevailed. He always was a wonderful kisser but this was different—hard, frantic, sweet.

The door burst open. Two men edged in, with white shirts, flat expressions and hands tucked beneath their blazers. Burke raised his head, arms tightening as he edged her behind his back. "False alarm, gentlemen," he said. "And I'd really like to be alone now."

But the taller man floated to the right of the bulky mail cart and the other cut to the left, both straining to see Jenna. Christ, they had guns—she could see them now. Her eyes widened.

"She's not a threat," Burke said quickly. "My...fiancée likes to role play."

She smiled, no longer caring about the guards, and pressed a big kiss on his mouth. The twitch of his lip made her grin. And of course, the word fiancée.

"Excuse me, sir," the tall man said.

Burke dragged his mouth off Jenna. "What," he muttered, his hot gaze holding hers, full of so much tenderness she couldn't stop grinning.

The guard to the left gave a nervous cough. "We need to hear the password, sir."

"Peanut," Burke said, still looking at Jenna.

Feet shuffled. The door closed.

"Peanut? I thought you were trying to forget us?" she asked.

"I was trying. God, I was trying so hard. Please don't freeze me out again, sweetheart."

"Technically it was you who left." She tugged his shirt up, slipping her hands over the warm skin on his back, needing to get close. "And I was the one who had to fly across the country, break into this hostile office and plead my case."

"You didn't bring Wally then?" He snagged her right hand, clearly distracted, his face softening with relief at its healthy appearance. "You flew here by yourself?"

"Actually it was Emily who encouraged me to come. She even sold her cherished wardrobe to raise enough money."

"For which she has my eternal thanks." He paused. "Can she do something else for us? Can she take care of the pony for another week? Then we'll fly home and figure out where to live."

Home. She blinked, her smile widening. "Really? I thought you might have to stay here—and I can do that—but you can live in Stillwater? I can still go to college?"

He pressed her back into his chest. "We're not giving up your porch, Jen. But I'd like to haul away the trailer. Build something bigger. That view was one of the reasons I fell in love with you. That and your butterfly tattoo."

He slid his hands beneath her shirt, proceeding to show some of the many other things he loved.

Chirp. His hand on her breast muddled her hearing, but she was pretty sure her phone was ringing. *Chirp, chirp.*

"I better get it," she said, her voice husky.

"Let me answer. Wally won't talk so long to me." But he smiled as he tugged the phone from her pocket. "Burke," he said.

Jenna opened two buttons on his shirt. Pressed her mouth against his skin, listened to his heartbeat, the deep rumble of his voice, knowing she was much too happy to talk anyway. *Oh, God. Thank you. Thank you. Thank you.* She felt like leaping and squealing and leaping some more.

"She's a little busy right now," Burke said, but his voice softened. He even sounded amused.

Not Wally then. Must be Em. She released a few more buttons, sliding her fingers over his chest, relearning his hard contours. Of course, she wanted to talk to her dear sister but not at this precise moment. Right now, she only wanted to get closer to the man she loved.

Be nice if he'd finish talking though. He sounded deep in negotiations. She waited another polite minute then gave his chest an impatient nip.

"All right. Red it is." He ended the call and tossed her phone on the desk. "Your sister will look after Peanut for as long as we want. And I think I just bought her a sports car."

"No!" Jenna's eyes widened. "You have to watch her."

"Not a problem. Today I would have bought her a small island." His mouth curved in an indulgent smile. "Because I happen to be in an exceptionally good mood, a very generous mood."

"I see." She tilted her head, pondering for a moment, but Emily was fine, Wally was fine, as were Peanut, Frances, even Stillwater itself. Everything was fine. Amazingly there wasn't a single thing or person to worry about.

Somehow, somewhere, benevolent forces had combined to make everything in her world align. It was almost too good to be true. Best of all, this wonderful man loved her. Knew her and loved her, in spite of her many faults.

She gazed into his tender eyes, eyes that were oddly damp, and sucked in a shaky breath, abruptly overwhelmed with emotion. "I'm just so grateful," she managed. "So h-happy."

"So am I, sweetheart," he said softly. "So am I."

***

About The Author

Bev Pettersen is an award-winning writer and two-time finalist in the Romance Writers of America's Golden Heart® Contest. She competed for five years on the Alberta Thoroughbred race circuit and is an Equine Canada certified coach. Presently, she lives in Nova Scotia with her husband and two teenagers. When she's not writing novels, she's riding. Visit her at www.bevpettersen.com

Printed in Great Britain
by Amazon.co.uk, Ltd.,
Marston Gate.